BANDITS BELOW

MARINE AIR-GROUND TEAM IN PURSUIT OF THE BANDIT SANDINO

(Based on Historical Events)

LT. COL DAVID BROWN, USMC (RET.)

Gold Award author of *Battlelines*

BANDITS BELOW

Marine Air-Ground Team In Pursuit Of The Bandit Sandino

Lt.Col David Brown, USMC (Ret.)

Kravitz & Sons
INNOVATORS IN PUBLISHING MARKETING AND ADVERTISING

Kravitz and Sons LLC
1301 Farmville Blvd, Suite 104
Greenville, NC 27834

Published by Kravitz and Sons LLC.

ISBN: 979-8-89639-350-4 (sc)
ISBN: 979-8-89639-349-8 (e)

Library of Congress Control Number: 2025915656

CONTENTS

Acknowledgements

I want to first recognize the Marines who lived to share the stories of their brothers fighting in Nicaragua during the late 1920s. These stories about camaraderie, unquestioning trust, leadership, superior training and weapon skills are fundamental in bringing victory to the battlefield. I also recognize the bravado of the nationalist, Augusto Sandino, who unwittingly leads a group of under-armed peasants against the Marines and the Nicaraguan Guardia Nacional.

I deeply appreciate the reams of US documents available about this "Banana War" conflict, without which the book could not have been written. US Marine Corps after action reports, *Marine Corps Aviation: The Early Years 1912-1940*, and Michael J. Schroeder's The Sandino Rebellion in Nicaragua were key research documents used to craft Bandits Below. Additionally, my gratitude is extended to Ms. Kara Newcomer of the Marine Corps History Division, who provided the majority of the photos used in the book.

In that early Marine Corps aviation is an integral portion of the book, I wish to profusely thank Mr. Jack Farrior who flew me in his bi-plane, a 1926 Great Lakes Navy trainer, executing the many aerial maneuvers used in this book—except, of course, the crash of "Old Green Nose." His flying instructor, Hilton Carson, and my friend, LtCol Chuck "Wimpy" Wimmler, USMC (Ret.), provided aviation tips on flying these early planes.

As with our earlier book, I credit Tiffany Holmes, my insightful daughter who is a distinguished literature and fine arts teacher, for wading deeply into the first draft. Then, after numerous other invaluable reviews, made polishing touches to the final draft.

I provided Marc Waszkiewicz with an early draft. Marc, in Vietnam, was my artillery forward observer and he has made it a life-long project to assist me organizationally. For this book, I credit him with helping to restructure it into four logical subdivisions. Marc's review was then examined by another friend, Swami Suddhananda, who provided, among other things, key advice: "Ignore what Marc wrote and just keep in the love scenes."

The manuscript was provided to Diane Rowland, a neighbor and professional teacher with no military background for her review. I thank Diane, not only crossing many "t's" and dotting a bunch of "i's", but for her demands to clarify the unexplained military terms or jargon. Diane constantly marveled about the young Marines on the battlefield, a point obvious to a person fortunate enough to go to war with them. I am grateful for her comprehension.

Once, near the final editing point, my niece Alison Nissen (a literary scholar and published author) successfully honed that which had been looked at numerous times with an eagle eye.

Finally, I want to thank three Marine Corps colleagues, Col Chris Wilk, USMC (Ret.), Gunnery Sergeant Gabriel Soleto, USMC, and Staff Sergeant Adel Abudayeh, USMC (Ret.). As both a career Marine and a writing scholar, Chris provided a professorial approach in his detailed analysis of *Bandits Below*. Gabriel's work on the cover and his graphics advice have been crucial for the visual appeal of the book. Adel designed the maps and other graphics for the book. Adel may be medically retired from the Corps as a result a nasty wound suffered in Afghanistan, but I will assure the reader that only active-duty blood runs through his veins. I am thrilled these three Marines were part of this dedicated team.

PREFACE

Today's Marine Corps air-ground team did not just suddenly occur. From the Corps' inception in 1775 through World War I, the ground guys alone perfect their own combat skills. But in the World War, aviators enter the combat stage and step toward the spotlight in the1920s by competing in and winning international seaplane races. Individual aviators gain national recognition. One of them, First Lieutenant Christian Schilt, who served in the Azores as a Marine Corps private and aerial gunner during WWI, is, in 1926, considered to be the Marine Corps' best pilot and wins second place in an international air race.

While the high-spirits of the 1920s characterized America's mood, in Nicaragua, anguish between the US-favored Conservative Party and its Liberal Party adversary darkens the skies of an impoverished nation in the wake of the 1924 election. Despite his reluctance, President Coolidge is forced to send additional Marine forces to Nicaragua as his Ambassador forecasts future hostility and danger to US citizens and investments. The most lucrative of these investments are gold fields, banana plantations, and, if built, a proposed canal through Nicaragua giving the US the exclusive right to operate the canal. The call for challenging the government and ridding his Nicaragua of all foreigners is championed by one young man, Augusto César Sandino. Articulate, confident and passionate, Sandino mobilizes his countrymen into a challenging force for the Marines. While his personal life changes from being a small-time rebel rouser to a married warrior to a national hero, the Marines consistently called him a "Bandit."

Deployed from the West Coast is Major Rusty Rowell, his VO-1M air squadron, and his desire to begin implementing close air support learned from the US Army in 1922. From the East Coast, the VO-4M squadron arrives headed by First Lieutenant Schilt and others to join Rowell's beefed up organization. They train extensively, honing Rowell's desired ability to provide the support needed by the Marine ground troops.

Intensity builds with Sandino's successes and multi-engagements involving the infantry Marines. The angels above and ground-pounding Devil Dogs below begin shaping the Marine air-ground team with coordinated aerial bombing, supported aerial machine-gun firing, aerial reconnaissance in support of infantry patrolling, and air medical evacuations. For his selfless heroism, First Lieutenant Schilt is recommended for the Congressional Medal of Honor in early January 1928 for an aerial-evacuation of 18 wounded Marines and Guardia soldiers while under enemy fire. This allows the remaining Marine Force to locate and destroy Sandino's secret, mountain-top headquarters.

BOOK ONE: EARLY MARINE AVIATION

(1917-1926)

Chapter 1: Legendary Marine Aviators

Pensacola, Florida, February 13, 1917. "Hell no! That's impossible. And don't give me any of that Bernoulli's Principle talk! No seaplane made can be looped—the pontoon make it impossible." Captain-select Alfred Cunningham groaned. "We're doing enough crazy maneuvers around here. My back is still screwed up from my nose-dive I took in November off the USS North Carolina." Cunningham, the dark-haired, debonair-looking, 36-year-old southerner was the Marine Corps' first aviator and designated Naval Aviator No. 5. Beyond flying, he emphatically believed in the future in Marine aviation as a necessary component of supporting Marines fighting ashore.

The Naval Deficiency Act of 29 August 1916 provided funds for the purchase of Curtiss N-9 Seaplanes

uscgaviationhistory.aopter.org

"I know I can loop it," countered the sometimes overly-confident Lieutenant Francis T. "Cocky" Evans. The dapper, former infantry officer with a petit handlebar mustache, added, "I know that the N-9 is strong enough to sustain a loop." The N-9 was the new, recently-delivered Curtiss-built seaplane. Pensacola had 25 of the N-9s. "And besides that, Commander Mustin made the launch from the ship three days before you crashed. You just had a bad launch. Well, I'll be doing a loop in the morning. It's the 13th—my lucky number. Just come and watch if you want!"

The next morning, flying alone at 3,500 feet over the Gulf of Mexico with a couple of cups of coffee in his gut, Evans's mind flashed thoughts from earlier aviation mishaps, to the requirement for Marine aviators to participate in Pensacola's aeronautic experiments. From his few naval officer buddies, who also believed the N-9 was built better than earlier seaplanes, to "Let's get on with this loop!" Evans eyes narrowed and his lips tightened as he pulled back on the control wheel as hard as he was able. For five seconds the nose of the plane lifted upward to a nearly vertical position. The Florida sun blinded Evans. The 100 horsepower Curtiss OXX engine strained mightily, unable to go higher or invert onto its back. As the fuel stored in its upper wing stopped flowing downward through the cockpit and the firewall, the engine abruptly stalled. Gravity slowed the ascending plane, turned it earth bound, then more and more rapidly pulled the weight of the heavy engine toward gulf's waters. The plane with its 53-foot wing span started spinning out of control. Slowly at first, then more rapidly in its second rotation. No American aviator had ever recovered from a spin.

As his mind focused solely on looping the plane, Evans was wholly unaware that his plane had begun to spin. To begin the second loop, he pushed his control wheel forward to gain speed and controlled the turning thrust with his rudder. That maneuver was a first in the brief annuls of American aviation to prevent going into a continuous, out-of-control spin resulting in certain death. Although Evans thought nothing of the feat, he smiled then whispered softly in the noisy cockpit, "Damn, that was easy. I almost had it! Let's do this thing again." His second attempt mirrored the first one. On his third attempt, he did something vastly different. He dove sharply, dramatically gaining far more speed than he had in his first two attempts. It was at this point that he pulled the wheel back sharply. Instantly, the hinged elevators on the horizontal stabilizer thrust the plane's nose upward. Within seconds, the loop had been completed and Evans eyes flashed sky, land, and sea. His made his loop and a hearty "Ha, ha!" blasted out from a man who did something that others thought could not be done. Flying back to the air station low enough and waggling the plane's wings when passing over the hangers to get the attention of others, Cocky Evans flew his N-9 skyward and looped once more to prove to all what could be done.

Evans, who had become a legend, not for his "loop," but for solving the spin-recovery problem, was sent on a tour of airfields to teach the spin-recovery methodology to all military aviators. Newly promoted Captain Cunningham found himself meeting in Washington the next week with the Marine Corps' Major General Commandant Barnett and his staff to prepare for the inevitable fight using aviation assets for the first time against the aggressive Germans.

The Marine Corps, on February 26th, less than two weeks after Evans's now-famous loop, established an Aviation Company at the Philadelphia Navy Yard. Cunningham had been ordered to organize the company for war. Eight months later, the Aviation Company split into two organizations: the First Aeronautic Company, under the leadership of Captain Cocky Evans, was to deploy to the Azores to hunt German U-boats in January 1918; and the First Marine Air Squadron was to deploy to France to conduct bombing missions sometime later.

San Miguel Island, Spanish Azores, May 5, 1918. "Frank," the youthful-looking aviator, Lieutenant Aaron Wilkins, called to his gunner, Private First Class Frank Schilt, as the two Marine aviators weaved their way from the briefing tent and through the oversized lifeboats resting listlessly on their sides on route to their Curtiss R-6.

Two Curtis R-6 of the 1st Aeronautic Company at Punta Delgado, San Juan Island Azores. 1918

National Archives, RG-127 Photo 529925

"Sir?" Private First Class Christian "Frank" Schilt responded looking over his shoulder already walking two paces in front of the Company's new pilot. Schilt was a solidly built man with a handsome face in an athletic, rugged sort of way. The 23-year-old Schilt, hailing from rural Richland County in central Illinois, always seemed to move faster than the others in the Marine Corps Aeronautic Company. This morning his square face, normally bearing a pleasant smile, looked serious.

US Navy Photo

"The skipper told us to fly our mission to the northeast and bomb the German sub that the San Miguel fishermen saw last night," Wilkins announced.

"Yes Sir," Schilt said while stepping on the left pontoon, "I want to give the bird a good look over before we take off."

"You ever see a German sub?"

Schilt, with his waterproof boots now wet as he stepped on to the port pontoon and his mind more focused on the underside of the plane's engine, responded, "I did about two weeks ago," he paused, "about fifty miles east of here. I was with Captain Evans. We were about five miles away from it when they must have seen us coming. I had the torpedo bombs ready to go, but the sub submerged by the time we caught up to them."

"The skipper said you are one of the best. He is about to promote you to corporal and recommend you for flight school. Where did you pick up your technical background to do all this?" Wilkins asked, his arms stretched outward for balance as he started climbing into the forward cockpit.

"Sir," Schilt interrupted, "if you don't mind staying with the mooring line, I want to double check the fuel line to see if the mechs have it tightened. There was a small leak this morning. Afterwards, you can uncouple us, and we can take off...Oh, yeah, I graduated from Rose Polytechnic Institute in Terre Haute, Indiana. Ever heard of it?"

"Wow, that's a great school. One of the best."

Ignoring the compliment about his school and pushing a metal panel closed, Schilt offered, "Okay to cut us loose, Sir, the fuel line looks good."

Minutes later the two aviators were at 3,000 feet in a cloudless sky searching for a German sub.

Chapter 2: Championing Marine Aviation

Marine Corps Barracks, Quantico, October 20, 1923. Pleased, yet mystified by the quick acceptance of their invitation to spend Saturday, the 20th of October, with the Marines, Marine Corps leaders looked forward to hosting President John Calvin Coolidge to Marine Corps Barracks, Quantico, Virginia. Commandant Major General John Archer Lejeune and the Barracks' Commanding General, Smedley Darlington Butler, had been friends for many years. They met in Quantico a week earlier to consider what, if anything, the 30th President, may have in mind. Coolidge, less than five months earlier, assumed the office of the president following the sudden death of his predecessor, Warren Harding. Lejeune and Butler could not believe that Coolidge, nicknamed "Silent Cal" for his quiet, steadfast and frugal nature, was visiting only to see the football game between Quantico's two-year-old team and Gallaudet University. Would it be the Corps' role in the Banana Wars? In China? Would he want to fold the Marine Corps into the US Army? Would the new boss want to eliminate Marine Corps aviation?

Lejeune knew the seldom-smiling, republican lawyer from Vermont all too well. In fact, the Marine Guards, stationed at the White House, already shared one incident with the Commandant that told him a lot about the man. Apparently, Coolidge buzzed for his bodyguards and they searched frantically for him throughout the building. They finally found him hiding under his desk laughing about the practical joke played on the guards. Lejeune concluded that it would be best to accentuate the positive about Marine expeditionary forces and Marine aviation and then address whatever the new boss had on his mind.

More rapidly than imagined October 20th arrived. Virginia's autumn is often considered to be nature in perfection. Foliage of saffron, scarlet, and marmalade blankets the southern landscape. A crisp breeze combined with a warming fall sun energizes its afternoons. The day was beautiful. Quantico, the small southern town 35 miles south of Washington, DC, and nestled beside the Potomac River, was an enclave surrounded by a bustling Marine Corps base. Along the town's narrow rail platform on this late November Saturday, a formal contingent of Marines stood at rigid attention.

The three-car train carrying President Calvin Coolidge and Commandant Major General John Lejeune that departed Washington's Union Station at 11:00 AM, squeaked to a stop in Quantico thirty minutes later. The president beamed as he appeared at the rear door of his, the train's final car. At that precise moment, the barracks band struck up "Hail To The Chief." Nearby were several hundred other Marines anxious to see their commandant and their nation's leader. In the front of the contingent on the platform was the commanding general of the Marine Corps Barracks, the wiry-thin Quaker from Pennsylvania and legendary two-time Medal of Honor winner, Brigadier General Smedley Butler.

Many considered General Butler to be the most complex Marine on active duty. To Marines, first and foremost, he was a hero. He would have earned a third Medal of Honor in the 1900 "Boxer Rebellion" had officers been eligible for that award at that time. Men working for him knew he was a demanding leader who drove all Marines to accomplishments beyond their own imaginations. This rang true for Quantico Marines as Butler had orchestrated the construction of Barrack's football stadium by the hands of every officer and enlisted man on the base.

Considered perhaps an oddity, he possessed uncompromising values against drinking that had grown prevalent earlier in the "roaring twenties" and increased during the three-year old prohibition law. He eliminated drinking on the sprawling base and in the adjacent small town of Quantico. Most Marines surmised Butler's Quaker background influenced his campaign barring alcohol. Still, each man ignored personal persuasions and accepted Butler's directive. Butler was a first class gentleman in every other fashion. With a raptor's nose and a glare so fierce, his men called him "Old Gimlet Eye."

Butler snapped a sharp salute. Following Butler's lead, all Marines saluted the Chief.

Casting an avuncular, ever-so-slight smile of immense pride, the 56-year old Lejeune stood behind the President. Lejeune's popularity was fathomless. Upon the close of WWI, he emerged as the intellectual and spiritual leader of the Corps. All loved him as he effectively championed the future of his beloved service. He was considered to be "The Marine's Marine."

The band's final note ended. Butler's saluting right hand crisply cut the air as it whipped to his leg. Others followed, the unified snap echoing into the morning. Coolidge's attempt to say a few words of greeting opened, "Morning, Devil Dogs." With that, a raucous eruption of cheers lasting prolonged minutes finally caused the President to look over his shoulder at the Commandant Major General, wink, and say, "Perhaps my greatest speech!" Immediately, he moved to Butler, his host, shaking his hand.

"You sure know how to motivate the men, Sir," Butler smiled.

Shaking his head while looking at the still cheering Marines, the President said, "It must be magic!"

"General Lejeune," Butler clipped while saluting his boss and good friend. Then to both, "Would you gentlemen care to join me for a light lunch at the officer's club before we go on to the game?" Both nodded. Immediately, they were whisked off to the base, one half-block away, in Butler's sedan. Mounted on each side of the sedan's hood, the two blue Presidential flags flourished in the air. Within moments, the party arrived at Commanding General's suite inside the relatively small, one-story O' Club.

Coolidge had accepted Butler's invitation to attend the game as he had a couple of agenda items to bounce off the two Marines. The first item he'd approached with Lejeune in the train ride to Quantico. It pertained to an idea to tighten up the city of Philadelphia from its upward-spiraling crime rate.

Sitting at their table with an enlisted orderly stationed just far enough away to prevent casual listening, the three began to eat their lunch of Manhattan clam chowder, various meats and breads for sandwiches, condiments, and chocolate ice cream made earlier in the day by two members of the Wives' Club organization. The president surveyed the spread, turned to his host and said, "Ahhh... yes...the Marine's idea of a 'light faire'." Coolidge smiled as he continued, "General Butler, I understand you come from the Philadelphia area."

Butler's parents actually lived in West Chester about thirty-five miles south of Philadelphia. Rather surprised, Butler nodded and confirmed, "That's right, Sir."

"No doubt you have been reading the current news that the city is having quite a difficult time with 'speakeasies'," Coolidge said, referring to the illegal saloons resisting prohibition restrictions. "This defiance has not helped their crime rate. Violent crime is up 74%. The mob is starting to take over much of what was legitimate business. Their mayor asked if I could provide a leader with a military background who could reverse their downward trend in safety. Simply put, they are looking for a Commissioner of Public Safety. They even mentioned you by name."

Butler looked deep into his guest's eyes while comprehending the President's unexpected announcement. His only registered response was confined to a single word, "Sir?"

Continuing, the President confirmed that he'd previously tested the idea with the Major General Commandant on the way to Quantico. "Please take a week to digest this opportunity. It means taking a leave of absence from the Marine Corps while in Philadelphia."

"I will, Mr. President," was all that Butler could manage.

Coolidge ate a forkful of salad, and then confessed, "I must tell you two that my Secretary of State, Hughes, is suggesting pulling back your legation guard in Managua."

Before continuing, he paused letting the two Marines adjust to the change in subject. "I take it you have been reading the Nicaragua legation bulletins? All reports are indicating that Nicaragua is ready to stand on its own."

"After their elections next year—I believe they are planned for October—you ought to plan on bringing those boys home. I don't intend to cut the size of your Corps. I'm pulling the legation out of Nicaragua because next year I will be running on a platform that will be fiscally conservative; thus, it's the politically correct thing to do. If it doesn't work, rest assured we'll send them back in," Coolidge prognosticated.

At precisely 12:30 PM, the lunch concluded and the VIP party returned to the sedan to travel on the flat, tree-lined boulevard to watch Quantico football team play Gallaudet University. Along the way Marines, seeing the shiny vehicle with its two flags waving in the air, stood at attention and saluted. After three quarters of a mile at the direction of a military policeman, the sedan abruptly turned right ascending an incline to the field level of the newly named Butler Stadium.

Before the sedan stopped, the three men examined the new stadium nestled into a hillside that stretched upward to the ornate trees gracing the landscape with their varied hues. "General Butler, did Marine officers and enlisted men dig this stadium out of this hill by hand?" the President asked his host seated in the front seat.

"Yes, Sir, they did. Many of the 'diggers' will be playing today."

In awe, the President murmured, "That's amazing."

Butler's smile remained as he turned quickly to the back seat explaining, "Rest assured, Mr. President, we did give them picks, shovels, and wheelbarrows."

As the sedan stopped for the second time allowing the passengers to enter the stadium, Butler turned to the President and asked, "Sir, before we get seated, would you mind meeting a Marine we recruited last year and promoted to corporal in January? His name is Jiggs. I am certain that he will be very honored to meet you. He's over here by the wall."

Corporal Jiggs-First Marine Corps English Bulldog

Lejeune smiled and shook his head as Butler introduced Corporal Jiggs to the President who could not help but laugh out loud upon seeing Butler's recruit. Butler explained that the corporal showed much promise as a career Marine.

Most members of this "All Marine" football team were permanently stationed at Quantico. In their first year, their record boasted more losses than victories. However, Butler had taken steps to reverse that trend.

The game concluded by 4:45 that afternoon. The Marines played well and beat Gallaudet University Bisons 61-00. The President and the Major General Commandant re-boarded the train shortly after 5:00 PM. Still perplexed about the potential of going to Philadelphia, Butler stood alone, saluting at rigid attention. Coolidge cupped a civilian salute. As they entered the car the President said, "You know, John, I was overwhelmed with the half-time air show. Your Marines' flying skills were so impressive. Where are you going with your aviation force?"

While removing their jackets, Lejeune, in his customary soft voice explained, "Mr. President, we're working together with the Navy on the acquisition of new planes and training pilots. The Marines are focusing on 'close air support.' We believe direct support of the ground forces will be crucial in future combat successes. The Navy is developing ways to land their planes on ships at sea and investigating the use of seaplanes doing far more than just racing.

"In fact, Mr. President, I don't know whether or not you heard that the US won an international seaplane race this past September?"

Coolidge cocked his head slightly to the right implying that he had not.

"It's called the Schneider Cup. As I understand it, that the next race will be here in the states since it always takes place in the country of the winner. In anticipation of a major seaplane race here next year, the Navy is evaluating the possibility of entering the event."

Chapter 3: 1925 Schneider Cup

Quantico, Virginia, October 24, 1925. Precisely at noon on Saturday, the day before the big international race, Frank and Elizabeth Schilt's Model-T Ford pulled up to Bill and Betsy Bailey's three-story, brick apartment building on the highest ridge overlooking the Quantico base. The Schilts lived two units away in an identical building. The Schilts, with Christian being two years older than Elizabeth, were both from the small town in Olney, Illinois, and had known each other since they were young. Schilt, now a first lieutenant, and Bailey, a second lieutenant, were assigned to the same aviation squadron and flew out of the nearby Brown Field below the apartment ridge on the southern part of the Marine base. The couples had become fast friends because they were married. Most of the other lieutenants in the squadron were single.

The men opened the doors of the car to let their wives scramble into the back seat before settling in up front. Schilt, who had kept the car running, put it in gear and took off. "Maryland," his thick baritone voice climbed above the car's motor, "here we come."

As they started down the hill toward the main gate, Betsy Bailey, the constantly-curious and bubbly newlywed who rarely sat still, chimed in with her first question, "Tell me again, what is this race all about?"

Frank Schilt, aware the question was directed at him, paused for a second to collect his thoughts, then answered, "Okay, Betsy, here's the five-minute answer."

Betsy's mischievous glance met Elizabeth's I-told-you-not-to-get-him-started smile. Directing her gaze back to Frank, her sly wink was not lost on Elizabeth.

"The Schneider Trophy, which we in the United States refer to as the Schneider Cup, is the international race for seaplanes. The first race was in 1913 and was won by the French with an average speed of 46 MPH.”

Betsy’s eyes widened as she mouthed an impressed “oh” to Elizabeth who giggled slightly in return.

“Why seaplanes?” Frank continued, “You see, most people believed that seaplanes would end up being the principal trans-Atlantic carrier and that this race would accelerate development. “Then, except the war years, the cup was exchanged back and forth by the Italians and Brits. Up to 200,000 Europeans attend every year.”

Hearing a slight break, Betsy inserted, “Well why is the race here in the US now?”

“Right, two years ago in 1923, an American by the name of David Rittenhouse flew a sleek craft designed by Glen Curtiss called a RC3. He won the event in the UK and brought the race to the US. He was timed at 177 miles per hour. There was no race last year, but the US is hosting the one tomorrow.”

Elizabeth gave Betsy an affirming nod. Betsy, in turn, raised her eyebrows. “That’s pretty fast!”

“You know, Bill,” Schilt added and looking across to Bill Bailey, “that bird had a liquid- cooled engine. Pretty neat, huh?”

Without waiting for his passenger’s response, Schilt went on, “All right, Betsy, here’s the rest of the story,” he said as the car started north up US Route 1 toward the capital.

Before Schilt could begin, Betsy injected while turning her head quickly toward Elizabeth looking for support, “We’re going to a ‘speakeasy’ tonight, aren’t we?”

Elizabeth smiled, but pursed her lips, and raised her eyebrows implying that she was staying at arm’s length for this discussion.

Bill Bailey snapped his head back to stare with a modest amount of frustration at his bride of six months. It didn’t matter though, Betsy, who by now had a big grin on her face, was proud of the fact that she injected the ‘speakeasy’ idea.

Frank Schilt, wanting to ease the situation, said “Betsy,” then he paused careful to include his wife in the conversation, “and Elizabeth, we'll see about going to Pauly's Restaurant—and pub." Schilt turned his head enough to ensure they heard, "Don't forget Pauly is a retired Marine Master Gunnery Sergeant, so it will be safe. Okay?"

Betsy, with a smile of victory on her face, said to her accommodating host, "That's great, Frank. Now what were you saying about the rest of the story?"

Chuckling almost out loud, Schilt agreed to continue, "All right then, there were no entries in 1924, so there wasn't a race. This year the Brits have entered two seaplanes. One is a Supermarine S.4, and the other is a Gloster Napier III. Italy has only entered one seaplane, a Macchi M.33. I don't know much about these planes or their pilots although I have heard that Brit's Napier entry is supposed to be pretty good.

"The US has three Curtis RC3.2s; the RC3.2 is a model upgrade to Rittenhouse's RC3. They should dominate. Two will be flown by Navy lieutenants and one will be flown by an Army lieutenant. His name is Doolittle, Jimmy Doolittle. He's already set all sorts of aviation marks and is probably the best pilot in the Army. All three are stationed at the Anacostia Naval Air Station in DC where they are getting special training in high-speed flying of seaplanes."

Always amazed that his friend seemed to know every detail about flying, Bill Bailey took his turn. "Frank, do you know who's flying the Navy's planes?"

"Not really. We can probably find out tonight. I understand there will be one or two Navy guys there at the same hotel."

Bladensburg, Maryland. Pauly's Restaurant, perched on the corner across from their hotel, was in Bladensburg, Maryland, about 10 miles north of Washington, DC. The couples drove directly to the hotel, checked in and headed to "Pauly's" for dinner and the Marine-renowned "piano" bar.

Pauly's Restaurant wrapped around both sides of the street corner. Booths lined the windows along both streets. The back of the restaurant had a more formal dining atmosphere, complete with small wooden four-top tables and a grand piano. The couples, upon entering, stopped cold.

Pauly's had become synonymous with good times. But all they saw was a partially full room. "I think there is an inch of dust on that piano," Betsy murmured, disappointment lacing her words. "Bill, I doubt if this is the place."

Bill Bailey patted his wife's hand where it rested on his arm. He leaned toward the host seating them, "I was told to ask for 'Tun Tavern II'."

A look of immediate understanding crossed the man's face upon Bailey's quiet words. "This way, Sir" he said sharply. He led the couples to a dark, narrow hallway. Stopping, their host merely motioned them on with his hand. Once they had moved past him, he turned and walked back toward the front of the restaurant.

Bailey assessed the dim passage only momentarily before plunging ahead, tugging Betsy behind him. The tunnel-esk hallway consisted of several turns but stopped at the top of a rather steep staircase. Careful not to hit their heads on the way down, the couples descended, ducking

low under the protruding ceiling. His expression still dubious, Bailey turned back to the others and with his eyebrows raised, simply gave a curious "Hmm?" Turning back, he opened the single door a few feet from the bottom of the stairwell. The scene on the other side stopped the couples dead in their tracks.

The Schilts and Baileys were delighted to find the place packed with Marines. Most probably from the Marine Barracks in Washington. What surprised them was the number of attractive young women who had just come from the "secretary pool" on Capitol Hill.

Once seated at a four-top table almost in the middle of the room, Betsy's eyes darted here and there. She smiled, "Elizabeth." Her good friend leaned in across the space between them conspiratorially, "Look!"

Elizabeth waited a few moments, peered coolly over her shoulder, then turned back with a cat-like grin, "Did you see their dresses? They look like the poster on the door."

"Flappers," Betsy agreed with enthusiasm. Both of the men's faces lit up, and they inspected the independent women of such notorious style with happy appreciation. Betsy playfully thumped her husband with the back of her hand, "Don't even!"

Within moments, a small, wiry man with lightning fingers took up his position at the piano.

As if on cue, several Marines and their newly-acquired dates gathered around the piano.

Frank Schilt said, "This is more like it," before taking a long, admiring glance around the room. His eyes weren't for young women but were reserved for the room's décor. Pictures of commandants and Marine Corps uniforms adorned the crimson-colored walls, which boasted gold stripes painted about every four feet apart. Dark mahogany paneling covered the walls from their midline to the floor. The effect uniquely mimicked the Marine Corps' colors.

"Well, I'll be damned!" A voice rose above the rest from behind them. "If it isn't good old Frank Schilt and Bill Bailey."

The men turned, grins breaking across their rugged faces. "Reynolds!" Schilt called.

"Welcome to Tun Tavern *the second*!"

"Bob Reynolds!" Schilt said enthusiastically. He stood, and the two men vigorously shook hands. While Bill Bailey and Reynolds did the same, Schilt pulled Elizabeth from her seat. "Honey, you remember Bob. We went to flight school together."

"Yeah, hi Bob," she smiled.

"And…who's this?" Reynolds asked, directing his gaze to Betsy Bailey.

"Bob Reynolds, meet my new bride, Betsy." He turned to Betsy, "Bob and Frank were instructors when I was in flight school."

"Sure!" Betsy nodded, "I've heard you talk about him." Turning to Reynolds, she asked, "So why do they call you 'Voodoo'?"

"Now…I hope you don't believe everything…," he started. While they laughed, Reynolds jerked his thumb toward the group gathered at the piano. "Listen fellows. I could use some reinforcements at the piano. I'm over there with a bunch of grunts!" he said affectionately.

"The Hymn?" Schilt asked. "Why didn't you say so?" Without waiting for a reply, he tugged Elizabeth from their table and nudged their way between several Marines.

Bill and Betsy Bailey joined them, "Don't mind if we do!" Bailey announced.

Reynolds placed his arm about the shoulders of a young lady with soft brown eyes and a fashionable "bob" styling her brunette hair. "Let me introduce you to my fantastic gal, Suzy. Suzy, this is Elizabeth and Frank Schilt, and Betsy and Bill Bailey."

"Hi," she said, nodding her head from her position on the other side of Reynolds.

They all nodded as the piano struck up the chords of a song familiar to everyone assembled. The gathered Marines broke into boisterous song, "From the halls of Montezuma, to the shores of Tripoli. We fight our country's battles on the land and on the sea."

Reynolds, Bailey, and Schilt broke away from the rest of the men singing the newly copyrighted and reworded Marines Hymn and shouted, "In the AIR!"

The piano player stopped. "Heys!" and "Ho nows!" erupted from the other Marines.

"Now I told you land lubbers how it should go!" Reynolds instructed.

"How's that, Voodoo?"

"In the air," Reynolds started.

"On land," Schilt, Bailey, and Reynolds all boomed out.

"And sea," Reynolds finished.

"Yeah, yeah, yeah! You flyboys are all alike."

"And how's that?" Schilt asked.

"Pretty and all that..."

"Very funny, Harriman!" Reynolds said, sarcasm lacing his tone.

"All right, all right," Bailey chimed in. "Shall we?"

The men's voices filled the room as the piano player struck the keys. "From the halls of Montezuma, to the shores of Tripoli. We fight our country's battles, "In the air, on land and sea..."

"Alright, men. Let's finish!!!" the piano man declared, as he pounded proudly on the keyboard.

Pauly's hamburgers were thought by many to be the best on the east coast. So after burgers and a couple more beers at "Pauly's Restaurant" with nearly half the of the Quantico squadron who showed up as the evening aged, the married travelers turned in for a good night's sleep. Most of the bachelors spent the entire evening around the corner piano singing "Over There" and other ballads with some especially good-looking Capitol Hill women. Pauly, the retired master gunny, invited the aviators back for his famous eggs benedicts breakfast in the morning at "0700." The Schilts and Baileys decided to accept the offer as they anticipated only a three-hour drive to race's start point at Shore Park Bay just few miles south of Baltimore. If they left by 8:00 AM, they should get there one hour before the race begins.

On a bright Saturday morning, with all its passengers full from a superb breakfast, Schilt's Model-T headed up Route 1 toward Baltimore. "About the race, Frank, where do they fly to?" Elizabeth asked, figuring she'd get in a question before anyone else this time.

Frank Schilt, ready with his response, explained, "The race is 350 kilometers or 218 miles and consists of seven legs, each about thirty-one miles. The general route is over the Chesapeake Bay, starting south of Baltimore at Shore Park Bay," he explained. "Then, they will fly south about ten miles toward Annapolis and east another ten miles to the eastern shore of Maryland before heading northwest back toward the starting point."

The passengers mulled over his answer before Schilt finally said, "We'll find out more when we get there, gang." He then switched the subject to Quantico's much-improved football team that was forecasted to play the Army in the President's Cup.

Shore Park Bay, Maryland, October 25, 1925. The Model-T with the Schilts and Baileys arrived at 11:15 AM. It was just a beautiful, windless autumn day at Shore Park Bay. Already, distinguished guests from Washington sat in attendance for the noon start of the race. Among them were the Chief of Marine Corps Aviation, Major Edwin H. Brainard, and the Chief of the Navy Bureau of Aeronautics, Rear Admiral William A. Moffett.

The Marine aviators, conspicuous in their brown leather flight jackets, along with several of the attractive women they met the night before at Pauly's were cheering the Navy pilots.

The two Navy pilots who had entered the race were dressed in blue flight gear. They waved to the rowdy crowd as they moved into starting position next to their aircraft. Flags from each of the countries were marched across the front of the bleachers with as much flare as the windless day would afford. The pilots, recognizing their signal, climbed into the cockpits while officials bugled orders through bullhorns.

Frank Schilt led the way up to one of the upper rows of the bleachers. Most of the Marines acknowledged the group and made space. Bill Bailey took up the rear, and when finally seated, their wives snuggled between them.

"Hey, Pete!" One of the Marines who had been at Pauly's the night before slapped his buddy. "That's Frank Schilt!"

"Oh, yeah?" Pete, a burly-necked, cropped-topped Marine, smirked, and twisted around to face Schilt. "I heard you should be out there flying for us!"

Schilt smiled confidently, tilting his head at the rowdy Marines.

"Are you kidding? Those blue angels wouldn't know what to make of a brown devil dog in their midst!" Bill Bailey flipped back.

The group's laughter preceded the grumble of propellers firing up in front of them. Betsy leaned into her husband, a smile lighting her, "It's time, right?"

He chuckled, nodding his head and pointing, "Here they go!"

The line of the six planes lurched forward, picking up speed and bouncing down the smooth water. Within moments, one by one, the planes leapt from the surface. They hummed out of sight, hornets on the horizon.

Each time the planes roared emerging from a distant tree line and swooped over the heads of the assembled masses, the crowd filled the air with cheers and hollers. The cheering for the navy pilots did little good since the two Curtis R3C.2 planes were unable to challenge the speed of the other racers. Navy Lieutenant Ofstie dropped out on the 6th lap and Navy Lieutenant Cuddihy gave up on the final lap. Most impressive, though, was the Lieutenant Doolittle's record-smashing first place with an average speed of 233 miles per hour. He beat the British entry who averaged 200 miles per hour.

Flying this Curtiss R2C-2, a young Army Lieutenant, James H. Doolittle-LARC/photographer unknown - Great Images in NASA Description, Public Domain, *https://commons.wikimedia.org/w/ index.php?curid=510366*

The rowdy Marine lieutenants had been cheering near the VIP bleachers. Their silence at the end of the race was as noticeable as their cheering during the race. Major Brainard watched the Marines as they lost interest in the post-race activities and turned their attention to one of their own who was being taunted in jest, yet with due respect by the men as they gestured toward the now- moored planes. Brainard eased off the bleachers and moved closer to the group to more accurately access the pulse of his aviators. One of the men with the name "Reynolds" printed on a patch on his left chest and a bright-looking young woman on his arm had broken from the group. Seeing Brainard, he smiled and said, "Afternoon, Sir."

"Afternoon to you, Mr. Reynolds," Brainard replied easily realizing he addressed the son of Hal Reynolds with whom he had served in Haiti in the early teens. Brainard had heard Hal's oldest son, Robert, had joined the Corps after graduation from Villanova and was in flight school about a year ago. "It's Bob isn't it?"

"Yes, Sir, Major Brainard," Reynolds said recognizing the head of Marine Corps aviation whose photo was on the wall of his squadron commander's office. "Sir, may I present Suzy Buchanan."

"Nice meeting you, Suzy." Pausing for a second while the young, seemingly shy woman smiled and said hello, Brainard asked, "Bob, how's your dad? I haven't heard from him since his Christmas card."

"He's fine, Sir. I'm planning to see him this Christmas, and I'll say 'Hello' for you."

Intent on his initial purpose, Brainard asked, "Reynolds, what's going on over there with the Quantico pilots?

Reynolds didn't understand what Brainard was referring to at first. Then he looked back at the group and understood. "Oh...that, Sir. They are harassing our best pilot, Lieutenant Frank Schilt. We all think he could have beaten those racers today. He's simply incredible!"

Brainard paused thoughtfully, "You're no doubt right. I've already heard he's one of our best. Thanks for the information, Bob. I'll keep it in mind. And nice meeting both of you."

Chapter 4: 1926 Schneider Cup

US Navy Headquarters, May 21, 1926. "Admiral Moffett, you have to support US Navy and Marine Corps entries in this year's Cup," Major Brainard said with a clear sense of urgency. "The Navy and the Marine Corps cannot let the Jimmy Doolittle and the darn Army win another cup. We'll be the laughing stock on Capitol Hill."

"I'd really like to get in the race, Ed, but after our boys gave up on, what was it the 6th and 7th laps last year, we'll look like fools who just know how to spend money on new aircraft for a race but can't produce any pilots!"

"I'll confess, Sir, that the Commandant is not going to quit on this." Brainard pressed, "He's pushing me to get a Marine aviator in there and win that darn cup."

"Who would you possibly put in even if we came up with another Curtiss racer?"

"We have a recently-promoted first lieutenant who's been flying seaplanes since he was a private first class in the Azores in 1918." Looking at Moffett who took a sharp interest in Marine aviation, Brainard continued, "Well, maybe you know him…his name is Schilt, Christian Schilt— he goes by 'Frank'."

"Oh sure, I know of him. Isn't he the young man who made the great aerial survey and mosaic map of Dom Rep you told me about a couple years ago?"

"That's the one, Sir. Well, he not only has nearly eight years of experience in flying, we consider him to be our best. Also, he has sent me some ideas on minor modifications he believes will assist in cutting down some drag."

"All right, Ed, I'll work on it and get back to you in a couple of weeks." Moffett eyed Brainard intently, "Come to think of it, it may be a month. I need to see if we have any spare money in our budget for another racer."

Marine Corps Headquarters, July 20, 1926. After two months of heated debate in the Navy Headquarters, the Marines are granted permission to participate in the Schneider cup. "General Lejeune," Major Brainard began somewhat gleefully, "we have a great chance to win the Schneider Cup. I just confirmed that Admiral Moffett is going to buy an upgraded Curtis RC3.4 and a Curtis D12-A. He is giving us their best RC3.2 from last October's race."

"What's the difference between the models?" Lejeune asked for clarification.

"Sir," Brainard said, "the RC3.4 is about three feet shorter than the RC3.2 and that means less weight; it also has a new engine which increases the horse power from 565 to 685. The D12- A is a dog; I can't believe the Navy will enter that plane."

"Wow, seems like the RC3.4 has quite an advantage," Lejeune remarked, questioning Brainard's enthusiasm.

"On paper, yes Sir, but I have Lieutenant Schilt already working on enhancements for our RC3.2. It's the same model Doolittle used to win the cup last year. Schilt's quite an engineer on top of being a superb pilot. The re-engineering is in the design stage. We are keeping the changes secret until the race. The modifications will help, but 80% of the race depends on pilot skills. Schilt is our best. This kid can fly in any weather condition. With hurricane season coming, who knows what the weather will be on the day of the race? I'm absolutely confident he'll give those navy pilots a race they won't forget!"

"That's fantastic, Ed. Make sure you keep me in the loop; I don't want to miss this one!" Lejeune added, "Let me know if you need anything."

Quantico's Seaplane Hanger, October 1, 1926. Schilt had drawn up all his proposed changes. He received an oral okay from Major Brainard and was now working with Technical Sergeant Ike Billingsworth and Corporal "Junior" Wilson in the back of the large wooden hanger beside the Potomac River. Billingsworth was feeling good with his recent promotion, particularly now that everyone informally referred to him as "Top" instead of "Gunny," even though he had been mighty proud to be a Marine Corps Gunnery Sergeant. Junior Wilson had more energy and engine-repair savvy than all the aviation mechs Billingsworth ever knew. From Schuylkill Haven, Pennsylvania, Wilson raced and repaired Indian motorcycles before enlisting. His younger brother and dad took over the motorcycle shop while he enlisted in the Corps to learn about aviation maintenance. Billingsworth was the senior aviation mechanic in Quantico and Wilson was the only mech he had full faith in for this project

Lt Christian F. Schilt standing on a seaplane at Quantico, October 1926-*Official USMC Photo #528078*

Schilt gave them each a copy of his changes. Billingsworth read aloud:

RC3.2 DRAG REDUCTION ACTIONS

1. Place fairings (sheet metal) on top of any loose fabric not aerodynamic.

2. Adjust wing-to-fuselage flying wires.

3. Modify struts.

4. Adjust controls.

5. Adjust trim.

6. Adjust rigging angle on wings.

Finishing, he looked up at Schilt.

Schilt said, "Remember this is secret. You are not to discuss it with anyone. We'll work on it three to four hours a night for the next three weeks. After working hours," he added.

Billingsworth nodded, "Yes, Sir. We got it."

"I want it covered each night with a parachute, Top. In three weeks I want to take 'er up. After that, if the changes become known, the Navy won't have time to evaluate them and make any duplications. Any questions, Junior?"

"No, Sir. I made similar mods like this to my Indian cycle; I can almost do them in my sleep."

"We'll start tomorrow. And, if any questions develop between now and then, we'll go over them tomorrow afternoon." Both men nodded before silently going back to work.

Naval Air Station (NAS) Norfolk, Virginia, November 6-13 1926. Schilt, Billingsworth, and Wilson had been at the NAS Norfolk for most of the past week preparing for the race and fine tuning the plane.

Schilt had flown the approximate course Tuesday and Wednesday. By Thursday, the race's turn markers were set, and he and the other planes had made their true-course practice runs.

On Thursday evening the racing participants—all six sets of them—had gathered for dinner and drinks at the Navy Flight Club. There were three Italian military teams and three American military teams—two navy and one Marine. Twenty NAS hosts attended as well. Over 50 men celebrated the forthcoming race. There was a clear amount of bravado coming from Navy Lieutenant Cuddihy's camp. Schilt and the other two Marines ignored the heady forecasting and bragging about Cuddihy's upgraded RC3.4. They focused on the race, a mere day and a half away.

The weather had been beautiful all week, even on Friday morning. The race was scheduled for the next day, Saturday the 13th. However, by Friday noon, a bank of clouds seen on the Maryland side of the Chesapeake confirmed that a front—predicted by the Weather Service— would worsen flying conditions dramatically. The now-visible nor'easter front would lower the flying ceiling, lower the temperature, increase wind gusts, and guarantee occasional showers. Nevertheless the race would go on as scheduled. Thus, at twelve noon all six aircraft were moored just off the launch ramp to start their mandatory six-hour float test. By midafternoon, without a blazing sun sparkling off the blue water, the six shiny, multi-colored planes looked pretty humble in the cold shower.

The planes were back in hangers by 6:30 PM Friday evening. By that time, Elizabeth Schilt and Bill and Betsy Bailey had arrived at the air station's Bachelor Officer's Quarters where both couples were staying for the next couple of nights. While Frank checked in, Betsy and Elizabeth discussed their new "flappers"—the dresses in vogue that they would be wearing that evening for dinner.

Meanwhile, in the seaplane area, the Americans worked in one hanger and the Italians in another. The Marine team dried and operated every mechanical item they could. Schilt set a three- person, all-night watch on the plane. Billingsworth had the first watch allowing Schilt to go to the Navy Flight Club to meet Elizabeth and the Baileys for dinner. He would be back at 9:00 PM and be relieved by Wilson at midnight.

With low-hanging clouds and penetrating dampness, Saturday morning looked just as gloomy as Friday afternoon. Yet a crowd of about 5,000 had gathered by 11:00AM. The VIP bleachers were under a shelter keeping those ladies and gentlemen dry. The other bleachers were masked by umbrella coverage. The rest of the crowd stood on the hanger side of the restrictive launch ramp. The planes and crews there were ignoring the light rain.

Corporal Junior Wilson called to Technical Sergeant Billingsworth, "Hey Top, look at that Cuddihy group. They sure don't look as cheerful as they did on Thursday evening!"

Billingsworth told Wilson to get squared away as he saw General Lejeune and Major Brainard coming their way. Schilt talked to Lejeune and Brainard for a few minutes pointing out some of the modifications. He introduced his crew to the officers. After saluting, Lejeune and Brainard returned to the VIP bleachers; Schilt put on his leather cap and climbed into the cockpit, while Billingsworth climbed up behind Schilt for a final double check of all wires, straps, and gas lines.

By 11:55 AM all six planes slowly throttled to the start line. The noise and back spray drowned out much of the loud speaker introductions. The rain eased off. The wind held at 15 MPH. The clouds formed a ceiling between 800-1500 feet over the course under which the aviators would fly.

At 12:00 PM, the flag was dropped by the starter. Instantly, the planes thrust forward. First, within 50 yards of the start line, Cuddihy's bird was airborne, followed by two of the Italian's planes; then Schilt's plane and finally the remaining two lifted off. In cloud cover such as this, the planes flew at a height slightly above the surface to about 300 feet. Then they quickly disappeared out of sight.

The announcer chatted about the entries until he received a radio report from monitors which happened frequently. Converting the kilometer measurements of the European race to mileage, the race was 217.6 miles long and divided into seven laps. Each lap had three legs. Doolittle's average speed of 233 MPH in last year's fair weather had him flying the total distance in 56 minutes with each lap taking about eight minutes. Each of the three 10-miles (plus) legs of the laps needed a bit more than two and a half minutes to complete.

Thus in about seven minutes the crowd could hear the roar of the three lead planes. Suddenly appearing just above the water's surface was Mario DeBernardi in the stunning single- wing Macchi.M.39. Close on his tail was Schilt, followed by the second Italian, Adriano Bacula, who was just behind Schilt. Dragging back in sixth place was the once-boastful Lieutenant

Cuddihy. A quarter a mile from land above the turn buoy, the planes made a gentle turn and soared higher in the air, 300 feet above the surface.

Elizabeth Schilt looked at Bill Bailey and asked, "Why does he have to fly so close to the others and so close to the water? It makes me so nervous!" Before Bailey could answer, Betsy Bailey added another question she thought was equally as important, "And why do they fly higher as they leave us?"

"You two know I am not the expert like Frank is, but this is what he's been telling me and what I learned in flight school. The big issue is reducing drag," Bailey started and the two women nodded knowingly. "When they are flying on each other's tail, they are 'drafting'—being sucked behind by the plane in front of them. Frank learned that when he was at Rose Poly in Terre Haute. He and his buddies went to the Indianapolis Speedway and that's all those car racers did."

The women continued to listen attentively as Bailey went on. "Also, they are flying just off the surface to get in what we call a 'ground effect'. You see, there's a cushion of air about the same height as the total wing span." Bailey looked at both to make sure they were following his explanation. They were, so he continued, "Now that cushion effectively increases the lift and, at the same time reduces the amount of weight the engines have to pull. That in turn increases airspeed.

"Here come the other three," Betsy interrupted. "Wow, they are up in the air; no wonder they are so slow!"

"Right, Betsy. Frank and the guys in front are taking advantage of the wind direction. You can feel the breeze behind us blowing right onto the front of their planes as they approach. They are playing the wind. When the wind blows along the surface, it is slowed by the friction of the surface. So, that's another reason they are flying low as they approach. At higher altitudes, the wind has less friction and its speed increases. And that's why the leaders fly low when they approach us and higher as they fly away."

Elizabeth concluded, "I still wish he wouldn't fly so close to the water."

"Look, here they come again, and now there's separation," Bill observed. "Five more laps!"

In another 35 minutes the wet crowd, boosted by the announcer, was cheering wildly as DeBernardi in his Macchi.M.39 came into sight to win the cup. He was clocked in another record- breaking speed of 247 mph and completing the course in just less than 53 minutes. Not to be denied, less than four minutes later, was Frank Schilt with an average speed of 231 mph; that time was only two miles per hour behind what Doolittle had done last year in nice weather. Bacula hung on to third place, a commendable three minutes behind Schilt. The last finisher was the US Navy's Lieutenant William Tomlinson and he was 35 minutes after Bacula. Cuddihy in his souped-up Curtis abandoned the race on the final lap. The only other entry, from Italy, dropped out on the 4th lap.

Schilt coasted to the ramp and Junior Wilson grabbed the mooring line. With the plane safely held by Billingsworth and Wilson, Schilt jumped off the pontoon and greeted the Commandant who was now at the bottom of the ramp with his hand extend to congratulate his young aviator. Schilt's young wife was running up behind the Commandant. Lejeune spent ten minutes congratulating Schilt and meeting Elizabeth. Just as he was telling Schilt that the Corps would need him soon flying in support of the infantry, the band struck up a zesty tune to signal the start of the awards ceremony. Lejeune turned to return to the VIP bleachers, leaving Frank and Elizabeth Schilt staring at each other pondering what the Commandant was implying when he noted "soon flying in support of the infantry."

Following the awards ceremony, Rear Admiral Moffett looked at Major Brainard with a congratulatory smile on his face and said, "Ed, you were right. Schilt can fly as well as anyone in our services— particularly in a tight race like this."

"Well thank you, Sir."

"But you know what, Ed?"

"No, Sir. What?"

"This was our last race; don't ask for any more racers. We just can't afford them," Moffett summarized succinctly.

"Yes, Sir. I understand."

"I assume that you have been keeping up with the events down in Nicaragua."

"Absolutely," Brainard said although he was not entirely sure of all the implications meant by Moffett. Brainard figured he could get a full update from the Commandant on the way back to DC.

"I'm convinced you're going to need Schilt down in Nicaragua way before he's needed here to win any racing cup!"

An hour later on the trip back to DC, Major General Lejeune thanked Major Brainard for his efforts in Schilt's race.

Brainard thanked the Commandant for his support then paused for a moment before asking, "Sir, I heard there was a 30-day truce in Nicaragua that seemed to fizzle. Is there anything else you can tell me about what's happening down there?"

"I know you get the Department of State daily updates, Ed, so you are aware that the revolution is at the boiling point. Despite the 30-day truce we arranged, both armies are engaged. With Mexico's support, the Liberal Army under General Moncada is getting arms, munitions and money. They will soon be strong enough to overthrow any Conservative government even a coalition government. In any case, the Liberals are not pro-US, and that's not going to do well for our investments there." Lejeune paused to collect his thoughts then added, "When the treaty between the Liberals and Conservatives expired on October 30th, President Moncada promptly resigned.

"That's the latest I received and that was from yesterday's OPS briefing. At any rate I am anticipating a sizeable Marine Corps force going to Nicaragua soon. We'll be getting the ball rolling on Monday."

"Yes, Sir. I'll make sure the air squadrons are ready."

CHAPTER 5: BOOZE, BOMBING, AND NICARAGUA
(Seven months earlier)

Naval Air Station Coronado, California, March 19, 1926. Smedley Butler's eccentricities flourished during the two years he spent in Philadelphia. He had taken to his job as Commissioner of Public Safety with such verve that national news banners frequently touted him as Philly's top cop. However, despite his notoriety, after two years Lejeune anticipated needing him back in the Corps; with the Marines now committed in China and possibly soon in Nicaragua again, Butler's organizational and leadership qualities were required. Lejeune's personal letter to his long-time friend let him know he was needed back on active duty.

A part of Butler wanted to continue as the police chief. He even thought about entering politics. Another part wanted to return to the Corps. Then, after a ruthless, rather indiscreet booze bust that involved a few prominent citizens of the city, Butler was threatened with both impeachment and a law suit. As a result, General Butler returned to active duty within a month and traveled west where he assumed command of the Marine Corps Base in San Diego.

The base's principal tenant was the 4th Marine Regiment, commanded by one of Butler's old drinking buddies in his younger years, Colonel Alexander Williams. A social welcome for the general and his wife was a mandatory military protocol. Accordingly, Colonel Williams invited the Butlers and key officers to his home on the nearby island of Coronado for a cocktail party to be followed by dancing at Hotel del Coronado. On paper, everything seemed ideal. However, neither the host nor the guest of honor anticipated the party's potential pitfall.

Williams had not changed; Butler had. Butler's old drinking buddy still drank whereas Butler had sworn himself to abstinence. Butler refused the alcoholic drink offered by Williams at the start of the party, then witnessed his host consume it himself. The situation immediately placed Butler in a moral dilemma: to immediately curtail all drinking and ruin the party in his honor, to go home, or to turn a blind eye to the party's consumption of alcohol. Buying time to collect his thoughts, Butler invited the officer he was sitting beside to join him on the porch "to get some air."

"Major," the heated, now flush-faced brigadier confessed when the two had slipped out into San Diego's balmy air, "I have fought against all aspects of alcohol for the past five years; so when I see an old friend serving and consuming alcohol—even in his own quarters—I am most offended. I'm sorry I dragged you outside and into all of this."

The tall, wiry, 42-year old major innocently replied, "Sorry, Sir. I guess I missed most of that." Truth be told, when a Marine Corps legend invites a younger officer anywhere, the opportunity is never refused.

Recovering, Butler drew a deep breath and asked, "Your name was Major Rusty…" He paused, "I don't recall your last your name."

"It's actually Ross Rowell, Sir," the copper-brown topped major responded. Rubbing his close-cropped hair, Rowell added, "Somehow the nickname, 'Rusty,' given to me long ago, stuck."

"Did you say you are an aviator?" Butler asked.

"I did, general. I'm CO of Observation Squadron 1, known as VO-1M. We are based right here at the Naval Air Station in Coronado."

Visible in his face, Butler's disposition improved as Rowell went on.

"The squadron had been in Dom Rep. When they redeployed last year, the birds were shipped straight here instead of to the East Coast. We now have six De Havilland DH-4B1s and one Jenny." Rowell's obvious prejudice toward their well-outfitted squadron rang in his tone.

"Isn't that a JN-4 something, Rusty?"

"JN-4B yes, Sir. The Jenny's been around since before the war. It's so easy to fly; all the squadrons use one for training." He added, "Later this year after we add a fighter squadron and an administrative squadron, we'll become the '2nd Aviation Group'." Here Rowell's high cheekbones and intense countenance transformed into an expression confident with deserved pride.

"As a matter of fact, Sir, here is something we did last year—flew across country in a couple of Martin bombers. You may have read about it when you were in Philadelphia," Rowell said handing Butler a photograph he had taken from the pocket inside his coat.

Marine Gunner Michael Wodarczyk, Captain H. D. Campbell, Captain R.A. Presley and Major Ross E. Rowell

Photo from Marine Corps History Division

"I did read about it! My apologies Rusty. Congratulations! You aviators are sure stepping up. I'm glad to see the 'powers that be' recognize your potential. When I was in Quantico, our aviators made all sorts of accomplishments. I figure CMG," Butler continued referring to Lejeune, "is going to want me out in China sooner than later. I wouldn't mind air support this time. Heck, when I was fighting the Boxers at the turn of the century, the Wright brothers didn't even know where Kitty Hawk was located," he added facetiously.

Both laughed at the irony.

"Rusty, as squadron commander, what have you been focusing on?" Butler asked as the reality of the alcohol being served inside slipped away from him.

Leaping with gusto onto his favorite subject, Rowell elaborated, "Sir, around 1919 or 1920, Lieutenant Sandy Sanderson, who was in Haiti at the time with our 4th Squadron, worked on an idea that vastly improves the kind of aerial bombing we did in France. We simply make a 45- degree dive," here Rowell's long, lean fingers and forearm mimicked his words in gesture, "on the target and release bombs at the low point. This hurls the bomb directly at the target from about only 250 feet."

"You know, Rusty, I actually attended one of his lectures back in Quantico. That's a fantastic improvement."

Clearly impressed by this aviation-savvy, no-nonsense commanding general, whose attributes seem to mirror his own, Rowell explained, "I was introduced to it at the Army Advanced Flying School in '23, and my squadron has been practicing every day we fly—as a unit. I believe this dive bombing technique will defeat an enemy seeking offensive superiority; I don't care if they are massing for an attack or ambushing a patrol from defensive positions. Timed right, we can dive on them one bird at a time so as to continually attack them for up to an hour. They will never have seen anything like it! It would be perfect in Dom Rep or China for that matter," Rowell concluded.

Butler was now lost in thoughts transferring the enthusiastic major's convictions into past battles and future ones. He lit up a cigarette, offered one to Rowell who refused it, took a long drag and exhaled. Thirty seconds later, he looked Rowell in the eyes and said in a hushed voice, "Major, I forecast that, by next year, you'll need to do that in Nicaragua."

"Nicaragua, Sir?"

Without saying a word, Butler crushed out his cigarette, looked deep into Rowell's eyes, pursed his lips, raised his eyebrows, and cocked his head slightly to the left. His message couldn't have been clearer: I am giving you a "heads up" young man—be prepared to go south!

BOOK TWO:
EXPEDITING MARINE FORCES

(1926-1927)

CHAPTER 6: SEA-GOING MARINES LAND IN BLUEFIELDS

The Caribbean, May 15, 1926. The Liberal Party's revolution and the threat of the growing Liberal Army in Nicaragua, now in its fifth month, had grown beyond the incipient stage. The revolution sought to rid the country of foreigners. US firms owned and operated several gold mines and numerous banana plantations in the isolated eastern half of the country. For their own safety, the Americans living in Eastern Nicaragua pleaded for help. Their pleads resulted in the US Navy deploying the *USS Cleveland*, with its US Marine detachment, from the Pacific to the town of Bluefields along the east coast of Nicaragua via the Panama Canal. In route, the *Cleveland* was to stop by Managua's nearby Pacific port of Corinto to pick up a representative of the US legation. Also, three replacements for the ship's Marine detachment, who were to have disembarked at Corinto on the previous day by a west coast commercial steamer, would be picked up at the port.

USS Cleveland-*NH 55170*

Captain Henry LeBlanc, the Marine detachment commanding officer, and his acting first sergeant, Gunnery Sergeant John Tackett, used the captain's launch to go ashore to meet the new Marines and the legation passenger. The *Cleveland* was anchored one half mile from the port because the dock spaces for this size ship had already been taken. On the way in, Tackett, having joined the detachment in Panama three weeks earlier and having never been to Corinto, asked the Captain who had been with the detachment for two years, "Sir, who is this fella' you're supposed to meet?"

"His name is Ward, George Ward," LeBlanc responded. "He's been in Nicaragua for a few years. He's from New York City and is smart as a whip. I've been to several briefings he's given but never spent any time with him." The captain looked at Tackett and asked, "Any particular reason?"

"No, just that we're pulling over to pick up one person—beside our Marines—and I just assumed he had to be important."

"I know he has been promoted a couple of times." Reflecting, the captain added, "I'll tell you, Gunny, from the assignments he gets, he's sure an important person for our government in Managua."

The Pacific port of Corinto was the only deep-water port on either of Nicaragua's coasts and was located 15 miles west of the larger city of Chinandega. Chinandega was 70 miles northwest of the capital city, Managua. Managua and Corinto were tied together by the country's principal rail line, which passed through Chinandega and Leon.

"What's Corinto like, Sir?" Tackett asked, trying to acclimatize himself to his surroundings.

"Well, Gunny, Corinto is a small town located on a sandy island. It's connected to the mainland by a road bridge and a railroad bridge. Most of us visitors remember Corinto's waterfront by its fishy ocean odor, as well as its sweaty and sometimes-sober stevedores."

General View of Corinto May 1927-*USMC History Division K-3-14*

The captain pointed, "The railroad station is just beyond the waterfront warehouses." Tackett nodded, following the captain's directional indicators. "Across the street from the railroad station is the *Restaurante de Corinto*, run by a local by the name of Daniel López. The restaurant is known for its spicy seafood specials, a favorite of sea-going travelers. Beer, fruit drinks, and fruit drinks with rum are the main drinks. You ought to try it when we have more time in port."

"Sounds good, Skipper," the gunny smiled.

The captain's lips curved into a smile, "Oh...and Gunny." He waited for the wide shouldered Gunnery Sergeant to look back at him. "Unless you plan on spending quality time in the head, trust the sign hung over the bar."

Corinto: docks, hotels, two ships-*USMC Official Photo Nicaragua 14-10*

Before the gunny could question his captain further about the sign hung over the bar, the launch skimmed over the gentle waves of the port and docked. By 11:30 the two Marines climbed out of the boat at the pier. LeBlanc told the coxswain that he would radio the ship for a pickup in a couple of hours. With an "Aye, aye, Sir," the young sailor saluted and turned the craft back out to sea.

"God, does this place stink!" Gunnery Sergeant Tackett muttered.

The two of them inspected the waterfront without seeing Ward or the Marines. Twenty or so stevedores were waiting in the shade of the closest warehouse for ox-pulled carts loaded with food and other stores for the American ship.

"You'll get used to it in no time," LeBlanc responded. Then after giving him a moment to look around, he pointed toward a warehouse and said, "The only other place to meet Ward and the others is the Restaurante de Corinto." The gunny nodded remembering the captain's cryptic warning. "It's just on the other side of this yellow warehouse." With that, he traversed on the path paralleling the rail tracks that led away from the waterfront. In a minute they arrived at the front entrance of the restaurant. A blue sign with the neatly painted words "Restaurante de Corinto" hung over the door.

The gunny inspected it, then observing that his captain took no notice of it, shrugged and followed him inside. Inside the dimly-lit restaurant were empty tables and a small bar with four stools. A short cheery looking man opened the swinging doors to what was obviously the kitchen and greeted the two Marines, "Hola my friends. And welcome to Restaurante de Corinto."

"Señor López, it is good to see you again," LeBlanc replied in perfect Spanish.

"Señor Capitán LeBlanc, it is good to see you again," López, responded. "I assume you are looking for Sergeant Howard and his two Marines."

"Si, Señor, we are."

Gesturing with a leading hand toward a doorless opening along a side wall, López, stated, "They are enjoying my 'Citrus Surprise' out on the patio."

"Gunny, meet Mr. López, and then check on the Marines. I'll settle up with Mr. López, for their stay last night." Explaining to Tackett he continued, "Señor López, owns the only hotel in town. We'll send out a Citrus Surprise for you unless you'd like a beer."

The gunny eyes darted past the captain toward the patio then paused at the back of the restaurant where they spied a faded sign over the bar written partly in English.

Gringos—No drink el agua.

Obviously, this was the sign the captain was talking about, Gunny Tackett reflected before focusing on the restaurant owner's eyes.

"Sir," Tackett said shaking López's hand. "And, Captain, I believe I will have that beer."

"Good meeting you as well, Gunny," López, responded, then turned to the kitchen and, in a much louder voice ordered, "Maria, dos cerezas, por favor." Lowering his voice while retaining his constant smile he added, "I assumed you wanted one as well, Capitan."

Tackett nodded to both men, then walked toward the patio and through the doorless entry to the patio.

"Thank you, Señor. How much do I owe you for the hotel?" LeBlanc inquired.

Suddenly, the sun coming into the front entrance was blotted out by a man in khakis and a short-sleeve white shirt who looked around the restaurant and without hesitation said with a smile, "Captain LeBlanc, nice seeing you again."

LeBlanc was surprised George Ward had recognized him; then, after thinking about it, realized Ward knew all that was going on in Nicaragua. Before he could respond, the six foot-one, black haired Ward greeted the proprietor, "Señor López, como esta?" The restaurateur returned his greeting before the three men sat at a table inside to discuss the revolution.

Outside, in the walled patio overcrowded with colorful plants, the six foot-three, two hundred and twenty pound Sergeant Joe Howard immediately recognized his future boss and stood up sharply. Caught off guard, the two privates looked at the new comer until Howard, pumped his left arm with his thumb raised, realized they should be standing as well. "Sergeant Joe Howard, Gunny," Howard said to the well-built, though somewhat stocky Tackett.

"Nice meeting you, Howard," Tackett replied to the much larger man with an athletic build, then visually inspected the two privates for a half minute. Obviously pleased, "You must be Elliot and Okonski—I'll be calling you 'Ski'," the gunnery sergeant declared. Tackett added as he pulled up a fourth chair from the closest table, "We have a few minutes; did you bring your record books?"

"Yes, Sir, Gunnery Sergeant," the bright, accommodating Okonski responded.

"Well, let's see them."

While the two privates scrambled to dig through their bags, Howard, who anticipated the request, handed his book to Tackett. Tackett immediately opened the book to the third page that recorded the service member's prior assignments. Looking up, Tackett inquired, "I see you played football with Quantico's championship team. What position did you play?"

"Tackle, right tackle, second string behind Lieutenant Joe Burger."

At that time Maria silently appeared with a tray containing a beer and glass and placed it in front of Gunnery Sergeant Tackett and murmured softly with a velvety, somewhat enticing, accent, "Compliments of Señor López."

The conversation inside continued with a town-to-town analysis of the Liberal forces' actions and the inactions or inabilities of the Conservatives, even with Chamorro in power.

Outside, Howard pressed Tackett to discuss shipboard life. "What's life aboard ship like, Gunny?"

Tackett didn't hold back and thus explained that their quarters below deck were fairly crowded, "You'll probably enjoy sleeping under the stars on the open deck with most of the other Marines as long as it doesn't rain. Chow is fairly good. They have a good cook. That reminds me, I need a replacement in the chow hall tomorrow. Ski, that will be you."

Ski nodded his head without any expression.

"Let's put it this way, Marines, you'll be darn glad when you go ashore in Bluefields."

Within minutes the visit was over. López radioed the ship and the coxswain of the captain's skiff launched his trip into port to pick up his passengers. On the way to the Cleveland, LeBlanc asked Ward about López, radioing the ship. Ward explained that the US embassy and the Nicaraguan government have been working together for the past eight years to constantly retain good communicators. A whole series of civilians—priests, doctors, department employees, police chiefs, missionaries, and more have been lined up to operate the long-wave radio transmitters. Ward summarized, "The system seems to work all right but, in the mountains, we still have to rely on horseback."

From Corinto, the *Cleveland* steamed south passing by Costa Rica, then east through the Panama Canal, and finally, north into the Caribbean Sea toward Bluefields, Nicaragua. The *Cleveland* was a light cruiser, one of four--sometimes five--ships in a "Special Service Squadron" that would have never been considered the US Navy's finest. Compared with what was being built after the world war, these ships were slow, under gunned, and old. The *Cleveland*, built just after the turn of the century, had two sister ships, the *USS Denver* and the *USS Galveston*. The flag ship of the squadron, the *USS Rochester*, built in 1893, was the oldest vessel in the US Navy.

As the enforcers of the US diplomatic arm, Marine detachments aboard the ships were sent ashore "to preserve the peace" or take on any other designated mission. That had been their traditional role for over 100 years. And, in the 1920's, there was a no more prevalent need for induced stability than in the politically unstable Central American and Caribbean countries. Hence, the *Cleveland's* visit to Bluefields in May 1926 was a normal operation.

With 50 miles remaining before dropping anchor off Bluefields, the Marine detachment commanding officer, Captain LeBlanc, gathered his eight non-commissioned officers (NCOs) and led them to an open area just below the bridge. This was the area frequently used by the ship's captain, Lieutenant Commander Thomas Ellington, for briefings, classes, and social events. Ellington was young for his rank and believed that shared information resulted in successful operations. Even ashore, LeBlanc would be working for him. Ellington had asked Ward to brief him, his chiefs, and the Marine NCOs about the situation prior to disembarking. Ellington and LeBlanc learned much from Ward in the past couple of days aboard ship. They were highly impressed with his savvy insight, in-depth knowledge of the Nicaragua's revolting Liberals, native Indians, and the US investments being threatened.

At 0800 on May 20th under cloudy skies, all Marines were set for the briefing. The ship's captain came down from the bridge. Gunnery Sergeant Tackett clipped out, "Attention on deck!" All Marines shot to the position of attention, somewhat surprising Ellington, the ship's Captain.

The Captain immediately, responded with, "At ease, men." Ellington smiled, impressed with the disciplined etiquette of the Marines as they sat back on the benches. In a moment, he stated, "Men, if my navigator has it right, at about noon, we'll be laying anchor off of Bluefields,

Nicaragua. You'll be going ashore to ensure the safety of the Americans and maintain the peace in the region. The Navy and Marines have landed in Bluefields several times in the past. Normally, we end up making this a better community than we found it. I don't envision anything to be different with this visit.

"Captain LeBlanc and I feel fortunate that Mr. George Ward from the US legation in Managua was able to sail with us. Mr. Ward has agreed to give us an update on the situation. So

… Mr. Ward."

Ward moved to stand in front of the Marines and asked, "Men, how many of you were in France eight years ago?" the 30-year old State Department employee asked.

Both Tackett and one other leathery-faced, staff non-commissioned officer reluctantly raised their hands.

"I think I'll start all over," Ward said pausing, smiling. "Good Morning, Devil Dogs!"

A collective chuckle mixed with "Here, here," from the Marines, helped break the ice and bring a morning smile to the Marine faces.

Ward added, "My younger brother joined the Corps in '18 and was sent to France as a replacement in 1919. He'd have killed me if I hadn't called you 'Devil Dogs'." The young diplomat opened an A-frame easel and placed a piece of stiff cardboard on the two small armatures. He tacked a map to the cardboard that represented eastern portion Nicaragua and measured three-by- three feet.

The men focused closely on the map hoping to pick up one or two important pieces of information that might be useful in the next week or two. The Caribbean Sea, painted in blue, dominated the entire right side or eastern portion of the map. A light shade of green, sharply contrasting with the blue of the water, portrayed the coastal areas and landward. It ranged variously in width as the coast jutted in and out. Inland, higher elevations were colored in tan. Many rivers, two quite large and so long they nearly traversed the entire width of the map, flowed into the Caribbean. Four coastal towns were identified. Rama was the inland village identified.

Ward glanced at the map silencing the men when he asked to the men and asked, "What's the first thing they tell you about Nicaraguan maps?"

"They are not accurate!" he said answering his own rhetorical question and evoking mocking wrinkled faces. "Well, I picked this one up a day before we left Corinto. While it's pretty good, never forget to verify your map locations and directions with every other navigational tool you bring with you to this country.

"What the map shows on the east coast is a sparsely populated region with two prime coastal towns, the largest being Bluefields up here toward the middle of the map."

Pointing to the lower part of the map, Ward said, "The Rio or river San Juan separates Nicaragua from Costa Rica. The river is significant as it is only about 160 kilómetros, or 100 miles, upstream to the huge Lago or lake de Nicaragua." Ward interrupted his answer to explain, "Don't forget the government of Nicaragua and others in Central America adopted the metric system of their standard of measurement about 17 years ago, so all of the maps and road signs are in meters not miles." Seeing the nodding of heads, he continued, "Anyway, cross that lake and you're about 30 land miles from the Pacific Ocean. However, here at the Caribbean end, you'll find Greytown that used to be San Juan del Norte; but since 1847, it bears the name of British Governor Grey of Jamaica who named it after himself."

Spotting a hand in the air, Ward paused, "Sergeant?"

"Sergeant Howard, Sir. Would it have been possible to put a canal to the Pacific in there?"

"Sharp question. As a matter of fact, the US Navy had been flexing its muscles in the Caribbean about the time Greytown was named. Right after that, in 1850, the US and Britain signed a pact to build a canal in Nicaragua with both British and the US Navies controlling its waters." Ward paused reflecting, "I have to add that in 1916, ten years ago, the US again signed a treaty with Nicaragua giving us the exclusive rights to build a canal through the country. Obviously, the best location would be down south here. "

Again, Ward pointed while referencing the map. "Let's go northward to Bluefields, our objective. Bluefields was named after the Dutch Pirate, Henry Bluefeldt who often hid in the large Bluefields Bay behind the promontory overlooking the Caribbean, called 'El Bluff.' This was in about 1610. After that, the native Kukra Indians were hired by both Dutch and British pirates to repair their boats. Soon trade began with the Europeans. Permanent residents came from Europe in the late 1700s. Banana plantations were started and enslaved Africans from Jamaica came to work the plantations. While slavery no longer exists, Bluefields gained a strong Caribbean influence at that point. Anglo and Moravian churches came and now dominate the Bluefields landscape. Believe it or not, Chinese immigrants are beginning to show up in Bluefields. So you are going into quite a hodgepodge of people. You'll find it dirty and, frankly, unregulated.

"I've talked about the Kukra Indians, but there are a couple of tribes worth knowing. The friendliest is the small tribe of Ramas who live on an island in the Bluefields Bay. The other is the Miskitos who live along the rivers and in elevated villages inland. They picked up their name because they sided with the British against the Spanish and were given 'muskets'—hence Miskitos." Ward added, "Although there are enough mosquitoes on the rivers to believe that's where their name came from.

"Corporal," Ward recognized a smallish, freckled-faced red head in the back row who held his right index finger raised as he sought to be called on.

"Sir, why are we going to Bluefields?"

"Another good question. Well, those two canal treaties caused speculation. US firms invested in various industries all over the east coast. We have banana plantations, gold mines, and land investments for future a trans-isthmus canal and rail lines. As motley as Bluefields is, it's the principal town Americans and Europeans go to when there is trouble. And, today, there is trouble all over the east coast."

Ward did not wait for the next question but continued on without pausing, "Five months ago, in January, the ultra-Conservative General Emiliano Chamorro seized control of the country in a bloodless coup, forcing the fairly-elected Liberal president, Carlos Solórzano to quit—capitulate—possibly to save his life. He lives in California now. His vice president, Baustista Sacaza, fled to liberal Mexico, a country filled with anti-Yankee sentiments, to prepare to return to power. From there he first appealed for US support which wasn't forthcoming since he was an ultra-Liberal.

"Chamorro, on the other hand, dismissed all the Liberal congressmen and had the remaining Conservative congressmen appoint him as provisional president. Today what's bugging Chamorro is the fact that the US and other countries are refusing to recognize his government. You see his coup was a violation of the 1923 Treaty of Washington. Constitutionally, Chamorro is not the legitimate president. According to the constitution, should an elected president step down, the presidency is assumed by the elected vice president. And that is the Liberal's, specifically Sacaza's, message: that he's the legitimate president. We cannot disagree with that. But now Sacaza is raising arms and his exiles are filtering in from Mexico with them. Our people in Bluefields indicate that newly-arrived armed Nicaraguans are beginning to live in town."

Ward smiled now, "We'll be landing at Bluefields by midafternoon. You will be here probably a couple of weeks. By that time, everyone on the east coast will know you landed and then things should quiet down. As your captain will remind you, we are there only to protect Americans and their property. The Conservatives supporting Chamorro won't be happy about our neutrality, but we must remain so."

Ward looked around at the attentive Marines and said, "Unless there are some questions, thanks for your time, and I'll see you ashore."

Lieutenant Commander Ellington thanked Ward for the informative briefing and told the men they would be served lunch before going ashore.

Captain LeBlanc dismissed the NCOs but, before he did, he reminded them of an inspection under arms at 11:00 AM.

At 2:15 PM, LeBlanc and Ward were on the first boat going ashore. Halfway in, Ward turned to Le Blanc and asked, "Henry, have you ever been to Bluefields before?"

"Not yet, George. I have been to Cabo Gracias and Puerto Cabezas, but it seems that every time we are slated to go to Bluefields, one of the other detachments lands just before us. Have I missed anything?"

"Well not really. I just wanted to tell you that if, by chance, your radio transmitter is not working and if any of you have a need to get a message to the ship, there's a Mr. Robert Satterwhite—he's a British citizen—who can help you. You'll most likely find him at 'Lola's,' ironically three houses away from the Moravian mission. He'll seem like he's three sheets to the wind; but there's no one better than him at transmitting Morse code, and he'll do anything for an American. So just ask him."

"Good tip, my friend, Thanks."

Chapter 7: A Presidential Call For Action

Nicaragua, June-October 1926. Following the two-week visit to Bluefields by the *Cleveland* in May 1926, Mexico announced its desire to replace the United States as the protector of Central America. In keeping with that desire, Mexico started arming of Vice President Sacaza's Liberal Army under the command of General José Moncada. Not recognized by the United States because of the coup d'état earlier that year and now attacked by the Nicaraguan Liberal Army supported by Mexico, President Chamorro felt threatened.

General Moncada established his headquarters in the east coast town of Puerto Cabezas earlier in the summer. He attacked south and threatening Bluefields in early August. After Bluefield's neutrality was challenged, on August 20 the town requested US support. A force of 100 *USS Galveston* Marines and sailors went ashore on August 27th to defend the town should it be attacked by the Liberal Army and to prevent rioting in the town by Liberal infiltrators.

By September, the high ground separating Bluefields Bay and the Caribbean, El Bluff, was occupied by a small unit of the Conservative army driven there by General Moncada's forces. The Liberal Army began a slow piecemeal attack on the Conservative positions from its first contact. The US enlarged the Bluefields "neutral zone" to include El Bluff on September 24th, thereby forcing both armies to withdraw inland about 80 kilómetros to resume fighting near the town of Rama.

At the end of September, the Liberal Army had achieved success by cutting off commerce and precluding Chamorro from funding his army. On October 1, 1926, the US legation's Envoy Extraordinary and Minister Charles C. Eberhardt, his newly-promoted deputy, George Ward, and his military attaché, Colonel Al Kauffman, had arranged a 30-day truce. As part of the truce, both sides would send representatives to Corinto for peace talks aboard the USS Denver. Marines would provide security of the port. However, the talks failed as the sides could not agree on a provisional president to replace Chamorro.

Chamorro resigned when the truce expired on October 30th. The resignation prompted the Conservative congress to select a Conservative senator by the name of Sebastian Uriza to act as the provisional president who would form a new government. The US immediately stated that they would not recognize a selection that was not supported by the Nicaragua constitution. Conferring with its European allies, in particular, Great Britain and Italy, the US insisted that the congress find a solution to their constitutional crisis.

Managua, November 1926. With skirmishes breaking out through the country, the weary congress reconvened and determined the only acceptable solution was to reinstate the Liberal congressmen ousted by Chamorro. Constitutionally, that would restore the government to its original status. On November 14, 1926, the reconstructed congress selected Adolfo Díaz, once the chief executive in 1912, as the country's provisional president. These actions satisfied the Americans and Europeans, and they immediately recognized Díaz's government. However, Mexico insisted that ousted Vice President Sacaza should be the country's leader and refused to recognize the Díaz government.

The very next day at 4:00 PM, Minister Eberhardt and Colonel Kauffman visited President Díaz in his presidential office. Eberhardt, a Republican, had been an industrialist prior to entering the diplomatic assignments for the United States. On March 12, 1925, he became the Minister to Nicaragua. Kauffman, who served with distinction during the Great War eight years earlier, was a true professional with a good sense of humor that Eberhardt enjoyed.

His secretary announced the visitors, "Mr. President, the American visitors are here.

Should I send them in?"

Díaz silently nodded his head.

As most top level meetings go, the agenda and purpose of the meeting had been predetermined. This meeting merely formalized Díaz's agreement that, if selected by the constitutional congress to take the country's reigns for thirteen months, he would do so as long the US would guarantee its support.

"Greetings, Minister Eberhardt," Díaz began. "And welcome Colonel Kauffman."

"Buenos Días, Señor Presidente,"

"Please be seated gentlemen," Díaz said, gesturing at the chairs.

After a settling in the chairs and making light talk about how many changes were made at the presidential office since the president had been here fourteen years earlier, Díaz opened the only envelope lying on the center of his empty desk and withdrew a single piece of paper. He studied it for thirty seconds then, somewhat hesitantly, passed it to Eberhardt.

Eberhardt looked at it for a moment and passed it on to Kauffman who watched it being typed in his office two days earlier. Kauffman said, "Looks good to me, Minister Eberhardt," and returned the paper containing a request for a treaty whereby the United States guarantees peace in Nicaragua and provides a specific number and mix of weapons needed for the Nicaraguan army. The paper also requested that a brigade of Marines be sent to counter the ever-growing Liberal Army. Eberhardt, now with paper in hand, said expectedly, "We will transmit your request tonight, Señor Presidente. The State Department and War Department are expecting it."

Naturally, the request had been negotiated by representatives of both countries during the past two months and agreed to by the US Secretary of State, Frank Kellogg, and former US Secretary of War, Henry "The Colonel" Stimson. The request would be forwarded to President Coolidge.

With a slight smile, Díaz said, "Mucho gracias, señor. Let me know the progress of my country's request."

"Si, Señor Presidente."

The legation headquarters were but a few blocks from Díaz's office; nevertheless, the American Charge d'affairés driver had parked his car in front of the presidential office building. The driver held the right rear door open for Eberhardt while Kauffman went behind the car and sat in the back seat behind the driver. Eberhardt directed the driver to return to the ministry.

George Ward greeted them as they entered the ministry. "How'd the meeting with President Díaz go, Sir?"

"No issues, no surprises, George. All as planned. Anything going on here?" Eberhardt asked.

"Yes Sir. I have both Mr. James Meriwether of the British consulate and Signor Viti from Italian delegation—who you met at Díaz's swearing ceremony—waiting for you. Both fear their citizens in Nicaragua are in grave danger."

"Thanks, George. Where are they?"

"I have them waiting in the reception room. They are having tea."

"Good. I'll see them immediately." Turning to Kauffman, Eberhardt said, "Al, get me the latest from Bluefields. I want to see what Moncada is up too. We may have to ask 'The Colonel' for the Marines sooner than we thought."

Bluefields, December 1926. Americans on the east coast found themselves helpless against elements of the Liberal Army and the packs of bandits following in the army's path. Daily, reports flowed to the legation, detailing destroyed American property. Sacaza returned from Mexico and claimed to be the leader of the "Constitutionalists" or, in his words, "the only legitimate government." He and his armed Constitutionalist supporters illegally collected taxes from Americans who complained to the legation. The legation formally protested to President Díaz who was helpless. The day after Christmas an American was killed at Puerto Cabezas, north of Bluefields. The legation relayed the reports to Washington, pleading for action.

Managua, January 6, 1927. Within the scope of the legation ministry and the Special Services Squadron authority, Marines and sailors from Special Services squadron in a coordinating manner were ordered to land at several coastal cities to safeguard US interests. *Galveston* Marines and sailors landed in Corinto and rushed by rail to protect the US legation headquarters and European diplomatic property in Managua. On the east coast, *USS Rochester* Marines landed on the east coast at Puerto Cabezas; *USS Cleveland* Marines landed at Bluefields; and *USS Denver* Marines split their force between Prinzapolca and Rio Grande.

Washington, January 9, 1927. President Coolidge took his oath of office in 1923 to preserve, protect and defend the Constitution of the United States. He and his predecessors interpreted this oath to include American lives and property anywhere in the world. Every afternoon since mid-October, Secretary of State Kellogg and Secretary of War Stimson would communicate with their representatives in Nicaragua. In turn, the secretaries would feed the president information about the deteriorating situation in Nicaragua during their morning briefings.

Coolidge soon became agitated with the Nicaraguan situation. In place was a legitimate government that complied with their own constitution. Yet this government was not respected nor recognized by the Liberals. While not wanting to be drawn into a war with the Liberals, their increased destruction of American lives and property challenged his oath of office, which he would never forsake. Coolidge concluded that direct action by the United States would be the only way to pacify the continuing hostilities and protect Americans in Nicaragua. He turned to the nation's most distinguished diplomat available for the task to solve this Latin-American dilemma, former Secretary of War Henry L. Stimson.

Stimson, a Republican and distinguished Yale College and Harvard Law School graduate, had been Secretary of War from 1911 until 1913. Unable to get Democratic President Wilson's support for reorganizing the Army, Stimson joined the U.S. Army in France as an artillery officer, reaching the rank of colonel in 1918. He continued his military service in the reserves, rising to brigadier general in 1922. Yet, in the Washington circle, he would always be referred to as "The Colonel."

By January 9th, the President met with Secretary of War, Henry Stimson, and Major General Commandant Lejeune, to discuss the size of the force needed to restore peace in the country. Coolidge had been sitting on the Díaz request for Marines, weapons, and a treaty guarantying peace in Nicaragua. Coolidge instructed Stimson to personally ensure that the two sides disarm until Nicaragua's 1928 presidential election. "Henry, keep in mind that I chose you because of your 'no-nonsense' reputation in the business world. And now I need you to get this Nicaragua mess cleaned up. I want you to get down there this spring after the Marines have things well in hand and get everyone to turn in their weapons. This way there's going to be no new outbreaks of war until…" Coolidge paused, shaking his head, knowing better. Anywhere in Central or South America the party out of power would challenge the party in power with a military takeover. He continued, "Well, let's get through the '28 elections. In the meanwhile, I want you to establish a national guard or police force of sufficient capability that we don't have to send the Marines in there every three months." He looked at the two men in the eyes and asked, rhetorically, "Can you two handle all of that?"

With a "Yes Sir, Mr. President" and head nodding, the Secretary and Commandant knew they had been given a green light to execute the plans they had been working on for the past few months.

Finally on the 10th of January, the normally quiet President let the US Congress know that, under no terms, would he let the situation in Nicaragua continue to deteriorate. He was sending in a brigade of Marines immediately and would be supporting the organization and arming of a Nicaraguan national guard to allow that country to maintain its own security. His order to execute those intentions was made official that same day.

Chapter 8: Marines Descend On Nicaragua

Bluefield Bay, January 11, 1927. "We will be landing in three hours," Lieutenant Colonel James Meade said as he looked at his three company commanders and staff officers gathered after breakfast in the officer's galley of the *U.S.S. Argonne*. "Each of you has received your orders. We'll be debarking as planned. For political reasons we can't land until the President speaks to Congress. That ought to be at 1100. I don't expect that all of the battalion will be here on the East Coast too long as Intel reports are indicating increased enemy activity near Managua."

"Sir, what's the latest on Liberal Army activities around Bluefields?" Captain Fred Buchanan, commanding officer of the 77th Company, asked. The 77th Company was going to occupy the outskirts of the town.

Meade looked at Technical Sergeant Larson, his intelligence chief, and without saying anything raised his eyebrows to redirect the question.

Larson jumped on the reflected question. "Sir, the last report from Captain LeBlanc came in at 0600. According to him it remains peaceful around town and on El Bluff, the high ground we just sailed by. If any activity is expected, it may take place at Rama, up the Escondido River."

"Thanks, Larson. Remember men, when we go ashore, Company 77th will secure the town first and occupy the two entrances into Bluefields. Anyone coming in and out with a rifle I want identified and his weapon taken." Looking at his quartermaster, First Lieutenant Shilling, Meade asked, "When is the USS *Meredith* coming with our follow-on supplies, so we can store the weapons we capture?"

Samuel Shilling III from Shillington, Pennsylvania, joined the Marine Corps as a result of prohibition when his family's brewery was mostly shuttered, answered, "Sir, she'll be in Guantanamo Bay for another three days and I do not believe we'll be able to store any captured weapons." Shilling added, "We just don't have the space."

"You're probably right 'Shilly'." Meade paused while contemplating. "Buchanan, find a good place to pitch the confiscated weapons in the Escondido river. We'll just record who we got them from and the type of weapon."

"All of you know that the 51st Company is debarking last." Then looking at his senior, highly confident captain, Gilbert Hatfield, who commands the 51st Company, Meade said, "Gil, once we get ashore and have the place secured, I want you to move out toward Rama. Depending on the roads and trails, I suspect you'll take four days to patrol up to Rama."

"We believe that we'll be there in two and a half days, Sir," Hatfield responded in a confident, yet almost challenging, manner.

"Just make sure you have enough supplies for a week. If we are to make a neutral zone along the Escondido, you'll have to clear each village on the way up to Rama. After that, you'll be living off the land. I suspect that in about a week the rest of us will be going to Corinto on the western side. So prepare your men for a lengthy stay."

"Sir," Hatfield acknowledged.

Panama Canal, January 28, 1927. After two weeks in Bluefields, the *U.S.S. Argonne* with its embarked battalion was ordered back to Corinto.

"Colonel Meade?" Lieutenant Howard Cartwright, the battalion communications officer inquired as he knocked on a door in the ship's officer country. A sign on the door read on two lines, "Lieutenant Colonel J. J. Meade, CO, 2nd Bn, 5th Marines."

"Come on in, "Howie," Jim Meade answered recognizing Cartwright's voice.

Cartwright opened the door, handed a naval message to his boss, and said, "Looks like they want us in Managua, Sir."

Meade put on his reading glasses and read the message carefully. On ticker-tape cut and glued to a single piece of paper was the message from the Commander Special Services Squadron that read:

```
SECRET
TO CO 2D BN, 5THMARS: UPON ARRIVAL CORINTO PROCEED BY RAIL TO
MANAGUA. ASSIST IN DEFENSE OF CAPITAL AREA. COL A. KAUFFMAN,
LEG MIL ATTACHÉ, OR MR GEO WARD, DEP MIN, WILL ASSIST IN
COORDINATING WITH LOCAL FORCES.
ON 1FEB27 ASSUME RESPONSIBILITY FOR DEFENSE OF CAPITAL.
SECRET
```

"Howie," Meade said looking up, "Have the 'ExO' and the 'OpsO'," referring to the battalion executive officer, Major Donald Black, and the battalion operations officer, Captain Luke Kelly, "report up here ASAP. Oh yeah, better have Shilly come to."

Managua, February 7, 1927. Minister Eberhardt. Colonel Kauffman, George Ward, and Lieutenant Colonel Meade met in an emergency meeting to review the current situation after the previous day's destruction by the Liberal Army of Chinandega, the rail city just north of the capital. Major Black and Captain Kelly accompanied Meade. Eberhardt opened the meeting by welcoming the Marines to Managua then called on Ward to update everyone with the situation in Chinandega.

"Yes, Sir," Ward stated and walked over to a city map of Chinandega. "To begin with, Nicaraguan troops have retaken the city. However," he said making a circle in the center of the map with his right index finger, "the core of the city is in ruins. The Liberal force was estimated to be 100 men. They literally went house-to-house and burned and blew up every structure they could.

"The city is in dire need of medical supplies, food and water." Looking at Lieutenant Colonel Meade, he added, "With the government troops already deployed, I anticipate your battalion's support will be needed as well as that of Admiral Latimer's Special Services Squadron. If there are no questions, at this point, I'll turn the briefing over to Colonel Kauffman."

Seeing Meade's hand raise a couple of inches above the table, Ward said, "Oh, excuse me, Colonel Meade."

"Thanks. Mr. Ward, can you tell me about the rail line and rail station at Chinandega? VO- 1M, the observation squadron from California, will be here by the end of the month."

"I can tell you that they burned the station, Colonel. It's totally gone. But, amazingly, they paid no attention to the tracks. The line's in good shape from Corinto to here."

Meade responded, "Good, thanks."

Kauffman followed and opened with, "Requirements? None are known yet. I suspect that the Nicaraguan army will survey the damage and get back to us tomorrow. Knowing what I do, they will want supplies of all kinds and manpower to handle it when it arrives up there. Like George said, the good news is, they didn't destroy the rail line. I anticipate you'll have to assist in loading trucks and wagons from the government warehouses and moving it to the Managua train station perhaps as early as tomorrow. How many men you'll need to escort the supplies to Chinandega is unclear at this point."

Kauffman continued: "We have been in touch with the Special Services Squadron. For security measures, we're keeping the *Cleveland* afloat in the Caribbean; the *Rochester* is going to stay in the vicinity of Bluefields; and we're bringing the *Denver* with its detachments back to Corinto to safe guard the rail line from there to Managua. As you know, Colonel Meade, the 51st Company is on its way back on the two ships. They will arrive in Corinto on February 18th to rejoin your battalion in defense of the Managua capital area.

"Your brigade from Quantico will be offloading in Corinto beginning March 6th and moving by rail and road to the capital area. We want that movement uninterrupted." Looking at Minister Eberhardt, Kauffman concluded, "That's all I have for now Sir."

"Thanks, Al," Eberhardt said. "Before we get to the Brigade's deployment, I should add that as of this morning we learned that

Secretary Stimson will be leaving Washington with his wife to force a settlement between the warring armies as early as mid-March."

"Colonel Meade, what's the latest on the brigade?"

Meade stood up and said, "Minister Eberhardt, the 2nd Marine Brigade has been activated and will be commanded by Brigadier General Logan Feland. For information, General Feland comes with a lot of combat experience; he had been the CO of my battalion, 2nd Battalion, 5th Marine Regiment in France during the War. The brigade's infantry will be comprised of the rest of the 5th Marines and 11th Marines. Marine regiments deploy with supporting artillery and quartermaster units. Sir, I received this photo last night. It has Commandant Major General Lejeune and our 2nd Brigade Commanding General, Brigadier General Feland reviewing the 5th Marines before they deployed from Quantico.

Photo Provided by USMC History Division

"VO-1M, the observation squadron I mentioned earlier, will be coming from San Diego, and it is planned that they'll be reinforced by VO-4M out of Quantico."

"What type of aircraft will they be bringing?" Kauffman asked.

"Sir, from what I know, VO-1M will be bringing six DH-4Bs De Havillands and VO-4M will be bringing six O2U-1 Corsairs. I understand that VO-1M will be shipping out on the 18th.

We should expect them here on the 26th, actually less than three weeks. They will be the first to arrive.

"As noted General Feland is planning to be here during the first week in March. The 5th Marines, with 1000 Marines, will be embarked on the *USS Henderson* with General Feland. Since the 11th Marines are just activating, I don't believe we'll see them until later this spring. And, Sir, that's all the information I have at this time."

"Very well Colonel Meade." Then addressing his military attaché, "Al, What is the latest on housing the Brigade?"

"Sir, there are a lot of issues being worked out with the host country. Our priority is on the observation squadron. We want to get them housed at the aerodrome, but some housekeeping and minor construction is needed first. I have been coordinating details directly with the squadron commander, Major Rowell. In the meanwhile, they will be using the softball park next to the aerodrome for their airfield."

Eberhardt looked around the room. "Well, gentlemen, this is not going to be easy. Bringing in 2,000 Marines in the middle of a civil war is going to drain all of us. We'll have to communicate effectively among ourselves. Colonel Meade, if ever you or your staff need to contact any of us at any time and that includes me, please do so without hesitation."

"Thank you, Sir," Meade responded.

Eberhardt finished, "Let's focus on getting help to Chinandega. After that, we'll concentrate on making sure Major Rowell's squadron gets situated here in Managua. All right?" Eberhardt looked at the serious faces with heads nodding in agreement. "Then gentlemen, that will be all."

Outside the Managua Aerodrome, February 27, 1927. Chief Marine Gunner Michael Wodarczyk, possibly the best flyer in VO-1M, walked up behind one of his oldest friends, Technical Sergeant Walter Heller, who was closely supervising the unpacking and assembly of the third DH-4B, and said, "Hey Walt, you had better be careful with old Green Nose!"

Managua Airfield-*USMC History Division*

Heller spun around, his concentration broken, "Ski? When'd you get down here to this lovely ball park?"

"I would have been here this morning, but I jumped off the train in Chinandega to check the damage those Liberals did. Really wiped the darn place out. I picked up this photo from the Marine cameraman assigned to a New York Times guy."

Train derailed by rebels Near Chinandega-*USMC History Division 132-3*

"Yeah, I saw that train too when we went through. I also thought it was pretty safe when I saw the Marines guarding the town." Spinning his head to the half dozen mechanics, Heller called out, "Hey you six, scratch one piece of paint off Green Nose and I'll personally see you are court- martialed."

Heller looked stern until he heard enough, "Yes, Technical Sergeant." He then turned back, so that the troops wouldn't hear, and said quietly, "Boy that bird takes more of my time than the rest."

"Well Rusty has been flying it for three years now, and he wouldn't take a new one if the Commandant came down here to personally gave it to him." Wodarczyk said about his boss, Major Rusty Rowell. "By the way where is the major?"

"He's over there in the airfield looking at takeoff areas. Hey, here comes another bird—it looks like yours. I have to get the next working party ready."

"Right, I want to stay around to see how you unpack that plane," Wodarczyk said now that it caught his interest.

Heller didn't skip a beat. "Smitty," referring to Corporal Roland Smitty who mostly went by Smitty to everyone, "I want you and your team up here now!"

Two minutes went by and the six men were assembled. Wodarczyk stood back while Heller took over. "Men, I want to hear you tell me how to reassemble an aircraft," he demanded. "First you, Smitty."

One by one each Marine mechanic stated the steps that they rehearsed a dozen times a day on the ship that took them to Corinto.

"First the fuselage." "Remove the box top." "Remove the box sides."

"Assemble the wheels and struts."

"Lift the fuselage from its cradle-CAREFULLY!" "Fasten fuselage to the struts."

And on and on until the wings were bolted back on, the flying wires and turnbuckles were adjusted; and fairings were screwed back on tight.

Wodarczyk smiled, shook his head, and walked out to the airfield.

"Good afternoon, Boss," Wodarczyk called out as he approached Major Rowell who was deep in thought looking at two of the mountain peaks in the skyline.

Looking back, he saw Wodarczyk and greeted him with a, "Oh, welcome to Managua, Ski." And, characteristic of the man with the reddish-brown hair who never stopped working, immediately added, "Seems like the prevailing winds are coming off the mountains from the north and east. So, we basically will be taking off from around third base and should be airborne over right field."

"Makes sense, Sir.

"How's Walt doing with the birds?"

Wodarczyk chuckled and said, "He's got those kids doing it by the numbers. He's threatened them with a court-martial if they scratched your Green Nose."

Rowell smiled at that line. "Ski, how about you and Walt meet me at the aerodrome in about 15 minutes? I'd like your input on how we'll rework the facility. Archibald," referring to his executive officer, Captain Stan Archibald, "is over there now and…well…We just don't want him getting too far ahead with the aerodrome project. I believe you know what I mean."

"See you over there then, Major," Wodarczyk said heading back to Heller and thinking about Captain Archibald whose potential seemed to run a good bit ahead of his performance.

Twenty minutes later Wodarczyk and Heller entered the aerodrome and joined Rowell, Archibald, Captain Frank Pierce, and Second Lieutenant Earl Thomas laughing at an old French bi-plane used during the world war. Two men, apparently the pilots, were explaining the antiquated features and joined in the humor about their aircraft.

Laughing the loudest was the youthful executive officer who, upon seeing Wodarczyk and Heller join them, said, "You won't believe this, Ski. But this bird and the one like it outside is the Nicaraguan Air Force!" Then he added that Mr. Stokes and Mr. Campbell were from Brooklyn and had been contracted to be the pilots. "Mr. Stokes tell these two gentlemen how low you go on your missions."

"Well, we are normally at 1,000 feet."

Archibald snickering said, "They never heard of 'glide bombing' or 'dive bombing'. But they agreed to be social members of VO-1M and tonight they are going to show us the town."

"Captain Archibald," Rowell interrupted placing a sober note on the moment, "there's going to be no liberty tonight for anyone until you get the galley functioning and berthing for all 85 of us." As all men now looked at the VO-1M's business-first commanding officer, Rowell made the priorities clear, "I want you officers to always look after the troops first, then the birds, then yourselves last. I trust you'll remember that. Technical Sergeant Heller, I want to get those birds in the air in the next 36 hours so we can start looking for those rebels. Now, are there any questions?"

The gathering disbursed immediately. Rowell pulled Wodarczyk and Heller aside to discuss the logical flow of maintenance for both their planes and the others coming from Quantico in the next couple of months.

BOOK THREE: NICARAGUAN COMBATANTS

(1926-1927)

Chapter 9: Sandino—The Perfect Antgonist

San Albino Mines, Nueva Segovia, May 15, 1926. The American-owned San Albino gold mine in the heart of the northern mining district in the desolated, mountainous Department of Nueva Segovia was, from the air, less than 30 miles south of the Honduran border.

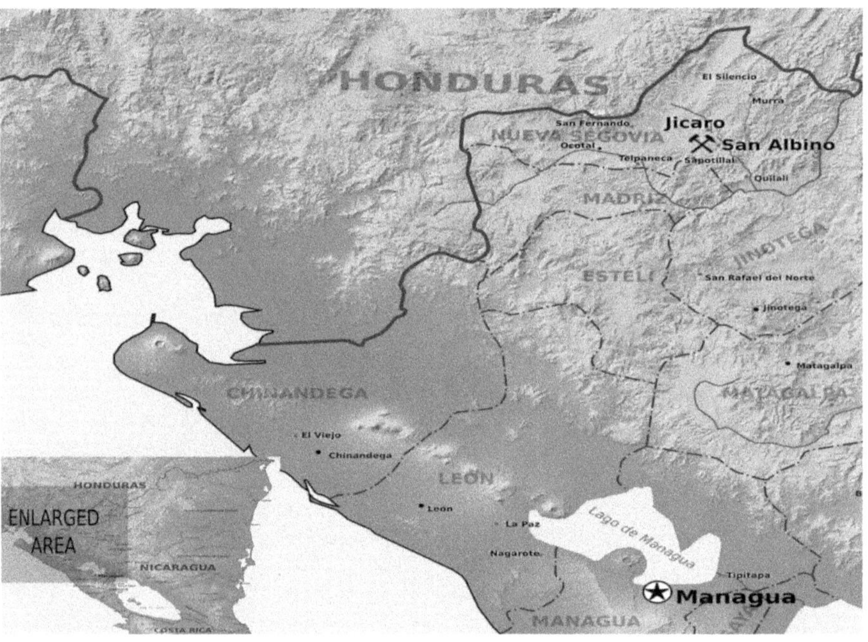

"Como se llama?" The American foreman asked the name of the five-foot-eight-inch, lean native in the country's official language of Spanish while sitting by a small table enabling him to note information with a pencil on a pad.

"Augusto Caesar Sandino," was the response stated in a slowly-delivered, articulate, though biting voice that rang with: "And don't forget it, Yankee!" Sandino's eyes penetrated. He didn't come across as the average peasant usually hired by the mine.

The foreman looked up warily. He could sense that a trouble maker was standing in front of him. The somewhat passive, local miners spoke mostly in their own Indian language. Yet the applicant standing in front of him probably could handle the work. The absentee rate had been high due to the annual Palo de Mayo *may pole* celebrations that drew the Indians back to their own villages where they took a month off from mining. Still, work had to be done, and he needed miners.

"Work experience?"

"Yeah," Sandino answered in a sarcastic growl.

Spotting the applicant's callous hands the foreman redefined his question, "I mean what type of work have you done?"

Sandino stared with rage down at the busy American engrossed with writing in his book. His stare emanated from the pure hate in his heart for foreigners, particularly Yankees. With that he responded, "I have worked around from the time I left Nicaragua in 1920. In Honduras, I worked at a US sugar refinery; in Guatemala, I worked at the United Fruit banana plantation; and most recently, I worked at an American oil company in Mexico."

Impressed, the foreman said, "Okay, be here at 5:30 in the morning. You'll be our time keeper. I'll expect accuracy from you as many miners lie about their work hours. I take it you'll need a place to stay. Find a bunk in the large building down the path at the river."

Sandino nodded and left. His belongings fit in a small, well-traveled, faded black-leather suitcase that he soon slung on a vacant bunk inside the large building. He went to the biggest man hanging around outside, opened his coat to reveal a pistol and, with his dark eyes piercing into the soul of the big man, said, "Watch the suitcase until I return."

The man merely nodded. Sandino took the path on the west bank of the river that led to Jícaro—the closest town about two miles away—to determine the contents of the small general store.

San Albino Mines, Nueva Segovia, June 15, 1926. The start of the rainy season had begun. At the end of the work day most of the miners gathered under the roof overhanging the front porch of the big bunk house. The innocent Indian mine workers were all uneducated, unworldly, and merely content to have a job. To them, it wasn't relevant who owned the mines. They were fed and had a dry bunk. In their simple world, life was satisfactory.

Sandino talked to them constantly. He started by sharing with them the events of his past— how he killed a man in 1920 before fleeing the country. "I am not afraid of anybody," he boasted. "Despite that, I have one true fear. It is a fear you should have, but most of you know nothing about," he preached. "The fear is the fact that neither you nor I have a voice in the direction of our country, our lives and our livelihoods. Foreigners, particularly 'Yankees,' have taken over our country," he gestured at the sign by the river directing visitors to the San Albino Mines.

He planned to kill a lot people. In fact, he planned on killing one person after the other until no more foreigners were left in Nicaragua.

"I will raise an army of loyalists," Sandino announced while pointing at the miners gathered that evening, "and when General Moncada comes from Mexico and initiates a true revolution we will ride to join him!" His admirers started to cheer, but he silenced them fearing the Americans at the mine would grow suspicious. "My friends, my brothers," he said in a hushed tone, "when that moment comes, we will help clear the path for Vice Presidente Sacaza to return to Managua as president—the rightful president!"

San Albino Mines, Nueva Segovia, October 15, 1926. The rainy season was over in October. Sandino's message had long since penetrated. He was joined by men who, in the future, would become loyal lieutenants. The first was "Sócrates" Sandino, his fairly-intelligent, younger brother who too had adopted a name from the classics. Santos López arrived next. López had studied to be a lawyer and was also from the Sandinos' birth village of Niquinohomo. Francisco "Pancho" Estrada, a merchant from Jinotega, 50 miles south of San Albino, joined Sandino's inner circle. Last, the more quiet of the men, is Juan Umanzor. He would as the guide for Sandino's force in the Segovias.

Francisco Estrada, Santos López, Sandino, Juan Umanzor and Sócrates Sandino-*From The U.S, National Archives*

Sandino's nationalistic rhetoric could be likened to "The gospel according to Sandino." His audiences grew. His followers could be found from as far south as his home town south of Managua to the Honduran border. Sandino, sensing a growing support from the men, intensified his message. Soon, he included the miners on his plans to raise an army and fight for the "Liberal" cause.

By this time, the miners also knew that Sandino's Indian-peasant mother's family name was Calderón. Since his childhood hero had been Julius Caesar, Sandino had changed his middle name from Calderon to "Caesar." In Mexico, when he was in Tampico, he met and rode with the world famous Liberal Poncho Villa. They knew he had saved a lot of money to buy weapons to outfit his army. Sandino and his now-close followers, who organized the evening meetings, were working on a plan to destroy the mine and ride east to join Moncada. The miners, under Sandino's cultivating thumb, recruited relatives and other locals to join up when the big day came.

"March, 1927" was finally decided as the month of the San Albino revolt. They had ten months. With fear, love, respect and conviction that Sandino was their rightful leader, the peasant miners all worked in secrecy to prepare themselves to fight. Sandino worked tirelessly to continue planting the seeds of his rebellion. When March came they would be ready.

Chapter 10: Sandino Flexes His Muscles

San Albino Gold Mine, Sunday, March 13, 1927. "Mis amigos," Sandino began in a somber, yet compassionate, tone, "it is a sad day for Nicaragua. I have just learned that the enemy of our country, the Yankee Imperialists, have recently landed in mass at Corinto. There are many men…and artillery…and airplanes being delivered and brought to Managua. Soon they will travel north from the capital to protect Yankee property. This mine will be guarded by the foreign pigs. You will be enslaved. If you resist, you and your families will be killed by the invaders.

"General Moncada, our Minister of War and army commander in Puerto Cabezas, needs the help of every able man to rise up and take arms against the Yankee imperialists. We need to fight… each one of us… until the invaders are no longer here. We need to clear a path for General Moncada to enter the capital in front of our legally-elected presidente, Juan Sacaza. Sacaza will assume the rightful control of the country for which he was legally elected in 1924. This, my friends, must happen. This, my friends will happen. This I pledge to you with my life and on the grave of my mother," Sandino said crossing himself, bowing his head and closing his eyes.

Francisco Estrada, Santos López, and Sócrates Sandino began slow pulsated clapping.

Soon others joined in. Cheers filled the air by the river bunkhouse.

Sandino opened his eyes, raised his head, then his arms and, as quickly as it started, the noise ceased. Sandino walked along the gathering of 30 men studying each of them. His eye contact was personal and almost deadly. Each miner felt relieved when he shifted his stare onto the man beside him.

Sandino spoke again. "Mis amigos, I tell you now; you must believe me for this is the truth. Today is a great day. For today is the day that I ride to join Moncada. Today, I lead my followers armed in to the battle for our nation's freedom. Today is the day we begin our glorious journey to the mountaintop of freedom. And tomorrow, my loyal followers, tomorrow is the day we ride into the battle of death. Death for the Imperialist Pigs. Death to every foreigner on this our sacred land. Tomorrow we drive them all from our country, the country we love and the country that is ours. Soon we will all be free and we can work, not as slaves, but as freed men. Our children will remember this day. We will give them the freedom to know that it was us, mis amigos, that on this day stood up for what is right! "Who rides with me tonight?"

His lieutenants, Francisco Estrada, Santos López, and Sócrates Sandino stepped forward and stood like pillars behind their leader. One man, then two more, then one by one as if on cue joined Sandino's group. The men smiled with approval and embraced one another as their friends joined friends. All but three joined Sandino.

As all stared at the three, the oldest of them walked forward to address the charismatic leader. "Augusto, my son," Rafael Hernández began, "my old heart wants to lead your army into that valley and raise this knife to decapitate the head from each imperialist soldier. But my body is no longer able to endure…even the trip to Puerto Cabezas.

"Comprendo, I understand, Rafael," Sandino said with compassion in his voice. "By arranging for me to buy our few weapons and munitions, you have already given much to our cause."

"Augusto, I speak also for Manny Sánchez, who without a foot, cannot possibly go with you. And I speak for José, now nearly blind. Both were great warriors in the past. We ask your forgiveness for not accompanying you on this great day. But rest assured, we three will be here ready to help you. We pray for your successes against the invaders."

Then Sandino did something none of his followers had ever seen before. He extended his right arm in an explosive manner as if he was jabbing in a boxing match. At the instance of full arm extension, his index finger pointed at Hernández's face with the rest of clenched fingers tight in a fist. Then he moved his extended arm slowly in the shape of the letter "S" while continuing to point at Hernández. The size of the "S" was about a foot high. When he finished, he said in a deliberate manner, "We fight for you amigo—and all the others we leave behind." This was a message he wanted sent throughout the country. He would plant the seed first in his home region, the Segovias. Sandino could not find a better threesome to begin spreading his gospel.

As he finished, he added somewhat parenthetically, "I will talk to you three after I speak to these brave freedom fighters." With that Sandino turned and faced the men he would lead in battle.

"Mis amigos, return to your villages and say your farewells. Bring what you can to survive the journey to Puerto Cabezas. We will travel light and fight on foot. We'll use the jungle as our refuge. The Yankees cannot use our jungles.

"We will meet this afternoon a la tienda, at the store, in Jícaro at 3:00. In the next two weeks the rest of you will have a weapon. From Jícaro we begin our journey to Puerto Cabezas. Tomorrow we'll pass through Murra, then onto the Coco.

"Hasta las tres de la tarde, amigos!"

Feeling the momentum, the men cheered once more before breaking up.

Francisco Estrada, Santos López and Sócrates Sandino joined the three who would remain behind. Sandino walked up and said, "Lo siento, I am sorry, but Señor Hernández we need your assistance once again."

"Si, mi General."

Caught off guard by the title he never heard before, Sandino took a breath before continuing. "Señor Hernández, I must impose on you one more time. I need you to begin taking dynamite—one stick every day. I will return soon with these men, and we will blow the mine.

"Si, General Sandino, for you and our country, my friends and I will be warriors once again. We are honored!"

"I am in your debt, Señor."

The Rio Coco, March 17, 1927. Nicaragua is politically divided into "departments" as opposed to states, territories or provinces. In the western half of the country, the most northern department is Nueva Segovia. Tall cliffs fall from the mountains into the valleys below. The near- country wide, mighty Rio Coco is fed by tributaries that lace the territory and draws

its waters from the Segovia Mountains—the Segovias—sending most of it north then east to the Caribbean Sea. With hardly any roads, the principal way to cross the Segovias is to follow trails cut by oxen or mules. Unlike the winter's cooler dry season, the summer's rainy season has clouds that almost always hide the sun's light. During the rainy season, torrential downpours lasting many hours make trails almost impossible to traverse. Pack animals often sustain injuries when sinking up to their bellies in mud. Landslides occur frequently. The height of the rainy season is July.

Reaching the Coco River in four days, Sandino and his 30 men fell precisely within the length of time forecasted by the dark-skinned Juan Umanzor, another Sandino confidant and the most experienced traveler to the east coast. Nicaraguans, such as Umanzor, who live in towns high in the rugged mountains and along the many rivers woven through the jungled valleys, are in their natural environment in the Segovias. Instinctively, they are able to subsist off the land. Umanzor's knowledge of the trails in the northern department of Nueva Segovia from Jícaro through Murra and Silencio then onto the Coco was arguably the best of all of Sandino's men. Umanzor discussed the planned seven-day trip with his new boss.

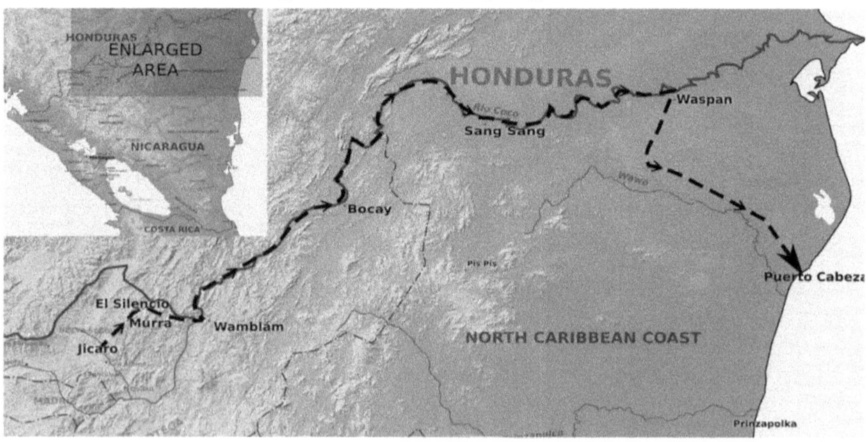

Sandino's planned trip from Jícaro to Puerto Cabezas in March 1927

The trip to the Coco went without difficulty. After three and a half days, Umanzor waited for his leader at the bottom of a steep trail. Upon seeing Sandino, he extended his right arm, pointed his index finger and made a foot-high "S" salute.

"Augusto," Umanzor greeted Sandino, "Augusto, here is the Coco!" Proud of his success in guiding his new leader through the mountains, Umanzor pointed to the river.

Sandino then moved past Umanzor to hear the babble of the mighty Coco. He smiled, looked back at Umanzor, and returned the "S" salute. He said, "Well done, Juan. We are on schedule."

The Coco was not roaring as it would be three months later in June, the first month of the rainy season. However, anywhere the river cuts through the mountainous Nueva Segovia, it is far more energetic than its navigable and more lethargic portion that begins at Wamblán.

"Si, Señor, Wamblán is only 16 kilómetros downstream. There, we will pick up enough pitpan canoes for our trip to the Rio Huaspuc. We can get resupplied at Bocay and Sang Sang as we go by those villages. We should arrive at Waspan on March 23rd as planned."

"Splendid, my friend. Now we'll give the men an hour to get water and wash up."

Sandino's Camp Near Puerto Cabezas, March 24, 1927. Sandino's four lieutenants, Juan Umanzor, Francisco Estrada, Santos López, and Sócrates Sandino were sitting around the fire as the sun was setting and were now talking about whatever had come to any of their minds. Estrada, the merchant, asked provocatively, "Hey Sócrates, you're the brother of Augusto, are you not?" Sócrates stared silently at the taller man without answering and wondered where he was going with his question. "Well tell me then, just why he is so distant today?"

"Francisco, tomorrow is perhaps one of the all-time biggest days in this great man's life. Meeting Moncada is a crucial step on the General's plan to rid the country of foreigners. You know that, don't you?"

Santos López, had known Sócrates from childhood. Prior to leaving San Albino, for the younger Sandino, it had been "Augusto this and Augusto that." Now for the past couple of weeks it's been "The General."

"Si, but he's really distant today. You know, Sócrates," Estrada paused, "I think he needs a woman!"

"Well, mi amigo, I assume you have just the woman for the General. Since you are from the grand city of Jinotega, I am sure you have some special young girl picked out," Sócrates said with cynicism and a brotherly challenge if the instigator wanted to continue. "We went through your city a couple of months ago, and I wasn't certain which looked better: your city's mules or the women!"

López, always the negotiator, interrupted rapidly, "Knock it off you two. Here comes the General!"

Augusto Sandino walked straight up to the fire not realizing he had been gone for over three hours. "Mañana, mis amigos," Sandino said with a quiet voice to his four deputies as he joined his confidants by their fire. Sandino had been gone for the best part of the afternoon reflecting on the important meeting with Moncada. "Mañana is the day we will join the Liberal Army to cast the invaders from our home land. I will ask to lead the cause in the Segovias.

"I cannot be denied this opportunity," Sandino continued. "As we know, there is no Liberal Army presence up in our mountains. The Segovias are our backyard. Only we and our people know our mountains."

"Si, Augusto," López said, "Mañana es el día."

"Si, hasta mañana, amigos," Sandino said and then went to his blanket to reflect some more. Lying down, he thought, when that happens, what role will I play? The governor of the Nueva Segovia Department? Head of the "Independent Sandinista Party?" Business person?

By 10:00 AM the following morning Santos López returned to the Sandino camp. "Augusto, General Moncada will meet you this afternoon at 2:00."

"Very well. We will ride together to meet him. How did he take my request to see him?"

"So-so, my friend. The truth is he knows little of you. Some of his generals did know of you and persuaded him to have the meeting," López confessed.

"Thanks, Santos, your information comes as no surprise. However, we will be ready for this afternoon."

Puerto Cabezas at Moncada's Headquarters, Same Day. In front of the old plantation house at the southern end of town were five uncovered wagons half loaded with furnishings, a clothing trunk, and a few boxes. Nearby, an "arriero," mule handler, tended to six large brown mules.

Sandino cocked his head toward López as he approached the house and asked rhetorically from the side of his mouth, "Someone going someplace?"

Inside, a minute later, Captain Juan Álvarez, Moncada's aide, entered the first-Floor reception room where Moncada was busy packing papers and books into boxes to announce Sandino's presence: "Sir, Señores Sandino and López are here to see you."

General José María Moncada Tapia, the 55-year-old member of the Liberal Party, was a teacher and journalist, until in 1910 when he took up arms in favor of the revolution that overthrew the Conservative government. He became part of the new government as minister of the Interior until the Conservative Party retook the government in a coup d'état. That revolution forced Moncada to emigrate to Costa Rica.

Continuing to pack and noticeably not interested in the visit, Moncada turned his head to say, "Please show the renegades in and tell the 'Chief' to attend as well." Moncada was referring to his Chief of the General Staff, Major General José Álvarez, the aide's uncle.

The two visitors looked like anything but mountain renegades. Sandino, small in stature, wore a wide-brimmed hat, typically worn by the upper-class business community; a two-pocket, casually-worn field shirt buttoned at the sleeves covering a contrasting white undershirt; tight riding trousers tucked into knee-high, leather riding boots; and a holstered pistol hung loosely down onto his right leg. It would be difficult for anyone to believe he had just come halfway across the country by foot and pit pan. López, a much younger man, was very handsome and appeared more as a urban professional on a country sojourn. Major General José Álvarez stared at the visitors upon his arrival in the room, no longer sure of what he was looking at.

Moncada now turned around fully and said in a condescending tone, "Mr. Sandino, I have been told you wish to talk to me. As you can see, I am busy packing to move my headquarters to Prinzapolka, a step closer to retaking Managua."

"Lo siento. I am sorry to disturb you General Moncada. I can see you are very busy." Sandino paused then continued, "I am here to offer the services of myself and my loyal men. We need but a few rifles and some ammunition. Once armed, we will be able to go with you to fight as you direct to rid the country of foreigners and to return Presidente Sacaza to his rightful position as head of our country."

"Just how many 'loyal' men do you have, Mr. Sandino?"

"I have only 25 with me but, in the Segovias where we are from, another 400 wait for me," Sandino boasted.

López silently wondered, just who is he counting?

"And do you have weapons for these men, Mr. Sandino?

"For some. Many have arms."

López thought, sure, machetes.

"Then, what do propose to do with this battalion of yours? How will it serve the Liberal cause?"

"General Moncada, you have recently fought units of the Conservative army against whom you have had great success here on the east coast. I congratulate you on your accomplishments." Sandino stopped his bravado tone and turned serious. "Sir, the American Marines have landed in force with airplanes, artillery, and many men. The Conservative army guarding the capital will be strong with these American reinforcements. You need an army on your northern flank to ensure you will be able to take our capital with minimum casualties. My army will guarantee your safety from any force north of you. The Segovia Mountains are controlled by the Sandinistas. That, Sir, is what I offer you."

Moncada paused to gather his thoughts before huffing, "Mr. Sandino, that is the most far- fetched and ridiculous proposal I have ever heard. What makes you believe you control the Segovias? I have fought in your mountains for the past 15 years with much success.

None of your peasants have arms. I do not need your help. You are a fool, Mr. Sandino, for coming this far expecting me to bend to such a preposterous request!"

Sandino did not move. His stare into the eyes of Moncada bore down the throat and into the heart of the general. Soon, the general's heart was being removed, pulled through the throat by this dapper man's mind. His eyes squinted with far more intensity than the general had ever seen. In the smaller man's mind he was eating the heart, chamber by chamber. Sandino suddenly relaxed. His transformation was over. He recovered sufficiently to say, "Then thank you, Sir, for your time and your interest in my warriors. I will leave you to your packing."

No one in the room missed that moment. In particular, Moncada gaped as Sandino left with López in trace. Álvarez simply raised his eyebrows as if to ask, "Did you see that?"

Moncada said to his chief, "I don't trust that bandit. See that he gets no weapons!"

Sandino and López did not talk on the way back to their camp. Upon arrival Sandino said, "Santos, I need some time to collect my thoughts. Tell the men to go to town and relax. I will meet with them here tomorrow at 9:00 in the morning. In the meanwhile, I will join you and the others for dinner tonight so that we can review our best next move."

Sandino Camp Near Puerto Cabezas, March 25, 1927. "I have just received the best news since we arrived at Puerto Cabezas," Sandino told the gathering of his men. "Two of our brothers stayed overnight with local women. When they awoke they saw American Marines from a ship offshore were rushing through the streets. The Marines are blocking several roads in and out of town." Sandino looked at his men who were more curious about Sandino's meeting with Moncada. Their eyes were now wide opened wondering what they were about to learn.

"Soon the Marines captured 35 Liberal Army soldiers left behind for security purposes. Their weapons were captured and are being thrown into the pond near the cemetery on the outskirts of town. Five of our brothers are now in the jungle observing the Marines.

"We will go into town this evening to recruit persons who want to join our cause. Many of the local men and women have expressed interest in joining us. We will dive for the weapons and bring them here. We will have achieved this part of our task.

"I have been asked to tell you about my meeting yesterday with General Moncada. I will tell you that when Santos López and I met Moncada yesterday he was packing to move his headquarters to Prinzapolka. He claims this will be his first stop he makes on the way to the capital. He did not want us to join him at this time.

"Once we have the weapons, that yesterday, had belonged to his soldiers, I am not sure whether we will travel to Moncada's new headquarters in Prinzapolka and again offer to join his army or return home and begin taking over the towns in the Segovias and continue to recruit to build our own army."

"I want you all to get a good rest today. We will not sleep again for a few days. At 5:00 this afternoon, we will meet again to give instructions on tonight's activities."

With that Sandino thrust his hand forward and made his "S" salute. This time his men, who had been practicing the same salute among themselves, returned his salute.

Chapter 11: Sandino To The Rescue

Pis Pis Gold Mine, April 1, 1927. A week later, the Sandino force stopped briefly at another American gold mine. The Americans who had operated the mine had gone to Bluefields for safety two weeks earlier. The miners fled to their homes along the Río Hauspuc, leaving the mine with a caretaker.

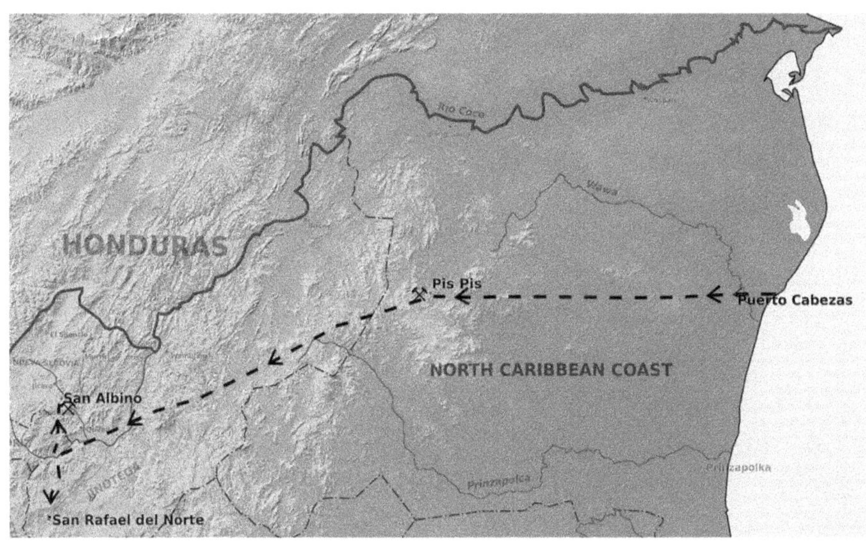

There they split up. Sandino and his brother Sócrates and two body guards waited at the mine for Estrada and López who, a week earlier, had been sent south from their camp outside of Puerto Cabezas to Prinzapolka to meet again with Moncada. Juan Umanzor continued with 64 others to Jícaro, the city near the San Albino mines.

Of the 64, two dozen were men who started at San Albino; fifteen were Puerto Cabezas locals including the two prostitutes the men slept with the night before the raid; and twenty-five were Liberal Army guards who couldn't see the difference between Moncada's cause and

Sandino's. From the east coast, the journey was about a 150-175 miles depending on the route taken. They estimated it would take eight days with the first third of the journey relatively flat with good roads. The remainder consisted of mountainous trails.

Attempting to comfort his older brother as the two sat alone outside the office of the mine "Augusto," Sócrates said, "Estrada and López should arrive by nightfall." No response. Sandino's mind was elsewhere.

Trying a completely different approach, the younger brother continued, "Augusto, we're set to begin a revolution, but I must ask you, have you ever thought about getting married?"

That question captured Sandino's attention. "Me? Of course, little brother," he said with compassion. "I guess I never told you, but I fell madly in love with a young Mexican woman in Tampico." He moved from the porch chair to a grassy area a few feet away, and relaxed by laying his head on the ground and gazing up at the stars. Free from his revolutionary passion, his mind wondered back two years before to the summer of 1925. Sócrates saw a smile come over his brother's face for the first time in weeks. "Her name was Angelina." Then Sandino told his younger brother of his short life with his one true love.

"Every night at 12:30 Angelina would close the cantina by cleaning the glasses and tables. I'd sweep the floors to help her with the work so we could leave the cantina as soon as possible. Within minutes we were up in that one-bedroom apartment three blocks away passionately kissing. Wow; we'd make love for hours. Dios mío, sometimes I'd only have two-three hours of sleep before going for work. But I never got tired! In late summer we talked about getting married. I'd grow old in Tampico and visit Nicaragua, once or twice a year. Angelina wanted me to become mayor of Tampico. We'd laugh at her suggestions then make love again."

Socrates, whose face bore a locked-on smile and whose eyes as wide as he could open them, had never heard his brother talk about his personal life before. Speechless, he was amazed beyond words. Then without notice he watched his brother's smile vanish.

Sandino continued, "I was so comfortable in knowing about the 1924 election victory of Liberals." Bitterly he continued, "That comfort disappeared six months later with the Chamorro coup. General Moncada and Vice President Sacaza had fled to Mexico to build an army. I told Angelina 'Looks like I'll be in Mexico during the next revolt.'"

The older Sandino's face suddenly tightened. His eyes squinted tightly—tight enough to hold back tears. "February 14th. I'll never forget that date. I was taking a nap after work, waiting until about 10:30 to go to the cantina and to meet Angelina. Tampico was a hot bed for Liberal thoughts, including Communism and anti-Yankee ideas. I remember Henrico wrapping violently on the door and screaming my name. I got up and said, 'Calm down Henrico; I can't understand you.' Then he told me. I can still hear his words, 'Three big American miners came to Angelina's cantina. They were drunk with whiskey. At first they accused customers of being 'a bunch liberal Communists. Soon the bar filled up with other locals from nearby bars who were heard about a potential brawl. The fight started around 9:00. It ended suddenly at 9:15 after a dozen gunshots. The three Americans laid dead on the cantina floor. Four locals were wounded, including Angelina who tried to break up the fight. Angelina is being taken to Doctor Blanco!' I ran through the streets to his office hoping for the best. My lovely Angelina died two days later."

His brother comforted him in a soft tone, "Lo siento mucho, Augusto."

Sandino sat up abruptly. His eyes overly wide open. He had just passed through the gates of hell once again. He had vowed never to think of that date again. How did he slip into that memory? Damn February 14th and all Yankees!

"My brother," Sócrates blurted out. "I hear mule hoofs in the valley below!"

They both stood up and within a few minutes Francisco Estrada and Santos López, arrived at the mine.

López came up to the senior Sandino immediately. Sócrates drew closer so as not to miss the news. Estrada turned the two mules over to the bodyguards then turned to join the other three.

"General," the former law student turned negotiator, announced, "Your plan was a good one. We found Moncada's camp in Prinzapolka. I asked Major General José Álvarez, who was meeting with two brigadier generals at the time, for an appointment with General Moncada. He asked why and I told him simply that we now possess over 50 weapons, that our force is growing, and that we still want to be his army in the Segovias. He told me to wait and went off to see Moncada.

"While waiting for Álvarez to return, we talked to Generals Francisco Parajon and López Irías. They agree that we should be armed and protect their northern flank. They have no one there. If the Conservatives gain a foothold there, Moncada will never reach Managua. They were going to be the vanguard for Moncada. They would be leaving camp tomorrow and ride to take Jinotega. They had heard about what you said to Moncada about the American Marines and the fresh Conservative forces coming 80 kilómetros away from Managua. They were understrength, having only about 300 men each.

"When Álvarez came back, he indicated that Moncada was impressed. Moncada did not want you to join up with him at this time. He said you are to check the telegraph stations and let him know periodically where you'll be. He may need your protection on his northern flank as you offered."

Sandino hugged López. "Santos, we accomplished everything. We have the weapons and a commitment to join Moncada. ¡Estoy encantado! I am thrilled! Thank you all for your efforts. And now amigos we will leave and follow in trace Juan Umanzor. I believe we'll catch up to him at the Coco. In any case, when we get to the Coco, we will split up. Sócrates and I will go south with mules to the closest telegraph station—that's San Rafael del Norte—and provide our status to Moncada. We will join you at the mines no later than the 5th of April."

Río Coco, April 2, 1927. "Augusto, please before we go, the men have sent for a photographer who wants to join us. His name is Jose Castro. Please join them in one photo. They want to be in a photo with you and their new weapons."

"All right Socrates, just one photo."

"Hasta luego, mis amigos; we'll see you about the 5ᵗʰ," Sócrates shouted back to his companions turning his mule to the left in trace of his older brother's somewhat hasty movement and now disappearance south along the river trail.

Thirty minutes later he caught up to the older Sandino and yelled over the noise of the trotting hoofs, "What's the hurry, Augusto?"

Sandino looked back at his younger brother without a smile and kept on riding.

Sócrates didn't quit, "What's the matter; did I say something in front of the others I shouldn't have?"

The elder Sandino abruptly halted his mule, causing Sócrates to have to veer sharply left to avoid hitting the stopped mule before halting his mount. Both mules were panting desperately for air.

"What?" Sócrates shouted with heightened frustration, as much to get his brother's wrath out of the way as it was finding out what had incurred the wrath in the first place.

Augusto said quietly, "I am not mad at you at all, Sócrates. But your question the other night at Pis Pis got me thinking. And damnit,

I am going to ask a woman—wait a moment, a gorgeous, intelligent woman—to marry me tomorrow when we arrive in San Rafael del Norte!"

Sócrates dismounted, headed for a tree stomp along the river edge and sat staring at the Coco. Sandino dismounted as well, figuring that the mules need a break, and this place was as good as any. Sócrates shook his head in disbelief, turned around and said, "You have got to be kidding me. Just like that. You don't even know her name! What's her name—this woman, my future sister-in-law?"

"Her name is Blanca, Blanca Arauz."

"And," still trying to come to grips with his older brother's intentions, "and just when were you going to share this information?"

"Well I just did little brother. Now I am ready to go, are you?"

"Hell no my general. I am not. Nor are the mules! We have a revolution to fight—which you are going to lead—and you are telling me you are going to get married. Just like that."

"Si. Porqué no?"

"When are you going to be married?"

"In May, next month, whenever Blanca is ready."

"Yeah, right. Does she know anything about this?"

"No. Should she?"

"You know, Augusto, you are a bright person. You'll be a great leader in our nation, but sometimes I believe you must have been sleeping when our mother was telling us about señoritas. Have you considered that she may not even like you?"

"No."

"Well, yeah. It's a possibility."

"Little brother, I'm more worried about her not liking you," Sandino said remounting his mule. "She may not even want you to be the best man in the wedding like I'm going to recommend," Sandino said riding away chuckling.

San Rafael del Norte, April 2, 1927. Shortly after the grand church's towering steeple came into view, the two mules and their mounts emerged from the pine forest, crossed the stream that ran beside the small mountain village of San Rafael del Norte and reached the first house that could be considered in the town. The local population believed that their village, the highest on all of Nicaragua, was the future "Jinotega" since they had a telegraph line connecting their little community with the rest of the country—for that matter the rest of the world. The town's mayor, Fernando Arauz, owned the telegraph equipment. Blanca, his 19 year old daughter, operated the telegraph. The church's Franciscan nuns who ran the village school believed she was one of the smartest young people in the village; she could not only read and write Spanish, she was competent with Morse code.

After riding by a few small wooden homes and entering the village center, the Sandinos saw the mountainous village more like a municipality. There were stucco-walled homes and stone fences that established property boundaries. The beautiful Catholic church, built by Franciscan monks from Italy in 1887, was at the center of the village. Next to it was the nun's convent. The telegraph office was several doors away. Four horses were grazing in the park across from the convent. The Sandino brothers dismounted their mules and let them graze in the park with the horses.

San Rafael del Norte Cathedral

Sócrates followed in trace of his older brother. As Augusto opened the front door to the telegraph office, a small bell suspended from the ceiling was hit by the door's top signaling to anyone on the back of the building that a patron had entered the small front room. The entrance separating the front room from the rest of the building had brightly colored bead strings dangling three quarters of the way to the wooden floor.

The hands of the telegraph operator, Blanca Arauz, divided the beaded strings. Sócrates stared in disbelief as the absolutely prettiest young woman he had ever seen appeared. His eyebrows thrust upward pulling his eyelids along. At the same time his eyes reached their largest opening capacity, his lower jaw fell open one-half inch. She looked at him curiously for a second, then to his brother who she recognized immediately and bubbled, "General Sandino. I was expecting you!"

The sometimes-grouchy older brother warmed immediately, "Señorita Arauz, como estas?"

"Bien, gracias, have you traveled far to see me?"

"Si señorita, I have come all the way from Puerto Cabezas only to see you," Sandino said in a flirtatious tone that brother Sócrates had never heard before.

"Mi general," Blanca shot back in an equally teasing tone, "your devotion carries me through the cold winter days. I would be lost without you. And who is this young man?" the young woman inquired making Sócrates feel very unimportant.

"Oh, I am sorry. This is my brother, Sócrates. After I told him of your beauty, he came across the country to meet you as well."

"I am flattered by both of you," Blanca responded

Sócrates smiled and gently shook his head not believing what he had witnessed since Blanca appeared a moment ago.

"Oh, General, I have a telegram for you. It's important. Please wait a moment."

"Señorita Blanca, I use to be 'Señor'—on occasion 'Augusto'—now it's 'General,' what's going on?"

"You wait. Mi papa wants to talk to you. I will get the telegram for you mi General Augusto—is that better?—then I will get mi papa."

Totally confused, Sandino said, "Go my little butterfly."

Blanca returned with a telegram which she immediately surrendered to Sandino.

She looked at Sócrates whose face had returned to normal, winked seeking his approval of her, and dashed out through the beads again.

"Sócrates, read this."

```
1 APRIL 1927
GENERAL SANDINO,
MY ARMY HAS SUFFERED TWO SIGNIFICANT LOSSES IN THE PAST WEEK
AT CHONTALES AND AT JINOTEGA. I AM NOW ACCEPTING YOUR OFFER TO
PROVIDE SUPPORT FOR MY NORTHERN FLANK.
I NEED YOU TO TAKE THE TOWN OF LAS MERCEDES AS SOON AS
POSSIBLE.
REPORT YOUR LOCATIONS. I WILL SEND FUTURE TELEGRAMS TO SAN
RAFAEL DEL NORTE UNTIL YOUR FORCE MOVES SOUTH OF THAT
LOCATION.
MONCADA
```

Sócrates' face sobered. "Unbelievable, Augusto."

With that the beads parted and the bouncy Nicaraguan beauty emerged followed by a fifty- something year old man.

"General Sandino, it is my honor to meet you, Señor," the San Rafael del Norte mayor said with undisguised admiration. "My name is Fernando Arauz; I am the father of Blanca Arauz."

"My pleasure Sir. I am Augusto Sandino, and this is my brother, Sócrates."

After quick handshakes Arauz continued, "The Liberal Army suffers defeat and you are called to the rescue by the Secretary of War, General Moncada. I am honored that you are able to use our telegraph services to save our nation. Blanca has said so many nice things about you.

With all the telegrams she sends for you to your father, Don Gregorio, she feels as if she knows you quite…"

"Papa!" Blanca interrupted loudly, "telegrams are private! I have never told you anything of their contents!"

"I know my dear. But you have told me of your respect…" Arauz paused and then added, "and fond admiration of General Sandino."

"Papa, you embarrass me," Blanca said spinning around and dashing through the beads.

"Oh my, I spoke too much. One minute, general, I will get my daughter back. Sócrates, I wish to talk privately with your brother. Would you allow Blanca to give you a tour of our famous church? We will join you two in a few minutes."

Sócrates could think of nothing better. He said to the departing mayor, "Tell her I'm anxious!" then looked at Sandino waiting for a blast from him.

"That's good, Sócrates, I wish to talk to Señor Arauz as well."

In a minute, the bouncy Blanca returned as if nothing happened. "General Augusto, my father said you are staying this evening before going to San Albino. I am very happy. Come Sócrates, I will show you nuestra iglesia bonita."

"We are?" Sandino asked as the younger two disappeared out into the street.

The bell rang again as the front door opened and closed. By this time Arauz had returned to the front counter where Sandino stood. "General Sandino," the mayor began, "I wanted to meet you for many months. I was at our church when you spoke there last July. Your message to free our country from foreign influences resonates so well with my message as mayor of this small village."

"Comprendo," Sandino uttered in a near whisper.

"We have 43 men who meet on Sunday afternoons—mostly ranchers and farmers—who agree with your message. They too support the Liberal cause and want no more foreign-owned businesses in the country and especially up here in the Segovias. As you may know we need rifles in the mountains to survive and to feed our families. These men all have rifles and are ready to defend their homes, this village and our nation. Your name was mentioned and they are ready to ride with you if you need them.

"I am honored Señor Arauz. As you can see from the message, we are needed at this moment."

"Yes General. I knew that. When will you be riding to Las Mercedes?"

"I plan to return with my men on the 10th. I invite you and your men to ride with me. How many men can I count on?"

"I will have at least 30 men and we will ride by your side, amigo."

"I am in your debt, Señor. Thank you," Sandino said extending his hand.

While shaking hands, both men stared deep in to each other's eyes silently pledging mutual support. When they released their grip, Sandino composed his words before beginning. "Señor, it is most unfortunate that my cause has consumed any time I have for my personal life. Nevertheless I do have personal feelings. So I must tell you that I use your telegraph probably more than I truly need to."

Arauz looked at Sandino strangely as if to wonder where the general was venturing in his thought.

"Since my first visit here last July," Sandino cleared his throat slightly, "I have fallen in love with Blanca, and I wish to marry her."

Arauz's pursed lips bore a slight smile that only a father would have when hearing what he just heard; his chin and eyebrows lifted simultaneously as if he had been offered a proposition that needed much thought. "Of course you know, General, Blanca is the most sought after young lady in this village," Arauz countered.

"Well, I can imagine that, Señor," Sandino said knowing he may be in a bidding war situation. Again I regret that I have no time to court your lovely daughter the way she deserves. Sócrates and I must leave before the sun sets."

"No, no, no, no, no." Arauz countered not wanting to lose a potential monumental proposition, "I insist you stay the night we have much to talk about."

"Well with your permission, I will talk with Blanca after dinner to see if she has interest in marrying me."

"Si," the father agreed, "I see no problems with that at all. I will talk to my wife, Maria, tonight, and we'll see what happens in the morning. Before we visit la iglesia, let me tell her that we will be honored by you staying for dinner."

The night came and went. The rooster crowed just before sunrise. Maria and Blanca had prepared a breakfast. Augusto and Sócrates rose and were ready to ride north to the San Albino mines without breakfast. They compromised with the ladies by agreeing to take the freshly made bread and coffee to eat as they rode.

Augusto asked to speak to Blanca alone. They went to the front room. He held her, and they kissed passionately as they had the night before. Sandino knew the chemistry was working for both of them. He pleaded, "Blanca, can you give an answer, now?"

"I can't. Not just yet. Soon. Maybe on the tenth when you pass through again," was her multi-sentence answer that only raised Sandino's frustration.

Exasperated, Sandino sighed. "Alright then, on the tenth. No longer."

She threw her small shoulders back, made a mock hand salute and said sharply, "Si, mi general!"

He looked at her in disbelief of her brazen, yet acceptable, response.

Then she kissed him again, looked him in the eyes and said, "Ride safe, my love."

In a moment, the Sandino brothers mounted their mules and headed north out of town on the road leading to the San Albino mines. Sócrates slyly asked, "Augusto, did you get any sleep last night? "

Sandino thought for a moment, turned his head to his younger brother, winked and said, "Sócrates, I believe that it is time for you to review with me those things our mother told us about women. I must have missed them all."

San Albino Mines, April 6, 1927. While the ashes from the explosion that closed the mineshaft entrances had barely settled, the noise from the near-surface explosion lingered in the ears of the revolutionary soldiers. All had smiles on their faces, having triumphantly witnessed the destruction of Yankee property.

"Manny Hernandez, again I say, 'Thank you, Sir' for all that you have done in our absence. I am truly grateful. Not only did you get all this dynamite, you fearlessly killed that nasty American foreman who tried to stop you. You truly are a warrior and revolutionary hero. Today I am making you the captain of the San Albino district. We, the Sandinistas, will leave here soon. But I will always know that you have things well in hand up here. Thank you my friend."

After exchanging "S" salutes, Sandino announced an immediate meeting of his general staff. They met in the office building of the mine, the same one in which Sandino applied for a job a year earlier. And the same one Sandino now called his general headquarters. "Manny, I want you to attend as well," Sandino tacked onto the announcement.

Now gathered, Sandino addressed the others, Juan Umanzor, Santos López, Francisco Estrada and his younger brother Sócrates. "We have all read the telegram from General Moncada.

The urgency of us moving to support the Liberal cause is obvious. We will depart the day after tomorrow, the 8th.

"First we will stop by San Rafael del Norte to telegraph Moncada and let him know we will be attacking Jinotega. Afterwards, we will go on to attack Las Mercedes. We need to acquire mules when we are in Jinotega. You have a day to prepare yourselves and the others. Are there any questions?"

Looking around he saw Estrada's hand raised. "Pancho?"

"I am in charge of supplies, am I not?"

"Sí."

"We will need to buy supplies as we get closer to Managua. Do we have the money?"

"Not yet, but we will when we leave Jinotega. I want you to take anything of value that can be used for buying food or anything we need."

"Juan?" Sandino said calling on his local guide and operational assistant.

"How long will we be gone?"

"As long as it takes, my friend. But I hope we'll be back in May."

Sócrates smiled, knowing his brother's secret intentions to marry Blanca Arauz in May.

"Augusto, Jose Castro wants to take a photo before we depart. You know, big brother, these are your first revolutionaries!"

Sandino above black line. *From The U.S, National Archives*

San Rafael del Norte, April 9, 1927. When 70 men and five women enter a small mountain village, the event, planned or not, is significant. At San Rafael del Norte on the 9th of April 1927 the significance of the event was heightened as 27 armed and mounted local men assembled, ready to join the travelers. These men committed themselves to support the Sandino cause.

The Sandino brothers rode on mules at the front of the column. The cheering grew in volume as the leaders arrived at the town center where many well-wishers gathered to greet them and to send off their own heroes. The open grassy square filled with horses. Other horses were tied up at posts along the street. The Nicaraguan flag was hung over the street on a rope tied between two the telegraph poles outside Mayor Arauz's office and home. The mayor, his wife, and several others stood on the front porch, welcoming the dismounting Sandino brothers with applause. The elder Sandino approached Arauz and embraced him. He looked around at the crowd, removed his hat, and waved it back and forth to greet the gathering.

"Welcome Señor Sandino. My men are ready to join you. Our wives have prepared a wonderful luncheon at the church for everyone. Please invite your men to join us at this time."

Sandino nodded his head and said, "Mucho gracias, Fernando."

"Perhaps," Arauz said conspicuously enough that both brothers could understand, "Señor Sócrates can assist the others to the church for lunch if you need to send a telegraph."

The brothers chuckled at the deception, and then Sócrates took over, giving instructions for the travelers to visit the church. Augusto disappeared into the telegraph office.

As he entered the small front room and barely closed the door, Blanca leaped into his arms. They kissed with the same passion as if they hadn't left each other. In a moment he looked deep into her eyes and said, "I missed you, Blanca. I missed you a lot!"

The tears streaming from her eyes conveyed her only response except the kiss that followed. Catching her breath, she finally blurted, "Yes, yes, yes, and forever yes."

Sandino, beamed and said, "I haven't even asked a question yet."

"Yes, you did, last week!"

"I love you, Blanca," Sandino said, wondering where in the heck that statement ever came from. Probably his mother.

"Oh and I love you so much, Augusto."

"May 18th, that's the date," she said.

"Date for what, my love?"

"Our wedding date, Augusto." The enthusiastic organizer began with rapid-fire statements. "I know you are in hurry, but you better be back for that date. The whole village will be here. Oh, and I want Sócrates to be your best man. I already contacted your father, Don Gregorio, and he and his wife will be coming to the wedding. I have arranged for the photographer and the priest will have the church set up with beautiful mountain flowers. And..."

Sandino placed his index finger on her lips and said in a patient tone, "Blanca, you will have everything done exactly right. I have total faith in you. I will return on the 18th. Now we need to go to the church as I have a long ride this afternoon. When we leave, telegraph Moncada to let him know that we will be going to Jinotega."

"Si, mi General," Blanca teased.

El Templo de Jinotega, April 12, 1927. General Sandino joined Monseñor Sánchez, head priest of El Templo who welcomed him in front of the church. El Templo was Jinotega's principal and handsome Catholic Church built in 1805 and was across the street of.

El Templo de Jinotega

Parque Central.

"Monseñor, I have given strict instructions to my men not to take anything belonging to your beautiful church. However, we will be taking items from your citizens who provided support to the Conservative Army in their victory over the Liberal forces two weeks ago. My men will fight with the Liberal Army until Managua is back in the hands of the Liberal Establishment."

"Thank you Señor General, I am in your debt. You are always welcome here."

"De nada, Monseñor."

"We will be on our way tomorrow and leave your lovely city in peace."

"I have a couple of persons I wish for you to meet General; will you please wait here?"

About that time Santos López walked up to Sandino. "General, I believe we have completed our search of the homes identified as Conservative supporters. Our takings are moderate, but Francisco Estrada is satisfied we will have enough to buy rations for two weeks. We have also acquired 12 horses and 20 mules. Actually, we have also been joined by three mule handlers and the 12 cowboys who own the horses."

"Excelente Santos. Please go to the telegraph office to see if Moncada has anything new for us yet. Tomorrow, I'll confirm our departure for Las Mercedes."

About that time Monseñor Sánchez returned, followed by two men dressed in dirty and wrinkled military uniforms who obviously needed a bath. Apparently held in one of the church's secluded basement rooms for a while, they squinted at the daylight. The Monseñor announced, "General Sandino, you know General Parajon and General Irías don't you?"

"We haven't met as yet, but my deputy here, Santos López, has met the generals."

López interceded, "You both look as if you need some attention. We have a nurse if you wish me to get her."

Francisco Parajon spoke first with a scratchy voice, "Muchas gracias, amigo. Estamos bien."

López Irías added, "Thank you Santos," recalling Sandino's bright deputy, "but we really need to clean up. We ran into a battalion-size Conservative force as we approached Jinotega that killed and captured our lead platoons. Before we knew it, we were nearly surrounded. We fought desperately to escape to the rear and were able to occupy defensive positions. In the morning most of our men deserted into the mountains and the Conservative force had strangely withdrawn to the south toward the capital.

"Monseñor Sánchez has been nice enough to hide us while waiting for your arrival. With your permission, General Sandino, we wish to travel with you on your attack in support of General Moncada."

"Of course General, the pleasure would be all mine," Sandino replied. Then taking charge, he directed, "Santos, please go the telegraph office to see if there is a message for us and have my general staff meet together for dinner here at the church at six."

"Si, mi General."

"Monseñor, please assist the two generals to get cleaned up and have a dinner prepared for ten at 8:00 this evening. I would like you to join us. Please tell your cooks 'thank you' in advance for us. We'll need privacy so the cooks should leave after they deliver the dinner."

"With pleasure, General Sandino."

"Generals," he said looking at Parajon and Irías, "please join us for dinner. We will discuss leaving Jinotega tomorrow and attacking Las Mercedes. Your thoughts and guidance will be deeply appreciated."

Both generals responded as if they had just had received an order from Moncada with a sharply accented, "Si, Señor."

Las Mercedes, April 18, 1927. "I am indebted, sirs, for your thoughts and insight. You were right. We encountered no resistance here at Las Mercedes. The Conservatives have again withdrawn," Sandino said to Parajon and Irías after riding up to the waiting generals. "Santos López said you wished to meet with me."

Parajon, less talkative of the two, shook his head in agreement.

Irías opened, "Si, General Sandino." Irías pointed, "Perhaps we should talk at the picnic table under the tree over there."

Not knowing what to expect, Sandino cocked his head agreeing and said, "Si."

After sitting, Irías stated. "General, since we met your deputy, Santos López, we have had great respect for you. Riding with you, as we have for the past few days, has allowed us to understand your compassion for our country. We respect your compassion deeply. In you, we see no political ambitions. No disrespect, Sir, but you have apparently not been in touch with our national politics for some while. It is in that sense, we are compelled to share some of our thoughts for your own safety."

"I am confused, Señor."

Irías continued. "Señor, you must know that Nicaragua's acting and interim president, Díaz, is an old man and will not run in the '28 election. His day has passed. We believe that our own Liberal Vice President Sacaza lacks the strength to defeat the Conservatives in a national election." Irías let Sandino think about that. Then he asked, "Who on the Liberal side is left to win the next election Señor?"

Hesitant as a school boy being drilled by his principal, Sandino weakly concluded, "Moncada?"

"That's right amigo. And we believe Moncada has a scenario planned that gets him elected into the president's seat next year. We know nothing specifically."

"Thank you for telling me this. You are right, I have been away too long."

"We must continue, Sir. There is more," Parajon said making his only contribution.

Irías started again. "General Sandino, you are a wild card and a huge potential road block in Moncada's path to the presidency."

Sandino's only comment was an unbelievable, "What?"

"Moncada did not want you armed and does not want you with an Army," Irías added.

Now that you have gained a force, General Parajon and I fear Moncada may want you eliminated."

"But why then would he want me to attack Boaco--our next objective?" Sandino asked.

"Boaco, General Sandino, is a Conservative stronghold. The mountains surrounding the city and the two-tiered hills upon which the city was built favor the defenders. Attacking the town will cause the attackers many casualties, my friend."

Irías concluded, "Sir, we recommend you bi-pass Boaco and go directly to Boaquito and confront General Moncada yourself. As you know Boaquito is only 32 kilómetros west of Boaco, near Managua."

Sandino pressed, "What is he doing there? Why hasn't he attacked the capital?"

"Before we left Prinzapolka to attack Jinotega, Moncada received a message informing him that the Americans were sending an important person to negotiate a treaty between both forces that would ensure a peaceful 1928 election. He planned to wait at Boaquito and would represent the Liberal government as the Secretary of War."

Sandino was quiet, allowing the message of Parajon and Irías to settle in. After a few minutes, Sandino said, "Will you join me and my general staff in about an hour to discuss our plans. I do not wish that they know what you said here at this point."

"We will meet you there then," Irías said in a quiet voice.

Chapter 12: The Peace Of Tipitapa Facade

US Legation Headquarters, Managua, April 19, 1927. Minister Charles C. Eberhardt started the meeting by welcoming the commanding general of the 2nd Marine Brigade, Brigadier General Logan Feland, and his principal officers. Feland's appearance bore a somewhat starchy professional look; his World War ribbons earned during the Great War while commanding the 5th Marines in the defense of Belleau Wood left no doubt that he brought with him significant combat experiences gained in France nine years earlier. Yet his manner and tone was pleasantly warm. Eberhardt was impressed the moment he met Feland in early March that the right man had been assigned to assist him in achieving the difficult tasks the State Department levied on him.

Eberhardt's face grew serious as he focused on the crucial and hopefully-successful peace negotiations set to begin in ten days after the arrival of the American special envoy, former Secretary of War Henry "Colonel" Stimson, "Gentlemen, we are on the cusp of stopping the ongoing civil war. Colonel Stimson, who you know well, departed the States on the 12th, and his ship is due to arrive on the morning of the 26th in Corinto.

"General Feland, your task will be monumental. You will be asked to collect and store thousands of weapons from both the Liberal and Conservative armies, provide security throughout the country, stand up a national guard, and ensure safe and fair elections next year. If all goes well, you'll be able to redeploy at the start of 1929.

"Colonel Kauffman, my military attaché, and Mr. George Ward, my deputy who I believe many of your commanders and your staff know, will be your day-to-day points of contact. Naturally I am available at all times.

Attempting to make a light moment, Eberhardt said, "Before Al Kauffman briefs you on the current Nicaraguan military disposition, I want to say that, after three years, he will have concluded his duty here in Managua on May 30th and is due to return to the States. So I want you Marines to work him extra hard so that we all get our money's worth out of him before he leaves."

Smiling eyes focused on Kauffman as he rolled his own upward.

"Kidding aside, General Feland, I'd like you know that Al has served the Legation well for those three years and I shall miss him immensely after his departure. "Okay Al, it's your show."

"Thanks for that memorable introduction, Sir," Kauffman said with a broad smile on his face as he placed a large, somewhat thick paper on an easel at the front of the room. Turning to the audience while pointing to the easel Kauffman opened, "Minister, General, gentleman, I have shown the Conservative forces in blue and units of the Liberal Army in red. As you can see the majority of both forces are in the vicinity of the capital. If you'll permit me, I'll make some opening comments about both forces and then open the discussion for questions."

Kauffman explained, "The Conservative Army, led by General Juan Toledo, is comprised of about 2,500, men. On the positive side, the capital-area forces have been successful against the Liberals.

Recently, from a telegraph we intercepted, we know that they just defeated two undermanned battalions of Liberals at Jinotega. Another Liberal force, led by Sandino, considered attacking the Conservative battalion defending nearby Boaco this week, but reconsidered because of the strong defenses. However, Conservative units sent to the east coast last year had been pushed around by the Liberals at will. Their lack of success has caused low morale until this recent turn around.

"The Liberal Army is led by General José Moncada, who also introduces himself as 'Secretary of War'. He has, purportedly, a slightly-smaller size force, perhaps 2,000 troops, that he had obtained on the east coast or recruited on his drive here to Managua. Most of his units are east of Managua in the Boaquito area. His troops are well armed, many with recently-manufactured weapons given to them by the Mexican government. He has about 11 or 12 general officers who are professional soldiers dedicated to restoring the Liberal government. I believe that, if facing the Conservative army alone, the Liberals could attack Managua and secure a foothold. Your Marine presence should prevent any ideas on an assault on the capital. I could add more but, first, I'd like to see if there are any questions."

General Feland looked around at his staff and commanders soliciting their inquiries. Captain Chris Worchester, the brigade's newly-appointed intelligence officer, was first to respond. "Colonel Kauffman, recently we've been hearing the name Sandino. Does he fit into this picture?"

"Thanks, Captain…. Sandino…. Seems that no one is sure about him. I believe he fits into the picture, but to what extent, I don't know. We know that he returned after a long absence. He had been in Mexico and other countries up north. He returned about a year ago. Unlike the Conservatives and Liberals who both welcome our help, Sandino has been 'rebel-rousing', if I can use that term. He has been calling for foreign military forces to leave and for the Nicaraguans to take over all foreign-own business. Actually, we intercepted telegraphs and believe Sandino will soon join Moncada at his Boaquito location. Even if Colonel Stimson can arrange a truce between the two major players, I'm not too sure Sandino will want to play into that hand. He may launch his own rebellion. I'd say to all, keep a close eye on Sandino."

"Major Rowell," Kauffman saw Rusty Rowell's finger rise and called on him with a smirk on his face. "I believe I know what question you are going to ask."

Rowell smiled as well, "Sir, I take it you know who may have shot four holes in my Green Nose while we were flying up in Nueva Segovia last week."

Everyone at the meeting knew Rowell's favorite plane was named Green Nose and that the hard charging aviator had been shot at last week.

"Thanks, Rusty. I checked on the incident. According to the chief municipal official at Ocotal—guy's name is Señor Arnold Ramirez Abaunza—there were six or seven armed rebels who had passed through Ocotal the day before, spewing anti-Yankee babble. Ramirez believes they were the ones who fired at you. Given the time frame they, most likely, were with the defeated Liberal Army unit at Jinotega. I'm sorry to hear about Green Nose; I assume the damage was repaired."

"It's flying again, thank you, Sir."

Looking to all the Marines, Kauffman said, "If there will be any future engagements, I'd place money that they will mostly be in the Segovia mountains. I'd even bet that the only adversary turns out to be Sandino."

The meeting continued with George Ward providing details on the planned truce discussions based on the very limited information the legation had been given. He was going to assist Stimson on a day-to-day basis, freeing Minister Eberhardt to keep in touch with the State Department.

Regarding the Marines, Feland reported that the 11th Marine Regiment arrived in country from the west coast two days earlier and was getting ready to store thousands of weapons and provide security around the capital. The 5th Marine Regiment was already providing security, particularly along the main rail line from Chinandega to Managua. They were preparing to deploy units north to the Segovia region as soon as a truce accord had been reached. Feland announced the recent arrival of Lieutenant Colonel Rhea, who would command the Guardia National if the peace talks go as planned. Finally, he was in the process of establishing a command post in the Tipitapa area to support the talks.

Minister Eberhardt concluded the meeting with summary thoughts about security issues and the continual need for effective communications.

Moncada's Headquarters, Boaquito, April 21, 1927. After confirming the futility of attacking Boaco without the promised support from Moncada, Sandino executed his alternate plan of following the Liberal Army to Boaquito. Sandino rode into the General Moncada's camp with Generals Parajon and Irías. The three shook hands. Generals Parajon and Irías rode away while Sandino dismounted and walked directly to Captain Juan Álvarez, Moncada's aide.

"I need to see General Moncada at once," Sandino demanded in a firm voice.

"Un momento, Señor General," the young aide responded.

Within seconds Moncada appeared as if on cue. "Welcome, General Sandino," Moncada said in an pompous way, extending his hand to greet him.

Sandino did not accept the outstretched hand. Instead, he squinted looking measurably into Moncada's eyes and knowing that this arrogant man had ordered him and his men into a death trap. They would have gone had he not been forewarned by Generals Parajon and Irías.

Moncada had seen the look before in Puerto Cabezas and hadn't forgotten its meaning. Moncada knew there was room for only one of them in Nicaragua. For now, however, he ignored the affront knowing they would have to work together if he was to eventually ascend to the presidency. "General Sandino, first I want to thank you for looking after my two generals, Parajon and Irías. Then I want to tell you that I am glad you are here to join us as we wait for the US special envoy to explore a possible truce and political solution until another election can once again restore out Liberal party to power. Your presence reinforces our army's credibility."

"General Moncada, I am confused. President Sacaza remains the legally elected president.

How could you possibly accept anything less than that?"

"Sadly General Sandino, we are a nation at war. We Liberals wish no less than to restore what was wronged when Chamorro usurped the presidency. We have struck back seeking to regain all that is rightly ours. Unfortunately, our war robs the nation of its wealth and unnecessarily takes the lives of its good citizens. I will meet with the US envoy and see what accommodations are offered by Díaz and the Conservatives. I will include you and the other generals in deliberations."

"Thank you for that, Señor. I do not like the position we are in, but I will wait to see what develops. Whatever develops, we must free ourselves of external interference by other governments!" Sandino said, stating his case.

"General Sandino, I invite you and your men to wait until the envoy arrives. He is planning to meet with us at the end of the month— another ten days."

"Si, Generalissimo," Sandino said, acknowledging the key position of his adversary.

"Very well. I have learned your force has grown substantially since you left San Rafael del Norte—you have nearly 300 men now I understand."

Sandino merely nodded in agreement.

Moncada continued. "I have made arrangements for you and your men to occupy El Comun, the hill not far from Boaco."

"I am surprised," murmured Sandino, acknowledging the danger lurking there. "A large Conservative battalion occupies Boaco."

"They did until yesterday morning. When you did not attack they withdrew to Managua. My army will be in the village in the morning. When I have the proposal points for the treaty, you'll be notified and will join the other general officers in Boaco. On El Comun, you will be fully supplied with food for your men and feed for your horses."

Not knowing how to measure Moncada, Sandino responded with a simple "Gracious. I will see to my men and wait for you. "

Moncada's Headquarters, Boaco, May 3, 1927. "Generals, generals, generals!" Moncada cried out raising his voice to silence the verbal dissension by his general officers— including Sandino— over the proposal he had brought back from his first meeting with Envoy Stimson. In that proposal, the country's provisional president Díaz would be retained in office until the November 1928 elections. Moncada was okay with that arrangement since it included a promise from the envoy of his support to have Moncada run for president—a fact not shared with the general officers. "What do you want me to take back to the negotiating table?"

Within ten minutes the generals let him know that most any arrangement would be good as long as Díaz was not part of any deal.

When Moncada left with the "No Díaz" counter proposal, Sandino leaned over to General Parajon and said, "I am very suspicious about what is taking place, Señor."

Tipitapa Truce Headquarters, later the same day. "I don't care what your generals want; Díaz stays 'til next November. The United

States is not moving from that position, Generalissimo!" Henry Stimson declared almost in a rage.

"I may be able to sell to them a Díaz-Sacaza compromise," Moncada countered.

"Díaz shall sit alone, General Moncada."

"Señor, you must assist me to help find a solution; otherwise, I cannot make an agreement."

Stimson, a byproduct of the ruthless American business world, offered, "The only thing I will do for you is to give you my word that, if an agreement cannot be reached to keep Díaz in power until the elections a year from November, the US will use force against any army or bandits trying to prevent that!"

Moncada thought for a moment weighing the wishes of his generals and the ultimatum notice just served by the former Secretary of War.

"The US will apply force?" Moncada asked. "You have the authority to declare such a commitment?"

Stimson looked the general in the eye and declared, "No I don't; but if you want me to put it in writing to convince your generals just how serious we are, I will do so."

Moncada gazed upward thinking. A letter would help. They surely would not be pleased at first, but he could sell them on the prospect of peace, time with their families, a Liberal-election victory, and positions in the army after the election. Looking back at Stimson and shaking his head in agreement, Moncada said, "A letter may help, Sir."

"You must surrender all of your weapons, is that understood, General?"

"Yes Sir it is."

"Very well, I will have the letter prepared. Please return at 5:00 PM this afternoon."

"Hasta más tarde, Señor."

Moncada's General Officer Conference, Boaco, May 4, 1927. Moncada announced, "You have all studied Stimson's letter. I have given you the night to consider the predicament we are in. Our options are to fight and risk all opportunities to peacefully win back the country or to turn in our weapons, make the most of our situation and get ready to take power in a national election 18 months from now."

The grumbling signaled that discontent still existed. Major General Álvarez stood up. "Generals, we have discussed our dilemma late into the night. Many of us have not visited our families in months. We must consider preparing to fight the American Marines that are here with their air planes and artillery. Their infantry outnumbers us. We may get help from the Mexican government, but we cannot count on their support in a timely manner. We know these things already. I say that tomorrow we begin turning in our weapons. We will do that on pace with the Conservatives so that our forces and theirs remained balanced. We will turn in our older weapons first."

The grumbling faded as, one by one, the generals agreed. They had agreed to meet in the morning to get details on surrendering the weapons.

Sandino hid his defiant expression under the wide brim of his hat. His thoughts were confusion by the sudden acquiescence by the other generals, the abandonment of the Liberal principles, and the continuing occupation by the North Americans. He had a lot to think about before he met with his general staff. He surely would not surrender his arms. How could he trick Moncada into believing he'd turn in his arms? Would he start a revolution alone? Could he alone defeat the North Americans? What kind of army could he raise? Could he get support from the people? From Mexico? From Honduras?

Trusting no one, Sandino left without notice.

Moncada's Headquarters, Boaco, May 12, 1927. "Generalísimo," the ashen-face Stimson began, "I am so disappointed in you. Five days ago, you told me that all weapons had been turned into the Marines. Now you tell me that your General Sandino did not surrender his or his men's weapons. How could you authorize this exception?"

"Many of his men come from the northern Segovia mountains and need their weapons to survive attacks by wild animals and to kill game for eating. I have fought there and know the Segovias. I am going to meet Sandino in Jinotega, and he and those men who live in the villages will be surrendering their weapons. Everything is under control," Moncada promised.

"In nine days I will board a ship to return to the States. I will leave your country believing I failed you, your country, and my country for not getting all the weapons turned over to the Marines. The revolution is not over. The fire smolders and a revolution will flame up once again."

"Señor Stimson, I cannot thank you enough for all that you did for my country. You single handily ended a very costly civil war. I believe, contrarily, that Nicaragua will enjoy peace and prosperity for years to come. I hope you will stay in touch to observe the benefits of what you have done."

"We'll see, General Moncada. We'll see."

Chapter 13: A Wedding In The Mountains

San Rafael del Norte, May 17, 1927. "He's not coming?" Sandino asked his fiancée, Blanca Arauz, mostly in disbelief. His father, Don Gregorio, had been there for all the important events in his life; surely he would not miss his wedding.

"Did he say why?" Sandino pressed

"Only that he was to meet with General Moncada in Jinotega tomorrow to discuss something important. Let me get the telegram and you can read it yourself."

Sandino nodded, believing only that the conniving Moncada had lured his own father into his web.

Blanca returned with the brief telegram that extended Gregorio's true regrets for missing the wedding, the note about an important meeting with Moncada, and the promise to see both Augusto and Blanca soon after the meeting.

"Blanca, my dear," Sandino explained. "Moncada cannot be trusted. He wants to be elected president next year. He has the Norte Americana's support, but he sees the Sandinista movement as a threat to his election. I believe he is doing everything in his power to see that my men and I do not interfere with his plans."

"I understand, Augusto," Blanca said nodding.

"Will you send a telegram to my father in Jinotega, informing him of our sorrow for him missing the wedding and telling him to be careful when dealing with Moncada?"

"Si. Ahora?"

"Si, por favor."

Sandino stood behind Blanca as she quickly typed the telegram. He was amazed by her skill and totally wrapped by her beauty and charm.

She finished, and spun her swivel chair around and asked, "Want to add anything?"

"No my love, just send it."

In a moment she stood up, looked Sandino in the eye and declared, "Now, Señor, you must promise me to clear your mind and pay attention to the details of our wedding. I want you to be able to greet all of my relatives, as well as my friends, by name. You must put the revolution in the back of your mind for the next few days. Do you think you can do that, Augusto? For me?"

"You are right, my love, I must do just that. Where do we begin?"

"We will meet with my mother right now who is preparing tonight's dinner for my immediate family, Father Juan, you, and Sócrates—if he ever shows up."

"Father Juan?"

"Si, you met him at the church last month when I was giving Sócrates the tour of the church's paintings."

"Now I remember; he was a very nice man." Sandino said chuckling to himself for not mentally disengaging from the revolution.

"I haven't seen your father since we returned. Where is Fernando?"

"He's visiting the men who just returned with you. But, Augusto, it's my mother we must see now!"

"Si, Blanca."

San Rafael del Norte, May 18, 1927. "Sócrates, how is papa?" the older brother asked.

Sócrates was with the latter group of Sandino's 300 men—those mostly recruited from Jinotega—and arrived a day behind Sandino in San Rafael del Norte. "He's not there yet. Tomorrow, perhaps." Sócrates continued, "I went to the telegraph office and, when I asked if there were any messages for 'Gregorio' or 'Sandino', the operator gave me the telegram you sent to papa.

"Later, Monseñor Sánchez told me that Moncada was also coming on the 19th with a company of Marines Americana to pay for and collect the weapons from our men. Those from Jinotega—about 40 of them—were looking forward to getting the money."

"Sócrates, thank you. We'll concern ourselves with our men and their weapons in two days; in the meanwhile, we're here to have fun and celebrate the wedding."

San Rafael del Norte, May 19, 1927. On a slightly overcast, yet warm, day in the southern Segovia mountains, the ceremony in la Iglesia Parroquial, the beautiful church of San Rafael del Norte, was magnificent. Colorful mountain flowers abundantly adorned the church. Most of the women of the small village were dressed in the white dresses they wore on Sundays and special occasions. And the marriage of their Blanca Arauz and Augusto Sandino was definitely a special occasion. The men dressed in their best attire, which did not look too much different than their everyday garb. Some brandished pistols. The children dressed in their good school clothes. Sister Gloria played the organ flawlessly.

Father Juan was magnificent. His blessings for the couple and wishes for a long and prosperous life together ignored the concern Sandino had confessed to him about the forthcoming personal sacrifices he was about to make on behalf of the country. Sandino had stated that he was ready to die for his cause; he begged Father Juan to look out for Blanca and any children should they be blessed with any.

After the hour-long ceremony, the couple posed for many photographs with twenty friends and family members. Sandino's jefes—chiefs—Francisco Estrada, Santos López, Juan Umanzor, and Sócrates Sandino attended. Also Pedro Altamirano, whose potential to serve prominently in the Sandino cause, stood noticeably in the front row near the newlyweds.

From The US National Archives

The celebration ended late in the evening. The day had been fun for all. Blanca was pleased even when he told her Sandino would be traveling north to nearby Yali later in the morning and that he wanted her to ride with him and his jefes.

They would ride in the morning, but that was still eight hours away.

BOOK FOUR: WAR IN THE MOUNTAINS

(1927-1928)

CHAPTER 14: OPPOSING GENERALS DRAW BATTLE LINES

US Legation Headquarters, Managua May 23, 1927. "General Feland, please have a seat, Sir," Minister Charles C. Eberhardt said greeting the 2nd Brigade Commanding General.

"And good morning to you, Minister Eberhardt," Feland replied while taking a seat on the same straight-back wicker chair he used for his one-on-one meetings with the head of the legation. Eberhardt used the sessions to learn the military consequences of fast unfolding events. As a matter of fact, he relished the meetings with the "CG" as Feland's insight often went way beyond commanding Marines.

"Coffee, General?"

"Yes, thank you. Your staff brews a fine pot of coffee."

"Did you see Stimson's report to the State Department?"

"I did."

Eberhardt poured the coffee from the pewter pot imprinted with the Great Seal of the United States imbedded on its side. He looked over the warm cup he placed on the edge of his desk within Feland's reach and said, "Logan, I believe the report had a few ambiguities that we need to talk about."

Feland silently nodded in agreement.

"I cannot agree with the report's statement that the war between the Liberals and Conservatives appears to be over."

"Likewise, Sir."

"His downplaying of Sandino 'not surrendering his weapons and reneging on the agreement' is the part that gets me. It runs counter to the intelligence we have on the Sandino threat. Do you agree?"

"Most certainly, Mr. Minister."

Eberhardt had grown accustomed to Feland's "Mr. Minister" formality despite his initial pleas for "Call me, Charles," when they were meeting privately.

"Our brigade's information and that of the Guardia Nacional folks believe that Sandino's magnetism will be able to generate a large enough following to challenge our brigade on a piecemeal basis when we're spread throughout the country. And based on the republishing of that Colombian reporter's interview in the New York Times and European papers, we also believe he has the ability to generate international support."

This time Eberhardt silently nodded.

Feland continued, "Our backdoor information indicates that the Stimson's report emboldened the Senate to demand the troops come home—all of them. The Commandant's message to us was, 'We'll probably be bringing the 11th Marines home as well as some support forces. He added that our mission to stand up the National Guard or Guardia and to secure the national elections would not change no matter how many grumbles would be heard from the hill."

"Well, General, that's good to know. I'd hate to be sitting by myself here without you Marines."

"Rest assured, Sir, we're not going to leave you 'high and dry'."

"That's quite comforting, Logan. What are your plans?"

"We're going to do two things. First, we are going to reduce bandit activity in all villages in the vicinity of the Corinto-Chinandega-Managua rail line. With your support, we'd like to send one of our more self-sufficient companies—the 51st—to Ocotal to force him, Sandino, out into the open. If we can eliminate him, we'll be free to concentrate on other tasks."

"That's exactly what we need to do, Logan. What can I do?"

"Nothing this minute. My staff has almost completed our plan. George Ward, your deputy, will be visiting with us tomorrow to get details. Then I believe that in a couple of days we both can get a complete briefing on their plans. I'll send you an invitation to visit my headquarters for the briefing."

"Excellent. I'll look forward to that."

Sandino Camp Near Yali, May 24, 1924. Mules, six to ten of them, could be heard moving at a gallop up the only road that passed through village of Yali toward the camp in the Jinotega Department. The camp, situated just east of the road was hidden in a tree line and was less than a half mile from the small village. The unimproved road was the principal route between central Nicaragua and Honduras. Soon two Segovians, who rode in front of a well-dressed gentleman, could be seen. Five others, also mounted on mules, trailed.

The commotion drew the attention of the campers, who emerged from the line of trees as much out of curiosity as they did to greet the riders. The riders waved their hats to greet Sandino and his jefes , his chiefs.

Sandino, recognizing the men, waved back. As they closed with Sandino, the lead riders suddenly veered left towards the other campers leaving the gentleman they were escorting to stop his horse in front Sandino.

Sandino greeted the gentleman with boyish enthusiasm. "Father! Thanks for coming to Yali." Sandino opened his arms to embrace his father, Don Gregorio, who was dismounting the large grey mule he had ridden from Jinotega. Both men looked deep into each other's eyes seeking answers to questions that pitted national security against family loyalty.

"Augusto, please forgive me for missing your wedding."

"Of course father. The wedding was beautiful."

"And so I heard."

"You did?"

"Si, I stopped at San Rafael del Norte figuring you were still there. I went into the telegraph office to inquire about you, Blanca and Sócrates. Señor Arauz described the wedding in much detail. I met Señora Arauz. Both are proud of their daughter and are very much in awe of you and what you mean for the future of our country. They are pleased for you and Blanca."

"That's wonderful, father."

"You know why I missed your wedding, don't you?"

"Yes, father," the son said with a hint of disappointment in his voice.

"Now, I know I made a mistake by missing it."

"A mistake?"

"Yes, a mistake."

"I arrived in Jinotega a few hours before Moncada and went to the telegraph office. They had the telegram you sent. I finally understood why that devious Moncada wanted to talk to me. He wanted me to talk you into surrendering all you weapons. Thanks for that warning to be careful about Moncada." He continued, "I went to the church and met Monseñor Sánchez. He holds you in the very highest regards. I might say as well as everyone I met."

As an additional thought Gregorio declared, "Moncada is truly an arrogant ass!"

Sandino smiled, much relieved from what he had heard.

"He and those Infantería de marina Norteamericanos collected a lot of weapons that our not-too-bright Presidente Díaz, paid $10 for. Your men told me on the way up here they all had turned any old weapon they could find and kept their good ones.

Turning in weapons, 1927-*USMC History Division*

Sandino quietly said, "Si, father, I know that. Let's go back into the camp."

"You have quite a following."

"Si, father, I know that too."

As they entered the tree line, Sócrates dashed up, "Papa, Papa!"

The three men walked to the camp's center, where Don Gregorio met and instantly warmed to Blanca, his brand new, bubbly daughter-in-law. He also met Pete Ramirez, a reporter from the <u>New York Times</u>, who had been granted an exclusive interview with General Sandino, "The

People's Hero of Central America."

Don Gregorio soon understood his son's objective for an independent Nicaragua. Up to a few months ago, Sandino harbored few ill feelings about the Infantería de marina Norteamericanos. But now, with them occupying the country's villages, the Marines would have to go. One way or another. It was merely a matter of time before he would strike.

CHAPTER 15: CHASING BANDITS AND REBELS

Matagalpa, May 29, 1927. "Gunnery Sergeant Robert Wilson," Captain Gilbert Hatfield said to the wiry senior non-commission officer of the 51st Company with a smile on his face, "We're going to get some bad guys!"

MATAGALPA- *from the US National Archives*

"Music to my ears, Capt'n!"

"Yeah," Hatfield went on, "compared to that two and a half day hike in the sun we had along the Rama River to that deserted river town, I believe we'll see some action this time. Let's get the men ready to leave tomorrow morning after breakfast.

"Oh, you know what? I want to brief them along with the officers and NCOs. With the exception of those men on security, let's all meet back here at 1830. In the meanwhile, Willy, inspect the men's feet and boots. I'm going to check on the mules."

"You're on, Capt'n, 1830."

For the past week, since they returned from Jinotega, 15 miles north of Matagalpa, the company had camped in the Morazán Park. In Jinotega, they had collected over 160 rifles from Liberal Army soldiers who had served with Sandino. They had also provided security for General Moncada during his attempt to have Sandino surrender his weapons. Sandino's mostly defiant refusal to even meet with Moncada caused the generalissimo to send Sandino's father, Don Gregorio, to talk to his son. Moncada also labeled Sandino "a bandit."

"See you at chow, Sir."

The pack-mules, thirty of them, were at the far end of the park. Hatfield assigned Sergeant Bo Becker of the 1st Platoon to supervise the training of packing the mules under the watchful eye and tutelage of the local arriero or mule handler who, while helpful, could not speak a word of English. Hatfield learned that Marines could learn to load a pack mule very easily and he did not want to have the mule handlers, with their language barrier, travel with the company to Ocotal.

"Sergeant Becker, is your platoon picking up the art of packing these mules as fast as Bill Henderson's did yesterday?" Hatfield greeted the head of his 1st Platoon.

"You bet, Captain. Sergeant Henderson said there wasn't much to it."

"All right, I have the Gunny checking on boots and feet before we take off for Nuevo Segovia tomorrow. Otherwise, are the men ready to go?" Hatfield queried the young warrior.

"They're all ready Sir," Becker replied. "You gonna give us the details of our mission,

Sir?"

"Right Becker, I plan to do that after chow at 1830. Hatfield concluded, "Well, just make sure your men can rapidly unload that

Browning and ammo if we come under fire on the way north. I heard that armed bandits are everywhere in the Segovias."

"Yes Sir, Captain," the sergeant replied.

Parque Morazán, Matagalpa, 6:30 PM, May 29, 1927. "Gunny, we have everyone accounted for?" the captain asked.

"Yes Sir."

"Men, as you all know, tomorrow we are leaving for Ocotal. That's the capital of the Nuevo Segovia Department. Ocotal is a good 100 miles north of here and only 15 miles south of Honduras.

"You also know, the country is crawling with bandits. They are mostly from the Liberal Army. They are dangerous. Two weeks ago a band of outlaws from the former Liberal Army, raided the village of La Paz, just south of Chinandega. As they started their looting, the La Paz detachment of Marines charged up main street to meet them. The Marines routed the bad guys, but not before Captain Buchanan and Private Jackson were killed."

Hatfield paused seeing the controlled rage flare in the faces of his men. They had all been rocked by the Buchanan incident. They knew that Buchanan was a friend of Hatfield's, and he would drop by to visit their captain on occasion. Jackson, a newly-joined Marine, was unknown to the men of the 51st. Hatfield continued, "I learned of another bandit story yesterday from Lieutenant Colonel Meade, when he gave me our orders to go north." Now their faces intensified while awaiting possibly more bad news.

"Before I proceed, let me first ask a question. Who has ever heard of Captain William Richards?"

A half dozen hands went up in the air. Hatfield looked around and stopped. "Corporal Rollins?"

"Sir, isn't he Quantico's pistol champ?"

"That's correct, Rollins."

"Well, three days ago while Richards had his detachment at El Viejo—just north of Chinandega—a notorious bandit by the name of Cabulla rode into town with a few of his cohorts. The Marines were in the town's only bar having lunch.

"The bandits finally came into the bar. They were all armed. Cabulla made all sorts of threatening remarks to the men having lunch. Typical punk!" Hatfield said as if spitting. "Then the stupid bully got really annoyed at Richards who was essentially ignoring him. He said, 'Hey Mister Norte American big shot! Are you paying attention?

"Richards didn't turn around but was looking at Cabulla in the bar's mirror. The irate Cabulla reached for his pistol. Before he got it half way out, Richards drew and fired his own pistol and the fat bandit fell dead on the floor."

While the Marines start laughing and cheering, Hatfield continued, "Richards turned around as if nothing happened. The other bandits charge for the door. One big Marine, a private from Texas by the name of Holmes, blocked the door and said, 'No olvides a tu amigo!' Don't forget your friend! With that, the now-humbled bandits were nearly in tears, repeating, 'Nosotros lo sentimos muchísimo' We are sorry all the way out of town."

When the laughter subsided, Hatfield announced, "Tomorrow, we are going to Ocotal, a far more dangerous town in the middle of the bandits' heartland. There are 43 of us and we will be waiting for a vastly smarter bandit than Cabulla. We will wait for Sandino and his men, perhaps 200 of them, to come. Sandino is reported at Yali just north of San Rafael del Norte to get weapons and recruit an army. When he finds we are in his mountains, he'll want us out.

"We'll have a fight on our hands. But remember one thing, Devil Dogs, like Captain Richards, we can handle anything they want to give us!"

Chapter 16: VO-4M Finally Arrives In Nicaragua

Managua Aerodrome, 3:00 PM, June 3, 1927. "You must be Frank Schilt," Major Rusty Rowell said as he approached the athletic looking aviator from Indiana, currently looking into one of the O2B-1 engine compartments.

First Lieutenant Schilt's head turned slowly toward the greeting to see another Marine in an aviator's jump suit standing between him and a grey sky. The crow-feet wrinkles emanating from the greeter's eyes and reddish-brown hair told Schilt that his future new boss had just announced his presence. "Sir, I am; and you must be Major Rowell."

Schilt casually pulled a slightly greasy towel from his rear right pocket and wiped off his right hand before extending it. "Pleasure to meet you, Sir."

"It's my honor, Frank. With that Schneider Cup, you have done a lot to put Marine aviation on the map. I want to thank you for that."

About that time the inquisitive young mechanic, who had heard the words "Schneider Cup," looked around the far side of the engine and over the prop of the aircraft at his new commanding officer.

"You're too kind, Sir," Schilt responded. Then looking to his right to see his curious mechanic, Schilt added, "And I could not have done it without the help of my dedicated mechanic, Corporal 'Junior' Wilson."

"Nice to meet you, Sir," was all that Wilson said before retreating back to the far side of the engine.

"And nice meeting you, Corporal," Rowell said, smiling to the young man he could no longer see.

Boeing O2B-1-*US Navy Photo*

Most of the flying community referred to the type and model of this aircraft as a "DH-4" because it had originally been designed by De Havilland in 1916 at the start of the world war. The US adopted the design and manufactured and shipped nearly 1900 DH- 4s to the war. By 1927 the US Army called the aircraft a "DH-4M-1" and used it as an air-to-air fighter aircraft and bomber. Rowell's six birds were an earlier series, DH-4Bs. The US Navy upgraded the aircraft and changed the designator to "O2B-1" when they started using it for reconnaissance, cross country, and night flying instead of as a fighter/bomber.

Rowell walked slowly around the aircraft, examining it scrupulously. Schilt joined him. "How did the birds do on the ship?"

"Fine, Sir. This one's leaking a bit of oil; but it's not from the trip down here."

"Frank, you know we are practicing 'glide bombing' or 'dive bombing' as we now call it.

Have you tried any of that?"

"Yes, Sir. You remember First Lieutenant Frank Pierce, now Captain Frank Pierce?"

"Sure I do. He left our squadron a year ago. I knew he was going to Quantico to assist in building the new airfield?" Rowell acknowledged.

"He's our senior observer now; I expect him to join us in a few months. Anyway, we have been doing nothing but practicing dive bombing. Captain Pierce was excellent at showing us the tricks—I should say 'all your tricks.' As a matter of fact all six of our O2B-1s have Lewis machine guns mounts fore and aft.

Rowell nodded pleased at what he heard and knowing that the source was more than credible.

"Did you hear that much of my squadron—VO-1M—is going back to Pendleton later this summer and that VO-4M—your squadron—will be joining the remnants?"

"Yes Sir. And we'll be designated 'VO-7M' I heard."

"Well Frank, looks like you have matters in hand. Thanks also for that. Oh, by the way will you and your other pilots be ready to fly with us in the morning?"

"We're looking forward to it, Sir."

"Great! We'll meet at the briefing tent at 0730. I suspect, as the rainy season approaches, we'll see more clouds. That may affect where we practice."

"We'll be there," Schilt said, then added, "Oh Major, I do have a question."

"What's that, Frank?"

"We had heard that if we stay down here for over a year, we may be able to bring our dependents down. Do you know anything about that?"

"Frank, that's up in the air. Initially we thought a significant force would be needed here. However, with the Conservative and Liberal armies surrendering their weapons, the long-term plans have been brushed aside. The 11th Marine Regiment, that arrived last month, is already packing up to return to Pendleton and deactivate. And that's why my squadron is mostly all going back to San Diego sometime this summer. So, there is no simple answer for you. If this guy

Sandino never surfaces, I'd say we'll all be out of here after the November '28 election. However," shaking his head, "if he's as bad as some people say he is, we may be here a bit longer."

Managua Aerodrome, 7:30 AM, June 4, 1927. The chatter and camaraderie blended with the "we can do this better than you can" bravado comments in the joint squadron briefing tent. Naturally competitive, the mood of the aviators seemed to soar in response to the sun's appearance. They knew it would be a good day for flying and they couldn't wait to show off their stuff.

All six O2B-1s from Quantico and the six DH-4Bs from San Diego were lined up for the morning flight and ready to fly.

Rowell entered the tent exactly at 7:30 AM. As the pilots rose to acknowledge his presence, he was quick to announce, "Have a seat gentlemen."

Major Ross E. "Rusty" Rowell *Official Photo USMC #3713*

The brief chatter while seats were being retaken ended sharply when Rowell opened, "We're honored to have the pilots and observers from VO-4M join us this morning. We're also lucky to have nice weather so we'll be able to make several runs today. It's my intention to make dry runs this morning with all birds. We'll plan on making about six runs each, and we can do that next to Lake Nicaragua. I should explain to our newly-joined aviators that we have been shying away from flying over the lake. Since, God forbid, should we have engine trouble over that lake and have to make a wet landing. Its shoreline is covered with alligators.

"We'll break for lunch after a critique of our work this morning; then we'll use live ordnance this afternoon in the southern part of the Segovia mountains. For you men from Quantico, the key to successful dive bombing is the constant, relentless attacks on the enemy, whether it's their soldiers or their fortifications. With that, our ground forces will be able to close with and defeat the enemy. Just how do we achieve a constant, relentless air attack?" Rowell asked rhetorically.

"First of all we do it as a team. 'Constant' deals with the timing between the planes attacking. Ideally, every 30-45 seconds between strikes should be sufficient to keep the enemy's heads down. With their heads down, our infantry Marines can move in on them. In the beginning, we'll attack from at least 1500 feet with the sun at our back or from cloud cover if that's possible. Then we'll lower the attack altitude to mostly 1,000 feet so as to maintain constant pressure.

"The 'relentless' part pertains to hitting the enemy until all resistance ceases, our Marines have taken their objective, or until we run out of ammo or need to refuel." Rowell paused. "Any questions?

Rowell looked around. His pilots were nodding their heads. They had heard Rowell's speech many times before and knew it well. The Quantico pilots were digesting Rowell's message.

"Seeing none…. this morning our attack formation will have Gunner Mike Wodarczyk in the lead attack plane. Lieutenant Schilt, I'd like you to follow Mike and place your birds in any order you think is best. I will be in Green Nose observing.

"I would like Gunner Wodarczyk to review our hand signals for diving, regrouping, acquiring new targets, and returning to base, among others. There's not but a dozen, and I'm sure you use many of the same ones; nevertheless, it's good for all of us to think alike… Mike."

Ten minutes later two staggered lines of six aircraft each saw pilots and observers climbing into the respective seats: observers in the aft seats and pilots in the forward seats. The sole exception was the lead plane, with Major Rowell flying Green Nose solo. Flying solo, he was in the rear seat and a 100 pound sandbag was in the front to balance the plane's center-of-gravity balance. The biplanes wobbled along the field toward the far end of the grassy runway.

Rowell led. His front two wheels straddled a two-inch-deep furrow into which his rear skid fell. Now the DH-4B faced into the wind and was on track to lift off. The noise of the plane rose modestly as the engine turned the prop faster. Within thirty yards, Rowell and the plane were airborne. Rowell kept the plane six feet off the ground while building up speed. After 100 yards and the plane flying about 65 miles per hour, the major gently pulled back on the stick and the plane soared into the air. At 2,000 feet he leveled off and circled the aerodrome. Five planes followed and the final six moved into line to take off.

In minutes, Rowell led the flight of twelve aircraft toward the fields adjoining the large lake. The major signaled the others to observe him while he dove toward the ground to mark the target. Seconds before he bottomed out of his dive and about 400 feet above the ground, he lifted a five pound bag of wheat Flour from his lap and dropped it. The bag fell toward the intersection of two very visible ox trails. Upon hitting five feet from the middle of the trail crossing, the contents exploded in a 15-foot high cloud of flour. None of the twenty two aviators— pilots and observer-gunners—above missed the major's accuracy. All were impressed and ready to duplicate his dive. They were eager to experience the body pressure shared by aviators: the 1.5 negative Gs as they dove losing half their body weight and the 3.0 positive Gs as their pulled up when their weight tripled.

Rowell joined the others who had been following Wodarczyk's aircraft making lazy circles above the ox trails. Rowell pointed a finger at Wodarczyk. Immediately the Marine gunner returned a "thumbs up" then flew another half mile before suddenly dropping down toward the Flour-marked intersection. Twenty-five seconds later Schilt followed. The first runs seemed easy and the diving planes looked pretty organized. However, as the number of dives increased, the intervals between planes ranged haphazardly between 15 seconds and 75 seconds. The pulling up angles varied and annoyed Rowell who loitered above. Rowell thought, interesting, Wodarczyk and Schilt execute each dive perfectly while most of the others struggled at times.

After 45 minutes, Rowell caught Wodarczyk's eye and signaled to return to base. The major led the way back to the field and descended toward the grass below. In preparation for landing, when he was about fifty feet off the ground, he eased his plane's rear skid down to a point slightly higher than the wheels. This maneuver caused his eye level to be three-feet below his huge engine thereby blocking his forward view. To overcome the inability to see forward, Rowell flew Green Nose in a slightly zigzag manner enabling him to see forward alternatively from both sides of the aircraft. Once about ten feet off the ground, he straightened the nose and blindly settled onto the grass. The others followed not far behind.

Back in the briefing tent Major Rowell began his promised critique, "Men, as a unit, our flight formation to the target area was, what I consider to be satisfactory. That formation will enable effective communications between pilots. When we arrived at the target area your 'circle the target' set up worked well; I could see that when flying up to rejoin the flight after I marked the target."

He paused looking around at the young lieutenants from Quantico and their equally youthful enlisted observer-gunners, none of whom he yet knew. Then continued, "As a team executing a dive-bombing mission, you did well in the beginning. Then, as you know, you lost your rhythm. The angle of attack and attack speeds started to vary. To compensate for these variables, you constantly accelerated and decelerated. All of this precluded the desired 'constant basis' that I talked about this morning. As a group, it was unacceptable. I will note, however, that I was impressed with our lead pilots, Gunner Wodarczyk and Lieutenant Schilt, who flew particularly well.

"On the bright side, I anticipate that you should improve rapidly. We will practice dive bombing techniques twice a day for the foreseeable future. You'll know when you are improving. Any questions?"

"Sir, Lieutenant Earl Thomas," the young Quantico pilot said identifying himself.

"Yes, Lieutenant."

"What do you consider to be the ideal speed and angle when we're attacking?"

"Under ideal conditions, and that's when the clouds and enemy fire are non-existent and when the terrain isn't a factor, you should attack at a 45 degree angle and achieve about 150 miles per hour at the bottom of your dive. This morning we had ideal conditions. This afternoon we'll be bombing in the foothills of the Segovias. The target's location along the ridges or in the valleys will affect our approach, and we are almost in the rainy season so cloudy conditions may exist. Clouds will be used to our advantage to mask the attack, but clouds definitely will require that our flying rhythm be nearly perfect—nothing like it was this morning. Thanks for the question, Lieutenant."

Looking around, with no hands in the air, Rowell said, "Well, seeing no other questions, let's break for lunch and plan to meet back here at 1300 hours."

Over the top of the babble of the departing pilots and observers about the morning flight, curiosity about what they were having for lunch, and liberty in the town after the evening meal, Rowell caught Wodarczyk's and Schilt's attention and asked them to remain.

"Frank, Mike, again, nice flying this morning. Our squadron is tasked to fly a reconnaissance mission daily, and I'd like you two to fly today's mission." Then pausing, he added, "Unless you would rather practice dive bombing this afternoon."

Both shook their heads declining the practice, communicating a clear, "No sir!"

"All right then, after lunch go to the OPS office to see Technical Sergeant Roy Jolson for a briefing. You'll be flying up north over the Segovias, so the cloud cover will be a factor from time to time. Stay together and work as a team. You'll be fine. Check in with OPS when you're finished for a debriefing, then look me up as I want to know not only what you achieved but how the birds flew."

"Thank-you, Sir" was the comment made by both officers who were thrilled by the assignment.

Managua Aerodrome, Late Afternoon, June 4, 1927. Schilt's O2B-1 landed in the field beside the aerodrome seconds before Wodarczyk's DH-4 and rumbled across the grassy furrows to be greeted by Corporal Wilson near the other five O2B-1s. Corporal Roland Smitty, who had been talking about the baseball game the two technical sergeants had arranged between the combined squadron and the departing 11th Marines while waiting for the returning pilots, split off and stood next to Green Nose waving his arms to direct Wodarczyk where to park his plane.

Smitty, from Los Angeles, had attended every Los Angeles Angels home baseball game since 1921 when the "Looloos" won the Pacific Coast League championship. Living a few blocks from the 15,00-seat Washington Park, he and his buddies knew how to slip in the broken panel between on South Hill Street near right field and never get caught. Naturally it didn't hurt that Al Smith, Smitty's father, was the head groundskeeper.

Keeping a watchful eye on their junior noncommissioned officers while standing at the large door to the aerodrome were the two technical sergeants, Walt Heller and Ike Billingsworth. Aircraft maintenance in Managua was in great shape for the foreseeable future since Heller and Wilson opted not to return to the States and joined Billingsworth and Smitty. But, this afternoon, their focus was selecting their team for the forthcoming ball game.

"How'd she fly, sir?" were the first words out of Wilson's mouth as roar of the plane's engine grew silent.

"No problem, Junior," Schilt replied as he unsnapped his harness belt and removed his aviator cap. "Flew absolutely fine."

Once on the ground, Schilt walked over to Wodarczyk, who already was out of his plane and talking to Smitty about a bit of "looseness" in the rudder control.

After Smitty's, "I'll tighten it." Wodarczyk looked to Schilt and smiled, "Neat area up there, eh, Frank?"

"Wow, that's some rough terrain; pretty from the air, though. It's hard to believe anyone lives up there," Schilt said as the two walked into the aerodrome to file their report with the operations section.

They opened a heavy wooden door with a large opaque glass panel. Painted on the glass, in black, hand-painted letters, was the words *Operations Office, Managua Aerodrome*. Technical Sergeant Roy Jolson sat at his desk smoking a locally-grown-and-rolled cigar and reading <u>The Detroit News</u>. His slicked-back black hair and prominent nose gave him a handsome, but inner-city, tough-guy appearance. At first meeting, he was quick to let strangers know he was from Detroit, the automobile-manufacturing capitol of the world. Jolson grew up in Detroit the son of a union organizer and assemblyman in one of the new auto plants built near there. By the time he was twelve, he had grown weary of his dad. He told his friends that his dad surrounded himself with a bunch of communists. He left home to join the Marine Corps and escape the liberal atmosphere at the age of 17.

Thirteen years later Jolson still loved to hate liberals and communists. He was quite proud, many times argumentative, of his conservative views. He fed on anyone with liberal views. Since Marines mostly harbored views similar, although not as pronounced as his, he satisfied his voracious appetite for consuming liberals by subscribing to *The Detroit News* and the *St. Louis Post-Dispatch*. Both papers had liberal leanings.

Now inside the office and through the light-grey layer of cigar smoke, Schilt saw three maps and six aerial photographs pinned to the wall.

"Gentlemen, how was your flight?" Top Joyner asked as he laid the newspaper on top of a stack of others.

Wodarczyk answered, "Fine Top, have you met Lieutenant Schilt, yet?"

"No, Sir. Nice to meet you, Lieutenant."

"Pleasure's all mine, Top. I see you have a newspaper. What's it say about Charles Lindbergh?"

"Tell you what, Sir; it's amazing that this communist paper has anything at all about the Lone Eagle. The bastards who write this trash are all a bunch of queers. To answer your question, though, they said he's just back in New York getting a ticker-tape parade. They're going to give him a Medal of Honor in the next two weeks, and they are talking about sending him down to South America to show the locals that the US is the modern and powerful country that we are. All of that in preparation of the Pan American Conference scheduled for January in Cuba."

Schilt, in awe of the detailed response and added commentary, said in amazement, "Thanks, Top. Maybe we'll get him up flying with us."

Realizing Joyner was on his high horse, Wodarczyk interrupted. "Top, the CO is expecting us, where's the After-Flight Reports?"

"Sure, Mr. Wodarczyk, the AFRs are at the corner of that table over there. Need a pencil,

Sir?"

Half an hour later… "You filed your reports with OPS?" the squadron commander greeted the two pilots who had just entered his office.

Wodarczyk confirmed that they had just done that with Technical Sergeant Joyner.

Turning to the powerful looking lieutenant, Rowell asked, "Well Frank, what did you learn on your first combat flight since 'the war'?"

"Well sir, I learned a couple of things. First of all, northern Nicaragua has dramatic mountains, cliffs, waterfalls, and tree canopies. I used to fly over the Appalachians and thought they were rugged, but the Segovias have them beat."

Schilt paused to collect his thought, "Then, I could not believe that I was almost blind from 1500 feet. We'd be flying along and I would be looking down enjoying the view when Mike would get my attention and point down. I'd follow him down and sure enough the roofs of three or four huts would come into sight. Then I'd see a trail leading to the huts, a camp fire, and finally, before pulling up, washed clothes spread out on bushes and left to dry. No people though—they were probably in the huts hiding."

"Good analysis Frank. We all improved our observation skills after we arrived. You'll be fascinated by your own improvement after a couple of weeks."

Schilt asked Wodarczyk, "Okay Mike, how'd you know there was a group of huts?"

Looking at Schilt, "Like the major said, you have to know what you're looking for. On that group of huts you just talked about, I'd been watching this trail as it came out of a valley. After a couple of miles it joined with another from the connecting ridge to the east. Within 500 yards there were the three bumps of a slightly lighter color which I took to be huts instead of trees. That's when I slowed up and signaled you to go down with me to take a look."

Schilt's head moved up and down wholly understanding the easy, but new way of thinking when flying a reconnaissance mission in Nicaragua.

"Did you find the 51st?" Rowell asked referring to Hatfield's company.

"Yes, Sir. They're camped about 50 miles south of Ocotal. They waived like all heck when we flew down on them," Wodarczyk added. "It's like they hadn't seen a friendly face in weeks!"

"You know, Sir, if we are going to get better at supporting those ground guys, we need to be able to communicate with them better. We can drop messages all day long, but we need to understand what they want," Schilt offered.

"You're so right, Frank. We have to be able to communicate from both the ground and the air. We need to set up a group of ground and air personnel to develop an effective way of communicating while we're here in Nicaragua. We can't ask the ground guys to haul all those fancy ground signal panels around, but we can probably do something else. I'll propose a meeting at the 'urgent' brigade meeting tomorrow to explore other options for them communicating with us."

Then remembering why he wanted to talk to them in the first place. Rowell asked, "Oh yeah, how did the airplanes fly?"

Schilt answered quickly that his was fine, "No problem." Meanwhile, Wodarczyk reported about the loose rudder cable and the fact that he believed Smitty had it tightened by now.

Chapter 17: Preparing For The First Battle

2nd Marine Brigade Headquarters, June 5, 1927. Brigadier General Feland opened the meeting, "Minister Eberhardt, Mr. Ward, we welcome you to our refurbished headquarters." As a side note, he added, "I don't know if you knew that Major Smedley Butler… now Brigadier General Butler… and his battalion staff used this same building when they were here in 1912. It's quite accommodating."

"It is very nice. And you have done a marvelous job in cleaning it up and making it functional once again."

"Thank you, Sir. Minister, would you like to make some opening comments?"

"No thank you, General Feland. Please begin."

"All right, Sir," Feland turned to his Intel Officer, "Captain Worchester, would you give us an assessment of the current enemy situation."

Captain Chris Worchester, the brigade's intelligence officer, rose, walked to the map with a pointer, and offered his assessment. He briefly reviewed the recent incidents near Chinandega at La Paz and El Viejo that he considered to be isolated banditry.

Worchester's voice deepened when he addressed his next subject, Augusto Sandino. He pointed to Yali on the map, "Sandino and his followers are believed to be gathering weapons and recruiting in the Segovias. At this juncture, they have 30-40 armed soldiers. They are camped, we believe, near Yali. That's based on the information we gathered from his father's, movements. His father, who met with General Moncada in Jinotega, was last seen 35 miles north of there near Yali. We tasked the 51st Company to search the area as they passed through Yali four days ago in route to Ocotal. There was no trace of Sandino and his gang.

"

"I don't believe Sandino will be ready to do anything noteworthy for a few months. He'll need to enlarge his army and train his recruits to be soldiers first."

Worchester paused and looked around. "Unless there are questions, I'll be followed by the OPS officer, Major Black."

"I have one, Captain."

"Oh, certainly, Colonel Meade."

"Do you have any information on Sandino getting any outside support from, for example, Mexico?"

"I don't at this point, Sir. Perhaps Mr. Ward does."

The deputy minister immediately fielded the question, "Colonel Meade, we feel quite certain that Sandino cannot sustain a large enough force to make any difference in the political environment here unless he has external support. He is getting an immense amount of good publicity from various interviews and is becoming the hero of liberals in the Caribbean and South American countries. This may lead to support in the future. But, that's all we have at this point, Sir."

Meade nodded his head understanding.

Seeing no other questions, Worchester turned to Major Black while passing the pointer and said, "Sir."

"Thanks Chris," Major Donald Black, the former 2nd Battalion, 5th Marines Executive Officer and now Brigade Operations Officer, said. Then looking at the two senior men, "Minister, General, based on the information you just heard about the reduced level of enemy activity and the political climate in Washington, we are currently redeploying the 11th Marines and are planning to redeploy VM-01 later this summer.

"The 5th Marines and the Guardia Nacional will focus on policing up the bandits and eliminating the Sandinista force. The two incidents Captain Worchester discussed near Chinandega are representative of the anti-bandit effort. This effort's initial priority will be focused on the capital region, the Managua-Leon-Chinandega rail line and Corinto port area. We'll expand eastward to the Boaco and Chontales departments in the future. We are relying on the local police to control the areas south of Managua, including Granada. There have been no bandit incident reports south of us during the past month.

"Regarding our efforts to eliminate Sandino, we are planning to go on the offense, break his popular support, force him out into the open, and destroy any armed group he presents. The 51st Company from the 5th Marines commanded by Gilbert Hatfield has already deployed and should arrive in Ocotal tomorrow or the next day. The various Guardia units moving up north, commanded by Major Vic Bleasdale, are about a day behind the 51st. We are also organizing a large mule train to take supplies that will be needed in the Northern Departments. Major Oliver Floyd will be leading that element when all the supplies and animals have been acquired. We are hoping that they will be moving north in the next couple of weeks.

"Our biggest challenge will be effective communications. Soon we'll have our 1800-man regiment spread throughout the western half of this country. In many cases, through the national telegraph system, communications will be sufficient to support the deployed units. However, when our units are on patrol, moving from one village to another, or located in mostly any small village, they will be without communications. In these situations, our air squadron will be both providing fire power to support them and filling the communications gap. Only last week, at the excellent suggestion by Major Rowell," Black paused to acknowledge the squadron commander sitting beside him, "we initiated looking into ways to improve ground-to-air communications. Once developed, we intend to make the air-ground communications training a priority.

"Last, though absolutely not the lowest priority, we are supporting Lieutenant Colonel Rhea in his effort to stand up the Guardia Nacional. Gentlemen, please recall President's Coolidge's guidance to Secretary Kellogg: 'I want you to establish a national guard or police force of sufficient capability that we don't have to send the Marines in there every three months.' To that end, we have identified the best weapons collected from both armies and are reissuing them to his recruits. We are providing training support, such as constructing and operating a rifle range and a pistol range. Along with Colonel Rhea, we have identified other deficiencies the Guardia has. These are in the areas of patrolling, defensive operations, communications, and field medical treatment. We are helping the Guardia Nacional officers who are American Marines correct these deficiencies.

After another fifteen minutes of detailed logistical and administration information, as well as summary comments by General Feland, Minister Eberhardt accepted the Brigade Commander's second invitation to speak to the attendees. His most surprising suggestion was in the area of getting along with the Nicaraguans. He told them about how the Nicaraguans had fallen in love with the game of baseball. In Managua, a five-team league had been formed. Looking at Ward sitting beside him, he offered, "If you are interested, George will be glad to assist you in scheduling games with teams in the league," ending the meeting on an up note. The minister's baseball suggestion was a pleasant distraction from the cloud of combat looming on the near horizon.

Sandino Headquarters, Jícaro, June 15, 1927. "Sir, just why does General Moncada, and now the American Minister Eberhardt, refer to you as a 'bandit'?" Pepe Jericó, the Colombian reporter from the Bogotá *El Tiempo*, asked Sandino.

Jicaro (To be renamed on June 13,1927 by Sandino, "Cuidad Sandino")

Photo from History Division given by Maj EN McClellan, USMC

Sandino looked up, thinking of the exact words, knowing that what he said would be heard around the globe, "Señor Jericó, if I am a bandit, the Norte American imperialists will be only helping Nicaragua search for a trouble maker. That would not gain any visibility in their press. If, on the other hand, they called me a revolutionary leader, then their Marines would be looking for a rebel. And, if they are looking for a such a person, it would mean two things: first, the Tipitapa Agreement would be considered to be a failure; and second, the act of chasing a rebel would be interpreted as 'interfering' with another country's internal business and that is not what Coolidge promised he would do when he was elected. The Prensa Norte Americana, their press, would love that.

"So," he shrugged, "they call me a bandit."

"You are so right, Señor," Jericó noted. "They are even calling your men, 'a gang of criminals.'"

"That's most offensive. My men are organized and idealistic, not a gang of criminals; they are prepared to die as patriots."

Sandino narrowed his eyes and lowered his voice as he always does when he gets serious, "Our purpose is solely to give Nicaragua back to the Nicaraguans. If Moncada gets elected next year, the Americans will be here for another four years. They will be stripping Nicaraguans of the wealth that rightfully belongs to them."

"Señor, it looks as if they already are starting to do that. I know you are aware that the Infantería de marina Norteamericanos has taken over this department's capital of Ocotal. Are you planning to do something about that?"

"Señor Jericó, I have written two letters to the Marine commander in Ocotal, a Captain Hatfield. I have warned him that I am the Latin-American David, and he is the North American Goliath. I am making plans to thrust him from Ocotal."

"And, how does he respond General?"

Sandino's laugh sounded similar to a brief snort. "He welcomes me to 'come and get' him.

His words mock me; they are both belittling and provocative!"

"Wait until he sees the recruits I now have. I am now up to nearly 300 men, perhaps more, who promise to ride with me."

"Are they armed?"

"We only have rifles for one hundred men at this time. We have a few machine guns and will soon be making bombs. Capitán Hatfield has no clue how much more powerful my army will be in one month. He will be destroyed."

"Bombs, Señor?"

"Si, if you stay for another week you will know all about our bombs."

"Yes, of course, General. But first I should like to file this story."

"Please do. Then, after you are sworn to silence for a week, you will be able to file a second story focusing on the capabilities of the Sandinista army."

"All news articles state the location where the articles are filed. May I state that this article was filed from Jícaro or will that give your location away?"

"Señor Jericó, two days ago at a ceremony, I renamed the town of Jícaro, 'Sandino City'.

Please use the new name as your filing location."

Sandino Headquarters, Jícaro, June 25, 1927. The rain had stopped soon after darkness engulfed the trail bordering the Río Jícaro. Yet the droppings from the trees had thoroughly soaked Rafael Hernandez's shirt. Hernandez, the old soldier, rarely failed to tell everyone he met that he is the "Captain of the San Albino District" and that he reports directly and only to General Augusto C. Sandino. Hernandez walked up to meet a soldier outside of Sandino's headquarters in Jícaro.

"Are you Hernandez?" the guard inquired.

"Si, I am Rafael Hernandez, Captain of the San Albino District."

"Wait here," the guard said unimpressed.

Soon, Francisco Estrada, Sandino's logistician, and the owner of the store two buildings away opened the door illuminating the wet loyalist and said, "Rafael, please come in. The General is waiting to see you."

"Gracias, Señor."

Sandino embraced his patriot. He offered a seat and a small cup of rum to warm him. He introduced Hernandez to Pepe Jericó, the Colombian reporter from the *El Tiempo*, who sat with a pad of paper and pencil, nearby but conspicuously apart from the space Sandino had for himself and his visitor.

"Are you ready my friend?" Sandino asked Hernandez.

"All ready, General."

"How many men from the San Albino Mine Company are there at this hour?"

"At the office, two, maybe three. No one lives in the bunk house after we blew it up in April."

"And the dynamite? How much did you bring?"

"Four sticks should be enough to blow the two shafts. We only used two the last time— with the rain, I brought a couple extra."

"Good," Sandino paused while anticipating his next move, then asked, "Rafael, how many sticks remain after we use these four?"

"Over fifty, Señor."

"Excelente, Señor! Please make sure they are given to Francisco Estrada en la mañana.

Right now we are going to blow up an American mine."

Looking at his watch, Sandino said, "Sócrates told me that we will leave at 8:00. The mine is only four miles away and we should be in position by 10:00 and back here by midnight."

"Vámonos!"

Near the Managua Rail Yard, July 10, 1927. As he approached, Captain Haynes McConnell returned First Lieutenant George O'Shea's salute and asked, "What's the count, George?"

"Sir, after the Leon train off loaded this morning, our pack-mule count is just over 100. We have 150 riding mules. And we're okay with both saddles and packs. Those were easy to buy here in Managua."

"That sounds great; I hope it calms the major down. Floyd has been a nervous wreck for the past week. He thought we could simply go to the brigade quartermaster to request 300 animals, do a 'right face' and 'forward march' up into the mountains with 225 Marines and Guardia!"

"We still are 25 oxen short—that's really what's holding us up. There's a cattle ship expected into Corinto from Mexico later this week that should meet our needs."

"I am going to tell the good major to anticipate leaving on the 15th. You have the ox carts, don't you?"

"Yes Sir, we have all 50 of them." Shea answered as his eyebrows shot up in the air twice, alerting McConnell that someone was approaching.

McConnell spun around and quickly saluted his boss, Major Oliver Floyd.

"What are we up to Haynes?" Floyd asked while returning the salute.

"All but 25 oxen, Sir, and we ought to have them by the 14th."

"The 14th?"

"Yes Sir and we'll be on the road by the 15th."

"God, General Feland is going to have our butts. Who the hell knows what that outlaw Sandino is up to after he blew up that mine? It's a good thing that Vic Bleasdale and the 1st Guardia Company left on time. They should be joining the 51st in Ocotal by the 15th."

"Well, keep me informed. I'm on my way to the brigade headquarters, and I'll tell Major Black the oxen information. Geez Haynes, double your efforts to make sure the men are ready to step out smartly on the morning of the 15th. Oh, and check with the Guardia as well."

Chapter 18: The Battle Of Ocotal-July 15 and 16, 1927

Parque Municipal, Ocotal, 11:15 AM, July 15, 1927. The cloud-covered Nueva Segovia Department capital was unusually still and deathly quiet. Throughout the morning, the hyper- kinetic Jefe Politico de Ocotal or mayor, Señor Arnaldo Ramírez Abaunza, would hustle out of the front double doors of the city hall, a building he reluctantly shared with Captain Gilbert Hatfield for the past week. Ramírez called the building. "La Commandancia." The Marines simply referred to the building as "the barracks." Whatever he was searching for had not arrived. The normally- loquacious little man would look around, appear to be listening for something, then quickly return back through the doors without saying a word. The more consistent activity was notably the Marines as they casually walked in pairs to the well in the Municipal Park to shave and wash up; to brush, feed and otherwise tend to their mules; and to sit on benches in front of the few stores that faced the scenic park and clean their weapons. The town's citizens had disappeared; either they left town or they were hiding inside their homes.

The noise of men on mules soon filled the air around this little mountain town that nestled on a sandy plain at the junction of the Dipillo and Coco rivers and the just below dominating mountains surrounding it. The riders had come from the south on the main road that passes through Ocotal and joins Nicaragua to Honduras, fifteen miles to the north.

Hatfield and his second-in-command, Gunnery Sergeant Wilson, both in their wide- brimmed field covers, stood in front of the creamy-colored, two-story stucco barracks that dramatically contrasted to the darker, less-remarkable buildings adjacent to it—waiting to greet their much-needed reinforcements. Within minutes, 50-some sweaty mules finally filled the street on the city hall side of the park and cascaded to a halt. Wilson saluted the tall Marine who had begun dismounting the lead mule.

Maj Victor F. Bleasdale of the Guardia Nacional of Nicaragua taken during the Segovia Expedition-July August 1927

Official Photo USMC #516898

Hatfield, recognizing his friend who had been promoted to major while working with the Guardia Nacional, extended a hand and said, "Vic. Good to see you!"

"You too, Gilbert. And greetings to you too, Gunny Wilson," the lanky Californian with a receding hairline said while returning the salute.

"Welcome to the mountains, Major Bleasdale," was Wilson's reply.

"You doing well, Vic?"

"Well enough for an old man," Bleasdale said with a smile. "Hope you are."

"I am. Vic, I have arranged for you and your men to occupy the large fort across the park," Hatfield said while shaking the hand of his friend. "By the way, how many men do you have?"

Major Victor Bleasdale turned his head in the direction Hatfield was pointing and said, "You know I'm here with Lieutenant Grover Darnell and Lieutenant Tom Bruce. Darnell's the CO of 48 Guardia soldiers. I believe you remember him from Dom Rep, don't you?" Bleasdale was referring to the other Marine still giving directions in fluent Spanish to two Nicaraguan sergeants. Grover Darnell, a Marine 1st Lieutenant, was the company commander of the 1st Company, Guardia Nacional de Nicaragua.

"Oh, hell yes. Grover was my XO in '23. Sure, I remember him!"

"As for me, I am the one-man advance party for Major Floyd's group, if they ever get out of Managua. "How 'bout you? How many Marines do you have?"

"We have 39, and we're over here at the barracks," Hatfield responded, nodding his head toward the building behind him.

Growing serious, Hatfield said, "Vic, I don't think we have a lot of time. So why don't you get the men settled, have some lunch, and come over afterwards. It's getting a bit spooky around here. Damnit, the bastards cut our telegraph line last night! We need to get our defenses set before tonight."

At that moment, Darnell moved into the conversation, "Yeah, what the heck is going on, Captain Hatfield? Did you scare all the natives away?" The lieutenant smiled, greeting his old boss who taught him all the basics of combat when he was a raw second lieutenant. "Ever since we entered Nuevo Segovia there were no people. None on the road; none in the huts; and none in the fields. And this capital city looks like a ghost town, sir." Darnell, a very relaxed and—like Hatfield—self-confident Marine officer, made subsequent warmer greetings to Wilson.

Bleasdale said, "I hate to break this reunion up men, but we better get going. Grover and I will be back in about an hour."

Ocotal City Hall, 12:30 PM. Light poured in through the eight-foot window to light up the office Hatfield claimed as his command post. It was quite sufficient for the five men standing near the office door. "Major Bleasdale, First Lieutenant Darnell, and Second Lieutenant Bruce, this is the Jefe Politico de Ocotal, Señor Arnaldo Ramírez," the host announced.

Bleasdale extended his hand to the little man dressed in a white shirt, looking more like a banker than one of the local cowboys, "Pleasure to meet you, Señor."

"Señor Capitán, the pleasure is all mine. Earlier today I was expecting a visit from Sandino and his men. When you rode into town I felt relieved."

"Buenas tardes, Señor Ramírez. Me llamo Grover Darnell"

"Sir, you speak our language very well. Nice meeting you as well Señor Darnell."

"And I am Lieutenant Bruce, Sir."

"I am honored Lieutenant Bruce. Correct me if I'm wrong, sir, but you have been in Nicaragua since 1924 helping my government. My friends in Managua have spoken highly of 'Gunny Bruce' from one of the ships. I finally get to meet you and now you are a lieutenant. Congratulations on your promotion"

"Thank you, Sir. I will be a lieutenant as long as I am with the Guardia."

Hatfield looked at Wilson and said, "Willy, let's move this table to the side, we'll only need the easel." As they moved the table, he added, "Have a seat."

Soon all were seated and Hatfield, standing by the easel, opened, "Sergeant Bo Becker, who has my 1st Platoon, marked this photo that the air guys dropped to us earlier today. It shows the town and its surrounds. You approached Ocotal from the south." Pointing to the bottom of the photo, "You passed through Totogalpa, so you know that road. As you can see, the road continues north into this valley," he explained raising his finger toward the top of the eight by ten-inch photo he held in his hand, "and through the city before it

Ocotal Looking North; 6-27; A.S. 2N Brigade by Order of The Bureau of Aeronautics-*Official Photo USMC*

begins uphill to the ridgeline and on to Honduras." Sliding his finger to the right side of the photo, Hatfield continued, "Now, the high ground to the northeast has a less prominent road that goes up to the small town of Mozonte only two and a half miles from here. From there the road continues to San Fernando and on to Jícaro, then to the San Albino mines that were blown up last month." Not on this photo, but just south of here, the Río Coco flows eastward. Of course, if you followed the Coco, you'd come to Telpaneca in about 15 miles and, in another 25 miles, the junction of the Río Jícaro. Handing the photo to Bleasdale, he added, "We'll pass tis around so that you all can see Ocotal from the sky."

"Señor Ramírez has told me that most of the town's population— over 1,000 people— support Sandino. Many have already joined him, bringing along their machetes."

"How many do you estimate have joined him by now, Señor?"

"Over 60 from here. But I believe 600 all total, Capitán."

"He expects Sandino to attack Ocotal at any moment. When he does, the rest of the locals plan to rise up against us."

"Gilbert, do you have anything else that corroborates this information?" Bleasdale asked.

"He wrote to me five times asking me to leave or surrender. Three telegrams and two letters. Willy, they're in the top drawer. Show them to the captain. He's got my name from the locals I assume," Hatfield said as Wilson handed the documents to Bleasdale.

Bleasdale looked closely at the letters, then looked up at his host. "Did you ever write back, Gilbert?"

"Oh sure. We knew he was on his way here for a couple of weeks. Three days ago I invited him to surrender."

"And what did he say to that?"

Wilson unfolded a piece of paper. "Take a look at the last letter with the drawing of one of his soldiers about to kill a Marine with a damn machete. That was his response. Now that sends a clear message, doesn't it?"

"Sure does. Wow!" Bleasdale said passing the letters to Darnell.

Sandino's Seal *Defense Dept Photo (Marine Corps 527136)*

Wilson said, "Lieutenant, read what the letter with the drawing says—in English, I know you can read Spanish, Sir."

"Where?"

"At the end, Sir."

"Oh, here. 'I remain your most obedient servant, who ardently desires to put you in a handsome tomb with beautiful bouquets of flowers.'" Darnell looked up to verify Wilson's satisfaction.

"And Lieutenant, here's what my captain wrote back, in Spanish, of course." Wilson smiled smugly while unbuttoning his left breast shirt pocket, pulling out a paper, unfolding it and reading: "Bravo, General! If words were bullets and phrases were soldiers, you would be a field marshal instead of a mule thief." Wilson then added, "Is that not the darn best response ever, sir?" Boasting of his own contribution, he looked at Hatfield and confessed, "I copied it, Sir...for history's sake."

Hatfield shook his head reluctantly accepting Wilson's plagiarism then redirected, "All right, let's get back to business." With that he unrolled a second piece of paper and pinned it to the easel. This one showed the city streets. "Sergeant Bill Henderson of the 2nd Platoon made this map.

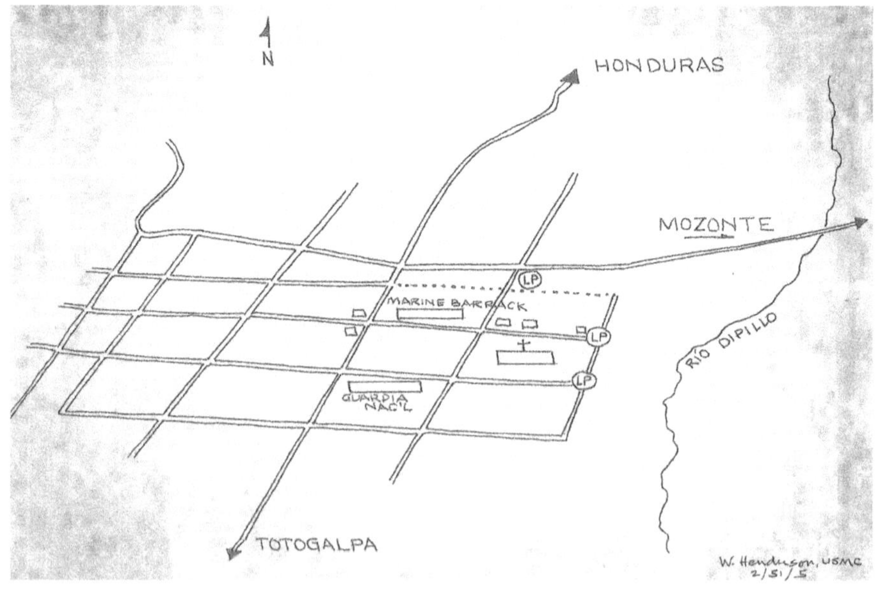

"You can see the principal avenues of advance into the town: the south road—the one you came in on; the north road that goes to Honduras; the road coming from Mozonte; and the eastern river trail. The road from Mozonte will be the most likely one used. Logically, when they get into our valley, they will spread out and cross the Dipillo River at several points since it's nearly dry." Pointing at the three LPs on the map, Hatfield continued, "We need to put listening posts along the Dipillo behind the church and at the gate at the Mozonte road. When the squad sees the attackers, they are to immediately withdraw to our defensive positions in the Marine barracks and the barracks your Guardia men are occupying," he said looking Darnell.

"I expect that any sizable attack will come from the southern side of the cathedral and flow into the municipal park and directly toward the building we are in," Hatfield said in deliberate tone. Then looking again at Lieutenant Darnell, he added, "Grover, they don't know you are here.

So, hold your fire. We won't open up with our BARs," pausing to explain to the mayor, "Browning Automatic Rifles and our Lewis gun from the center two balconies until the last moment. When we do, let 'em have it! You got that?"

"I do, Captain."

"Before then, we'll slow anyone attempting to enter the park with sharp shooters on each of the outside, second-floor balconies. Each will focus on a specific street corner. Any comments?"

Bleasdale asked, "How many men does Sandino have?"

"Like the mayor said, best we could figure is about 600, maybe more. We figure he has only 60 to 100 rifles, a couple of machine guns and, after hitting that mine, a couple of cases of dynamite."

"Vic, when do you think Major Floyd will be here?"

"He was hoping to leave today and, with that circus he's dragging with him. If they make 15 miles a day, I'd be surprised! I figure they'll take six to seven days to get up to this department. By the way Gil, you see any of our airplanes?"

"Oh, yeah. Every day there are a couple come flying over the town. We wave to them, and they dive and wave back."

"Good. We had met with them a couple of times prior to my departure and came up with a dozen messages with tee shirts. I'll show Gunny Wilson what we agreed on so then we'll both have the signals."

"Great," Hatfield said, "Who knows if we'll ever need their support? Now let's get the men out in all positions, double check the firing positions so that we are not shooting at each other, and fit in one rehearsal just before dusk in case anyone is trying to watch us from the mountains."

With Sandino in Mozonte, 6:00 PM. Mozonte, two and a half miles up into the mountains above Ocotal, has several vantage points from where the view of the Ocotal valley is spectacular. Over 750 men occupied the small village. They were located around the village in three groups. One group, comprised of 60 former Liberal Army soldiers, was armed with rifles and had two machine guns. The second group had 100 members and was made up of recently joined men from Ocotal. The third group had nearly 600 persons and was divided into the five segments—each segment consisted of men from the same town. Other than the soldiers, all men were armed with machetes although 20 of the men from Jícaro who had worked in the San Albino mines also carried satchel charges made of dynamite.

Sandino Flanked by Two Lieutenants *Defense Dept (Marine Corps) #5262*

Most of the men knew only that General Augusto C. Sandino was consistently neat, short in stature, and trim. Had they been able to see his face under his wide-brim hat, they would see the look of fierce determination. His staff had not seen him look as serious since his meeting with Moncada in the beginning of May.

Sandino had recruited Pedro Altamirano to lead the assault on Ocotal. Colonel Simon Jirón and Captain Colindres would attack Ocotal's "aerodrome" and blow up any airplanes and the landing field. General Salgado will drag out all "Conservatives" for trial and execution. Rufo Marin would take his men to the road that leads to Honduras and set up an ambush.

The plan was that, at midnight, the men from Ocotal would begin infiltrating in pairs. They would cross the Rio Dipillo at various points. Their knowledge of the town, its streets and homes, would allow the others to approach the village behind them and establish control rapidly. Behind the locals were the men from Jícaro carrying the satchel charges. They would blow breeches in any blockade that was set up to stop the assault. Altamirano and the former soldiers would overrun the Marines. After the attack, their job was to ensure every Marine captured or wounded was tried, found guilty, and hung.

"Are the men ready, Pedro?"

Altamirano looked at is subordinates.

Rufo Marin sharply answered, "Si, General."

Captain Colindres mumbled, "Si Pedro."

General Salgado and Colonel Jirón sharply nodded their heads.

Leaders of the machete-armed groups and the soldier groups looked at Pedro Altamirano, nodding their head. The fierce-looking big man with the domineering handlebar mustache glanced back at Sandino and grunted, "Si."

Sandino summarized, "I will follow you to the bluff on this side of the Rio Dipillo. It's about 1200 meters from the city's north gate. The assault should commence by 1:30 AM. We will attack the Commandancia by passing on the southern side of the Iglesia Nuestra Señora de la Asunción. By morning, the city will be ours and the trials of the surviving Marines will be over. Fight well comrades, tonight we will be drinking Yankee blood." For nearly a minute he looked into the eyes of his leaders as they prepared for their first battle in the Sandinista cause. He made his "S" salute and said, "Que vaya con Dios."

Ocotal City Hall, 10:00 PM. "Bill, hear that?" Sergeant Bo Becker asked his friend of the same rank, Bill Henderson, who had just joined him in the front of the Marine barracks.

"No, what?"

"Hush! There it is again."

"Oh yeah. Oh yeah. What the hell are they yelling?"

"Sounds like 'Death to Marines!' Where's the gunny?"

"He's in there BS'ing with the captain and the major. I'll get him."

One minute later the five Marine leaders were on the street listening to the cat calling from the ridge road leading to Mozonte, perhaps a mile outside of Ocotal's north gate. In a minute Arnaldo Ramírez appeared at a ground-floor window with his hand cupping his ear.

"You will die Marines," the words drifted down from the hills. Bursting out from the front door and running up to the group, Ramírez said, "Si! Si! That's what I was listening for this morning! They are coming tonight!"

Becker announced, "I am on the way to Hawthorne's and Blanco's squads near the North gate."

Henderson said, "Right Bo, I'm going inside to check on mine as well."

"Gilbert, I better make sure the Guardia is ready," Bleasdale said spinning around to cross the park.

Hatfield, now alone with Ramírez, said, "Come on Señor, let's get inside. It's time to double check the firing positions upstairs."

Ocotal, 12:15 AM, July 16, 1927. Corporal Ben Hawthorne, Becker's 1st squad leader, slipped beside his fully-alert men in his squad lying below the two-and-one-half-foot wall that delineates the town's northern edge and the road leading up to Mozonte. Soon he was beside his last man. He continued another thirty-five yards until he reached Private Teddy Obleski, a new kid from New York City and the first man in Corporal José Blanco's squad. Recognizing the Marine, Hawthorne whispered, "Hey 'New York,' where's Blanco?"

"Two more men down, Corporal," came the whisper with a *new yak* accent.

In a minute, Hawthorne crawled next to Blanco, "You picking up anything José?"

"Yeah, Ben. One of my guys, Private Williams, heard some movement. Then he thought he saw some shadows. Later he saw some more. They were coming from the Dipillo riverbed. I told 'em to blast them if they get challenged."

"Okay, I'm going back to the barracks. Stuff's getting spooky."

"Right, we better get going. The Gunny wants all the fighting to be done in the park in front of the barracks. So, he'll be pissed if we engage those bad asses out here."

Ben Hawthorne said, "See you back at the barracks, José."

In a millisecond Williams leaped over the wall and blurted, "Corporal José, I just saw two men, each with a rifle."

"Get the rest of the men over there," Blanco said pointing to his left. "I'll get the guys up there and then let's get our asses back to the barracks!" In less than five minutes, Blanco led his men back through the streets, as rehearsed, across the park and into the Marine barracks.

Becker arrived in trace of Blanco's squad. The Gunny stood at the door accounting for all his men. Becker dashed through the door, prompting Gunny to ask, "Is that all of your Marines, Becker?"

Becker shot back, "Did Hawthorne make it back, Gunny?"

"Yeah, he's in."

"Got them all then, Gunny."

Becker saw Blanco looking a bit annoyed. "What's eating at you, José?

"Ah, the Gunny made me post a sentry outside. I guess all the firing positions were occupied upstairs so I obviously had at least one extra man."

"Who'd you put out there?"

"Williams. Who else? He's got the best eyes and ears in my squad."

Upstairs four balconies jutted out two feet from the upper rooms. The end balconies had expert marksmen armed with M1903 Springfields whose principal targets would be anyone near the two closest street corners. A two-man Lewis machine gun team was assigned at each of the center windows to rake the park when required.

Suddenly the Marines at the balconies could hear explosions coming from the vicinity of the aerodrome. They looked at each other with heightened senses then intensified their search of the park and streets below.

Corporal Ollie Blackburn, one of Henderson's squad leaders and the platoon's top marksmen, was upstairs kneeling on the ceramic tile floor of the right most balcony. From there, the 24-year old from the Appalachian Mountains of western North Carolina had a commanding view of the street corners adjoining the northern portion of the park. His assistant gunner and spotter was Private Joe Buffalo. Buffalo was a Pueblo Indian from New Mexico. He had been with the company for three months and was simply known to all as "Chief." Blackburn and Buffalo bonded within days. Tonight they focused on a single street corner.

Nearing the park, the attacking Nicaraguans moved through the few streets in search of the Marines.

"Chief, see any movement down at the far corner?" Blackburn asked.

"No, but I thought I heard talking coming from over there to the right. Can't see anything.

Stupid tree's blocking my view!"

"Keep listening, Chief. If you see any movement, let me know."

"Wait a minute, wait a minute," Blackburn whispered. "What do we have over here?" Then, answering his own question, "Seems like a couple of guys are setting up a machine gun—probably a Lewis."

From below the Marines could hear Private Williams challenge, "HALT. WHO GOES THERE?"

Blackburn's M1903 Springfield had been resting on the recently-added rock wall at the front of the balcony. Its five-round clip had already been inserted, and Blackburn's bolt had already placed its first round into the chamber. The corporal slipped his left hand under the rifle's stock. Now all that remained was to aim and shoot.

Through the dark he could easily see the white shirts of the two soldiers. He had already had his rifle's rear sight adjusted for the 75 yards distance to the street corner where two Sandinistas were now lying beside the Lewis. Talking softly to himself, though loud enough for Buffalo to hear, he muttered, "Easy Ollie, ea-zzz," all the while squeezing the trigger.

The round exploded from the Springfield muzzle. In the next second, the former Liberal Army soldier's head that once was next to the Lewis violently jerked back while the caliber .30 projectile entered his cranium just above the left eye and exited the back of the his skull.

"Got 'em," Buffalo said in a matter-of-fact tone as Blackburn moved the bolt back and forward chambering the second round.

As the second Sandinista gunner grabbed the Lewis, Blackburn's second round tore apart his spine and came to a stop in the man's right thigh.

"Number two down, Corporal."

"Just like shootin' them darn squirrels up in the mountains, Chief."

As the men watched for any movement in the park below, Henderson commanded. "Keep alert men. Wait until I give you the word to open fire!"

Four minutes later the Sandinistas charged into the square in mass from the southern, far side of the church. Waiting until the invaders reached the center of the city park, Sergeant Henderson finally shouted, "Here they are, Marines. Commence firing!" The Marines immediately fired from the six windows of the building.

What the attackers did not know was that the Guardia, across the square, had a plain view of their backs. Now caught in a deadly cross fire, the 30 Sandinistas were killed within minutes.

Suddenly, all was still.

North Gate, Ocotal, 2:30 AM. All armed Liberals went back to the north gate awaiting further instructions. Altamirano, like the bull that he was, fumed grotesquely. He snorted profanity. His force had just been cut in half. He had lost two key leaders; Rufo Marin, who should have remained on the road to Honduras but couldn't resist joining the fight and Juan Colindres who had already helped blow up the aerodrome. Talking to Colonel Jirón, he ordered, "Simon, take four men and harass these Norte American Yankee pigs. Do not expose yourself and get wounded. Sandino is finally here. He and I must review our approach to defeating the Norteamericanos now that we have the Guardia to deal with as well. We'll need to reorganize. After that, I'll come up to your position. If you hear bugles, come back to this location. Comprende usted?"

"Si, Pedro," Jirón said then left.

At 0330 hours the bugles sounded. The sporadic firing stopped and soon the city square fell silent again.

Ocotal City Square, 3:58 AM. Captain Gilbert Hatfield came down the stairs and joined Sergeant Bo Becker and Corporal Jose Blanco who were waiting anxiously by the front door for

Private Teddy Obleski to return from the Guardia's building across the square. "Anything of Obleski?" the captain asked.

"No, Sir. Nothing yet."

"How long ago did he go?"

"About 20 minutes, Cap'n."

"In about ten minutes we'll send a couple of men over there to see if he's okay," Hatfield said, turning toward the rear of building.

"Cap'n, there's someone running our way. I can hear the noise by the well. Listen," Becker said with an optimistic smile. He turned his right ear toward the park's center to focus on the sound and raised his right index finger above his head as if it was an antenna.

Obleski burst out from the shadows of the park's small trees and into the street fifteen yards from the building's recessed front door when the first round of the enemy's rifle exploded from its muzzle and tore through his shirt below his extended left arm. The bullet's path ripped the Marine's left lung and exited his right chest.

Obleski looked to his left instinctively searching for the weapon that he heard. At the same time a volley of three more Sandinista rifles tore into his falling body.

The Marine rifle fire from the upstairs balconies exploded at the Sandinistas, enabling Becker and Blanco to dash five yards into the street and recover Obleski's body.

By this time all four street corners erupted in bandito rifle fire. Altamirano's tactic was to simultaneously fire diagonally across the park from each corner at the Marine barracks and Guardia's barracks while advancing near to the center of the park. At this point all four firing elements would assemble, turn, and assault the Guardia barracks as one force.

"Keep working them, men," Gunnery Sergeant Wilson shouted to his marksmen as Sandinistas advancing into the center of the park were being picked off one at a time. Wilson worked with the men on the ground floor while Hatfield directed the action on the second floor.

In fifteen minutes only Pedro Altamirano and three others escaped the Marine's second slaughter. Altamirano had been wounded in the shoulder.

Sandino's Headquarters, Outskirts of Ocotal, 6:30 AM. Standing on top of the knoll beside the Mozonte road, 1200 meters from the city's north gate, stood General Sandino. Looking at the wounded man approaching him and recognizing Colonel Simon Jirón Colindres leader of attack on the aerodrome, he asked, "How bad is it, Simon?",

"No bones broken. The arm will be fine in a couple of weeks."

"I'll get the doctor to look it over," the leader said to his comrade.

"Sócrates, assemble the general staff and five town leaders. I will talk more to Altamirano.

I have ideas of what we should do next. I believe we can get them to surrender."

"Augusto, several of the town leaders are down by the bridge with their men. Give me 30 minutes until I get the your staff and the town leaders back here."

"Si. Let's meet at seven o'clock."

Managua Aerodrome, 7:00 AM. The two DH-4 biplanes piloted by Lieutenant Hayne "Cuckoo" Boyden and Chief Warrant Mike Marine Gunner Wodarczyk rumbled across the grassy airfield and lifted off to make the morning reconnaissance flight up in the Segovias. Standing by the aerodrome to ensure the planes took off without a hitch were Corporal "Junior" Wilson and Corporal Smitty, the Air Squadron's best mechanics. However, this morning their focus was less on the launched reconnaissance aircraft and more on the baseball tryouts scheduled to take place at 1600 hours in the field in front of them that is now used as an airfield.

"You know Smitty," Wilson said, getting his friend's attention, "I don't care what Heller says, if these tryouts are to be realistic, we have to mow this grass before 1600.

Agreed. I'll borrow that grass cutter from the Nicaraguan Electric Company this morning, and we can get it cut during lunch. Manny told me he'd help me any time I need him."

"Don't we play the Electric Company in September? By the way, who's Manny?" Wilson asked.

"Manny? That' Manuel Gonzales. Seems like he knows everyone in Managua. He's captain of their baseball team, the shocks, and comes over here to the airfield to make adjustments to our electrical power almost weekly. Good guy. Yeah, but, ya know, I don't know why we are having tryouts. Captain Archibald has most of the darn positions selected."

"What do you mean?" Wilson said turning his head abruptly.

"Tell ya what I mean. Sergeant Knoff told me that he's gonna play first base. He said, 'Archibald's already picked guys for several positions.' I believe Billingsworth and Heller are going to have a fit about that when they find out."

"Smitty, let's go see them in their office and give them a heads up."

Two minutes later in the office of the two technical sergeants.

Billingsworth looked up over his new reading glasses, "What's up with you two?"

That was enough to get Heller's attention who looked up as well.

"It's about the baseball tryouts this afternoon, Top."

In the next twenty minutes the two technical sergeants knew that, to hit a ball well, a person had to be able to see the ball accurately, hit to all fields, hit well even with two strikes against him, run fast around the bases, and know how to steal a base.

They both also learned that a good defensive player must know where the ball is going as soon as it leaves the bat, get a good jump on the ball, charge the ball with good speed, make good decisions because he knows the game, and have a strong and accurate throwing arm.

Junior Wilson summarized, "Remember Top, a hitter knows that the bat and the ball are his friends."

Shaking his head, Billingsworth smiled and said, "Hey, get some chow then get back on the line, Wilson; we have birds that need attention!"

"Right, Top," Wilson said and then headed for the door with Smitty right behind him.

Smitty almost had the door shut then opened it as fast as he could and said, "And Top Heller, always remember, in order to play defense, the player must know that the glove and the ball are his friends!"

Smitty shut the door as quick as he could without either technical sergeant having a chance to react and said, "We made our point Junior. Now they know a bit more about baseball."

Marine Barracks, Ocotal, 8:10 AM. "Captain, you better come up here!" called Gunnery Sergeant Robert Wilson from the top of the stairs.

Hatfield stopped talking to Mayor Ramírez and indicated he would be right back. At the top of the stairs Hatfield saw the gunny in the room to the right, "What do you have, Willy?"

"Take a look at that street corner, Sir," Wilson said pointing to the right. "The chief said he saw it a couple of minutes ago."

Hatfield saw the white flag tied to a four-foot long tree limb. "Willy, keep an eye on him. I don't trust that wily bandit," referring to Sandino. He then added, "I'm going to get the mayor involved with this one!"

"Señor!" Hatfield said getting Ramírez's full attention. "There's a man holding a white flag out there," Hatfield said pointing toward the corner. "I want you to find out what he wants."

Looking shocked that he was now being forced into a dangerous situation, Ramírez's eyebrows rose sharply. "Si, I will talk to him from the front door, Captain Hatfield."

Hatfield, listening to the conversation between the mayor and the messenger, already knew the information the mayor brought him. "Señor, the messenger has come with two letters. One for you and one for me."

"Please tell him he's safe and have him deliver the messages to the front door. I'll tell the men to Let him pass."

Ramírez ripped open the sealed letter and read silently. In a minute, he interrupted Hatfield reading his letter. By this time Gunnery Sergeant Wilson had joined them. "Listen to this Señor" and the mayor announced, "Señor Arnaldo Ramírez Abaunza, I know you are caught in a most remarkably-difficult situation. Your heart is wishing for a safe ending to this battle. If you get Captain Hatfield to surrender, I will make you the 'Director of Safety and Protection.' Please consider my offer seriously; I will not make a second one. Your loyal friend, A.C. Sandino."

He looked at Hatfield and Wilson and said, "Captain Hatfield, I'd rather be mayor."

Wilson, anxious to find out what the letter to Hatfield contained, said, "Read yours, Sir."

Hatfield nodded his head in agreement and translated as he read, "My Dear Captain Hatfield, I commend you on your heroic defense at Ocotal. You and your men are very brave. Unfortunately, I know you are out of water and unable to get the park's well. Soon you will need water. We have over 600 men. You have less than 100. The odds are overwhelming against you.

We have you surrounded. Surrender within the hour, and I will spare your life. Most respectfully, A.C. Sandino."

Hatfield went to his desk, and pulled a pen and ink bottle from the upper right hand drawer. In one moment he finished and said, "Want to hear my reply?"

"You bet, Sir."

"All right." He looked back at his response and read, "Señor Sandino, Marines don't know how to surrender and, water or no water, we will stick it out until captured or killed. We will commence firing as soon as your bearer of the truce flag turns the nearest corner."

"That's great, Sir," Wilson said, proud to be working for the Captain. "Would you mind if you let me copy it? You know—for history's sake? Oh, read it again in English. Thanks."

In minutes, the messenger was headed back to Sandino with Hatfield's response.

Nuevo Segovia Air Space, 08:10 AM. During the first portion of their flight, clouds kept pilots Boyden's and Wodarczyk's DH-4s below 2,000 feet and above the rolling tobacco fields and banana plantations. In July, at the start rainy season, cloud cover precluded flying at higher altitudes. Once they reached the Segovias they were forced lower, under 1,000 feet above the rugged mountains. As a result, the two pilots stayed with their flight plan, which was to trace the road between Managua and Ocotal, passing over the towns of Trinidad and Condega. Their mission was to recon Ocotal, the capital of Nuevo Segovia. 'Ops' concern was why the wire transmissions from Ocotal had been silenced for two days.

The two planes exchanged the lead every 20 miles on the 125-mile flight. This enabled both pilots and their observers, Sergeant Hank Keller with Boyden and Corporal Harold Dibling with Wodarczyk, to focus and refocus their view of the countryside theoretically enhancing what they were seeing.

Dibling, in the lead plane, first saw the whitish buildings of Ocotal and pointed to the town ahead. The other three aviators followed his outstretched arm to see the small town nestled beside the Coco and Dipillo rivers.

As Wodarczyk's plane crossed the Río Coco, Dibling focused on the city's Municipal Park adjacent to the large cathedral and yelled over the engine noise, "Ocotal must be having some sort of festival."

Wodarczyk looked down and acknowledged yelling, "Yeah, something's going on." He slowed his craft, and pumped his raised fist, signaling Boyden to catch up.

Boyden flew beside him and then looked down himself. By placing his index and middle fingers up to his eyes then pointing down, he quickly singled for both to dive in on the town to see what was happening.

The planes dove from the sky straight toward the Municipal Park since hundreds of people had filled the square. Coming under 500 feet while flying over the park, they saw a panel message, tied to upstairs' porch railings of the Marine barracks signifying, "SANDINO ATTACKING." Before pulling up, they could see that most of the men surrounding and in the park had machetes and many were mounted on mules.

Back at 1000 feet Boyden leveled off once again. He banked his plane west away from town. Wodarczyk followed not knowing what the flight leader had in mind. Now at the outskirts of the city, they were flying over Ocotal's small aerodrome and saw the destroyed buildings.

Boyden pointed up indicating for Wodarczyk to remain at his altitude, then sharply banked again and within minutes landed beside the aerodrome. He left the plane's engine idle.

Two men hiding in some bushes nearby darted out to the Lieutenant. Boyden calmly walked up to the men and asked, "Que pasa a Ocotal?"

Boyden's young observer, Sergeant Hank Keller, watched in awe as his pilot listened patiently to the very demonstrative peasants babble excitedly. Within minutes, the lieutenant was climbing back into the DH-4 and tightening his seat belt. As he did, Keller, asked, "What he say, Lieutenant?"

"Sandino has the Marines and the Guardia surrounded and will be attacking and killing all of them soon. He's already killed all the townspeople known to be Conservatives."

Hearing those words, Boyden turned, ran to the aircraft, climbed into the cockpit, powered the engine, taxied, and soon joined Wodarczyk's loitering DC-4. Boyden pointed to Ocotal, clenched his fist—the signal for enemy. He then motioned Wodarczyk to attack the enemy and indicated that he was going back to Managua for more support. He would see the Chief Marine Gunner back at the airfield. The two split, each with urgent missions.

Looking back at Dibling, Wodarczyk yelled, "Are you ready to make history, Corporal?"

"Living the dream, Sir. Let's do it!"

With that, Wodarczyk and Dibling launched the first American air power close air support on an enemy force. For a prolonged 20 minutes, Wodarczyk and Dibling released a torrent of machine gun fire on each approach and continuously strafed over and over again the machete- armed, local Sandino loyalists who first set eyes on their leader up in the village of Mozonte the afternoon before and who had slipped back into Ocotal by crossing the Rio Dipillo throughout the night. Now, gathered in the central park next to the cathedral, bullets were tearing them up without mercy. On each run, the DC-4 dove upon Sandino's fighters faster than they could effectively escape into the open streets. One and two men were cut down and killed and two or three others were wounded as men fell in front of each other, blocking the swift exit for all. Trapped and climbing over their own men, Sandino's forces ran from the attacking Marine plane, too slowly for them all to escape. Screams of immense pain filled the air that once possessed the bravado shouts of "You will die Marines." Finally, having run out of ammunition, Wodarczyk broke off and soared skyward, headed south to Managua.

Marine Barracks, Ocotal, 10:20 AM. "I'm sure they'll be back, Corporal Hawthorne. They'll be back," Hatfield repeated to assure his young squad leader an hour after Wodarczyk had run out of ammunition. In the meanwhile, make sure your ammunition is evenly distributed and you are ready for an assault on our building."

Bounding upstairs, Hatfield found half of his 2nd Platoon still looking out the windows at the dozens of dead and wounded Nicaraguans and a half dozen mules in the close intersections. "See anything out there, Sergeant Henderson?" Hatfield asked the platoon leader.

"Looks like they are dragging the wounded out of the Park and across to the church, Captain. I was worried that one of their snipers might get too close and hit the right-hand window. So, I told Blackburn to make sure that he and the Chief stay back away from the window."

"When is the last time you redistributed ammo?"

"'Bout an hour ago, Captain."

"All right, I don't know when they'll attack, probably after sundown. Make sure your men are ready!"

Sandino's Headquarters, Outskirts of Ocotal, 12:15 PM. "Pedro, can I help you?" Simon Jirón asked his boss Pedro Altamirano.

"No, Simon. It is you I am concerned about. How's your head?"

"It rings constantly. But I should be okay in a couple of days. The doctor said the wound was like a concussion. Thanks for carrying me out, Pedro."

"De nada mío amigo. General Sandino wants to see me. I will check on you later."

In Sandino's tent he asked, "You wanted to see me, Augusto?"

"Si, Pedro, please sit down. Have you had any rest?"

"Probably as much as you, General."

Sandino gently smiled. "Pedro, we are about to finish our attack and make Ocotal our headquarters for the next month. You and I will be able to sleep once our job has been completed. In the meanwhile let the men enjoy a two-hour siesta. Afterward we'll lead them down into the town and destroy the Marines and Guardia."

"Augusto, do you expect any more planes? That last one killed and wounded more than a dozen men."

"The Marines fly those planes with great skill. I miscalculated that. I thought they would fly like the two Nicaragua Air Force pilots. But, to answer your question, I don't believe they will return—at least I hope not. Get some rest. Have the men ready," Sandino said, glancing at his watch, "2:15. We attack by 3:00 this afternoon."

"Si. Augusto."

Managua Aerodrome, 1:35 PM. The five DH-4s had been armed with enough 17-pound bombs and belts of machine gun rounds that some doubting mechanics questioned if they would ever get off the ground. Rowell was going to lead the mission. He had chosen Boyden, Wodarczyk, Lieutenant "JC" Harmon and Lieutenant Earl Thomas as pilots. His executive officer, Captain Archibald was furious for not being selected. Rowell merely explained that, "If something happens to me, Stan, then you have to take over the squadron." Archibald knew he was not as good a pilot as those chosen, accepted the major's contorted logic, and told the major that he would do a good job in Managua until the major returned. Rowell left all the east coast aviators behind because they had not had sufficient flying time in the DH-4s—a plane that could carry more munitions than their O2B-1s.

Major Rusty Rowell completed the briefing and said with a firm face, "All right men this is it. Let's give them our show!"

Ocotal, 2:35 PM. Fifteen miles away from the municipal park, the low roar of the five DH-4s fill the air. It sounded like drummers alerting circus goers that a death-defying event was to occur.

Sandino was about to mount his mule, ride off the knoll again as he had at 3:00 am. He would join Altamirano and his brother, Socrates, and arouse the pre-battle passion needed by his 500 mounted and foot soldiers near the northern main gate and the Río Dipillo bridge. He frowned when he heard the sound.

The growing noise silenced the attackers' call for "Death to the Marines!" As one, they looked skyward. They had seen the lethal damage one plane had done earlier this morning. This sounded like many more planes. Frozen in their disbelief, they didn't move.

The men in the Guardias' barracks and Marine barracks were ready to participate in a great battle. Their resolve was unquestioned; the supply of their ammunition was in doubt. Grim-faced, they were ready. They too heard the distant drone as well. Could it be? Could it be more help was on the way?

Sandino's general staff had grown to 30 persons. While saddling his horse, he called back to the tent he used to meet and greet people as an aide held the reins. "Where's López?" Sandino barked to anyone listening as his top administrator emerged from the tent followed by Francisco Estrada, "Santos, pack up the tents. Get ready to move back up to Mozonte. Francisco," he commanded who was now by López's side, "Get the wounded on stretchers and hide them under the trees below."

"Everyone to the river bed! Everyone to the river bed!" were the useless commands from Altamirano and the other leaders of the sombrero-covered, untrained army of rebels recruited for this attack. In disarray, these intertwined groups acted more like caged fighting cocks then a disciplined military unit. They literally ran into each other—mule into mule and man into man.

Major Rusty Rowell, flying his favorite DH-4 Green-Nose, saw the white buildings of Ocotal. It was precisely as described by Lieutenant Boyden: "Ocotal is a small town cut into the hills with a town square and a large cathedral immediately to the east of the square. 200-300 mule-mounted rebels were in the streets." He looked back. The other four flew in the precisely prescribed formation. He looked forward again; the sombrero-covered men had clustered in the open space near the Río Dipillo bridge. He looked back again to Mike Wodarczyk and signaled to begin the dive bombing. With that Rowell broke formation and dove 1,000 foot into the center of the massed rebel force.

Wodarczyk was on his tail thirty seconds later. Boyden followed. Harmon's, then Thomas's DH-4s followed in a mechanical sequence. Each bird had four, 17-pound bombs mounted on their wings. The pilots in the front cock pit fired measured bursts from their fixed machine guns until they had to shift both hands to their stick and complete the dive. The observers released one bomb on each dive then grabbed the swivel machine gun and continued the grinding on the panicked, wounded and dead men below. The unrelenting bombing consumed forty-five minutes.

The once-surrounded Marines and Guardia knew the planes had to be slaughtering the rebel force. From the Guardia's barrack tower, Lieutenant Grover Darnell's spotter observed the carnage. He raced down to describe what he saw: "Hundreds of bodies, many wounded. It's awful. The mules…. Then he broke down and sobbed.

Major Victor Bleasdale, who was by Darnell's side, said "Take care of him Grover, I'll send a messenger over to Captain Hatfield."

Sandino, safe on top of the knoll, could barely watch. His grief overwhelmed his disgust. Will they ever stop even long enough for me to help the wounded? I beg you stop. My men, my brothers! Socrates, my brother! For God's sake stop!

After the bombs were expended, the planes continued using only their machine guns. For the next thirty minutes the observers blazed at those attempting to run eastward across the Río Dipillo past the "General's" knoll and onto the tranquility of their homes in Jícaro, Ciudad Antigua, San Fernando, and the other peaceful mountain towns. They, too, were torn down without mercy.

Out of ammunition, the planes grouped in the sky over the city, turned south and headed home. Their noise faded, and the village grew quiet.

Ocotal, Late Afternoon the 16th. Sócrates and Pedro Altamirano had sought shelter under the bridge and remained safe there until after the planes departed. They rushed to the knoll where fresh mounts waited for them.

Not far away, the doors of the Marine barracks and the Guardia's barracks flew open. Platoon-sized units swarmed over to the park's street corners like bees. Their anticipated chase of the rebels would only be slowed by maneuvering through the mass of the dead and dying.

Hatfield took over.

"Lieutenant Darnell, use your men and take charge of helping with the wounded."

"Lieutenant Bruce, there are snipers firing from the church; get them to surrender if you can."

"Willy," he called. referring to his gunnery sergeant and pointing toward the North Gate, "take the company and chase after those rebels trying to escape, but go no further than the north gate."

"Señor Ramírez, get the villagers out here and begin burying the dead."

On the bluff, outside of Ocotal. "Sócrates and Pedro," Sandino cried out, "Thank God you are safe." They were the only words Sandino uttered that late afternoon. Then, Sandino, disgusted, rode alone eastward up into the mountains in defeat. Unaware how the slaughter of his men would help him in the future, he vowed never to directly confront Marines again.

By dusk, the battle of Ocotal was over. With over 200 men killed by the successful aerial attack near the Río Dipillo. Another 100 lay wounded and would die in the next few hours.

The Commandancia at Ocotal following the fight.-*History Division Official Photo 5224-9*

The aerial photo below, provided by the USMC History Division and taken in May 1927, has a #3 on the Commandancia or Marine barracks. Corporal Ollie Blackburn was most-likely positioned in the upper balcony beyond the flag. Pedro Altamirano, who led the first attack past the church at #2, entered the central park. His men were cut down by Marines from their building (#3) and the Guardia in their barracks (#1). Numbers are on the 1927 photo.

Bullet-Swept Where Sandino Tried to Set Up Lewis Gun

Defense Dept (Marine Corps) 5224-5

Grave of only Marine killed in Ocotal battle taken on Decoration Day 1928

USMC History Division

CHAPTER 19: LOOKING FOR THE BANDIT SANDINO

Four Miles South of Trinidad, July 17, 1927. The 2nd Marine Brigade's plan to eliminate Sandino in the Segovias, was to break his popular support, force him out into the open, and destroy any armed group he represents. This required sending a large, mule train with months of supplies north from Managua to support and sustain the deployed Marine and Guardia combatants who will execute those Brigade's plans. Heading this campaign and leading this logistics movement is Major Oliver Floyd.

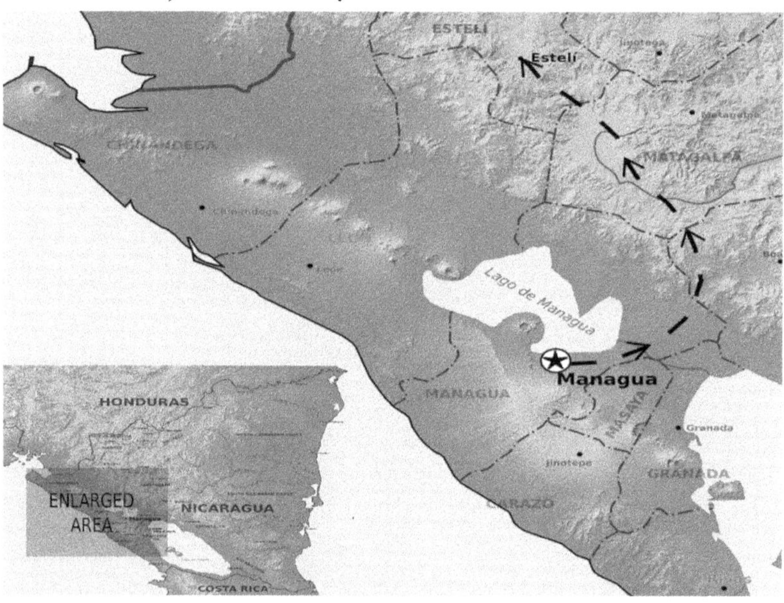

Planned route for 2nd Marine Brigade's Column moving North Under Makor Olive Floyd

Captain Haynes McConnell, the detachment quartermaster rode his mule back from the small mountain town of Trinidad and excitedly waved as he approached Major Oliver Floyd. "Sir," he called out, "there was a message sent by the brigade waiting for us up at the telegraph office. You better read it."

Floyd opened the message and started reading.

```
SECRET
FROM: CO, FIFTH MARINES
TO: CO FIFTH MARINES FORWARD
SUBJ: OCOTAL
1. OCOTAL SURROUNDED BY OVER 500 SANDINISTA REBELS ON 16 JULY.
AIR SQUADRON BOMBED, HIT MANY REBELS. ACTUAL EFFECT OF BOMBING
UNKNOWN.
2. NEED YOU TO EXPEDITE YOUR ARRIVAL AT OCOTAL.
SECRET
```

Floyd looked up at McConnell, thought for a second or two, and then said, "Where's O'Shea?"

"The lieutenant should be back there about a mile," pointing toward the rear of the two- mile-long caravan.

Maj Floyd's column in Route to the Segovias July 1927- *USMC History Division*

"Send someone back and get him…Never mind Haynes, I'll find him. I want to have him take fifty mounted Marines and ride to Ocotal as soon as possible. You and I will be there in a couple of days with the main body."

Twenty minutes later… "Right, Major, I understand," responded O'Shea, comprehending the urgency of the situation described by Floyd.

"So, here's what I want you to do, Lieutenant," Floyd explained. "I want you to take your men and ride to Ocotal as fast as possible. Take enough food and water for two days even though you will probably get there tomorrow. When you arrive, report to Major Bleasdale. I am sure he has things under control. I want you to be alert for a possible ambush as you approach Ocotal. We just may have angered a wild animal if you know what I mean, George."

"Yes, Sir."

"Oh, and stop by as you come to the front of the column; if I have anything else for you, I'll let you know at that time."

"Sir!" O'Shea acknowledged in the affirmative.

Ocotal, July 19, 1927. First Lieutenant George O'Shea's 50-man patrol arrived at the Río Coco bridge, the southern entrance to Ocotal, an hour before sunset on the following day. Escorted to the Guardia's fort by Corporal Jose Blanco who met the patrol's leader at the bridge, O'Shea reported to Major Vic Bleasdale. "Sir, we made it in time for chow, didn't we?"

Bleasdale smiled broadly and said, "Welcome, George. I had a feeling the major would send you. How are the mules?"

"The mules did well—a bit thirsty and definitely hungry—just like the men, Sir."

"We'll get you set up. The Guardia will assist your men. They'll need a good night's rest because we'll be sending you out tomorrow morning; you'll be patrolling east after the remnants of Sandino's bandits."

"Where is Grover?" O'Shea asked referring to his friend, First Lieutenant Grover Darnell.

"He was checking on his outposts. I expect him to be back any minute now for a meeting here at 1930 with the 51st…. Oh, you ought to attend that."

"Sounds great Sir. I'll be back."

O'Shea left Bleasdale's office, went into the office hallway and called, "Private Toro!"

Private Rafel Toro, who had joined the Marine Corps after stowing away on a New York- bound freighter from Colombia, was not the classic Marine infantryman. He had wanted to join the US Navy upon arrival in New York since his father had been in the Marina de Colombia. When he saw the sign in a first-floor window of a Broadway Office building that read, "Join the Marine Corps," he believed that he was at the right place. The English for "marina" must be spelled, "Marine" he reasoned. Eight months later, after assuming the role of Lieutenant O'Shea's body guard, the 19-year old Spanish-speaking Colombian answered O'Shea from about five feet behind, "Si, mi Lieutenant!"

O'Shea spun around somewhat surprised and said, "Toro, get Sergeant Glasser, pronto!"

Mozonte, July 20, 1927. "Lieutenant, if any of Sandino's men are here, they must be hiding," Sergeant Charles Glasser, the Chicago native, summarized as he walked in through the front door of the cathedral. "With five years in Dom Rep and Haiti, I can definitely smell dem rebels. Sir, I can't smell a thing!"

"I agree," O'Shea responded. "We've been here for a little over a week without a rebel in sight—and that's what I told the major in the message I wrote him yesterday. Well, maybe tomorrow."

"Tomorrow?"

"Right. Tomorrow we've been ordered to leave at first light for San Fernando. That's the next town to the east. It will be another hard ride in the mountains. Only about ten miles, but they won't be easy. Major Floyd will be following in trace with the main body. Once we clear San Fernando, we'll continue 10 to 15 miles to clear Jícaro. His message was that we'll establish and occupy an outpost at Jícaro. He was planning to continue a few miles further to the American- owned San Albino mines."

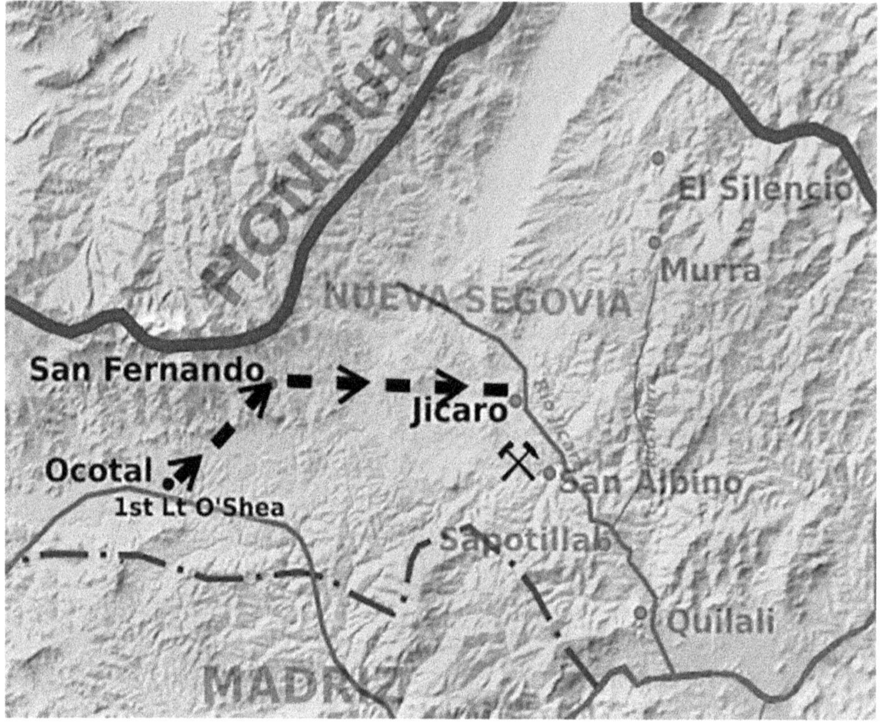

Planned route for First Lieutenant George O'Shea's in pursuit of Sandino

"You want me to pass the word to the men, Sir?"

"Sure. Have them check their mules tonight. Tell them that we'll be leaving at first light. You take the lead for the first half ride to San Fernando, and I'll take the lead to finish up the ride."

Outskirts of San Fernando, July 29, 1927. First Lieutenant George O'Shea and Private Toro had already moved to the front of the column an hour earlier when a rifle shot passed over their heads. The shot was fired from trees along the unimproved road that seemed more like a wide rocky path than a road. Those trees were on the third hilltop, at least a half mile away.

Mountain road in the Segovias -*US National Archives*

"Rebels, Señor!" Toro exclaimed.

"Let's go!" O'Shea called back and sped up his mule.

The column picked up its pace but couldn't catch O'Shea and Toro.

"Lieutenant, hombre on foot," Toro said, pointing to a man now only one hill away. The man was running, seemingly for the safety of the town.

"Claro, hay otra!" O'Shea shouted then thought, now he's got me speaking Spanish!

As they reached the crest of the third hill, the two Marines realized that the town was only 100 yards away. In that same moment the first round fired by one of the forty rebels who lay in wait for the Marines passed between them. O'Shea turned back to rally his men. Toro rode forward fearlessly into the ambush. The rebel fire intensified. While firing his pistol, Toro caught a round in stomach as he passed through impact area of the rebel's ambush. His '03 Springfield remained slung over his shoulder. He dismounted in the town's center and sought shelter behind a water trough.

His charge allowed the others, led by O'Shea, to overrun the rebels who couldn't escape.

Eleven rebels were killed.

O'Shea dismounted by the water trough and ran to Toro's side. "Como esta amigo?"

Toro holding his bleeding side murmured, "Ees nothing, Lieutenant."

At that time, the "doc" arrived. Toro, the only US casualty, received his full attention.

"Doc" was a bright, enthusiastic former rifleman by the name of Conwell Leinbach who had rapidly risen to the rank of corporal. Actually he was a 22-year-old graduate of the University of Pennsylvania. Corporal Leinbach aspired to become a surgeon once he left the Corps and his parents assured him a scholarship to U of P's medical school. His compassion and intuitive knowledge of medicines and healing not only earned him the nickname of "Doc," but had him assigned to care for the medical well-being of O'Shea's detachment on a permanent basis.

"Doc, I'm going to take the men to Jícaro. Take good care of him. He's a real hero."

Jícaro, July 29,1927. "You couldn't save him?" O'Shea demanded in disbelief full-well knowing Leinbach had done his best. O'Shea spun away reflecting on the impact Private Rafel Toro had on him personally and how the loss of this affable, brave young man would affect his detachment. A Navy Cross, definitely a Navy Cross. I'll write it up tonight and give to Major Floyd in the morning, he thought. O'Shea turned back around, placed both his hands on Leinbach's shoulders, and looked him deep in his eyes. "Connie, I know you did all that was possible."

"Thanks, Sir." Leinbach said quietly.

O'Shea gave a final reassuring squeeze on Leinbach's shoulders then lowered his hands.

Leinbach, who had waited with Toro until the Floyd's main body arrived, added, "Lieutenant, the major wants to see you." Pointing up the street, "He's over by the Tienda d' Estrada."

At the Tienda d' Estrada's doorway, O'Shea greeted the major, "Sir, good to see you."

Major Oliver Floyd looked at O'Shea standing in the under-stocked country store. "I heard you encountered no resistance here in Jícaro."

"That's right, Sir. Someone fired a few wild shots about half way between San Fernando and here, but we waltzed right on in here. The town is uninhabited, except for that half-witted teenager. Someone was here 'cuz they sure made a wreck of things!"

"They sure have. I've never seen anything like it." Getting serious for a second, Floyd said, "George, I was sorry to learn about Toro's death. I don't believe any other officer in the Corps had a bodyguard; although we probably should have one at times. You have my sympathy. You lost a very brave young man. Are you going to write him up?"

"I was going to recommend him for a Navy Cross and write it up tonight, Sir."

"Great. I'll support it."

"Thanks a lot, sir. My men will appreciate that."

"George, I am going to keep you here in Jícaro. It is all part of General Feland's plan to occupy Sandino's homeland. You may as well stay in this store for a while. It's central and pretty big."

"Where's the owner, Sir?"

"I talked to a half-witted local about a half hour ago. He claims the owner, I believe his name is Francisco Estrada, was called to Managua for a business meeting of some sort. Hasn't been back for a couple of months."

"Right, Sir. My men will be glad to stay dry and clean up."

"I just received this message," Floyd said handing it to O'Shea.

SECRET
29JUL27
FROM: COMMANDING OFFICER, 5TH REGIMENT
TO: MAJOR FLOYD
SUBJ: EL CHIPOTE
1. INTEL HAS LEARNED SANDINO'S COMMAND POST AND STRONGHOLD IS
IN THE MOUNTAINS NEAR YOUR POSITION. STRONGHOLD'S NAME IS "EL
CHIPOTE."
2. YOU ARE TO LOCATE AND DESTROY EL CHIPOTE.
SECRET

Floyd said, "So I'll be out of her in the morning and going south for a couple of days to the San Albino mines. We have to find that bandit!"

The next morning…

"Morning Sir," O'Shea greeted the major while offering him a piece of paper. "Before you leave, would you please take a look at my proposed citation for Toro. I can make adjustments if necessary."

"Sure George," Floyd said looking at the single sheet of paper.

The Navy Cross is presented to Rafel Toro, Private, U.S. Marine Corps, for extraordinary heroism in battle when on the occasion of an engagement at San Fernando, Nicaragua, 25 July 1927, during an insurrection in that country, while performing advance guard duty in an important expedition into Nueva Segovia. Private Toro, accompanying his commanding officer, rode ahead into the town and on being attacked, fearlessly proceeded against tremendous odds, returning the fire, and at the risk of his own life materially assisted in holding the enemy in check until the arrival of reinforcements. Although receiving wounds at this time, which later resulted in his death, Private Toro continued in the fight to the last displaying that type of grit, determination and courage which characterizes conduct above and beyond the call of duty.

"Looks really good, George," Floyd said quietly, shaking his head in amazement of the heroism exhibited by the Marine private and at the sadness of his death. "I'll get it back to the Brigade."

Mine Office, San Albino Mines, August 6, 1927. "Sir, this dispatch just came through from the CO of the Fifth Marines," the eager, private first class radioman said as he entered the adjoining room that Major Floyd used as his command post.

"Thanks, Smith," Floyd said in a receptive voice. "It's quite amazing just how fast the goldmine company paid to repair the telegraph line from San Rafael del Norte to here after Sandino blew it up."

Floyd opened the message and said to no one in particular, "Well, well, well. Looks like the Intel boys won't quit." Looking up at the Marine, Floyd ordered. "Smith, have Sergeant Albright come up here. I want to talk to some of the locals."

Soon afterwards… "Sir, you wanted to see me?" Albright, Floyd's Intel Chief, asked eagerly.

"Take a look at this Chief," Floyd handed the message to the sergeant.

"El Chipote, Sir? They still believe there is such a place? You know, Sir, the American who has worked this mine for over 20 years says that he doesn't think Sandino has a place called 'El Chipote.' You heard of it all the way down to Quilali. I frankly doubt it exists."

"Tell you what Albright. One last try. Remember those two old timers that are hanging around all the time who seem to know everything?"

"You mean Rafael Hernández, the old guy, and his buddy, Manny Sanchez, the guy who's missing a foot?"

"Yeah, they're the two."

"Round them up, I want to ask them some questions about this 'El Chipote'."

"No problem, Sir. They are always hanging around the office eager to help out when they can. They are outside now; I'll get them."

The monsoon rain beat down on the roof of the office while Floyd and Albright asked the nice older gentlemen about 'El Chipote.'

In his broken Spanish, Floyd said, "All right Señor Hernández and Señor Sanchez, let me summarize: You both know of El Chipote. But it is a place that does not really exist. It is a far- away place found only in mythical stories. Is that true?"

"Si, Si," both said approvingly with broad smiles on their face.

Hernández added, "Now you know more about Nicaragua than most outsiders, Señor."

Standing up, proud of his Spanish-speaking ability, Floyd said, "Gracious amigos."

"De nada, Señor major," Hernández said retaining his smile.

Outside, Hernández winked at Sanchez as they walked away from the building.

Sanchez, limping on his crutch, looked at Hernández, Sandino's Captain of the San Albino district, and laughed, "You wily old bastard! Wait until I tell the others that El Chipote is a fairy tale!"

```
SECRET
6AUG27
FROM: MAJOR FLOYD
TO: COMMANDING OFFICER, 5TH REGIMENT
SUBJ: EL CHIPOTE
1. INTERROGATED LOCALS. "EL CHIPOTE" IS MYTHICAL HEAVEN IN
MOUNTAINS.
2. OCOTAL SECURE. HAVE POSTED MARINES IN JÍCARO, TELPANECA AND
MURRA.
3. SANDINO NO LONGER A THREAT.
4. WILL RETURN TO YOUR LOCATION IN TWO WEEKS.
SECRET
```

Ocotal, August 21, 1927. "Gilbert," Major Oliver Floyd stated, "you and your men did well here the last month, and I have put you in for a Bronze Star Medal. I don't know where we'd be if Sandino had taken this town."

"Thank you, sir." Hatfield responded, "I have a number of citations for exceptional gallantry under fire for officers and men of both organizations. Lieutenant Grover Darnell, Lieutenant Tom Bruce, and

Major Bleasdale as well as several men from both organizations. After that air attack, Sandino ought to be licking his wounds until the end of the rainy season. Oh, and I believe the people of Ocotal seem to be warming up to Grover's Guardia."

"Did you hear that this morning the Fifth Marines okayed my recommendation to leave Vic Bleasdale in charge up here in the Segovias?

Hatfield shaking his head, said, "I did; Vic told me."

"He now has good communications with Lieutenant O'Shea over in Jícaro and Lieutenant Keimling in Telpaneca thanks to our air service and the telegraph. Even if he's out at one of the other outposts, he'll be able stay in touch with Grover Darnell here in Ocotal. The brigade has even promised daily mail drops and supplies. They are expecting engineers to start building small airfields at Jícaro and Telpaneca."

"When do you think we'll go on the offense, Sir?"

"I figure we'll be back in force once the rainy season is over to flush out Sandino," Floyd said with confidence. "There are other considerations, you know?"

"Such as, Sir?"

"Well, I can't figure out what's going on with the Navy. Now that Rear Admiral Sellers has taken over the Special Services Squadron, he believes we are just chasing an unsupported bandit. I believe there is a war a brewing." Floyd added, "He sent the 11th Marines home. He is sending General Feland home soon. We will be fighting a revolution with only the 5th Marines, the ship squadron Marines, and the aviators." Pausing to calculate for a few seconds, he then continued, "I guess we ought to add the Guardia as well. But we're spread thin. We really are."

"Hey, enough of that. Are your men ready to return to Managua tomorrow, Gilbert?"

"For a hot shower and liberty? You bet, Sir."

CHAPTER 20: THE SEARCH FOR EL CHIPOTE

O'Shea's Headquarters, Jícaro, August 19, 1927. The headwaters of the Río Jícaro are found in the jungles of the rugged Segovian mountains a few miles south of the Honduran border. The river flows south passing by Jícaro and the San Albino mines. At Sapotillal, it is joined by the Río Murra. At that confluence, the Jícaro deepens and flows faster, racing by the small town of Quilali 10 miles further south. From Quilali, the Jícaro begins its final 12-mile leg feeding into the mighty Río Coco.

Lieutenant George O'Shea's mission was to patrol the entire 100 kilometers of the Río Jícaro basin searching for and destroying Sandino, his men, and his headquarters, called El Chipote. In early August, Major Bleasdale sent Lieutenant Tom Bruce, nine Marines and seven Guardia to Jícaro to beef up O'Shea's detachment in the eastern Segovias.

At O'Shea's meeting table in the small Jícaro store and after having skimmed Bruce's two- page patrol report, O'Shea looked up at Bruce and said, "Thank God you escaped unharmed, Tom. And you, as well, Mr. Alexander," he added shifting his glance up into the eyes of the civilian visitor. "I am very glad that you were able to join the patrol outside of Murra. You two are to be credited with superb courage, outstanding patrolling, and very effective leadership."

"George, I'll tell you the truth. Without Ed Alexander's knowledge of this part of Segovia, we wouldn't have made it back here."

"Thanks," Alexander said deflecting the compliment, "but a lot of credit goes to your Marines and those Guardia troops. They really worked like a team to escape from those Sandinista ambushers. A lot of people say that the Guardia…," Alexander stopped abruptly at the sound of a knock on the office door.

"Yes?" O'Shea responded to the knocking.

The door opened and Sergeant Charles Glasser stood looking into the room before responding, "You wanted to see me Lieutenant?"

"Right. I wanted you to hear the post-patrol report first hand. We waited for you."

"Well, thanks Sir. And welcome back Lieutenant, Mr. Alexander."

O'Shea asked, "Then you know Mr. Alexander?"

"Not well. We only met just before they took off for Murra."

"Oh, all right. Well, Mr. Alexander is from Pennsylvania with the Pittsburgh Exploitation Syndicate. In fact, he's the assistant manager. He lives in Murra and has been working around there for three years."

Glasser, obviously impressed, offered, "I'm sure glad you are helping us and not the other guys, Mr. Alexander."

O'Shea said, "Tom, why don't you start at the top?"

Bruce began, "Suits me, sir. All eighteen of us left for Murra two nights ago at 2300. We took one extra mule to meet any contingency. After six hours of pure darkness and unrelenting rain on that mountainous 'Ridge Trail' north of here, the mules were really tired. About 0500 we came across two locals who we pressed into supporting us. We left one of our mules at their farm and traveled the remaining three miles into town.

"Murra sits in a narrow valley cut into the mountains. It's nowhere as big as Jícaro—39 homes—and we searched them all. I should have told you that, when we arrived, the village was vacant. Has been so since Major Floyd rode into Jícaro. Turns out one of the two locals knew that the people were all hiding out at a farm not too far from there. Mr. Alexander knew an older lady—one of the town's people—who he trusted, so we asked one of the two locals to go and bring her back. We gave him copies of General Feland's August 9th Proclamation. I'm not sure they could read that, so before the farmer left, I explained that we intended to stay in the Segovia until we were rid of Sandino and his band of rebels.

"Didn't take long for the guy to return with the lady. She told us that the rest of the locals were under the impression that Sandino has not demobilized and as a matter of fact he was nearby."

"Sandino had been in the town?" O'Shea asked.

"Sure was! At least his men were." Alexander answered. "All the houses were left in good shape, 'cept mine. The rebels drew all sorts of nasty things on my walls and destroyed all my furniture. Don't think they want me to come back anymore."

Bruce added. "We stayed overnight at Ed's place; it sits on a little hill on the edge of town. Just after midnight our guard challenged a group of men on mules. They yelled, 'Sandino,' and took off. The guard fired at them and forced them to leave behind a mule they had stolen from Ed earlier.

"So, I decided to take an alternate route back here to Jícaro. We left at 0800 and didn't get a half mile out of town when our rear guard was attacked by 10-12 snipers hidden in bushes no further than 30 yards off the trail."

"Thirty yards, sir?" Glasser questioned.

"Hell, Sergeant, we must have ridden right by them and never saw them. You might want to make a note of that."

"Sure will, sir."

"They killed a mule out right and wounded another. We were lucky though; the closest they got to any of us was putting a hole in one of the Guardia's hats.

"We fired back at them immediately. They yelled, 'Viva Sandino!' and fled.

"But, with all that firing, seven of the mules got spooked and went back to town. I took Corporal Neel and Private Turner back, and we recovered the mules. Unfortunately, when I returned, I had to shoot the wounded mule—hell, he was bleeding like a stuck pig. Afterwards, we rolled him off the cliff beside the trail.

"We took off again, cautiously now. In about a mile, our front guard sighted a lot of armed men—maybe 30 of them with red handkerchiefs around their necks—to our left front. They were moving to our left." Bruce paused for an instant and looked up toward the ceiling while replaying the event in his mind, then continued, "Perhaps 200 yards away. We halted and took cover. Soon they fired on us. We returned fire with rifles and rifle grenades. They immediately ran into the tall trees beyond. We could see we killed two and wounded at least five of them."

"Tom, that's what we have to do—prove our superior firepower. I'm not talking weapons here. I mean our marksmanship!" O'Shea interrupted. "Obviously they aren't near as good as we are with a rifle."

"You're right, George, and we have to keep up our marksmanship training."

"Sorry, Tom, please continue."

"Well that was about it. Again, thanks to Mr. Alexander's knowledge of the terrain, we returned with no casualties."

"What conclusions should we draw?" O'Shea asked the others. "I'll need to put some of them in my report to the brigade."

"Sandino's alive and well," Alexander blurted out.

"You're right, Ed," O'Shea said noting the comment down in a notebook.

"They're not good marksmen," Glasser said. "At least not this group. But they are good at camouflage or at least blending into the terrain. I was thinking about those snipers, Sir."

"Right, I'll add that."

"They operate in platoon-sized groups," Bruce mused aloud waiting for O'Shea to jot down the last comment. "But, you know what, George? In all of the three encounters—Ed's place, the ambush, and then when we saw them on our left flank—they never wanted to close with us. Funny, because the last time they had us outnumbered two to one. I wonder what's that all about?"

"All right, Tom, get your men some chow and rest. I'm sure we'll be at this soon again."

Twelve days later… O'Shea smiled when he received his orders. In them, the intelligence section had refuted Major Floyd's notion that Chipote was an imaginary and mystical kingdom. As it turned out, the major learned that his information was from Rafael Hernandez and Manny Sanchez—two of Sandino's operatives.

"Sergeant Glasser, you are not going to want to hear this, but I am taking most of the men down the river to Quilali in search of the bandit. You have to stay behind."

"What?"

"I'll be leaving Corporal Cook and his four men behind with you to help mind the store."

"You have to be kidding me, Sir."

"Look, this is our northern-most location. I have been told that we cannot let anything more happen to the San Albino mines, three miles south of here. So Sergeant Glasser, if anything happens here or at the mines, I want you to join up with the security force hired by the American mine company. Together you'll be able to hold off until our airplanes come your way or I can get back. And, if you need him to translate, Cook speaks fairly fluent Spanish—not that it will help much with this Segovian slang."

"When are you taking off, Sir?"

"Tomorrow…about 0800."

"Well then, if you don't mind Sir, I'm going to gather up Cook and ride to the mines. I want to make sure we know any possible ambush sites if the bandits attack the mines again and try to block our support. I also want to meet the mine foreman and his security team."

"Sounds good with me. I'll have Corporal Barron go along so that he can take the lead on tomorrow's patrol."

Ops Office, Managua Aerodrome, September 1, 1927. "Captain Archibald, where's Sergeant Knopf, Sir?" Technical Sergeant Roy Jolson asked the squadron's executive officer, who was dressed in his flight uniform and ready to fly.

"He's not feeling too well this morning, Roy—thought you knew that."

"Anyone else flying with you, sir."

"Nope, just me and the sandbag."

"Well, sir, your wingmen are First Lieutenant Thomas and Sergeant Dowdell, his observer."

"Oh yeah. Thomas's a pretty good aviator; I've flown with him before. Where are they now?"

"I've already briefed them. They went for chow."

"Sir, look at these two cartoons I clipped out of that liberal *St. Louis Post- Dispatch* paper. Bastards. The first one appears on July 24th implying that we're a bunch of killers with all the dead Nics laying all around. The second one was on August 7th. The pinko bastards titled that one, 'Salesmanship.' Our bombs have destroyed the Latin American Trade Conference?" Jolson questioned, raising his hands, palms up, to his shrugged shoulders. "I'll tell you Sir, if they have their way, we'll all be saluting that bastard Joseph Stalin in ten years!"

Archibald was studying the cartoons. He casually asked, "Has Major Rowell seen these yet?"

"Not yet sir. I'm going to put them on my wall. He'll see them then."

Switching subjects Archibald said, "All right Roy, what do you have for us this morning?"

"We have O'Shea's 21-man patrol arriving at the junction of the Ríos Jícaro and Murra sometime this afternoon. Tomorrow they'll be moving toward Quilali and, if all goes well, they should actually arrive there by dusk tomorrow. According to the Intel guys, Sandino's headquarters, called El Chipote, is in the vicinity of Quilali. Lieutenant Thomas's and your mission is twofold. First, you are to provide direct air support to the ground patrol. Scout ahead for enemy ambushes and ensure they are well off logistically. They will be using the color panels we dropped off last week in Jícaro. You are up to speed on the panels aren't you, sir?"

"Oh sure, I taught the pilots last week as soon as we received them from Quantico."

"Okay then, the second part of your mission is to make your own reconnaissance of the area. Sandino's headquarters has got to be somewhere in those mountains. Follow the trails that lead to the rivers. Take notes so you can brief me when you return."

"Can do easy, Roy," Archibald said using a current colloquialism. "Anything else?"

"Well, our mule train arrived at Ocotal two days ago. So, if you need fuel or parts, you won't have come back here to top off. And, I guess that's all, Sir."

"Okay, Roy. I'm going to get some chow, and then we'll take off."

"Yes sir. Have a good flight."

Five minutes later in the aerodrome mess…

Captain Archibald announced his presence as he approached the two seated aviators, "Morning Lieutenant Thomas and Sergeant Dowdell."

Both men stopped eating, stood up at the four-sided table, and offered Archibald a seat.

"Thanks, I will join you," Archibald said as he placed his steel food tray on the table that contained two eggs "over easy" and toast generously covered with a creamy, grey-colored gravy mixed with ground beef. The Marines affectionately referred to the toast and spicy gravy concoction as "SOS." Archibald's right hand held a large cup of black coffee that he placed next to the tray.

"Burns," Thomas started, referring to Tech Sergeant Duffy Burns, the mess sergeant, "can make some great SOS, can't he sir?" Lieutenant Thomas offered.

"We're lucky to have him." Archibald said. "They wanted to hold him at San Diego when we loaded aboard ship, since he is so fine a chef, but Major Rowell pleaded our case."

Dowdell asked, "Sir, any word on getting new aircraft to replace these ancient DeHavillands?"

"No word yet; although, we have raised our concerns about their flight worthiness."

"Gosh Sir, if our mechs ever run out of banding wire, all our birds will be grounded."

"Well, Marine Corps aviation is here to stay, so we'll be getting new birds just like the ground guys get their new toys."

In between bites the captain asked, "Speaking about the ground guys, we have challenged them to a field meet on the 15th," the captain said, looking at Dowdell's huge shoulders and puffy muscular fingers. "Have you two entered any events?"

Dowdell replied with enthusiasm, "Sir, I signed up for the shot-put. I was by far the strongest guy in my high school class!"

As Archibald was saying, "That's good," Burns approached the trio with three brown paper bags.

"Here are your three sandwiches just the way you ordered them, Captain—corn beef on rye with mustard."

"Thanks Burnsie, you're the best!" he said taking his bag.

Thomas and Dowdell looked surprised but gratefully grabbed their bags.

Archibald stood up and said for anyone to hear him, "Aviators can't fly on an empty stomach." After swigging down the last of his coffee, he said, "All right, let's get those creaky old DHs in the air!"

Río Jícaro Trail, September 1, 1927. O'Shea gave his patrol order: "Corporal Barron," referring to Corporal "Woody Barron, the first section leader, "you'll have the lead. Leinbach," referring to Corporal Conwell Leinbach who acted as the patrol's pharmacist mate or doctor, "and I will follow in trace. Jack," addressing his second section leader Corporal Jack Sumner, a 21-year old scrappy kid from Beaver Falls, Pennsylvania, 40 miles north of Pittsburgh, "you bring up the rear.

"I expect that we'll be seeing more rebels anytime now since we picked up the Murra river trail back there at the junction. The intel message I received from the airplane told of enemy activity near Quilali. I'm guessing that's only seven miles further south. Pay attention for ambushes—both from the front and rear. Woody, you have the front and, Jack, you have the rear. Watch out for anyone trying to join us from behind." Seeking to confirm the section leaders' understanding, O'Shea looked at both men and asked, "Got that?"

Sumner raised his right index and caught the lieutenant's eye.

"Jack?"

"When that plane dipped down on us yesterday, did he drop you that report?"

"Right. It darn near hit Woody's mule square on the head."

Barron added immediately, "That pilot or the guy in the back seat missed me by two feet. Those guys are good but we have to watch out for their messages! Wow, had it hit me, I would have had a doosie of a bump on my head!"

Sumner, wide eyed and still marveling at the modern method of communicating by using airplanes, simply added, "Amazing."

"Hey look!" Summer blurted out. "Here come two more."

Patrol members eyes immediately shifted skyward first toward the noise then at the sight of the two bi-planes watching out for their well-being.

O'Shea broke the spell announcing, "All right men, let's saddle up and move out in 10 minutes."

800 Feet in the Air. Lieutenant Earl Thomas gave a 'thumbs up' to Captain Archibald flying 300 feet to his right, confirming that both he and Sergeant Dowdell had seen O'Shea's mounted patrol below. Then, as planned, the two planes flew a triangular observation patrol in search of Sandino or any of his compatriots. They would fly a few miles southeast to Quilali, then peel to the left and fly a 30-mile trek northeast above the Río Murra passing by El Chipote Mountain to the small town of Murra. Technical Sergeant Roy Jolson, the operations chief, had warned the aviators, "Be especially alert on this leg of the patrol because it takes you passed the El Chipote Mountain. Sandino's El Chipote Headquarters could be one in the same and the headquarters will be heavily guarded." The third leg of the trip was 25 miles long would have them fly due east to Jícaro before turning southeast and fly along the Río Jícaro and back over Lieutenant O'Shea's patrol.

Lieutenant Thomas flew in the lead plane. As planned, he flew over the west bank of the Río Murra and inland, searching trails and tributaries, or anything that was suspicious. Trailing about a half mile behind was Captain Archibald who would patrol in precisely the same manner on the east side of the Murra.

Thomas and Dowdell flew without incident nearly ten miles over the west bank of the river. Archibald questioned Jolson's admonishment as he too saw nothing. Soon the juices burning his stomach reminded him that he had a wrapped-up corn beef on rye sandwich tucked below his seat in a brown bag. The more he thought about the sandwich, the more he resolved that this was precisely the moment to consume it. Holding the stick with his right hand, Archibald's left hand carefully slipped between his legs to retrieve a brown bag. In a moment, his teeth sunk into a good portion of the speckled rye bread holding the two-inch thick, reddish-brown meat. Bright yellow mustard squeezed out from below the top piece of rye bread. "Umm um," the captain said under the roar of the DH-4's engine. "Damn that Burnsie knows how to… What the hell's that?"

The captain heard the noise of a bullet whistle nearby. He looked up above his head and saw with amazement a one-quarter inch hole in his upper wing. Archibald carefully placed the half sandwich back into the bag on his lap. He flew his plane upward 500 feet, banked to his right and then flew down closer to the river to study the same area he had just flown over.

"Who the hell shot a hole in my wing?" he asked himself. "Wait a minute. Wait a minute." His mind directed his focus onto a mule just off the river trail. "Let's check this out," he thought to himself.

In a moment, a man in a sombrero popped up from behind the mule with a rifle and fired a shot ripping through the lower wing.

Archibald squinted his eyes. His lips pursed and teeth tightened as he thought, "Why that bastard. I'll show him."

This time his plane soared upward to 1,000 feet, banked and flew back down toward the earth. Half way down, Archibald realized his gunner wasn't in the back seat to shoot at the enemy. "Shit!" he said at the height of his frustration.

He could see the unflinching rebel reload his rifle and place it on his shoulder pointing the weapon at the diving plane. Now in self-defense, Archibald instinctively grabbed the brown bag from his lap and threw it at his apparent assassin to distract him, banked left over the river and zoomed upward toward the grey clouds and safety.

"Damnit," he thought, "my sandwich. I'll show that little ass."

Knowing where Thomas and Dowdell would be, he cut across the triangle to intercept the other plane. He signaled them to fly with him to Ocotal, loiter above while he would get a .45 caliber pistol and anything else he could to assault that cocky rebel.

Thirty minutes later he was armed with a borrowed .45calber pistol and 12 small-sized coconuts flying on an empty stomach toward the devilish rebel. The rebel, apparently now out of ammunition, made a run for the underbrush. Archibald got off four coconuts on his first dive. Then on his second dive shot a clip of .45 caliber rounds in the jungle area that had swallowed up the rebel and his mules.

Loitering over the attack scene, Thomas and Dowdell, while eating their sandwiches, laughed without control. Thomas looked back at Dowdell and yelled over the engine's noise, "Wait 'til we get back and tell them all about this!"

200 yards West of the Río Jícaro, 4:00 PM. At a road junction five miles north of Quilali, Corporal "Woody" Barron raised his right arm sharply upward toward the cloudy sky while reining in his mount. His closed fist signally for all to stop their forward progress. He then pointed his rifle toward the front for a second, pulled it down, and flashed four fingers at his lieutenant. O'Shea hustled forward and upon reaching his first section leader verified, "You have four rebels?"

"Yeah, well, Jonsie did. About 200 yards up. They were armed and went to the left."

"All right, let's take the left-hand road and see if we can catch up to them."

In ten minutes Barron halted the column again. Both he and O'Shea were 15 yards behind the point man, Jonsie. This time Jonsie was pointing to a house on a hill 1,500 yards to the front. Just then two men came out of the house and watched the Marines, defying them to do anything at that distance.

O'Shea yelled, "Jonsie! You two other Marines. Fire on those cocky bastards!"

The noise from the '03 Springfields filled the air for 90 seconds then tapered off. Forty rounds were fired forcing the two rebels to run toward a crest before disappearing.

O'Shea was quiet for a minute while assessing the situation. Finally, he said, "Woody, it's getting pretty late. Go on until you find a good defensive spot, and we'll camp there for the night."

"Will do, Lieutenant."

O'Shea's Camp, 7:00 AM, September 2, 1927. Jones, 100 yards from camp, sat relaxed, watching his mule grazing nearby. He had his section's last watch. Been there on the road since 0400. Suddenly the face of the 20-year-old tightened. Men talking...in Spanish. nearby. Private

First Class Jones's mind processed the sound. His motor senses went on full alert. Jones, while instinctively grabbing his Springfield, looked toward the sound. "There. Five of them on the hill 200 yards away! Oh, my God! One's aiming at me!" Jones fired before his next thought could be conjured up. Then again. And once more. Finally, he looked beyond his rear sight to see the fifth man scrambling down the backside of the hill.

Jones's focus never left that hill. He mounted his mule. Soon, he heard mule hoofs pounding on the dirt road coming from camp. O'Shea brought his mount to halt. Corporal Barron and five other Marines followed. Jones could see the lieutenant was ready for a fight.

"Over there, Lieutenant!" Jones said pointing toward the hill. "I counted five of them, Sir.

They had rifles."

O'Shea had heard enough. With his pistol holster unflapped, he looked back at the other mounted Marines and roared, "Let's get them!"

An hour later, emerging from the jungle, O'Shea was greeted by Leinbach and Sumner. "Any luck, Sir?" Sumner asked.

"None. The jungle is so damn thick inside. You'd not believe it. The mules even get tied up in it. And there are tens, no hundreds, of paths crossing each other. Once the rebels get inside that jungle on foot they immediately have an advantage."

"We'll have to note that, Sir," Sumner said dutifully.

"Connie, wait until you see Woody's face. He must have got caught up in the vines. Looks like he was trying to kiss a bobcat. You'll have your work cut out for you cleaning that guy up."

O'Shea paused while mentally shifting gears, "Jack, anything going on in Quilali?"

"We saw about five men—one of them had a rifle. Looked like they were in a hurry to get out of town. Don't know why, 'cuz they didn't see us."

"All right. Let's mount up and get into town. We'll break up into twos and search each house," O'Shea said looking at Barron riding up to join the trio.

Sumner took one look at Barron's sweated and quite bloodied face, laughed and said, "My god, Woody, what's the other guy look like?"

O'Shea, taking control, asked, "You the last guy out?"

"Yes Sir," Corporal Woody Barron replied in a rather subdued tone.

Quilali-*Official US Marine Corps No. PB10535*

The four Sandinistas leading a pack mule saw the mounted Marines as they closed on the town. The Sandinista soldiers cut the packs from the mule and disappeared into the jungle beside the river. O'Shea's detachment ended up with corn and beans, not exactly what they had hoped to get.

The supplies, propaganda, and deserted houses discovered in Quilali and on the way back to Jícaro led O'Shea to conclude in his patrol report that Sandino was preparing for a counter offensive in the vicinity of Quilali and that they had been near El Chipote. He attached a sketch showing where he believed El Chipote was located, specifically on a flat spot between Chipote Mountain, located east of the Río Murra, and the small village of Manchones.

Diplomats and commanders in Managua concluded that Sandino was raising an army sufficient to overthrow the coalition government.

Chapter 21: While The Boss Is Away

Major Rowell Goes on Leave, September 10, 1927. Rowell, looking directly into his Executive Officer's eyes, declared, "The war is heating up. Despite that, our new brigade commander, Colonel Gulik, has ordered me to take the 30 days leave that I have been putting off for the past two months. He sees the war heating up later in the fall, and he wants me back here then. In my absence, Captain Archibald, I want you to ensure that the squadron's flying integrity remains at the highest point possible. That includes keeping these old DH-4s in the air. Do you feel you can handle that, Captain?"

"Oh, yes Sir."

"Stanley, I am dead serious. Much as I would love to go home to see my family, I will not do so if you have any doubts."

"I am ready to step in for you, Sir."

"Very well then. I want you to brief me at 1700 on just how you will conduct the search for the El Chipote fortress since we are in the middle of the rainy season and the cloud cover is intensifying. If I am satisfied, I will be leaving for Corinto in the morning. Any questions, Captain?"

"No Sir."

Aviators vs. the Infantry, September 15, 1927. Nicaragua's Independence Day is September 15th. To celebrate the day, Colonel Gulik and the 2nd Marine Brigade hosted an "athletic event" between the aviators and members of the 5th Marine Regiment. Eleven events were scheduled including the shoe race, 5-mile bike race, 3-legged race, sack race, egg toss, shot put, and tug of war. Colonel Gulik put up $100 prize money; between $5 and $10 would be awarded to the winner or winning team of various events.

Junior Wilson and his soul mate, Corporal Smitty, had competed in the egg toss, but their egg broke on the last toss. They won the three-legged race.

3-Legged Race in Nicaragua-Official History Division Photo

"Junior, would you look at that?" Smitty said with a smirk on his face as he pointed toward the midpoint of the sack race where Captain Archibald was jumping up and down like a college cheerleader while running and shouting for the aviation sack-race team. "Lord, have you ever seen such excitement. He's a real character."

"He was doing the same thing over at the shot put event—the one that Frank Dowdell won by five feet. My gosh, ever since the skipper left for the states, Archibald seems like he 'found the light'."

"Found the light? I agree. Even if the technical sergeants won't ease up on us, the thought of Archibald's half-day work routine was great! Maybe he's not too goofy after all."

Wilson, with his motorcycle racing experience was one of five aviators entered in the five- mile bike race. "Oh Smitty, my bike race is supposed to start at 1115 hours—that's 20 minutes from now. It's the second last event. We already won 13 out of the 17 events; I'd hate to blow this one. Come on over to see if you can see any more adjustments to the bike that will give me an edge—my victory is going to be our beer money for tonight."

"Sure, did you find those tires Top Heller brought with us from San Diego?"

"Right, Smitty, what a guy! He even helped me change the tires."

The aviators went on to win 16 events, including the bike race, where Junior Wilson gained the lead over a corporal by the name of Travis Martin—a grunt being assigned to the Ocotal detachment—during the final two laps of the race. After the race Wilson and Martin bonded immediately. Turns out they both raced motorcycles back in the States. Wilson assured Martin that once he gets to Ocotal, all he had to do was send a note to him asking for anything. If it was in Managua, Wilson would get it for him.

Lieutenant Harmon Loses the Flagship, September 16, 1927. Two flights were scheduled for the next day from the Managua Aerodrome. Lifting off at 9:00 AM were two planes on a mission to reconnoiter the Murra-Quilali area specifically searching for Sandino's fortress, El Chipote. Lieutenant Frank Schilt and Captain Frank Pierce, pilot and observer, were in one of the O2B-1 aircraft. Lieutenant Earl Thomas and his observer, shot put champ Sergeant Frank Dowdell, were in the second O2B-1 aircraft. Both O2B-1 planes were equipped with Lewis machine guns, mounted fore and aft. This fire power was a safety blanket for aviators flying in the eastern portion of the Segovian region—since, by now, every aviator knew about the uselessness of throwing sandwiches and coconuts at the enemy.

The second flight was a three-bird supply run to Ocotal and was led by the infamous acting commanding officer, Captain Stanley Archibald. The captain and Sergeant Oscar Knopf flew in one escort plane and Gunner Mike Wodarczyk and Corporal Dibling flew in the other escort plane. Lieutenant "JC" Harmon flew solo as he was transporting supplies to Ocotal in the third De Havilland. Harmon's aircraft was Major Rowell's favorite plane, Green-Nose or No. 6393.

Technical Sergeant Roy Olson, the OPS Chief, conducted the pre-flight mission briefing. The pilots and observers knew the aerial routes for both missions. Olson provided a reminder for escaping if any aircraft was forced down by weather, the enemy, or mechanical problems. "Remember pilots, after you hit the deck and you are able to move, you help the other aviator out of the bird and then you get the Lewis guns and other weapons out of the plane before the Sandinista bastards come out of the hills and claim them."

Technical Sergeant Ike Billingsworth, the maintenance chief, briefed the aviators on the unbelievable flying record of the squadron. With a 90-hour weekly flying record, no De Havilland or O2B-1 ever had a forced landing. "I read of the obsolete and historical 'DHs' in a recent aviation magazine I got from the States; but here in Nicaragua those birds are even more modern than the oxcart and are still making history! Have a safe flight, men."

All five aircraft lifted off within ten minutes of each other and flew north toward Jinotega where they split. Schilt's flight continued north toward Quilali and Murra while Archibald flight broke to the northwest toward Ocotal.

Ocotal 12:00 PM, September 16, 1927. "Thanks a lot Lieutenant, maybe later," Sergeant Knopf said to Lieutenant McQuade, the new commanding officer of the Ocotal detachment. All Marines knew of Lieutenant McQuade, the all-Marine football star with Quantico's championship football team. He had been written up in the Leatherneck and other military magazines several times. Truth was that Knopf, Harmon, and Dibling simply wanted to meet the football star, who had invited them to stay for a couple of days in Ocotal with "real Marines." Everyone laughed, knowing they did not want to remain overnight in this mosquito-infested mountain town. The aviators soon started up their planes for the journey back to Managua.

Wodarczyk's and Archibald's took off first. Harmon, with a bag of mail and a sack of fresh-cut coffee beans for Tech Sergeant Duffy Burns, followed about a minute later.

"What the heck was that backfire, Blanco?" McQuade shouted at his newly-promoted sergeant—one of the decorated heroes from the July battle.

Sergeant Jose Blanco, walking next to the lieutenant, whipped around. He had heard the noise as well. "Look, Lieutenant!" Blanco blurted, pointing at a dissipating puff of black smoke following

Harmon's plane. The plane was 50 feet in the air and had just crossed the Río Coco south of the aerodrome.

McQuade instinctively barked, "Sergeant take some men up there immediately to secure the wreckage!"

Two miles further south and at 800 feet, Knopf routinely turned his head to account for all the planes. He could see Harmon's aircraft struggling to get airborne. Black smoke belched from the engine and spewed along the side of the plane. He poked Archibald's right shoulder with his index finger, and yelled, "Captain, Green Nose ain't gonna make it!"

The captain whipped the plane around and dove toward the struggling plane. Seeing the pending crash, he raced for Ocotal's airfield to obtain a couple of mules for he and Sergeant Knopf to get to Harmon and what would be left of Green Nose.

In the meantime, Harmon feathered the engine over a cactus hedge and hit a grassy knoll covered with shrubs and cactus, no doubt saving his life. The landing gear snapped off and the plane continued sliding into several small trees. It finally came to rest on its propeller with the tail in the air. Harmon, shaken, scrambled out of the plane. He reached up from the ground and jerked on the ammunition box locking strap so hard that when it broke free, the box scraped the right side of his face.

DH-4 Lost in Nicaragua: 1927: *Official Photo USMC*

Twenty minutes later, Sergeant Blanco dismounted first. The rest of his men formed a perimeter around the crash site. Harmon, looking more disheartened then injured, despite the blood still trickling along his right cheek, sat forlornly on the ground with his arms wrapped tightly around his knees. He was 30 feet away from what appeared to be a totally destroyed plane.

"Lieutenant, are you okay, Sir."

"Sergeant, you'll never understand. You'll just never understand. None of you will," Harmon said with emotion.

"What sir? What won't I understand?"

"This is Green Nose. I killed Green Nose! My career is ruined."

At that moment, Sergeant Knopf's mule came to a halt beside the lieutenant. "Nice landing, Lieutenant!"

Harmon looked up at Knopf with Corporal Dibling dismounting next to the sergeant. "What the hell do you mean, Knopf?"

"Sir, Captain Archibald saw how you expertly avoided that cactus hedgerow and got safely over here. He was definitely impressed and wanted me to say so."

"Huh?"

Knopf now looked at the plane and said, "Beside that Sir, looks like we can salvage the engine and the controls."

"You sure?"

"Yeah, sir, and I guess we'll be guests of Lieutenant McQuade for a couple of days after all."

Chapter 22: Sandino Attacks The Telpaneca Outpost

Sandino Headquarters, El Chipote, September 16, 1927. "For two months, Francisco, we have been planning our revenge on the Yankees and their constabulary puppets. I have selected you, Señor, to lead our first attack on their outpost. Our revolution must stop the shedding of blood of innocent Nicaraguans.

Marines patrol on mules from Telpaneca-*Official Photo USMC*

"We have interviewed our brave compatriots by the hundreds and have concluded the most vulnerable of their detachments is in the village of Telpaneca," Sandino said not only to his friend but also to the dozen men who had gathered for the briefing. "I know you know this village along the Coco. The enemy only established an outpost there last month."

"Si, General Sandino, I know the Telpaneca well," Colonel Fernando Estrada, the former merchant from Jícaro, responded in a confident tone. "I have often traveled through Telpaneca on the way to Managua. I am honored to lead this attack."

"Very well, you will lead 200 of our brave men on horseback. Another 25 men will be with your supply train. I have ordered the supply train to go no farther than San Juan de la Coco. Juan Colindres, Carlos Salgado, José Díaz, Tomas Melgara, and Porfino Sánchez will lead your deploying units. You will attack under the cover of darkness on the 19th and leave Telpaneca before sunrise. You must be deep in the mountains before their airplanes can fly there from Managua.

"I have asked Jefe Pedro Altamirano to review your attack plan and to assure me that you will have all the weapons and supplies you will need."

"Si, mi General."

"We must not misjudge the enemy as we had in Ocotal."

"Si, mi General."

"One more thing Francisco. I want you to use the name, 'Carlos Estrada' in any report you make about this attack."

"Carlos?"

"Si, Francisco. The enemy must not know who we are and where we are from—especially when they have occupied your tienda in Jícaro." Gently smiling now at his trusted friend, Sandino said, "Ve con Dios, amigo. Go with God, friend."

Detachment Galley Storeroom Telpaneca, September 18, 1927. "Russell, you in here?" Private Handzlik whispered as he entered the storeroom where two young cooks and a few messmen had cots.

"Yeah," I have been trying to get to sleep since 8:30. What time is it anyway?"

"Must be 10 by now. I can't see anything out there. This darn place gets so dark at night.

Hell, it's amazing I found my way back here at all."

"You got your weapon handy, Russ?" Then Handzlik added, "Sergeant Eadens says it's too quiet out there. Most of the villagers don't seem to be around."

"Yeah, Slick. Now let me get some sleep!"

"Oh, all right. What are we serving for breakfast in the morning?"

Russell's snoring provided the only answer.

Río Coco's Edge, Outside Telpaneca, midnight, September 19, 1927. "Francisco, all the men are across," Juan Colindres whispered, adding, "Carlos has our horses ready for when we leave in the morning."

Asking an unnecessary question, Estrada replied, "You the last one?"

"Si. On our north side. Díaz and Porfino should be across the river on the other side of the bend by this time."

"All right, you and Tomas start getting the guns in place. We have exactly one hour."

12:30 PM, September 19, 1927. The twenty-four sticks of dynamite, wrapped tightly together, exploded behind the Marine barracks. It jolted the 25 Marines and the 20 Guardia who lived across the street from any degree of entombing sleep. Even while the fireball dimmed, the shadow of the rebel who set off the explosives danced eerily in celebration along the rear wall of the Marine's building. Yet the rebel was in full view of Private Irwin, the sentry posted in the large open courtyard to protect from any attacks from that area. Irwin's Springfield fired and the shadow made its final thrust into the air, a crescendo marking the first Sandinista casualty.

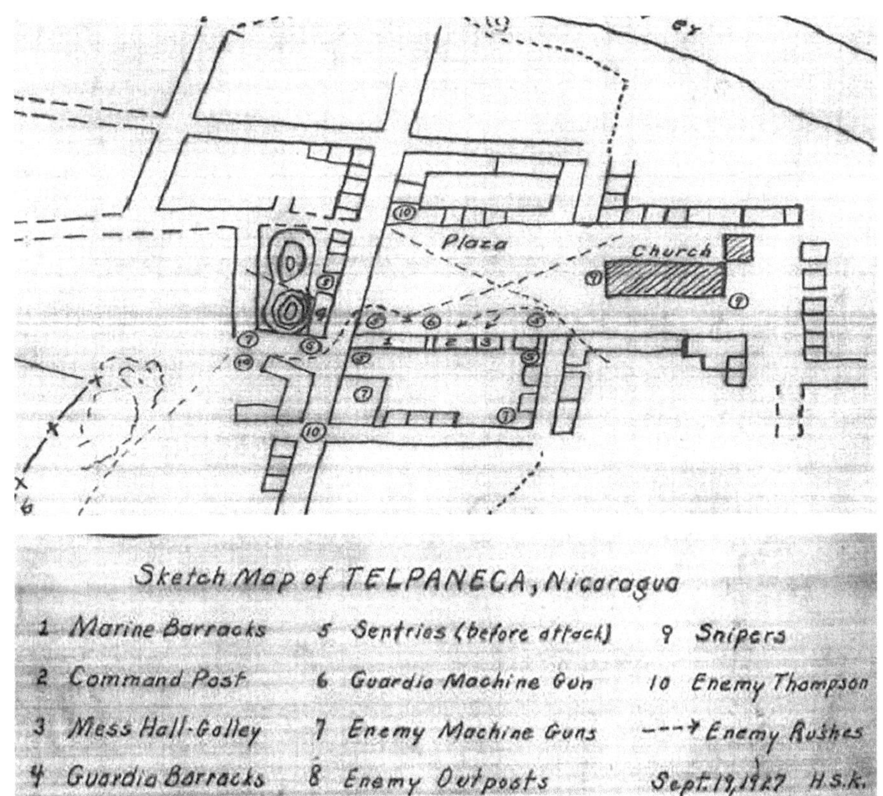

Herman Keimling After Action Report-*The Sandino Rebellion Nicaragua 1927-1935 PC27.09.22 Peard*

The front door of the galley's storeroom flew open. It was accompanied by an inarticulate scream made by a small Nicaraguan mountain man. His rifle fired in the direction of the noise he had heard from the outside twenty seconds earlier. His bullet nicked the now-rising Private Russell in the left shoulder, causing him to fly back into his cot with a distinctive grunt. Handzlik, awakening from a deeper sleep, observed his fearless friend fire while half way standing, reload and fire twice more before again being hit, this time in the chest. With his knees buckling Russell placed his rifle on the floor, collapsed back into the cot, tried to cry out in pain only to have his plea become muffled from the blood that was rushing into his right lung and flowing from his mouth.

"Russell!" Private Handzlik screamed rushing over to his friend's cot.

Three minutes later when Russell stopped gurgling, Handzlik dashed outside like a madman screaming after Russell's killer.

Soon he heard Sergeant Alva Eadens yell, "Handzlik," from the adjacent 600 square foot house, referred to as the command post.

"Handzlik, get your ass in here!"

Traumatized, Private Handzlik turned around and ran toward his noncommissioned officer, pleading to be understood, "They killed Russell, Sergeant! They killed Russell!"

Bursts from the three rebel Lewis machine guns failed to drown out the noise of bomb and hand grenade explosions emanating from the plaza in front of the barracks and from the open courtyard now being vacated by Private Irwin.

Private Glaser was dashing out to his post in the courtyard from the barrack's rear door to join Irwin when he caught a glimpse of his compatriot dashing behind a group of rebel soldiers attacking the command post.

Inside the small building, Marine First Lieutenant Herman Keimling, the detachment's only officer, wore captain's bars as the head of the Guardia Nacional detachment. Within moments of the initial explosion, Keimling had loaded his pistol, dressed and was crossing the room from the front to the courtyard door. He approached the door only to find it mostly blocked by his muscular sergeant. Eadens's fast-moving arm blocked the lieutenant's forward progress. Keimling, while grunting, "Whatha," then saw a charging rebel 25 feet from the door.

The rebel's rifle was fixed under his right arm, pointing at the door until a guaranteed sure hit could be achieved.

"Hold it Cap'n, here they come again!" the large sergeant said in a steady voice. Eadens wheeled his Springfield, confident of his marksmanship, fired, and watched the assaulting Segovian stagger, mortally wounded.

The falling rebel's finger remained on the trigger as the pain soared throughout his body. He grimaced as he fell. While his hands tighten to offset the pain, his rifle fired and hit Private Glaser coming up behind him.

The other rebels fled as both Eadens and Keimling came out into the courtyard firing. Outside now, Keimling looked around and assessed the situation. Eadens joined Irwin firing at the fleeing enemy.

"Sergeant Eadens, give me a hand with Glaser!" He then added, "Irwin, cover us while we pull him in. Then get back in the building with us."

Once inside the two men laid Glaser, now in shock, on a cot; his right leg, bleeding profusely, had two gaping bullet wounds. Irwin entered the room while still looking out into the courtyard. Keimling grabbed two grenades from his left hand desk drawer. "You two stay here, one with Glaser and one covering the courtyard. Keep the front door locked. I'm going out to check on the men."

Keimling stepped back in the courtyard. As he did, he saw a line of eight charging, machete-wielding rebels running at him. When they got to 65 feet away, Keimling threw his first grenade. Three enemy on Keimling's left blew up in the air.

The five remaining, alcoholic-high farmers huddled.

Eadens ran to the door to help. In amazement, he watched the lieutenant stand nonchalantly while watching the crazed men break their huddle and release an even more shrill-pitched yell. Now, as the charging line of five men was 40 feet away, Keimling threw his second grenade to see it fall in front of the rebel in the line's center. The man stopped abruptly. Without logic of any sort, he froze to stare at his imminent death. His two drunken compatriots on either side amazingly stopped as well. The grenade exploded and the three men flew upward and outward. The two on the flanks dropped their machetes and ran.

Eadens paused, then called out subtly, "Nice job Lieutenant."

The attack's initial fervor dwindled. Keimling would spend the rest of the night splitting time with the Guardia and the Marines. Several wrote after action reports that told of their admiration of their leader. They all commented on his encouraging words and his joke-telling ability.

By the morning the rebels were gone. Their dead were dragged to the river and thrown into it or taken up into the mountains. Russell and Glaser were the only Marines and Guardia casualties. Collectively, the detachment estimated 25 rebels were killed and 50 were wounded.

Sandino wrote a report about this attack most likely after having gathered the information from his fellow warrior, Colonel Fernando Estrada. It is published in his *Account of the Battle of Telpaneca of 19 September 1927* and concludes: "the eighty deaths of which I speak were those of the enemy alone."

Chapter 23: Meanwhile, Back In Managua

Ops Office, Managua Aerodrome, September 21, 1927. By 11:50 AM the four pilots and their observers were completing their post-flight reports:

"Situation in Telpaneca secure."

"Fresh graves for two young Marines dug in the cemetery south of the town." "Dropped food, supplies, munitions, mail."

"Searched trails and mountains for attackers with negative results."

The Ops Chief, Technical Sergeant Jolson, who constantly called for detail in the reports, kept saying, "Gentlemen, we don't need to have a book written about the mountains between Telpaneca and Quilali, I already know they are steep, and you can't see though the canopy. Tech Sergeant Burns is going to close the galley by 1300. We need you in your baseball uniforms and on the trucks by 1315."

Managua Ballpark One Mile from the Aerodrome. The Nicaragua Electric Company and umpires had been at the field for thirty minutes by the time the three cargo trucks loaded with the aviators rolled to a stop. Captains Archibald and Pierce; Lieutenants Schilt and Thomas; and Technical Sergeants Heller, Billingsworth, and Jolson had arrived fifteen minutes earlier and occupied the bleachers.

The other bleachers already over flowed with hooting and hollering Nicaraguans. Baseball was the key entertainment for the now undefeated "SHOCKS" from the Nicaragua Electric Company.

The rowdy aviators jumped off the rear of the trucks carrying bags of bats, balls and other necessities. They sported their new uniforms consisting of shirts with the word "BOMBERS" on their backs, black leather belts, and pin-stripe pants tucked into their knee length socks. Smitty and Wilson had pulled every string at both San Diego and Quantico to get the uniforms.

Archibald, the self-appointed team manager, walked over to talk to Captain Vickers, the team captain, for a final conversation. Top Billingsworth worked with the batters, while Top Heller focused on fielding. The BOMBERS no longer looked as unorganized and uncoordinated as they had during their first practice in August. Somehow, the uniforms seemed to help a lot.

Other than the battle up in Telpaneca, everyone focused on the game for the past few days.

Archibald posted the starting line up at the mess hall's black board two days earlier.

STARTING LINEUP FOR THE BOMBERS
1st Base—Oscar "Deputy Dog" Knoff
2nd Base—Duffy "Cookie" Burns
3rd Base—Robert "I love you no shit Roberto" Reynolds
Shortstop—Cpl "No Other Name" Smitty
Right Field—JC "Green Nose" Harmon
Left field— Junior "Speedway" Wilson
Pitcher—Frank "Shot-put" Dowdell
Catcher—James "Hawkeye" Dibling
Relief Pitchers—Don "Skipper" Vickers and Earl "The Pearl" Thomas

By precisely 1400 the Nicaraguan umpire yelled, "Ply Bol" and both sides erupted in a cheer.

The Bombers were the visiting team and battled first, so the Shocks took the field. As they did the Marines could hear a mix chorus of "Buenos Suertes" and "Muere Bombers."

The game was pretty well balanced until the top of 8th inning when Junior Wilson hit a ground double to left field allowing Harmon and Reynolds to score putting the Bombers ahead 9-6. The Shocks came back with a run in the bottom of the 8th off of an error made by Duffy Burns.

The Shocks held the Bombers scoreless in the top of the ninth. The Shocks took the field trailing 9-7. Earl the Pearl Thomas took the mound. He had two outs and the best of the Shocks' batters, a fellow by the name of Hernández, was at bat. The tension was pervasive. With the call of each pitch, one side would cheer or the other would book.

Baseball game in Nicaragua-*Official History Division Photo Nicaragua Collection*

Finally, with a full count, Hernández hammered a line drive to short. The athletic Junior Wilson gracefully fielded it and fired across the field to Oscar Knopf who placed his glove on the shoulder of the sliding Hernández.

"You're out!" called by the American umpire, a sergeant from Brigade headquarters.

The crowd noise erupted and the Shocks' manager stormed the field in protest.

Captain Vickers followed to hear the plea.

Pretty soon the crowd and players became quiet awaiting the final verdict. That lasted until a Marine spectator threw a firecracker at the conference.

With that, the home fans rushed the field. They charged the conference, yelling in a strange obscene language.

Escaping the bedlam, the Bombers ran to their trucks.

Finally, safe on the departing trucks and roaring in laughter at the winning outcome, they immediately looked forward to the next baseball game between them and the Nicaraguan Railroad Company's team, "the STEAM."

Chapter 24: Fliers Meet A Determined Enemy–October 8 and 9, 1927

Managua Aerodrome, 8:30 AM October 8, 1927. "Dibling," Sergeant Frank Dowdell, Lieutenant Earl Thomas's observer, called out.

"Yeah, Sergeant Dowdell."

"Did the Gunner tell you where we're going this morning?" Dowdell asked referring to Chief Marine Gunner Michael Wodarczyk.

"No, just to be ready to go by 1000. I suspect we'll be patrolling along the Río Murra and Mount Chipote looking for our bandito buddies like we had been for the past few weeks."

"I don't know how far we'll get. Weather-wise we've been pretty lucky the past couple of weeks," he said, pausing to look north toward the mountains. "It's still the rainy season, you know." Then turning his head back at the aerodrome Dowdell said, referring to the pilots, "Here they come now. Ought to know in a moment or two. Looks like they have the XO in tow."

Captain Stan Archibald, the executive officer acting as the head of the aviation squadron while Major Rowell was on leave in the States, walked out of the hanger with Thomas and Wodarczyk and stopped by the two observers. Looking at the four Marines he said, "You all have a good flight. See you when you get back. Oh, and don't forget, we have a baseball practice scheduled for 1600 here in the field."

They all made a "see you then, Sir" kind of comments and climbed into their DeHavillands with the two pilots briefing their observers.

In moments, the two DH-4s lumbered into the air, fully stocked with ammunition for their Lewis machine guns and sandwiches made by Cook First Class Duffy Burns. They flew north in search of Sandino's hideaway and checked on a morning patrol, heading toward Ocotal from Jícaro.

East of The Río Murra at The Foot Of El Chipote, 9:00 AM. "Señor Rivas, how did you escape death at Ocotal when my papa did not?" the 11-year old Manuel Aguirre asked.

José Rivas, the 50-year old mule driver or "el arriero," holding the reins of the lead mule in a three-mule pack train headed for Sandino's camp, looked down compassionately at the bright, orphaned boy. "Manny, I was fortunate not to be slaughtered by the airplanes like your brave father and those other national heroes. My job as uno arriero was to stay with the mules at the general's headquarters. The airplanes only attacked the men in the town. Your father was my good friend. That is why the general asked that I adopt you."

After three or four minutes, the inquisitive youth started, "Señor Rivas, my friends say you are a good shot with that rifle of yours—the one in the mule's pack," the youth said while pointing to the stock of a rifle barely visible on the right side of the pack.

"I'm a fair shot, Manny." Rivas said modestly.

"They tell me that you darn near shot a plane two weeks ago, Señor," the youth said, attempting to solicit a daring story.

"Got close I believe. The trick is to duck into the jungle on their second run. The worse thing they can do then is throw coconuts at you."

O'Shea's Headquarters, Jícaro, 9:00 AM. "How are the malaria cases?" First Lieutenant George O'Shea queried the visiting Navy physician, Doctor John B. O'Neill, who had just walked into his office.

O'Neill, a handsome, athletic-looking, recent graduate from Baltimore's Johns Hopkins University School of Medicine, was studying tropical diseases as an intern. He was on a six-month assignment with the 2nd Marine Brigade in Nicaragua. O'Neill raised his eyebrows, looking seriously at the Jícaro commander. "You have to be in the worst area in Nicaragua, George. Think about it. You sent your 10-man patrol out for Ocotal at first light. Most of them were pretty much malaria free. But here, you're down to two healthy Marines, plus yourself and six others weakened but recovering from the disease. The Guardia is not much better. They have four with a touch of malaria.

"It's the cool mountain air. That's the principal cause of your high malaria rate. When I return to Managua, I will file a report about the health hazards here in Jícaro."

"Well, I am glad you came up here; I thought I was doing something wrong."

"You're okay. You are all taking the prescribed quinine. I have already requisitioned additional mosquito netting. Upon my return I will look into the need to have anyone stationed here. Though, Lord, the enemy must be suffering with malaria as you are."

"Well, John, I am glad you are here for these couple of days. Not much going on Saturday nights. I'll be anxious to hear what's happening down in the big city. By the way, I have a superb corporal here by the name of Leinbach, Conwell Leinbach. He plans to attend a medical university when he gets out next year. I assume you two will be talking shop later."

Trail Junction, 10:05 AM. "Manny, be still." Rivas said placing his extended index finger to his lips.

His newly adopted son froze looking nervously at Rivas.

Rivas pointed southwest towards Quilali where he could hear the drone of airplane noise.

Soon young Aguirre heard the noise as well.

"Get way back in there where it's safe," Rivas said in a deliberate manner. "Take cover, my son," Rivas said more emphatically while walking to the mule's pack and slowly withdrawing the rifle, his eyes searching skyward. "Now, Manny!" he ordered.

Rivas remained defiantly in the open path-junction with three mules, daring to be seen. He was bound and determined to avenge the many friends he had lost back on July 17th.

Above the Río Murra, 10:15 AM. Wodarczyk was flying 500 feet below the clouds in the lead aircraft looking for hidden trails at the base of the El Chipote. Thomas flew within sight of the Río Murra about a half mile behind and to the west of Wodarczyk. The enemy could be anywhere. But trails always provided first clues as to where they may be. Both Thomas and his observer, Dowdell, kept an eye on Wodarczyk and Dibling.

Crest of Chipote Mountain-*5025 Defense Dept. (Marine Corps)*

Suddenly the lead aircraft dove towards the ground. Immediately Thomas pulled his stick to the right to learn what Wodarczyk had seen. Wodarczyk's plane had flown toward a the junction of a path and was pulling skyward by the time Thomas and Dowdell could see three mules and a sombrero-covered bandit with a rifle.

Thomas had time to yell back to Dowdell, "I'll bet that's the same dude that Archibald was throwing coconuts at! Get ready to fire!" With that Thomas banked the plane and began his descent. As he approached, the man fired his rifle. The bullet sounded as if it hit near the engine. The plane jerked upward. Thomas instinctively pulled up to assure his plane was flyable.

Smoke spewed from the engine. Thomas banked left to clear the area. Surely he did not want to land near Chipote. Flying over the Río Murra the engine sputtered. "Don't think we can make it, Frank!"

"Hold her up long as you can, Sir!"

"Gonna try to get over the mountains toward Jícaro!" Thomas shouted holding tightly to the shaking stick.

Losing altitude and at 400 feet the plane's smoke trail was quite visible as it crossed the Río Jícaro three miles north of Quilali. Wodarczyk flew in trace calculating his next actions. "Dibling!" he shouted turning around to his observer.

"Sir?"

"Their plane will crash. Draw a map to show where. Got that?"

"Roger, Sir!" Dibling answered affirmatively.

Wodarczyk saw what Thomas was trying to do. "He's trying to clear the mountains!" he shouted back to his observer.

With two prominent hilltops on either side, the plane attempted to climb up the ravine between them. "Frank, hang on we're going in."

With that, the DeHaviland hit the tree tops. Its wings were ripped away immediately. The fuselage plowed like a small train through the trees. In seconds, it was caught in a bottom layer of underbrush and simultaneously stopped on the ravine's rising slope.

"You have that, Dibling?"

"Yes, Sir. It's two hills east of Sapotillal Mountain."

"Good. Now if they made it, we are going to draw a map for them so they can get to Jícaro.

Start doing that now, and I'll fly over the site."

In the downed plane, Thomas asked in a quiet voice, "Frank, you okay?"

"Not sure, Lieutenant? Let's try to get out of here."

As the two dazed pilots opened their seat belts and climbed out of their barrel-like cockpits, Wodarczyk's plane buzzed overhead flying just over the broken treetops.

Thomas attempted to wave, but was too late as Wodarczyk had already flown past the crash site. Almost out of the plane, Thomas said in a weak voice, "Frank, we can't forget the guns."

"Right, Lieutenant. I'll get mine."

"I have mine," Thomas said as Wodarczyk's aircraft roared overhead and was gone in a flash. After their crash and the other plane's noise they barely heard the message weight fall through the trees. The small missile landed 10 feet from where the propeller had been mounted on the plane.

Dowdell raced over to it, bent over and opened the leather message holder. "It's a map, Sir.

Tells us where we are and where Jícaro is."

"Let me see, Frank," he replied as a raindrop hit the map.

Trail Junction, 10:20 AM. "You got him, Señor, you got him! Bueno! Bueno!" Manuel Aguirre shouted while bursting from the underbrush.

"You were supposed to take cover. Why didn't you?"

"I did," showing the cut he acquired on his right forearm.

"I didn't mean here in the underbrush. I meant back by the big trees. You have much to learn my son."

"Lo siento, Señor."

"We will discuss this later, Manny. Do you know how to get to the camp from here?"

"Si señor, it's up this trail--maybe a mile. Do you mean Chipote?"

"Si. Do you know where the general's office is located?"

"Si, Señor."

"I want you to run there as fast as you can. Tell General Sandino that the plane was headed toward Sapotillal ridge. I will stay here with the mules for three hours in case his soldiers need me to point the way. Then I will come to the camp myself with the mules. Now you go!"

"Si, mi padre," the youth said running up the hill to Chipote. "I will be telling all my friends about my new father's bravery."

O'Shea's Headquarters, 11:00 AM. "We must be getting some mail," O'Shea said after hearing what seemed to be a DH-4 attempting to land on his roof.

"Wow! Are all the mail drops that close?" Doctor John O'Neill asked.

"Nah, Doc. Something's going on." O'Shea said standing up. "Let's see."

O'Neill rose immediately and followed the lieutenant out the office door to the former store's main room.

Corporal Neel came rushing through the doorway of the old tienda with a message sack in his hand.

"Here, Lieutenant," Neel said with his arm outstretched.

O'Shea rapidly untied the sack containing two small pieces of paper. The scribbled note on the first one was readable. O'Shea read out loud. "DH-4 down on Sapotillal ridge, 3 miles N of Quilali, 1 mile W of Jícaro river. 2 aviators. 2 Lewis guns. Much ammo. Request you attempt to rescue. Will meet you along Jícaro 3 Miles N Quilali at 0900 tomorrow. Returning to home for additional birds."

Then he showed the others the hastily drawn map with a bold X in a ravine between two rather steep hills.

"Corporal Sumner!"

"Sir!"

"I want you to take two NGs on the best mules we have and get that patrol back here.

They're camping near San Fernando tonight."

"Yes, Sir."

"If I am not here when you get back, I will have left you and Sergeant Glasser specific instructions. Do not rest until you return here with the patrol."

"Got it, Sir."

Looking at the doctor, O' Shea said, "John, I need you to come with us. No telling what condition those aviators are in."

"All right, George."

"Connie, you stay back with the sick and maintain vigilance until Sumner comes back with Sergeant Glasser and the patrol."

"Yes, Sir."

"Neel, get Sergeant Melendez over here pronto! Oh, and get what mules and horses we have saddled up and ready to go."

As Corporal Neel spun to go to the Guardia house, O'Shea said, "Doctor, how are your boots,? We'll be going by foot most of the way."

"They're Marine-issue and broken in for the past month."

"Good, because the more I think about it, the more we cannot wait for the patrol. The bandits are all over the place. If those pilots have a chance at all, we better get going.

"All right then," O' Shea murmured to himself while contemplating his next move. "PFC Welch, it's 1130. Pass the word to the men that I want all able men assembled in the street and ready to go by 1145.

"Oh!" O'Shea said turning around toward the front door, "Buenos Dias, Sergeant Melendez. Have you heard what has happened?"

"Un poco, Señor."

"John, you better get ready. Travel light, although we'll be gone for a couple of days." Looking at the Guardia sergeant, O'Shea began, "Melendez, the plane brought this message.

Trail Junction, 11:45 AM. Rivas, the arriero marksman could hear the horses and mule hooves over the sound of their war cries from the top of Chipote. This was not unlike their shouting when first they entered Ocotal nearly three months earlier. Manny must have run all the way, he thought. Soon, nearly 150 riders neared the trail junction.

Sócrates Sandino pulled his horse to a halt next to the mule handler, forcing the others behind him to bunch up into one another, particularly those still coming down the hill trail. "You are Señor Rivas, our hero?"

"I am Rivas, Señor."

"You have excited the whole camp. My brother is very pleased. He waits for you at the top. More than three hundred men will follow to help capture the two aviators. Your son says you can confirm the direction their smoking plane flew."

"Si, Señor Sandino. They crossed the Río Murra north of here, perhaps two kilometers further up. I am sure they crossed the Jícaro south of the Murra Mountains. I didn't see or hear much after that since they become lower and lower in the sky."

"Es bueno, Señor."

"Pero, Señor…"

"Si, Rivas?"

"I did see the other plane dive a couple of times. I am not sure but it must have been close to Mount Sapotillal."

"Es muy bueno, Rivas," Sandino said. Then turning his anxious horse to the saddled men, Sandino shouted, "Vamos amigos!"

Río Jícaro Trail, Seven Miles North of Quilali, 5:30 PM. O'Shea raised his right arm in the air and clenched his fist, the accepted military signal to stop. Then he spoke to the Marine non- commissioned officer immediately in front of him, "Corporal Neel, get up front and tell the point to hold up. We'll be staying here for the night."

"Sir, while I'm up there, do you want me to post security for the night?"

"Right, I'll take care of the rear security."

"John," he now addresses Dr. O'Neill, Doctor O'Neill, "if you don't mind, check the men, including the NGs. We've gone about 10 miles, and we need the light to find the aviators. Right now, I'm concerned about malaria flare ups and bad feet."

"Sure thing, George."

"While you are talking with them, pass the word we'll be moving out again," pausing to look up at the sky after feeling the first drops of rain coming from a very dark and threatening sky, "at 0630."

"Will do. Somehow I am not suspecting a good night sleep."

Ops Office, Managua Aerodrome, October 9, 1927. "Captain Archibald, may I request you stay back here, Sir," Technical Sergeant Roy Jolson pleaded to the squadron's executive officer who was all ready to fly. "I could really use a hand. Damn Brigade's already peppering me with Status Report requests. I am having a hard-enough time working the flight schedule. Despite the weather reports, every one of our pilots are confident that they alone can find both the plane and the pilots! Bottom line is I could sure use your help managing the situation."

Always, Archibald thought to himself. Always I am to stay back to mind the store. When I was a lieutenant I could fly, all I wanted. Darn!

"Weather? I thought the dry season started last month."

"It may have, but the rain god up in those high mountains didn't get the word."

"All right, how many flights do you have scheduled?

"I have three flights of two birds each scheduled this morning. They are an hour apart. By the time the third flight leaves, the first flight should be on the way back here to refuel."

"Who's leading the first flight?"

"I have Gunner Wodarczyk leading the first flight. He already knows where he'll meet the patrol from Jícaro. At that point, they'll be about a mile away from the crash site. By the time the patrol gets near the crash site, Lieutenant Schilt will be there with the second flight. We should be able to keep two birds on station all day—weather permitting."

"How about the third flight?"

"Lieutenant JC Harmon is a good friend of Lieutenant Thomas. I've asked him to lead that flight."

"That makes sense. I am going to the field to watch Mr. Wodarczyk take off, and then I'll be back."

"Thanks, sir. I really appreciate that."

Río Jícaro, Three miles North of Quilali, 8:00 AM. The patrol moved four miles in the light rain. "Corporal Neel; hold 'em up. This is where we'll meet the plane. May as well rest. I'm sure we'll have a busy day." Then O'Shea added, "Before you do, better post security fore and aft."

"Will do, Lieutenant."

"George, I can see just how valuable these planes are to you guys out here in the jungle," Dr. O'Neill said, "and, of course, they couldn't begin to locate their pilots out here without you."

An hour later. The noise of one of the two DH-4s flying overhead filled the river valley. The lead plane suddenly broke away and dove in on the waiting Marines. Its arrival awakened the six sleeping Marines and Guardia soldiers.

Corporal Neel held a retrieved the message, "Damn near got me, Lieutenant! I'm getting to hate that, Sir."

O'Shea smiled and said while opening the message, "Well, let's see how close we are."

"Says we're one mile due east of the crash site. Unfortunately, we have to go back a little over three miles to get to the base of Sapotillal ridge. From there we can access the road and trail system along the ridge. Here's the really bad news—the ridge is socked in, and they will not be able to support us up there." Then pausing to evaluate the information for a few seconds, the lieutenant looked up and said, "All right Neel and Melendez, let's get the men saddled up and going."

Two hours later the patrol had left the Río Jícaro cart road and was well into the climb up toward Mount Sapotillal. The road rose at a steady rate, frequently avoiding the crests of small hills that dotted the sides of the mountain.

Near the top, a native woman was walking down the road toward the patrol.

Melendez, walking beside O'Shea, announced, "Lieutenant, I will talk to the woman."

O' Shea nodded in agreement and held up the patrol.

After listening to the mountain gibberish from the woman for five minutes, O'Shea finally interrupted with some impatience, "Sergeant Melendez, we have to get going. What'd she say?"

"She heard the plane crash yesterday señor, but she did not see any pilots."

"Well, thank her and let's get going." Then refocusing, "See that house up there about 250 meters. It's on the hill."

"Si, Señor."

"You and I are going to talk to anyone who is there."

"Si, Señor."

The two patrol leaders entered the small mountain-top house fifteen minutes later. They came out in about four minutes. Once outside, O'Shea asked his men posted along the narrow road if they saw any movement up the hill in front of them. "Nothing," was the collective answer, most of them remained noiseless with heads moving left and right.

O'Shea looked at his point man. With his right index finger pointing skyward, he snapped his wrist. And with that the lead Marine started moving up the hill.

The road stopped after weaving in and out around several hills. Taking its place was a wide trail. Now strung out along the mountain trail, the patrol skirted one particularly-steep hill near the summit on the hill's left side. Beyond that, the principal trail took a decided turn to the right.

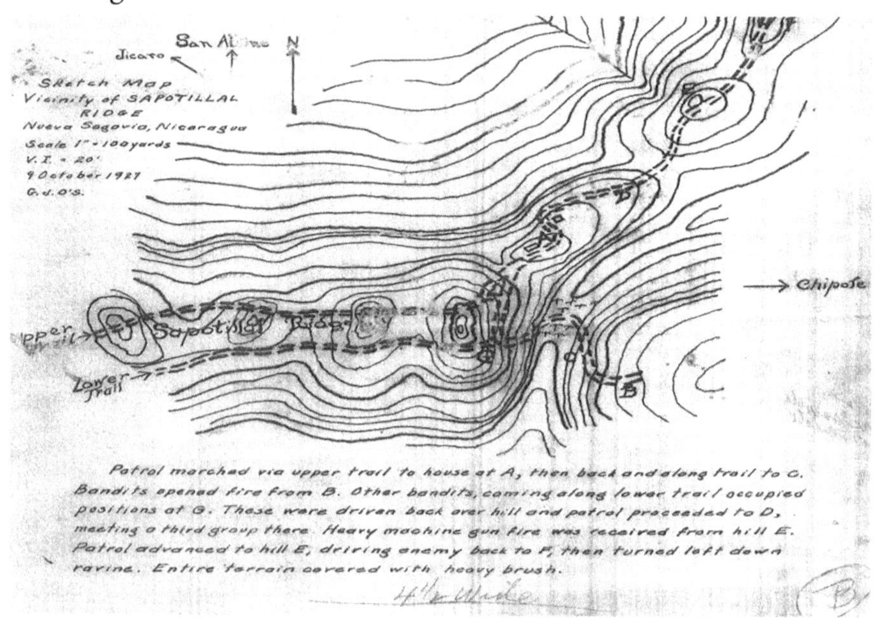

**Sketch Map of Fight at Sapotillal Ridge-*9 Oct 1927-*
NA127/38/30/93.55

230

Precisely at the moment the advance guard began following the trail's right turn, an enemy force fired on them blocking any forward movement. From their left on another hill, 200 more bandits opened fire. The enemy's vast fire superiority convinced O'Shea that the bandits had possessed plenty of ammunition. Soon, from behind them another 100 bandits opened fire.

With enemy now on three sides and a steep hill on the fourth side, O'Shea yelled, "Neel, we're going to turn back and run the smaller force off that hill to our rear."

Melendez, sensing the redirection over the noise of the fight, started barking commands as well. "Vamos! Vamos!"

The small patrol was caught in a crossfire. Making matters worse for the patrol, a bandit observer directed others where to throw hand grenades and dynamite bombs.

Dynamite Bombs *USMC History Division #SN-8*

"Save your ammo! No automatic fire," O'Shea yelled. "We're attacking the small hill."

The high volume of war sounds filled the damp mountain air. The firing from the rear continued relentlessly as the men reached the road again and attacked the hill occupied by 100 bandits in the direction of the Río Jícaro. Sergeant Melendez, trying to reach the front of the assault, fell dead with a bullet in his head.

Private First Class Welch cried out, "Sir, watch out! Hit the deck!" as a dynamite bomb landed between them. They both leaped away from the bomb and landed on the ground. The bomb exploded upward injuring no one. O'Shea charged forward while Welch waited for the bandits, following in trace of them. Soon he rose, grenade in hand with pin pulled, and threw the explosive. Three bandits died while Welsh hustled up to participate in pushing the bandits off the hill. Private McKenzie, the rear guard, fired and killed three with his Thompson. Immediately, the firing from the rear stopped.

Corporal Neel fired rifled grenades clearing a path for the frontal assault being led by O'Shea. Now back on the road, the lieutenant flipped grenades into the right side of the brush, seemingly filled with enemy riflemen.

Private Struck reached the road and ran up beside O'Shea to begin clearing the left side. Within a minute, he saw an enemy stand up ten yards in front of him aiming his rifle at the lieutenant. Struck shot him through the throat with his pistol. Over the gurgling noise, O'Shea said, "I owe you one, Struck."

Private Green, in a hollow between two hills, found three men hiding in a banana grove.

He killed two and wounded the third.

The Guardia soldiers, equally as deliberate as the Marines, took careful aim before shooting and advanced under cover.

At this point, O'Shea assessed the situation and calculated his next move. The horse with rations, the horse with the blanket rolls, the saddled horse, and a saddled mule had been killed. Only one horse remained. The narrow, tree-covered trail heading north to the San Albino road and to safety was his choice. "Private Golak, take the point. Keep on the alert and get us the hell out of here," O'Shea directed.

Within 200 yards, Private Golak raced back to his lieutenant and said, "Lieutenant, I spotted a whole bunch of them two hills away coming down the trail towards us!"

The athletic Doctor O'Neill, who had acquired a pistol, led the initial charge up the first of the two hills. Half way up the hill he was held up by a machine gun raking the trail. O'Shea called out, "Get Neel up here with his grenade rifle, Golak."

A loud "Sir!" was Golak's only response.

Neel, nearby, ran forward. "Where is the machine gun, Doctor O'Neill?"

"See that big tree with no branches?"

"Yeah."

"He's just behind and to the left of it."

Within a moment, Neel maneuvered to the branchless tree. "Hey Doc. Watch this!" With that Neel's rifle fired and 20 seconds later an explosion on the hill silenced the machine gun's fire. Neel poked the doctor on the shoulder, smiled and said, "Pretty neat, eh, Doc?"

But the noose tightened. Three Guardia were killed. Their weapons and ammo were quickly recovered by the remaining Guardia.

Above the noise of the rifle fire, O'Shea shouted to O'Neill, "John, these bandits are closing in. Our guides deserted and my compass fell off back there somewhere. I hate to do this but we have to leave the trail and cut through this thick under brush. It's our only chance if we're getting out of here."

"I agree, George. Let's do it!" O'Neill responded.

"All right, Neel keep the men and the NGs close together. We can't afford to get split up. We'll never find anyone who gets lost." With that, at 5:45 PM, O'Shea dropped left and disappeared fast down a very steep ravine that headed north out of the Murra mountains. The others followed one at a time with Corporal Neel last.

O'Shea led his patrol through the underbrush for the next 29 hours paralleling but avoiding the Río Jícaro road, fearing that it was too dangerous. At 11:30 PM on October 10th, the men on patrol suffering from exposure, complete exhaustion, bruises, cuts from thorns and insect bites arrived in Jícaro. Sergeant Glasser took one look at them and said, "Holy smokes, Sir. We'll take over from here!" Then looking at his dependable corporal, Glasser ordered, "Leinbach, assemble the men!"

As Leinbach moved out to assist the returning patrol, Glasser looked over at O'Shea and asked, "What the hell happened, Sir"

Sipping on some much-needed water, O'Shea said in a subdued voice. "I don't know. As soon as we got to the top of Sapotillal Ridge, we encountered over a hundred bandits. Dozens on various hills. We lost all the animals and had three NGs killed. The trails were totally blocked. We were lucky to escape through the jungle to get back here. Go out and help Leinbach. I need a couple hour sleep."

Chapter 25: Rowell Returns From Leave

CO's Office, Aerodrome, October 13, 1927. "A half day work schedule?" Major Ross Rowell said while slowly placing the squadron order on his desk and looking up at the captain braced at attention.

"Welp," was Archibald's attempt to get a word in edgewise.

Rowell shook his head in disgust. "We lose two aviators, and you're giving the men a half day off?"

"Only if their work is done, Sir."

"When, may I ask, would the work be done while two men are missing?" Silence.

"And Green Nose. My bird. Gone. What do you have to say about that?"

"Sir, Lieutenant Harmon did a great job. I saw him miss that hedge row. Good flying, Sir.

We did save the engine and some other components, Sir. It wasn't a total loss, sir."

Rowell did not say a word. He didn't have to, his raised eyebrow expressed his doubt.

"Sir, it must have been contaminated fuel from Ocotal."

"This report, captain. The one from the legation and the brigade MPs. Have you seen it?"

"Oh, yes, Sir. Yesterday, Sir."

"You know of the 'The Cantina Cowboys.' I assume?"

"Well, I may have heard of them, Sir." Then quickly adding. "But I didn't think they existed."

"Apparently the Cantina Cowboys rode in with stolen mules, threw firecrackers, and tore apart the 'Campo de Amour'. Do you know the bar, Captain?"

"I have been there a couple of times, Sir.... err before my wife Jeanie came down."

"And their mules were found near the aerodrome. So they are our guys."

"Perhaps, Sir. I interrogated all the suspected men and they all denied any involvement even though each of the suspected men were on liberty that night."

"Then last week Harmon wrecks another plane at Ocotal. I take it he did all he could."

"Oh, yes Sir. The oil pump had sheared off and the motor burned out. JC made a perfect landing in a nearby field. He didn't even break a shock absorber."

"And two nights ago, according to the log book, Private Detra almost became a casualty. A dead one. He came back from liberty by himself. I thought I had a standing order never to go on liberty alone," Rowell said shaking his head.

"Sir, I know he almost got sliced to pieces by that drunken villager swinging his knife. Sixty-nine stitches. Good thing Rosy, err... I mean Corporal Dykes, came along. He darn near killed the native—took that guy 24 hours to come to."

Leaning back on his chair and feeling more relaxed that Archibald actually did as well as he did, Rowell said, "Stan, I understand you did all that you could do. I am just glad I'm back. Now, before I go to the Brigade OPS briefing this afternoon, tell me everything we're doing to find Thomas and Dowdell."

Chapter 26: The Search For The Missing Aviators

Detachment Headquarters, Matagalpa, October 15, 1927. "Thanks for hustling over, Bob," First Lieutenant Moses Gould, Commanding Officer, Matagalpa Detachment, said while greeting his Guardia counterpart. "Looks like the war is really gearing up."

Matagalpa taken on May 11, 1927-*Official Photo USMC #k-3-28*

"How's that, Mo?" asked Second Lieutenant Robert Hogaboom.

Gould said, "Hey, do you recall O'Shea's report we intercepted off the wire, two days ago about his encounter on Sapotillal Ridge?"

"I do."

"Well, based on that report, the Brigade sending us north to locate that plane and the pilots. Here, take a look at our orders," Gould said handing the teletype document to the Guardia officer.

Skimming the directive from the 3rd Battalion, 5th Marines, Hogaboom said, "Ol' George really must have run into the bulk of the rebels. According to these orders, we'll be pushing north first thing in the morning. Oh, and I see there's another patrol coming south from Jícaro led by Second Lieutenant Chappell. You know him?"

"Only that he recently started patrolling from Ocotal."

"How long do you figure we'll be gone for, Mo?"

"I figure it will take 10-11 days to get to the wreckage. 'Til we get back?" Gould eyes quickly looked up toward the ceiling while calculating then refocused on Hogaboom, "You'd better plan that we'll be gone for a month."

"All right," Hogaboom responded. "I have 50 mules and five horses. How 'bout you?"

"We have 35 mules and six horses. How many more you think we'll need?"

"I'd say another 30 mules. What do you think?"

"That ought to be good."

"I'll get Sergeant Álvarez on renting the other mules from the locals ASAP."

"Sounds good. Let's get ready to take off at 0600 tomorrow but plan to meet back here at 1900 to finalize patrol details."

One Mile North Río Coco October 25, 1927. Gould's patrol consisted of his 25 enlisted Marines, Lieutenant Hogaboom and two other Guardia officers, 40 Guardia Nacional soldiers and 119 mules and horses. The patrol passed through valley-city of Jinotega on October 19th and reached the Rio Coco six days later.

Jinotega; Taken October 1927- *USMC Historical Division*

A young Marine corporal on horseback rode up to Lieutenant Gould shortly after a DH-4 dove down on the patrol. "Sir, the plane dropped this message."

Gould opened and then read the wrapped message. Looking at the bearer of the message he said, "Corporal, ride up front and ask Lieutenant Hogaboom to join me here. Looks like we have to go west, cross the Río Jícaro, pass through Quilali, then the plane should be about two miles further west. Tell Sergeant Mason to head west until he reaches the Río Jícaro; then ride north and find a place to cross the river. Remind him that we're in bandit country. Tell everyone to stay alert for an ambush."

"Aye, aye Sir," the corporal said then turned his mount around and rode to the front of the column.

Jícaro, October 25, 1927. After a brief recovery, Second Lieutenant Clarence Chappell, 24 enlisted Marines, Dr. O'Neill, one Guardia lieutenant and 15 Guardia soldiers had been directed by airplane message to begin their patrol from Jícaro on the 24th. They patrolled south for six hours, holding up at Jícarito. The next day they

239

departed Jícarito at 7:AM and were told to hold up at the ranch owned by Antonio Lopez at 10:00 AM. Now that the skies had cleared, the "air service," a common reference to the squadron, was coordinating the movement of the two patrols.

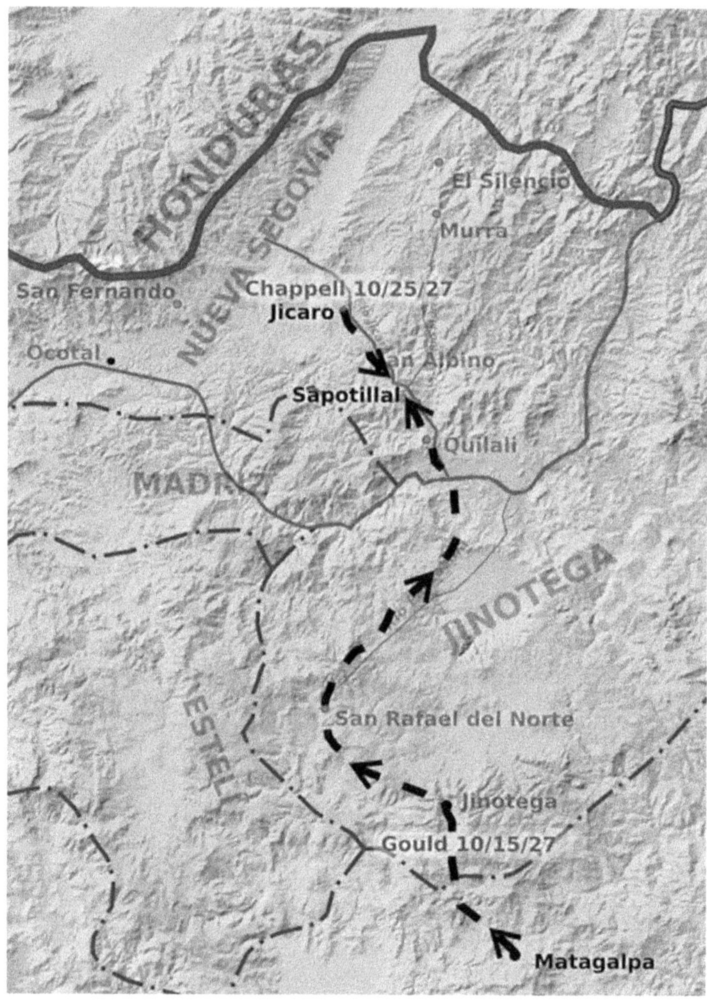

Chappell-Gould Patrols October 1927

However, despite the air-dropped message at 4:30 PM telling him to begin closing in on the wreckage, Chappell held his position as he had heard several explosions ahead of him. He reasoned that night movement would be more treacherous than fighting in the morning.

Ops Office, Managua Aerodrome October 26, 1927. Technical Sergeant Roy Jolson looked up to see his boss enter his office. He put down his lit cigar, snapped to attention, and said, "Welcome back, boss."

"Thanks, Top. I understand you have had your hands full," Major Rowell responded.

"That's not the half of it, sir. It's hard enough with us losing four planes and two pilots, but now that Colonel Gulick has the brigade they are requesting one report after another. Thank God Captain Archibald is here; he's been a savior."

Looking around the room, Rowell saw that the bulletin board with the editorial cartoons

"Another American Aviation Accomplishment"- *Diane Rowland*

clipped from the St. Louis Post Gazette now had a third one. Rowell studied the clipping for a minute. Then, without looking back at Jolson, the rusty-haired squadron leader asked, "Technical Sergeant Jolson, you obviously want to post these editorial cartoons. Why do you want to do that?"

"Well, Sir," the question caught the man with the mid-west accent off-guard. "You see, Sir. Well, the liberal bastards are making my boys look like the bad guys. And I resent that, Sir!"

"How many people did we kill in Ocotal, Top?"

"Give or take, 300, Sir."

"And how many, do you believe, were innocent civilians? You know, men with no guns."

"I figure a bunch, Sir. But they were hanging out with the wrong crowd."

Rowell, shaking his head said, "That's the problem, Top. Think about the unions in Detroit. I know you believe them to be communistic. You have said that many times. Supposed the car-plant owners bombed one of the plants where they knew there were many union organizers there and 100 innocent workers were killed. Who comes out as the good guy and who comes out as the bad guy?"

"Well, Sir that, that just wouldn't happen."

"You're not answering my question, top."

"Well, sir…"

The Ops office door opened and three aviators walked in. "Welcome back, Skipper," Chief Marine Gunner Michael Wodarczyk said with a cheery voice.

Rowell shot a glance at Jolson, ducked his chin and raised his eyebrows for a second, implying, "Think about that." He then turned to greet the trio.

"Good morning, men."

"Sir," Wodarczyk answered, "we're not interrupting anything? Are we?"

"No. No, you are not, Mike."

"Nice seeing you, Major," First Lieutenant Frank Schilt greeted his boss. "Sorry you had to come back to this," cocking his head to the map showing Sapotillal ridge with the prominent "X" at a ravine, clearly designating the location of the Thomas-Dowdell crash.

"Sir, are you flying up with us this morning?" Wodarczyk begged.

"I was planning to fly north, if Top here can spare a plane."

"Oh, yes Sir, we have one. Sorry it's not ol' Green Nose."

The major shot a menacing glance at the technical sergeant.

"Really, Sir. I am sorry."

Wodarczyk sensing the awkwardness in the air said, "Sir, have you met Captain Carl Byrd?"

Rowell, also realizing the sensitive atmosphere he himself had caused, said, "No I haven't." He smiled and said, "Welcome to the squadron, Carl."

The rugged-face, mature man replied, "Thank you, Sir."

Never having heard of his name, Rowell asked, "You been flying long, Carl?"

"No Sir, I just picked up my wings two months ago." Byrd paused understanding the new wings and his looks just didn't fit logically. "You see sir, I have been in the Corps since 1917 and I have always wanted to fly."

"That's great." Rowell noted. "Want to fly with me this morning?"

"Why, yes Sir. I would be honored."

"Then good," Rowell said. "Let's fly up to Sapotillal ridge this morning to assist those two patrols."

Sapotillal Ridge, October 26, 1927. At 7:00 AM, Chappell's patrol moved out in search of the missing plane and pilots. The wreck occurred two weeks earlier. Lieutenant O'Shea's after action report on his patrol established the fact Sapotillal Ridge was crawling with bandits. As a new lieutenant, Chappell approached his mission cautiously. They set out to climb a small ridge rising generally toward Mount Sapotillal. Soon, there was an explosion 800 yards in front of them. His second in command, Sergeant Shumate, continued moving forward, down into the saddle of the ridge he was following. Shumate held up the forward movement at the bottom of the saddle. In front of him was a clearing with a vegetated hill on the other side. Shumate directed his Marines to draw the enemy's fire. They fired at likely ambush spots. In response the enemy shouted "Sandino," "Sacasa" and "Chamorro."

Chappell organized the fire on the enemy for a short while. Soon a second group of enemy soldiers who closed behind the Marine patrol fire on them from the small hill they had just come down. Chappell directed an assault back up the hill, took the hill, set in a defensive position and displayed his ground panels to wait for the planes.

From 1000 feet above Sapotillal Ridge, Rowell had Byrd fly the plane up to Quilali, where Wodarczyk's gunner/observer Corporal Dibling threw a message that directed Gould's large patrol to go two miles west along a road they had just crossed. The message concluded that the crash site would be to their right up in the ravine.

Wodarczyk, who was commander of the flight, veered north to Sapotillal ridge where Chappell's patrol should be. The other planes followed. As they approached the ridge, Chappell's distress message, spelled out on panels, came into view. The planes circled the hill across from Chappell's and soon saw the enemy soldiers nervously gazing back and running off the hill, fearful of the air threat above them. Wodarczyk signaled to attack.

Byrd's first dive on the enemy showed a cautionary hesitation of the new aviator. Over the roar of the plane's engine, Rowell yelled to Byrd that he would make the next dive. With all Marine planes having flight controls in both fore and aft cockpits, Byrd simply singled he was giving up the stick. With that, Rowell took the plane up to 1500 feet passing through small puffs of clouds, executed a full loop so smoothly that the new pilot in the front hardly was aware it had happened, and dove in a 45-degree angle on the enemy. Half way down, he fired 20 rounds from his Lewis gun. At 200 feet, he released one of his 17-pound wing-mounted bombs. At 100 feet, he ended the dive and firmly pulled the stick back to his seat. Byrd felt the positive three Gs immediately and could barely raise his arms when he felt a firm tap on his right shoulder and another yell from the rear cockpit, "You got it!"

Welcome to Marine Aviation Captain Carl Byrd! Lieutenant Frank Schilt thought after he witnessed what Rowell had just done. Wodarczyk hadn't missed it either. Both veteran pilots, now forty yards from each other, smiled, shaking their heads. Wodarczyk pointed west toward Ocotal and signaled they would refuel.

At the Ocotal aerodrome, Major Rowell called to Wodarczyk and Schilt while the others were busy turning the hand pump on the barrels. "Mike, Frank, if I'm not mistaken, Lieutenant Chappell is going to hold until we redirect Gould to his location. Once together, they can safely move to the wreckage site."

"So, Boss, you want to fly over Chappell's patrol, verify that he's still there, then go on to Gould's patrol?"

"Right, Mike. Then Frank, you drop a message directing Gould over to Chappell. Neither patrol will be ready to move until the morning. You two return tomorrow and then vector them to the plane."

"Got it, sir."

Wodarczyk watched Rowell walk over to talk to Byrd who was assisting Corporal Dibling and Corporal "Junior" Wilson in refueling the three planes. "I figure Rusty will have some more instructions, eh Frank?"

"No doubt, Mike."

"Damn, am I ever glad he's back."

"You're right about that my friend!"

Sapotillal Ridge, October 28, 1927. Relying on the aviators, First Lieutenant Moses Gould finally linked up with Second Lieutenant Clarence Chappell two days later. "Mo, great to see a friendly face!"

"Right, Chaps, likewise. Sure are a lot of bad asses 'round here looking for us," Gould said winking at the younger lieutenant on his first patrol. Gould then cast his more-experienced eye on Chappell's men and mules. "Hey, how are your mules? They look a bit tired out."

"Tell you what, Mo. They should be. Haven't been watered for two days.

"Mine need a rest as well or neither of us will have them when we need them."

"By the way Mo, I want you to meet Dr. John O'Neil. He has been with us since we left Jícaro. If your men have some medical needs he will be able to help them".

After two days of rest, on October 30, they followed the guidance of the aviators and found the wreckage of the airplane. It was mostly at the floor of the valley between two fingers coming off the ridge. The motor and all its metal parts were intact; the machine guns were missing. They assumed that the pilots escaped as there was no sign of them.

The combined patrol reached Jícaro on the first of November after encountering an estimated 250 bandits six miles south of Jícaro near the village of Espino. Two Guardia Nacional soldiers and six mules were killed in that 35-minute skirmish.

Gould's report, made the following day, expressed his opinion; that the two aviators were dead; the air service was invaluable in coordinating the patrols; the 250 bandits who fought near Espino were protecting Sandino's headquarters of Chipote; and a large Marine force of at least 150 men would be needed to take Chipote.

Office of the Department Commander, Department of Nueva Segovia, Ocotal. The number of Marine detachments and Guardia Nacional companies had grown substantially in the past three months. The detachments were now in Ocotal, Telpaneca, and Jícaro. All had companies of Guardia Nacional assigned to them. Three other Marine detachments were being planned with priority going to Quilali followed by one at Jalapa and one at San Albino. To coordinate these detachments, a Department of Nueva Segovia was created by the Brigade commander, Colonel Gulick. Captain R. W. Peard from the 5th Marines became the first to command this northern division. Stationed in Ocotal, Peard's first operation was the Chappell-Gould patrol.

Gould's patrol report, sent from Jícaro on November 2nd, forecasted events to come. Chappell was to remain in Jícaro, while Lieutenant Gould was sent on to Ocotal.

On the afternoon of November 5th, First Lieutenant McQuade, detachment commander at Ocotal, knocked firmly on the frame of the open office door of the Department Commander. Peard looked up at the muscularly-built, Quantico football star, smiled, and said, "Come on in, Mac. What's up?"

"Sir, I thought you may want to know that Lieutenant Gould's patrol just crossed the Río Dippilo Bridge. They ought to be here any moment."

"Great, Mac. Let's get out there to welcome him."

As the captain and lieutenant emerged from Department headquarters building, they could see the horses and mules being formed up in the street by the mounted Lieutenant Gould on his two-year- old black bay. The horse was showing signs of fatigue from the last leg of the journey as the sweat foamed on its neck. They had departed Jícaro the previous morning, stayed overnight at the Orosi Ranch and, in the last hour, passed through the small village of Mozonte that overlooks Ocotal. It wasn't a long journey, however, the mountain road followed the ever-changing elevations and was always taxing on the animals. "Sergeant Mason," the lieutenant called out to the husky Marine who had been bringing up the rear.

"Yes, Sir."

"I am going to file my patrol report. Take care of the men and the animals."

"Will do sir."

Gould dismounted, gave the reins of his horse to a corporal next to him, walked over to Peard and McQuade, saluted, and said, "Greetings gentlemen."

Peard returned the salute and responded, "Welcome back Lieutenant Gould."

McQuade added, "How was your patrol, Mo?"

Gould shook his head and noted, "They didn't teach me any of this at Quantico."

"Come on inside and tell me about it. We're dying to know."

Gould told about Chappell's adventures of encountering the enemy protecting Sapotillal Ridge on the 26th, then being saved by the aviators. Shaking his head in complimentary amazement, Gould described the continual support from the aviators who were instrumental in finally tying the two patrols together. They then discovered the wrecked airplane and headed toward Jícaro. Gould related their encounter with

250 bandits before reaching Jícaro. At that point, Captain Peard offered Gould a local beer. "Want one, Mac?"

"Sure, Sir."

As Peard handed both lieutenants a beer, he asked, "So the two aviators, Thomas and Dowdell, simply disappeared?"

"Well I'm not too sure about that, Sir."

"Oh?"

"Señor Presentación Ortiz, the guy who owns the Orosi ranch, told us last night," Gould interrupted himself, "you know the man, don't you, Sir?"

"Sure I do. I've stayed at his ranch a good half dozen times. Nice man."

"Indeed. Well, according to Ortiz, they are both dead."

"How's he know that?"

"Ortiz talked to a brother of one of Sandino's men who was at the spot where they killed them, when they were killed."

"Whoa, does anyone else know this?" Peard asked.

"I doubt it. Ortiz just learned about it last week. And we were the first Americans to stop there since Clarence Chappell stopped there three weeks ago."

"You're right, you were."

"Apparently, the two aviators removed at least one Lewis machine gun after they crashed and attacked some bandits coming toward them. They killed four bandits."

"Good for them!!" McQuade interrupted with a sinister smile.

"When they ran out of ammo, they fled northwest along the valley of the Río Jícaro with only their pistols. They ran into two locals and forced them to guide them to Jícaro. One of the locals suddenly wielded his machete on the aviators and cut one of them badly on the neck. The other aviator shot the guy. But in the confusion the other local escaped. He informed Sandino where the pilots were. The pilots hid in a cave because the one cut had lost a lot of blood. Sandino sent 25 men after them. Apparently they were easy to find —with the blood trail and all. After a small firefight, they were both killed."

"And Ortiz believes that was a true story?"

"Sir, well sort of. Ortiz told us that the man who told it had no idea he would be telling it to any Americans. Then he gave me these two photos and he would not reveal his source. At any rate, he received two copies of both of those late last week."

1stLt Earl Thomas-*The US National Archives*/ US Marine Corps Bandit Series 5214-6

"Why, that's Earl Thomas! Jiminy Christmas! I just met him last month!"

"And this one."

Bandit Antiaircraft (Lewis Gun)

Official Photograph, Photo Section Aircraft Squadron; West Coast Expeditionary Force U.S.M.C.

"Sir, note the Lewis gun on the right. It could have come from Thomas's plane. These guys are gearing up to fight our air service."

"No doubt! I have to pass this on to the brigade. They will be soon be sending us after Sandino. They have to know that we are too thin here to conduct and sustain a large operation against Sandino. In a few months, once we're really into the dry season, and Quilali, Jalapa, and San Albino have detachments, we'll be able to go after him."

CHAPTER 27: AIR-GROUND COMMUNICATIONS

Managua Aerodrome, November 10, 1927. The six-foot, one-inch, black-haired Charge d'affairés had parked the ministry's shiny new Ford sedan in a space marked "VIP" early on the morning of the Marine Corps' 152nd birthday. George Ward, whose younger brother had been a Marine at the end of the big war, was well aware of the importance the day had to all Marines. As he carefully closed the door to the vehicle and looked around, he sensed the orderliness of the airfield complex, the cleanliness surrounding the aerodrome; the short road leading from the aerodrome to the grassy, well-marked airfield with nine bi-winged aircraft parked in a neat row; and the gold-and-scarlet-painted signs designating specific locations for a sundry of flying activities. Twenty aviators were standing by two other planes at the edge of the airfield. While orderly, the only thing that was non-military was a 40-foot wide, ten-foot high canvass banner hung by rope on the side of the that read:

Ward smiled; the baseball league was the result of Minister Eberhardt's project assigned to Ward. The visitor spotted a man walking from the hanger and immediately recognized his host, Major Ross Rowell.

"Happy Birthday, Major."

"Thanks. And," pointing subtly with his thumb at the side of the aerodrome, "thank-you for coordinating the baseball league. It means a lot to my men," adding, "You're going to the Marine Corps Birthday Ball tonight, aren't you George?"

"You bet, Rusty. I haven't missed one since 1924. Best party in town!"

"What kind of show are you doing this morning?"

"I picked up an idea for a mail pickup system when I was home on leave that enables our ground guys to give us messages, maps, letters home and the like. I have Mike Wodarczyk and Frank Schilt. You know them, don't you?"

Raising his eyebrows at a question Ward thought was elementary, "Rusty, who doesn't?"

"Right. Well, they're going to demonstrate the pick-up technique."

"Great. this will be interesting. Seems like there's nothing you guys can't do."

"Let's go out and join them."

Rowell and Ward greeted the men, many of whom Ward came to know in baseball uniforms. Rowell, the consummate innovator, educator and leader of the air squadron, provided the latest from up in the States. Immediately afterwards, Wodarczyk and Schilt and their observers, Corporal Dibling and Captain Frank Pierce, climbed into their planes. As usual, Wodarczyk was flying his DH-4 and Schilt flying his O2B-1, Corsair.

The ground-package recovery technique was quite simple. Two men on the ground would stand about 12 feet apart. Each man held the bottom end of an eight-to-ten-feet-long pole high in the air. A rope, loosely tethered to the top ends of both poles, was suspended between them. The "package" was tied to the middle of the rope.

The concept was that the pilot would target the two men holding up their poles while the observer would lower his own rope. A baseball-size device, tied to the bottom of the observer's rope, would catch the ground rope and rapidly wrap around it three or four times. The observer would feel the tug and immediately pull in his rope into the plane with the package.

Smitty and Junior Wilson, newly-promoted sergeants, emerged from the crowd with their jury- rigged poles. The sergeants fastened the horizontal rope to the end of their poles. Technical Sergeant Walt Heller joined them with the "Package" that turned out to be Dibling's leave orders.

Laughing at his own trickery, Heller said, "Hey men, wait 'til Dibling gets this—you all know that he's been begging for leave for the past three months."

Rowell, who had signed the leave orders the night before, jested, "You sure have faith in the pickup Top. Because I won't sign them again"

The tight group of men laughed at the funny twist given to the first pickup.

Wodarczyk dove down on Smitty and Wilson and leveled off near the aerodrome at about 60 miles per hour and 200 yards away from the poles. The sergeants, standing rigid, felt like the plane was going to hit them. As the plane approached, their eyes widened and jaws opened. Dibling was holding the rope hanging from the left side of the plane. The wrapping ball, dangling at the end of the rope, was more behind the plane then below it.

Mail Pickup System developed by Marine Forces in Nicaragua, 1927-

USMC History Division from the manuscript of General Wilburt S. Brown, USMC (Ret.)

Smitty saw the ball was more on his side than Wilson's. He yelled, "Junior, this way a bit!" They shifted two feet and seconds later the plane came and went. The two looked at the end of their poles. The rope was gone. They never felt it go.

Schilt had the harder pick up. From a simulated mountain side, the maneuver would prevent the leveling off flight pattern that Wodarczyk had just made and would require a 45 degree dive- bombing swoop. Captain Frank Pierce would be forced to let out 45 feet of rope unlike Dibling's 25 feet of line. Rowell had chosen Captains Archibald and Byrd as the pole holders for this event.

Rowell asked both men for their soft covers—because of the wind they would face. They gladly obliged. The CO turned his back to Archibald and Byrd and, while showing the hats to the others, was given a sack by Sergeant Wilson. He opened the bag and like a silent comic asked his audience if they wanted the hats placed into the sack. They enthusiastically urged him on. He did so and slung the sack to Wilson to tie it to the rope held by the pole men. Rowell never missed a trick: his newest pilot with his most senior pilot giving up their own hats as part of the test.

The two captains were soon standing with their suspended rope high in the air bravely watching Schilt's Corsair diving on them. Was this how the bandits felt as bi-planes fell closer and close onto their position? The other twenty aviators and Ward slowly, yet unconsciously, backed away five yards, then fifteen yards, then 30 yards. Rowell remained, closely watching in order to critique the event. As the plane bottomed out fifty feet above them, Byrd stared defiantly into the eyes of apparent death. Archibald's eyes had been closed tight five seconds earlier.

Then came the great noise of the engine, followed by a long gust of howling hurricane-like wind that kicked up a cloud of dry dirt. And suddenly the plane was sky bound. Archibald opened his eyes. The rope was gone. He looked at Byrd who just shook his head at the precarious nature of the task. Both looked at the men who walked into the circle again. The lieutenants cheered for their braveness, cynically laughing with their eyes shut tight.

"Captain Archibald and Technical Sergeant Jolson, get the men started at training this technique. We'll break for lunch at noon."

"We're on it Major," Archibald responded with confidence having been one of the first to execute this new technique.

Ward and Rowell walked back to the parking lot. Ward began the conversation, "Hey Rusty, glad to see you back."

"Thanks. Good to be back."

"Your men finding anything out about El Chipote?"

"Not yet. I've asked George O'Shea up in Jícaro to draw a map where he thinks it is. I'm going to pick it up tomorrow using our new technique."

"Is he schooled up on the technique?"

"Right I, dropped instructions yesterday. Should work, he's excellent at picking up new ideas. By the way, what's going on back at the ministry?"

Ward remained quiet for a moment, then started. "Rusty, I never told you this. You understand?"

Rowell silently nodded.

"President Chamorro is putting pressure on Eberhardt to get Logan Feland back down here again."

Rowell's eyebrows shot upward, "What brought that on?"

"Well, Chamorro is comfortable with Feland."

"And not with Gulick?"

"It's not that so much. He believes if Sandino gets any stronger, he—Chamorro—may lose his support in the upcoming election of deputies and senators. It's scheduled for the 20th—ten days from now. If he has to call on the US, he'd rather have Feland here with all his connections back up in the States than have a colonel with few political ties."

"What's Minister Eberhardt saying?"

"My boss is fearful he'll be replaced or indirectly working for Feland instead of the other way around."

As they arrived at the ministry's car, Ward said, "Not a word, Rusty"

"Trust me, George, that story is going nowhere!"

"All right, Happy Birthday. I'll see you tonight."

"Look forward to it , George. Now I have to get back to my men so that no one wrecks any of my birds."

Every pilot and observer practiced both scenarios. All ground personnel, including the admin clerks, held the poles. Actually there were several misses and a few precarious dives. The pickup ball missed Technical Sergeant Jolson by inches. By 1500 Rowell was satisfied and announced liberty call. He wished them a "Happy 152nd Marine Corps Birthday."

Chapter 28: Finding El Chipote

Echevarria's Headquarters, Sapotillal Ridge, November 11, 1927. "General Echevarria," Major Carlos Quesada said, entering the borrowed mountain home belonging to Antonio Salgado.

"Si, Carlos?"

"General Sandino has arrived."

"Bueno! Gracias." The general in charge of the Segovia military district said as he left his desk to walk through the front door to greet his esteemed visitor.

"Hola, mi general. Thank you for coming from Chipote."

"Manuel, thank you for caring for these loyal boys."

"Señor, let's go inside and have some coffee."

"Excelente, Manuel. Me gusto."

Once inside and with a cup of coffee in hand, Sandino asked, "Manuel, I want to know about your supplies. Do the men have enough grain? Enough salt? Tell me about their ammunition and weapons."

Echevarria detailed the requests from his deployed commanders and the amount of the supply support received by the quartermaster. "Señor, our biggest problem is a lack of grain like beans and sorghum. My soldiers can cut and eat corn. We don't have grinders for sorghum."

"General Echevarria. I want you to invite all the women you meet to grind any grains. If they do not want to come on their own, oblige them with force. If there is no corn field in their village to make tortillas, send them to me. In Chipote, I have more than a hundred men who have not eaten. I can use them and they will be rewarded in the future. It is necessary that we all help each other now."

"Si, comprendo."

"Tell me about your plans for defending Chipote," Sandino asked as he had on each earlier visit.

"Si, Señor. We anticipate the most likely attack on your headquarters to come from the south. Most likely from Quilali. We occupy the Sapotillal ridge and, from there can prevent movement coming south from Ciudad Sandino or "Jícaro" as the Conservatives still call it. From the ridge we will stop any enemy coming north from Jinotega or traveling east from Telpaneca. We have dug trenches in the hills around Quilali and believe we can hold the enemy in the town from our trenches."

"Believe, General?"

"We know we can hold them in the town, Señor!"

"Comprendo. Please continue."

"Once contained in Quilali, we will begin moving our men from Sapotillal ridge to pre-designated positions. Half the men will block the roads coming into and going out of Quilali while the rest will cross the Rio Jícaro and the Rio Murra and travel up pre-designated positions at the foot of El Chipote. If we are forced to defend El Chipote, we will fight to the death. But, trust me, General Sandino, they will never get that far."

"Si, Manuel," Sandino acknowledged pensively.

"Let's see, I was going to discuss their air support. The closest refueling station for their airplanes is Ocotal. They are making a landing field in Telpaneca but, according to loyalists, are having trouble without engineering equipment. So, I believe their air support will be limited."

"All right, General Echevarria, I will return next week and ask you what progress you are making, especially with getting women to grind the grain. My boys up at the headquarters are hungry."

"Si, mi general."

Jícaro, November 11, 1927. Sergeant Charles Glasser, O'Shea's senior NCO, and Corporal Conwell Leinbach, O'Shea's super grunt and acting pharmacist mate, shouted aloud as Rowell's DH-4 ruthlessly roared by them at sixty knots. As the plane's roar faded away from Jícaro, the two looked upward at the location where the rope with the bag containing O'Shea's map was, an instant before, suspended. The detachment Marines and Guardia National soldiers cheered, whooping it up after seeing the pick-up demonstrated. "Holy Moley, Lieutenant! Did you see that?"

O'Shea smiled and winked at Leinbach and Glasser as they walked to the porch of the Detachment Headquarters, "Good job, you two."

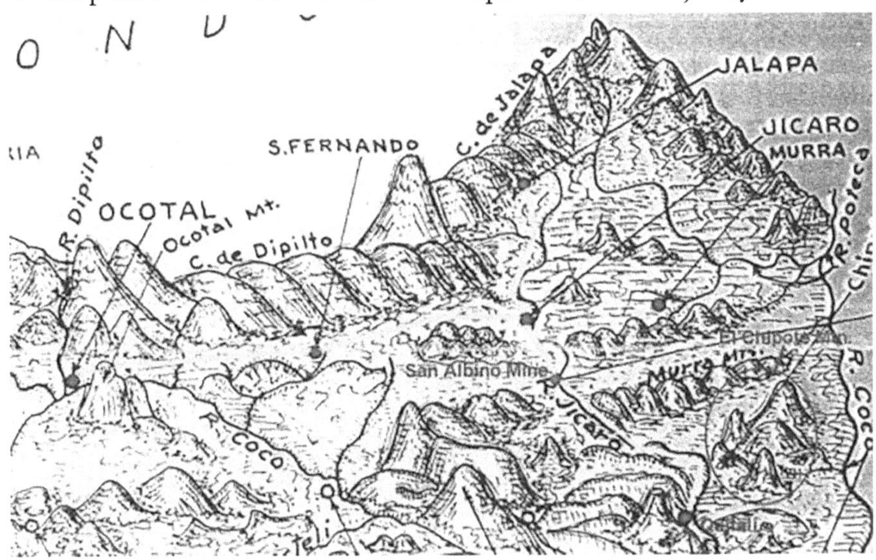

Map of Neuva Segovia, Monograph of Nicaragua, *USDS*
817.00/72941/2

Neuva Segovia, November 11, 1927. O'Shea's map proved to be invaluable. With it, Technical Sergeant Jolson laid out a comprehensive aerial reconnaissance plan that methodically combed every inch of terrain from the Río Murra to the prominent mountain east of it. Finally, on the eleventh day of the search, November 23rd, Captain Archibald's and Chief Marine Gunner Wodarczyk's took their turn to patrol. They had been up north twice before without success. The last time was three days earlier. The rainy season had ended, yet the clouds in the mountains clung to the highest tops requiring a search of the land from an altitude well within range of small arms.

Sergeant Oscar Knopf, Archibald's gunner, and Corporal Dibling, Wodarczyk's gunner, maintained sharp vigilance of possible ground

259

ambush sites, occasionally checking the ammo locked in their Lewis machine guns. Silently watched by hundreds of Sandino soldiers under cover on Sapotillal Ridge, the two planes crossed the Río Jícaro at Quilali at 10:35 AM. Three minutes later, they crossed the Río Murra where they banked south to look for paths or any other signs of activity.

Knopf spotted the hoof-beaten trail junction where Rivas, the mule driver, stood to shoot down Thomas and Dowdell. One trail visibly led up the mountain. Knopf tapped Archibald's shoulder and yelled for him to retrace the flight path and follow a suspected path. Complying, Archibald banked the bird, picked up the trail and led both planes up the mountain.

Flying further east than anyone in their squadron had flown before, the pilots flew directly over the trail leading them up the mountain. All four aviators saw the large flat area half way up the mountain at the same time. The four-to-six acres of level terrain was mostly covered with a low canapé. The roofs of four barracks-like buildings, hidden by trees, were barely visible. The planes would have to cross the small plateau in order to continue following the trail up the mountain.

As they flew across, small puffs of smoke rose from the canapé. Soon the cracks of passing bullets snapped nearby. On cue, both planes rose sharply skyward before looping at 1,500 feet. As trained, they dove recklessly towards their bandits, pilots' guns a blazing. Within 100 feet, the two planes soared upward allowing the observers their turn to fire.

By 11:10 AM, both planes were out of ammo. Dibling saw Archibald's signal to return to Managua. And, just as quickly as they appeared, they were gone.

By 12:30 PM, the pilots knew El Chipote was no longer a hidden sanctuary. They had found it ten miles northeast of Quilali. Strangely, the fortress was not on Sapotillal ridge—two miles northwest of Quilali as many thought.

"Top, I want that flat area bombed daily," Rowell directed at 5:00 PM after returning from the hastily-called meeting by the brigade's operations officer. "G-3 Ops is organizing a force to go over land from Jinotega and a smaller group from Telpaneca. They'll meet in Quilali and, from there they will attack Sandino's headquarters on the El Chipote mountain. We will be their eyes, ears and guardians from the skies."

CHAPTER 29: THE BATTLE FOR QUILALI

Livingston's Campsite, Matagalpa, December 19, 1927. "Ours will be the main attack force," stated Captain Richard Livingston, the leader of the joint Marine and Guardia Nacional patrol. "We have 114 Marines and Guardias. When we reach Jinotega tomorrow, we'll pick up the detachment there. That'll be Second Lieutenant Alex Hunt from the 5th Marines and his infantry platoon of 37 troops.

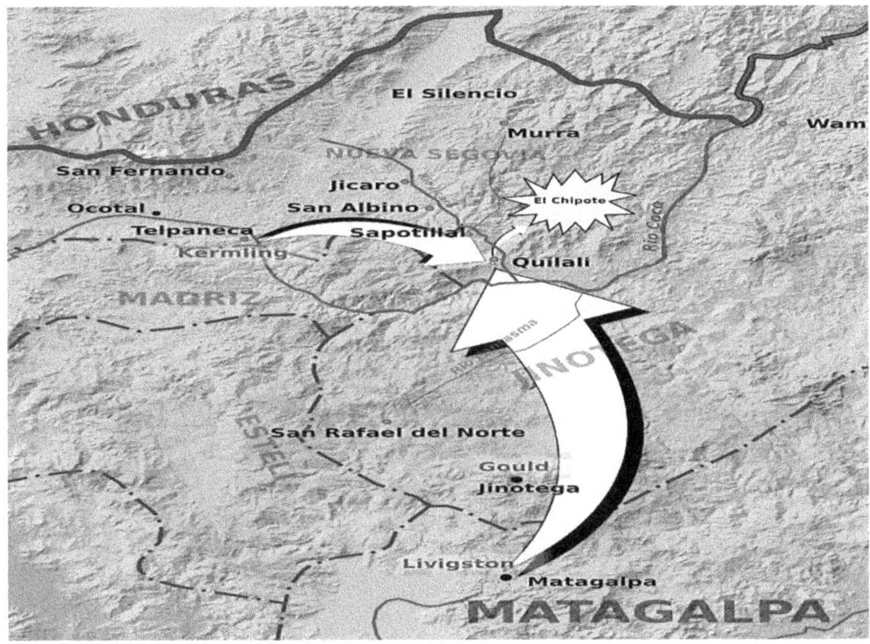

"We will be reinforced in the little mountainous town of Quilali by a patrol led by First Lieutenant Meron Richal, who will be coming from Telpaneca with another 50 men and supplies.

"Our mission is to attack El Chipote, approximately 10 miles east of Quilali, destroy Sandino's Headquarters, and capture or kill the bandit." Livingston paused to further study the intelligence report that accompanied the patrol order dropped by the Marine Air Service on the previous day.

Lieutenant Bill Minnick, the Navy doctor assigned to the patrol, used the pause to study the five other men sitting around the table, who would lead this patrol. In no particular order were: Gunnery Sergeant Fred Coryall, a career Marine last stationed at the San Diego Recruit Training Command and Livingston's number one enlisted man; Senior Chief Elliot Walker, his own deputy, who seemed solid enough to be successful on his first really-challenging patrol; First Lieutenant Moses "Mo" Gould, commander of the Matagalpa Detachment with much experience "up north" and for now Livingston's second in command; First Lieutenant Hempfill, a quiet, pipe-smoking Marine first sergeant who wore a single silver bar on each side of his shirt's collar signifying his leadership role with the Guardia unit he would lead on the patrol; and Second Lieutenant "TJ" Kilcourse, a newly-joined officer who seemed different than all the other Marines as he was openly against most everything that was going on in Nicaragua.

In the past two days Kilcourse had not been happy with the American foreign policy that led to the Marine's involvement in Latin America, specifically the fact Marines were in Nicaragua fighting somebody else's war. He believed General José Moncada was a drunken, over-sexed crook. In his diary, which he constantly quoted, he severely questioned the leadership of General Feland, who was slated to return to Nicaragua in January to again become commanding general of the 2nd Marine Brigade. He believed that the general, previously, fought the war from his office in Managua. Further, he believed Feland would be a puppet of Moncada.

Livingston passed the intelligence reports to Gould.

At that instance, Second Lieutenant TJ Kilcourse shot a "just-what-I-told-you" glance at Lieutenant Bill Minnick reminding him of the intelligence report that reported Sandino's had 600 to 1,000 men in the Sapotillal Ridge-Quilali-El Chipote area.

Livingston looked up and said, "We should arrive at Jinotega sometime tomorrow afternoon. Hard as it may seem, I want you and your men to keep a close eye on the mules. The road between here and Jinotega isn't too bad but we'll be stretched out over a mile, so keep watching the mules and the muleros. We cannot afford to lose the supplies on their backs. After Jinotega there are no easy roads; just a lot of bandits. Our point must stay alert!" Looking around he saw Kilcourse shaking his head. "Lieutenant?"

"Nothing Sir?"

"Do you have a question, Mr. Kilcourse?"

"Not for you, Sir. I simply find it difficult to believe that 150 Marines are going after 1,000 Sandinistas."

"Lieutenant," Livingston replied in a noticeably stern tone, "you have read all the reports about the bandits' inadequate training, poor marksmanship, and lack of discipline, have you not?"

"I have, Sir."

"In the mountains, we will not be fighting a force five or six times larger than us in a conventional campaign. Rather, on the tight mountain trails, the war will be fought squad against squad. We will eliminate them one squad at a time. We call that a war of attrition."

Now embarrassed Kilcourse offered, "Sir, I understand," in hopes his simple answer would diffuse the captain's mounting anger.

It did not. "Lieutenant Kilcourse, if you do not wish to go on this patrol, please let me know. You will not have to. Upon my return, I will personally draft papers to ensure your career in my Marine Corps terminates immediately. Do you have any questions, mister?"

Reprimanded and embarrassed, Kilcourse looked at the floor and shook his head indicating that he had none.

"All right then. We break camp at zero six hundred. Gunnery Sergeant Coryall?"

"Sir," the gunnery sergeant asked as the others cleared the room.

"Do you have time for a glass of bourbon?"

"I'll make time, Sir."

Livingston reached into a pack, poured shots in two small glasses, and handed one to Coryall. "Gunny, is there anything I should know about Lieutenant Kilcourse?"

Pausing to be careful that his answer would reflect on his long-term experience and not his more- junior rank, "Nothing in particular, Sir. I've seen many lieutenants who struggle to fit into our Corps. Some make it. Some don't." Then cogitating a bit longer, Coryall added, "You might want to give him a chance, Sir."

Matagalpa; May 11,1927-*USMC History Division*

Jinotega-Matagalpa one-half mile outside of Matagalpa- *US National Archives*

Jinotega, December 20, 1927. By 1:00 PM, Livingston's patrol arrived at La Catedral de Jinotega's, the handsome Catholic Church across the street of Parque Central. There, as planned, was Lieutenant Alex Hunt and his 37 Marines waiting for the patrol. Livingston greeted Hunt with obvious enthusiasm. "Lieutenant, welcome aboard. I will be counting on you to make a significant contribution to our patrol and its mission to destroy El Chipote."

"Yes Sir, I'll do my best!"

"Have you met Mo Gould?"

"Yes Sir, while passing through Matagalpa on the way out to my battalion," Hunt said reaching his hand out to shake Gould's. "How you doing, Mo?"

"Another great day in the Corps, Dan," Gould said winking his eye.

"Good," Livingston continued, "then meet Gunnery Sergeant Coryall. He will be the patrol's senior enlisted man. Lieutenant TJ Kilcourse, who is in charge of the rear guard and the mule train, should be arriving here soon along with Lieutenant Bill Minnick, the patrol's doctor, and Senior Chief Elliot Walker."

"Nice meeting you Gunnery Sergeant. This here's Sergeant Stevens, my platoon sergeant."

After the introductions, Livingston said, "Lieutenant, stay around. I want to brief you on your mission." He added, "Gunny, how about you and Sergeant Stevens plan where we are going to bivouac tonight."

An hour later…The rear guard and the pack train continued filing into the mountain town. As if on cue, their demeanor morphed as they rode on into the park, hearing instructions being bellowed by the former drill instructor. Coryall's baritone commands raised the audio antennas of the young Marines. That stimulus returned much of the anxiety each had possessed as a recruit. They now approached the camp site far more erect on their mounts and serious-looking than they had been three minutes earlier while riding by the cathedral.

Kilcourse spotted the captain as he, the doctor, and the chief passed the magnificent gothic cathedral. "Over there Bill," Kilcourse pointed. "Guess Captain Livingston is with Lieutenant Hunt."

Livingston, asked, "How did the pack train do, Lieutenant?"

"Still more problems with the loads on the mules. These men do not know how to load a mule's pack. And between Zeledón's ranch and here, at least eight muleros disappeared."

Looking at Captain Livingston, Hunt piped up. "Sir, if you don't mind, my platoon has been patrolling up here in these mountains for three months. Not sure, but we may be able to offer some assistance in packing the mules."

"Have at it Lieutenant. I'd love that," Livingston smiled. "Lieutenant Gould, how about you and I wander over to the telegraph office to see it there are any messages or any other information we can pick up?"

Later that evening, Lieutenant Kilcourse reported to Livingston whose tent was pitched next to a picnic table, "Sir, you wanted to see me?"

"Yes Lieutenant, please sit down."

"Sorry about the other night Sir."

"TJ, you've been doing a good job with that mule train and rear guard. I am going to forget about that incident. But, I want to make it perfectly clear that any doubts you have in the future about why we are here or anything else, you bring them up with me first."

"Yes Sir."

"I don't want any officer throwing around lose comments like you did without first discussing them with me. You got that?"

"Yes Sir."

"All right then. That's the end of it. I am required to report our progress on a daily basis. Can you type?"

"Yes Sir, 42 two words a minute."

"Well good. I am very slow and I believe anyone who reads what I type will quickly look for an interpreter 'cuz they won't believe it's English. So, first thing every morning, stop by and I'll give you a hand-written draft. You type it and get it ready to be picked up by the air service."

Ops Office, Managua Aerodrome, December 28, 1927. Technical Sergeant Roy Jolson handed the package to his commanding officer's outstretched hand. Jolson's somber face spoke volumes about the contents of the package. "The weather cleared today for the first time since the patrol left Matagalpa. We plucked this package from them at 1115 this morning." Jolson paused then added, "Must be rather rough up in the mountains, Sir."

Major Ross Rowell, took the package, went over to the map table by the window, pulled out the contents of the package and read:

Dec. 20. - Made Jinotega total 9 miles. Trouble with train due to lack of
experienced packers. Muleros deserting in route - apparently afraid to
go with us. Arrived Jinotega 1330. Lt. Hunt with 1 infantry platoon of 36
men joined us. Left 3 mules Jinotega.

Dec. 21 - Broke camp 1100 - made 9 miles made dry camp - trail across half
dry swamp - going bad in places. Two mules died - one lame   advance
guard halted at 1600 - train and rear guard arrived 2200 - camped on
prairie 3 miles south of Paso Real.

Dec 22 - Broke camp at 0930 a.m. Camped at Paso Real at 1530 made 3 miles
Roads bad - mud knee deep - mules down continually. Rear guard arrived
in camp 2200. Mules in poor shape because of bad going. Men working hard
but impossible to make time. Plane sighted at 1030 but he did not get our
signal. Manuel Gonzales taken prisoner and held on suspicion of spying
- tells many conflicting stories. Muleros deserting. Lack of experienced
packers badly handicap us.

Dec 23 - Broke camp at 0900 - only 22 muleros still with us. Roads bad
- advance guard camped at Embarcadero at 1430. Plane dropped mail at
1030. Prisoner Gonzales escaped from Lt Hunt s rear guard at 1900. Rear
guard arrived in camp at 1900. Distance covered 6 miles. Lost 3 mules
during days march from exhaustion. Health of command excellent - morale
excellent.

Dec 24 - Xmas Eve - Broke camp at 0900 crossed Guale Mts. in rain & fog.
Altitude 4500 feet. Roads almost impassable - mud waist deep for miles
making it necessary to cut new trail for at least 1 3/4 mile thru woods
in order to get thru. Five mules falling over cliff and lost with cargoes.
Advance guard made camp at Guale at 1500 - distance made seven miles. Men
in good shape - animals exhausted. All men sent back on trail to assist
mule train in. 1 1/2 sections on train unable to make camp remained out
all night. Everyone wet and covered with black gummy mud from head to
foot. Equipment covered also. Worst day yet - conditions indescribable.
Plane dropped mail at 1030. Officers slept in native shack - filthy -
young pig crawled in and parked beside Lt. Gould.

Dec 25   Xmas. In camp at Guale - part of train still out and coming in
slowly all day. All available men sent out to assist in bringing them in.
Rear guard arrived in camp at 1900 - from 0900, 24th to 1900, 25 , making
seven miles. Animals exhausted   equipment and stores smashed - broken -
and torn. Shoes of men falling to pieces - heels off - stitching broken.
Men s feet in bad shape in several cases because of continual immersion
in mud and water. Necessary to camp over one more day to reorganize and
allow animals to recuperate. Morale of command exceptionally good. Men
are working cheerfully under most trying conditions. Two planes over
camp at 1045 dropped mail. Christmas dinner, slum and hard tack - same
old pig pen to sleep in   Men bathed - first since Dec 19.

Dec 26 - still at Guale reorganizing. Planes over at 1030.

Dec 27 - Broke camp at Guale at 0900   some mules still in bad shape.
Advance guard arrived at La Brellere at 1600. Distance ten miles. Roads
bad most of way. Cut 1 mile of new trail thru woods because of bad
swamp. Rear guard arrived in camp at 2350. Three mules died in route of
exhaustion. At 1700 two shots fired from house at La Brellere and replied
to by 4 rounds from 37 mm gun. House deserted upon our arrival but
showed signs of recent occupancy. Planes over at 1030. Weather clear.

Lieutenant TJ Kilcourse Diary Entry -*Michael J. Schneider's The Sandino Papers, 2007-2009*

"Technical Sergeant," Rowell said addressing Jolson.

"Sir?"

"I will be going to Brigade headquarters to discuss the patrol's reports. I should return by 3:30 PM. I want to brief the officers and key staff NCOs at 4:00 PM in the hanger classroom. Things are heating up!"

"I'm on it Sir!"

Marine Detachment, Telpaneca, December 29, 1927. While Captain Livingston's patrol was moving North from Matagalpa to Quilali, Lieutenant Richal's organized his 50-man patrol in Telpaneca with plans to join Livingston in Quilali on New Year's Eve.

"I wish we were going with you, Meron," First Lieutenant Herbert Keimling, the Telpaneca commander shouted cynically to his old friend as he stood at the back of the officer's quarters in his green undershirt, khakis, and boots, "It's time to get rid of the bandits!"

While synching his mount's forward girth strap on cavalry-type Phillips pack sack, First Lieutenant Meron Richal looked over his mule's back and laughed, "Right, Herb. Tell you what my friend, we're running a little bit early; we'll give you time to pack up and join us. Is that okay with you, Tom?"

The "Tom" was Marine First Sergeant Thomas Bruce, who wore silver bars on his kakis shirt collar signifying that, while serving as he was with the Nicaragua Guardia Nacional, he held the rank of first lieutenant. Bruce, who had been in Nicaragua for three years and had been decorated for demonstrated leadership and courage during the July battle of Ocotal, joined in the fray. "I doubt if we'd need them Lieutenant. I've heard that, when they get more than a mile from here, they get lost."

Sergeant Alva Eadens, Keimling's second in command, chimed in while looking at the now paused airfield working party, "Gentlemen, we are nearly finished with our airfield. On the way back, be sure to drop by. We'll have direct flights to San Diego and Miami."

Bull cart or Oxcart or bulloc cart used for hauling dirt to fill holes in the landing fields-*USMC History Division 48-3*

The twinkle in the four leaders' eyes ended when the voice of Gunnery Sergeant Edmond Brown, 150 yards down the trail and leader of the advance guard, could be heard, "Main body move out!"

Lieutenant Richal planned on two days to get to Quilali. All members of the 50-man joint Marine- Guardia Nacional patrol knew, that as they approached Sapotillal ridge and its lethal fingers, they most likely would encounter more than a few supporters of Sandino.

South of Quilali on Camino Real, 30 December, 1927. "We should be there by noon," First Lieutenant Mo Gould said at 9:30 AM over his left shoulder to Captain Richard Livingston. Livingston's 151-member patrol slugged single file along the two-foot-wide "road", called the "Camino Real." It was the main route leading to Quilali from the south.

The Río Jícaro, 100 yards to their left and 100 feet below the men, flowed south toward the Río Coco. Quilali was on the other side of the

Jícaro and about 1,500 yards north of them. The road skirted the steep mountain above them. Where the Río Jícaro sharply turned west, the road disappeared into an old banana grove with extremely heavy underbrush.

The patrol stopped abruptly. Gould, immediately behind the four-man point guard, silently moved forward. The third man had assumed a kneeling position and was generally looking forward over the barrel of his Springfield. As the lieutenant crouched beside him, he whispered, "Watson saw some movement in that grove up yonder," referring to Private James Watson, who was the Patrol's pointman.

"Stay here, I don't want the main body and mules moving into this open area before we can secure that thicket ahead."

Gould spun around retaining a crouched position, looked at Livingston, and pointed his right hand toward where the movement had been noticed. That act triggered the Sandino force, consisting of

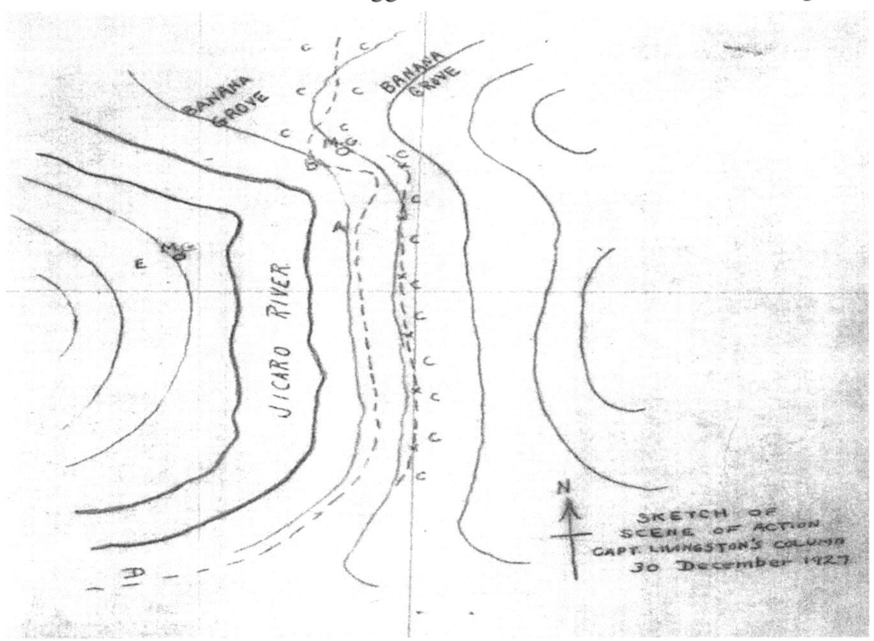

Sketch of Scene of Action, Capt. Livingston's Column, 30 December 1927. Gould's "not to scale" map attached to his 31Dec27 after-action report. A-location where point spotted movement at B. C-enemy positions above trail. D- not explained. E-enemy machine gun position-*PC-DOC 27.12.31 GOULD*

400 men, to open fire. From 100 feet above the lead men, the first rifle fired. Watson never knew what hit him as his body rolled down twenty yards below the trail stopping short of the river. Bullets, dynamite bombs, trench mortars and mountain battery gun filled the narrow gap that the river had cut through centuries earlier. The patrol's lead element was annihilated in the first minute. All four men on the point were killed. Miraculously, Gould made it back to Livingston with a slight wound where a bullet grazed his left shoulder only to find both the Captain and Gunny Coryall seriously wounded.

The pipe-smoking Lieutenant Hemphill was shouting to eight of his Guardia soldiers as they burst through the carnage and passed Gould returning to bring forward Marine machine guns and men with grenades. Hemphill's initial presence caught the enemy by surprise. The Guardia soldiers immediately fired on the bandit machine gun across the river, which soon fell silent.

The concealed enemy riflemen above the trail were not affected by the now-quiet supporting machine gun. They continued to emerge from behind piles of rocks firing their rifles and throwing dynamite bombs all the while creeping easily through their two-foot-deep trench line. Gould arrived back at the open area only to witness Hemphill and one of his Guardia troops being blown up by a dynamite bomb that exploded on the trail between them.

"I have Hunt enveloping up on the hill, Captain."

"Good," Livingston, going into shock, said in a noticeably weakened voice.

"We just have to continue counter firing until he gets in position."

Livingston nodded.

With that, Gould directed the fire by his Marines and the six other Guardia soldiers at suspected positions above.

After about 40 minutes a noise from up the hill could be heard. Soon the noise became clear, mad yelling, frightening and bold, from rebel-shouting Marines filled the air above the enemy trench. Fearing instant death, the frightened enemy ran from their trench line and the battlefield fell silent.

Hunt left a four–man team up in the trench formally occupied by Sandino's force for security and came down with the rest of his platoon to replace the advance guard.

"Nice work Dan," Gould greeted his friend.

"Thanks, Mo. Sergeant Stevens is setting in security in front. How's the captain?"

"Not good. Has a bullet lodged in his shoulder; but he ought to make it. The gunny is about the same—took one just below the knee."

"You look like you caught something in your shoulder."

"I'll be fine. It's only a flesh wound. Hey, did you see what direction the enemy was going?"

"Looks like they were headed for Quilali, Mo."

By 2:30 PM the five dead Marines, one dead Guardia soldier, and eight seriously wounded were loaded onto the mules or stretchers for the final hike into Quilali. The 18 ambulatory wounded marched unassisted along with the 118 not wounded. The two Marine aircraft that arrived after the fight, kept the enemy on the run. Nevertheless, the movement was slowed by the ever-more cautious point. The exhausted men arrived in the deserted village of Quilali at 10:30 PM.

Inside the village's small church and lying on a stretcher, Livingston asked Lieutenant Minnick, "How bad are the men, Bill?"

"Richard, get some rest. I'll give you a report in the morning."

Northwest of Quilali at Sapotillal Ridge, December 31, 1927. After taking a 20-minute break at noon, Richal's 50-man patrol from Telpaneca began its final leg into Quilali. "Only six more miles, right Lieutenant Richal?"

Marines on patrol in search of the Bandits-*Defense Dept Photo (Marine Corps) #527782*

"That's right Private Hooks, keep on going. We'll be there before sundown."

"Where's First Sergeant Bruce, Sir?"

"He's up there with the point, Hooks. Want to join him?"

"Don't think I'm ready, Sir. I believe I'll stay back here with you and Gunny Brown. But thanks anyway, Sir."

"Hooks, you are ready. Let's you and me take the gun team forward to give him a hand if he needs one."

"I don't know, Sir," Hooks said hesitantly.

Meron Richal turned to the men behind him with the machine gun and Stokes mortar and said in a voice loud enough to be heard 50 yards away, "Let's close it up, Gunny. We need that fire power forward."

The advance guard, led by Corporal Wallace Henry, was 50 yards beyond the junction on the trail that leads to Quilali and below the dominate hill. The young Marines, scouring the flanks of the route ahead of them, were suspicious of their easy movement so far.

With them, First Sergeant Tom Bruce slowed his pace, then stopped while looking up the hill to his right. Bruce's thumbs slowly flipped open both covers on his .45 caliber pistol holster to begin withdrawing the pistols. The Marine beside him saw this movement. Richal, now 40 yards behind Bruce, did as well. The bandit whose slight movement Bruce had observed did as well. The bullet tore through Bruce's neck milliseconds before its firing could be heard by all occupying the road, the two hills beside the road, the field, and the Lopez house to the right flank of the rear guard.

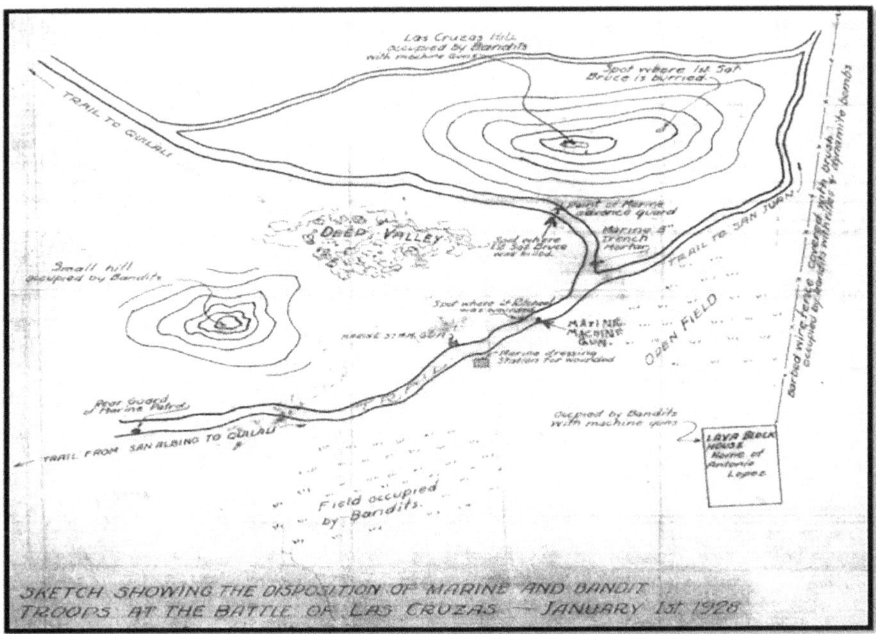

GySgt Edward Brown's sketch showing the disposition of Marine and Bandit troops at the Battle of Las Cruzas, January 1st, 1928-*PC-DOC 28.01.04 BROWN*.

The thrust of the bullet lifted Bruce's body into the air and snapped his neck bone. Before he fell lifelessly on the dirt road, Richal was barking orders, directing Gunnery Sergeant Brown to assault the small hill to their left rear.

The men in the advance guard stared in shock at Bruce's broken body with its head laying grotesquely on its right shoulder and blood pulsating from the open wound three inches into the air. The young Marines knew they had to recover Bruce's dying body. Anticipating their concerns, Richal yelled "Get back to the junction and cover the Stokes crew! We'll get him later!"

For twenty minutes, sporadic rounds kicked up the vegetation harmlessly near the forward firing positions of both forces. The weapons seemed to be more noise generators than lethal instruments of war. That soon ended.

A bullet cut Richal down as it tore through his left eye. He fell to the ground holding his face. Private Hooks looked over at the lieutenant. As he did a bullet cut through his right tricep. "Unh? Lieuuuutenant," he paused, then recovered, "you okay, Sir?"

From the road, Corporal Henry yelled to the mortar crew, "Get off two more rounds then fall back to the machine gun." With that, Henry helped the felled lieutenant move the forty yards back to the perimeter that Gunnery Sergeant Brown was forming.

"Get that gun in action!" Gunnery Sergeant Brown bellowed while in a crouching position.

"Eetz jammed, Gunny," Guardia Corporal Mendez snapped.

The rear guard set up the 37-mm gun and knocked huge holes in the walls of the Lopez house. In doing so, 10-15 enemy inhabitants scattered. Soon, the enemy soldiers nearby who initially were concealed in the field, withdrew in a noticeably-undisciplined manner.

Mendez's adroitness cleared the machine gun jam and it too began scoring hits on the larger hill in front.

After an hour, the battlefield went quiet. The only noise came from the same two airplanes that had earlier chased away the withdrawing enemy from Livingston's patrol. Once they appeared overhead, Corporal Morris Elwood, a Guardia Lieutenant, dug out panels from the lead mule and directed the aviators toward the enemy. Richal, face covered in gauze, said, in a somewhat in an exhausted voice, "Gunny, get a patrol out there to recover Bruce."

"Right, Sir," then looking around he spotted Elwood going back to the mule. "Elwood, take some men and secure that house over there across the field and post a team on the road to our rear."

"Gotcha, Gunny"

Seeing the blood on the face of Corporal Wallace Henry, Gunnery Sergeant Brown asked, "Henry, how's that head wound?"

"It's nothing, Gunny. Just a good scratch on my cheek. Probably won't be able to shave for a week. "

"Yeah, all right. Get a couple of men and bring back the first sergeant. Better bring something to carry him back in. The lieutenant tells me he is pretty messed up."

"Right, I saw him."

An hour later Corporal Henry, his face ashen, stood in front of the gunnery sergeant who was standing beside the prone Lieutenant Richal. "The bastards cut him to pieces," Henry said almost crying.

"What?" Brown said looking into the pale face and wet eyes of the corporal at the same time a "What?" came from Richal as he attempted to stand up.

Sobbing, Henry stuttered, "They drug him 50-75 yards to around the far side of the hill and macheted him. We covered what's left of First Sergeant Bruce with that blanket."

Brown put his hand on Henry's shoulder and said, "Let's go over to your detail. I want to talk to all of you. Where are your men?"

"They right over here, Gunny," the Corporal said in a whisper pointing to the men sitting on their packs at the bottom the large hill.

Brown walked over to the six men who assisted Corporal Henry with First Sergeant Bruce. Compassionately, he reminded that they are being faithful to each other, to the Country, and to the Corps. First Sergeant Bruce would have appreciated their remorse but would have reminded them that, if their mission is not complete, they are to stay alert, be a Marine and keep moving. Brown convinced them that he too was both enraged and sickened by Bruce's death, but he had to focus on getting all of the patrol to Ocotal. He assured them that Bruce will have a memorial service once we are all back in Managua. Then he ordered them back on the hill to finish their job and properly bury the First Sergeant.

After that, Brown went over to see his wounded Lieutenant.

Beside Richal, Hooks was the only other Marine seriously wounded. Fifteen mules had been killed in the fight and three escaped. They still had 99 mules. Brown resolved that, in trying to control the remaining mules and the vital supplies they carried, there were too few men to ensure security for the patrol's final six-mile leg, should they get ambushed again. Brown opted to hold his current position until he was reinforced.

Exhausted, Lieutenant Richal fell asleep and would not awaken until the morning.

Quilali, New Year's Day, 1928. The message dropped from the aircraft the day before informed Livingston and Gould about the ambush on Richal's patrol and the fact that they needed reinforcements in order to reach Quilali. The accompanying map indicated they were located six miles to the northwest. In exchange, the plane picked up a report that told of Doctor Minnick's insistence that the injured had to be evacuated, that the joint patrol needed supplies, and that a replacement commander before they could continue on their mission to destroy Chipote. The brigade would have to solve that problem. The Quilali force could not.

First Lieutenant Gould summoned Second Lieutenant Hunt. "Alex, I am sending you out to assist in bringing in Richal's patrol at first light tomorrow. We have been assured that you'll have air cover both ways. Any problems with that?"

"No, Mo, we'll be ready to go."

Hunt's platoon linked up with Richal's patrol by noon the next day. They gave First Sergeant Bruce a field burial and departed at first light on the 3rd. By midafternoon Hunt arrived back in the village town of Ocotal, surrounded by towering hills that had been divided by the Río Jícaro. The one-time confident, now combined two-patrol force had been out numbered, out fought, and immobilized by Sandino's irregulars. Their outlook was bleak and would remain so until, in their minds, a large enough force could come to help them fight their way out of Quilali.

That night Lieutenant Kilcourse wrote in his diary:

Jan 2 - Lt Hunt with 34 men sent to Richals aid at 0745. Orders reared
rec d to evacuate - Richal apparently shot up. See copy of letter
in this book addressed to Brig. Comdr. this date in reply to order to
evacuate. The Brigade has been led into a situation that is intolerable
by misleading reports and information from so called intelligence
officers who either have no military knowledge or are covering their own
lack of information or inactivity by writing reports calculated to please
the Brigade Commander. This town, Quilali, is from a military standpoint,
untenable. It is surrounded by hills, sitting as it does in the bottom
of a cup shaped geographical formation, and can be raked by machine
guns from a dozen or more hills surrounding it. It will take at least a
battalion to make the town safe at present - and then the question of
supplying this battalion is an enormous one. It cannot be supplied over
the trail we came - it took us 12 days to make it over trails beyond my
description. To supply a force here from points north or west is equally
difficult - all supplies would have to be brought in by pack train which
would require heavy guards to protect them - or strongly held points
along the trails they are to follow to insure their safety.

Such far flung lines of communication are unsound from a military
standpoint. And dope furnished by the Brig. Comdr. relative to the
military situation is so far wide of the truth as to be astounding. I am
personally of the opinion that information furnished by the Brigade is,
more than anything else, responsible for the greatest military blunder
the Marine Corps has made in many years. Regardless of the fact that
we have reached here in spite of enemy resistance, he has won a moral
victory at least that will do much to enhance his prestige and boost
his morale. If we can withdraw from here without further serious losses
and take a position along a line that will at least insure us a service
of supply, we will be lucky. We have been living on native beef which
we rounded up, for three days   that and coffee. We are entirely out
of supplies - Richal s failure to get through with the rations he is
bringing, has left us high and dry. However, we are still in the ring,
and tho Lt Gould and myself are almost nervous wrecks from the strain,
we are still in the game. Sleepless nights - lack of proper food - and
worry over the safety of the lives of our men are leaving marks on us
that we will carry forever. Planes have dropped us a message telling us
that Lt. Hunt, with the platoon we send out to help Richal s column, has
made it and that the combined column, will move out at 0900 tomorrow to
join us here. Lord knows we need them. All other orders relative to our
movements have been revoked - we are busy trying to clear a field for
a small plane to land and take our wounded off so they can get proper
care. Planes particularly active today strafing ground in all directions.
They will cover the march of combined column of Hunt and Richal - now
Hunts command - here s hoping they get in safely. It is hell to think of
sacrificing lives of any more of our men for a cause in which they have
not the remotest interest.

Lieutenant TJ Kilcourse Diary Entry with three minor author corrections-*Michael J. Schneider's The Sandino Papers, 2007-2009*

Chapter 30: Schilt Solves The Quilali Problem

Ready Room, Managua Aerodrome, January 3, 1928. "The 5th Marines are organizing another patrol to rescue the Marine and Guardia force in Quilali," Rowell announced to gathering of the key players of the air squadron. "Once together, they'll decide if they will be able to attack Chipote or move to a stronghold for the rest of the winter. For now the biggest problem is extracting the wounded.

"We know that our new Tri-motor Fokker has the lift capacity; but, hell, the closest airfield that we could land that plane is Ocotal and the wounded cannot be moved that far over land."

"Sir, our De Havillands are far too old to push them for multi-missions up there in the mountains," Captain Stan Archibald added, condemning his boss's favorite plane.

Rowell's eyebrows shot upward to indicate his surprise at his XO's comment.

"The captain's right, Sir. I can barely keep them up in the air," Technical Sergeant Walt Heller, Rowell's maintenance chief, quickly added to diffuse any potential issue emanating from Archibald's blunt statement about the decrepit De Havillands.

First Lieutenant Frank Schilt appeared to be distracted. The others in the squadron's "Ready Room," next to Technical Sergeant Roy Jolson's Operations Office, were listening intently to their squadron commander who sought solutions to what appeared to be a hopeless situation in Quilali.

Schilt stood up and drifted over to the wall that held a recent photo of the new O2U-1 Corsairs that they had just received. He stared at it silently.

Rowell noticed that his squadron's superb aviator was not engaged in the discussion. Rowell's other great pilot, Chief Marine Gunner Michael Wodarczyk, observed his boss, then turned to observe Schilt. "The 02B-1s are out of the question," Rowell said almost without thinking. "We must all find the closest landing field—or construct one—if we are to assist with the wounded."

"I don't know, Sir," Schilt said turning around slowly. "I believe I can get in and get them out."

"Frank," Wodarczyk challenged, "how many times have we flown over that village? You know that the main road going through the town is only 15 feet wide—at it largest. How can you get your Corsair in there?"

Schilt responded, but only to Rowell. "Sir, all we have to do is drop engineering equipment and have the Marines take down the houses on either side of the main street. That will widen it another 35-40 feet. Plenty of wing space."

Quilali 1927: *Official Photograph US Marine Corps No PB 10535*

"Frank, your birds don't have brakes and the level part of the road running through Quilali is only 150-200 yards long. That's not long enough for you to stop," Rowell added empathetically, knowing that his outstanding officer must not have thought of that.

"I don't see that as a problem. I will give Mo Gould instructions. Every time he comes here in town for a briefing, all he talks is about rodeos." By this time the men from out west knew what Schilt was talking about. The pilots from back east looked at each other like, "Huh? What am I missing?"

First Lieutenant Schilt in front O2U-1-*Defense Dept (Marine Corps) 5262*

Schilt quickly explained. "You see, a bucking horse can't be stopped at once. He's got to be slowed first. What you try to do is have a man on either side grab his flank strap and try to loosen it. If they miss two other guys do the same thing. Finally, they get the strap off and bring the horse under control."

The eastern pilots were clueless about what Schilt just explained. The western pilots nodded their heads confirming, that's how it's done. Two of them agreed, looked at each other and said, "Yep, that ought to work."

Schilt said, "Gould can place successive sets of Marines along the road, and they'll be able to grab my wings to slow me down."

Archibald said, "Frank, all that may work, but the Corsair's thin tires are going to lock up in the mud. We can call this the dry season down here in Managua but, up there in the mountains, you know it rains darn near every day."

The big, self-confident engineer from the Rose Polytechnic Institute smiled confidently as he recalled his modified Curtiss that took second place in the Schneider International Seaplane Cup. "Sir," he said, pointing to the print, "if I am not mistaken, the 02U-1s come with two sizes of tires. The bird you have been flying has the thin tires like our old 02B-1s. But this print shows the wider tires like your DeHaviland's. I am sure we have a set of those wider ones in storage. If not, we can put DeHaviland wheels on one of our new planes."

Billingsworth, knowing his old boss won the day, smiled, winked and gave Schilt a "thumbs up".

Rowell was quiet for a moment then said, "Captain Archibald, round up all the engineer equipment to knock down those huts. Start delivering it this afternoon."

"Yes Sir!"

"Top Jolson, work up an operational plan to suppress any fires coming from those hills looking into Quilali. I will conduct a rehearsal over them tomorrow and the 5th."

"Sir."

"Billingsworth, you and Heller work on getting those larger tires on right away. As a matter of fact, get tires on a second 02U-1 bird in case we need it." Both men shook their heads.

"Lieutenant Schilt and Lieutenant Lamson-Scribner," whose nick name was "LS", "work up that note to Lieutenant Gould, get it up there and make sure they know what the hell is going on," he added to his two Quantico pilots who had been close friends for years.

"I am going to Brigade ops and tell them that we'll begin the extractions on the 6th. They will have to get some replacements up there. So the extra couple of days to round them up will work for them." Rowell paused looking at his men then asked, "Any questions?" he asked, looking around at his pilots. "All right then, we have a lot of work to do. Let's get going!" He added, "Frank, LS," nodding his head for the two designated pilots to join him.

As they approached, Rowell said, "This will be a hell of a show. LS, I want Frank Schilt to fly these runs. You'll be his backup if something goes wrong. Think as one—you two usually do. Let me know if I can do anything."

"Thanks for your confidence, Sir," Schilt said with a determined look on his face.

Quilali, January 3, 1928. Schilt's message dropped precisely in the center of the narrow road that cut Quilali in half. Corporal Wallace Henry scooped it off the road and hurried it into Gunnery Sergeant Brown. Brown gestured to Henry to give it to Lieutenant Gould, sitting nearby.

"What type of plane was that, Henry?" Gould asked while opening the pouch.

"I believe it was a Corsair, Sir. A bit newer looking than the other ones. I saw it as it flew away. The pouch darn near hit me."

Gould smiled, suspecting that Schilt was involved. He knew this message was going to tell how they would get out of Quilali. He unfolded a typewritten note and read out loud. "Mo, here's the plan. On the 6th we'll begin extracting your wounded. Within an hour or two today you'll be getting engineering equipment. You need to widen the road running through the center of town by removing houses on both side of the road. I will be landing my plane on the road. My wing span is 36 feet. Take down enough houses on both sides to give me at least 50 feet although 60 feet would be better.

"Mo, you know my Corsair doesn't have brakes. We discussed that before when I flew you back to Managua in October. Remember how you told me they stop bucking horses at the rodeos? I need you to have Marines staged in the second half of the road to stop me. I will be on the ground for no more than twenty minutes. Anticipate I'll bring in one or two replacements. Also, there will be supplies in the rear cockpit. After removing the supplies, you'll load the most seriously- wounded men in the rear cockpit. We'll get them to Ocotal. Should take 40-45 minutes. We anticipate that the new TA-1 tri-motor transport will fly them to Managua. I can take out two lightly wounded men if they are standing. I should be up there by 0900 on the 6th. I'll try to get in four or five pickups that day. We are contemplating four flights on the 7th. The flights on the 8th are mostly dependent of how well we did on the first two days. We'll do a mail pick up tomorrow morning at 1000. Let me know if you have any questions, and tell me about the condition of each man you anticipate I will be picking up on each flight. Semper Fidelis, Frank." Lieutenant Gould smiled, satisfied that he knew.

Brown stuttered, "He, he wants us to do what?"

Quilali, January 5, 1928. By January 5, the wide wheels were on both planes. The test flights were successfully flown by Frank Schilt and Frank Lamson-Scribner. Rowell and six other aviators made several passes skimming over the most likely firing positions that the Sandinistas would use to fire down on Schilt on his approaches and his take offs. There was no visible enemy activity. Schilt's afternoon flight over Quilali generated a hand-written note expressing his satisfaction with the widening of the road, identifying the specific location for the first set of Marines to begin slowing his aircraft, and confirming 9:00 AM for the first landing.

Lieutenant Mo Gould had trained six Marines and six Guardia soldiers in the art of slowing a brakeless plane that would be rolling at the first two Marines at 20-25 miles per hour. Navy doctor Lieutenant Bill Minnick had prioritized the evacuations. He had Lieutenant Meron Richal, whose condition had become critical, slated for the first flight. Lieutenant Alex Hunt's platoon was responsible for local security at both ends of the town. Gunnery Sergeant Ed Brown and Corporal

Elwood's squad would off-load supplies and guide the arriving passengers to Lieutenant Gould's Quilali command post. Kilcourse's men would provide the stretcher bearers and assist Senior Chief Walker and Doctor Minnick in loading the wounded men into the rear cockpit and tightening the safety harness.

By 8:50 AM on the 6th the clouds that engulfed the valley during the evening, now lingered near the top of the hills. Sandino, General Echevarria, Major Carlos Quesada and 200 men had been in place for over two hours. From their firing positions, they could easily witness activity in the small mountain village that now appeared to be in ruin.

The noise of six Marine aircraft could be heard in the direction of the Río Coco fifteen miles to the south. As planned and rehearsed, the planes flew beside the hills that rose from the banks of the Río Jícaro-- three on the east side and three on the west, 30 seconds in trace of each other.

A knot grew in Sandino's gut. The memory of Ocotal hadn't faded. He looked nervously as the lead plane flew directly toward his location. Echevarria hadn't been at Ocotal in July. He could here Sandino mutter, "Los diablos, los diablos." He remained exposed, but lowered his profile to match that of Sandino as the plane sped by. As the third plane passed overhead, Sandino stood erect and spotted a single plane flying low and slow, up the Río Jícaro valley. "Echevarria."

"Si, mi General?"

"There is your target," he said pointing down at a slow-flying biplane.

"Si! Begin Firing," he yelled.

The event hadn't been anticipated by Echevarria's men, much less rehearsed. The sporadic firing that began was quickly quieted by the second pass of the six escort planes hammering at the rebels' firing positions.

"Here he comes! Get ready," Gould shouted to the Marines and Guardia Nacional troops on either side of the street. All eyes focused on the plane heading directly into the village and the space cleared for them in its center. Its deafening roar blanketed all other sounds.

Schilt reduced the engine's power one half mile south of the village and glided toward the waiting Marines, trusting the success of the rehearsals at the aerodrome. He planned to touch down at 40 miles per hour. The sporadic firing stopped when the plane had descended to the final five feet, lower than the roofs of the village houses. The first half of the muddy street would slow him to 15- 20 miles per hour until the first set of Marines could slow the plane to half that speed. The final set of Marines had to be able to arrest the plane and prevent him from crashing at the end of the widened path as the street dropped precipitously into the valley at the north end of the village.

Schilt quickly glanced down at the speedometer as it approached the muddy street. 40 miles per hour precisely! To land the plane, he had to come off the level flight, lowering the plane's tail section sufficiently for the tail skag to first engage the muddy street below. The tail skag is the foot-long prong that keeps the tail section off the ground. In doing so, the engine would mask his forward view. Normally, at an airfield, he would compensate by steering the plane ever-so-slightly left and right to see forward from the forward sides of the cockpit. He did this by pushing the stick a tad bit left and right. Today, Schilt had time only for a quick left push on the stick to ensure his right wing was far enough away from the small houses on that side of the street before quickly straightening out. In that instant, he saw the first two Marines with their legs slightly bent in a racer's position, their arms stretched out toward the plane, and their fingers spread wide. He continued to push the stick forward feeling the wheels engage the mud. He cut the power to an idle rate. Blindly, Schilt concentrated. He was ready for anything unexpected.

Soon, he felt jarring, simultaneous thumps on his wings casting his head forward about three inches. His perpetual slight smile broadened, knowing the first two Marines made solid contact. Four seconds later he heard a second, less pronounced set of thumps on his wings and the forward movement of the plane slowing to a stop. Schilt looked left and right to see two panting young Marines. He raised his goggles and said, "Fine work, men!"

"Mo," Schilt said smiling while climbing down from the plane to the approaching First Lieutenant Mo Gould.

"Great landing, Frank. How bad were they shooting at you?"

"They tried, but Rowell's boys kept them hiding in their trench line. Say, your men did an outstanding job in stopping me."

"Great, we rehearsed it a couple of times."

"Hey, I need to add something."

"Sure, what?"

"Since I don't have any room to turn around on my own, could you get the last two men to grab hold of the horizontal stabilizer, lift the aft end of the plane up about a foot to get the tail skag off the ground, and walk the plane around clockwise? I'll help with the prop and vertical stabilizer."

"No sweat. Want to do that now?"

"Right, if all four of us do it, I won't have to use the engine."

Occasional ground fire could be heard from the mountains. That noise contrasted notably with the disciplined fire from the Lewis machine guns used by the pilots and directed at the Nicaraguans who crouched in trench lines near the top of the hills surrounding the village.

In the next moment, a swarm of six Marines, led by Gunnery Sergeant Brown, dashed for the plane as the Corsair's Pratt & Whitney Wasp engine idled softly. Schilt provided instructions to Brown who passed them on to his men. Jammed into the aft-seat area were six boxes of critical medical supplies. The men removed the boxes. Soon each man departed carrying a box on his shoulder.

Senior Chief Walker and Doctor Minnick approached the plane. In trace were four Marines carrying a stretcher with the blind Lieutenant Richal whose vital signs weakened daily. Schilt rushed forward to instruct Minnick on strapping Richal into the rear cockpit. Minnick conveyed the instructions to the four stretcher-bearers.

As the men finished, Brown raced back to the plane and yelled, "Take care Lieutenant Richal. I'll look you up when I return to Managua!"

Schilt stole a glance at the passenger he believed to be unconscious. Richal's right wrist slowly rose from the seat compartment above the fuselage snapping upward to show a clenched fist and a raised thumb."

Brown added, "You get 'em, Devil Dog!"

Satisfied, Schilt then climbed into his forward seat and strapped in. Lieutenant Mo Gould dashed out to the right front of the plane to salute this gutsy American hero. Schilt, whose head was the only part of his body above the fuselage, returned the salute and gave Gould a thumbs up.

Within a half, a minute the engine started with a deafening roar moving the plane forward. In fifty yards it lifted off the mud road and leveled off at five feet in the air, gaining speed for another fifty yards. Soon the plane arched upward with the speed of a race car. The snapping of bullets passed perilously near the plane and continued for nearly a minute until Schilt was 1500 feet in the air and a mile out of town.

Rowell's six plane contingent sped home to the Managua Aerodrome to refuel, leaving Schilt and his weight-burdened Corsair alone for a minute. A single biplane, precisely like Schilt's, shot down from above and soon flew beside Schilt. Schilt looked over and cast a big grin. Lamson-Schneider, grinning, saluted his close friend. The plan had worked.

An olive-drab truck with a similarly-colored canvass top that had on it a red cross painted over a white square met Schilt's stopped aircraft at the Ocotal airfield. Two pharmacist mates and a doctor rushed to the aircraft and retrieved the slumped Lieutenant Richal. Four Marines, one carrying a collapsed stretcher emerged from a cargo truck parked beside the ambulance truck. Within four minutes, Richal was on the way to the makeshift field hospital inside the aerodrome. At the same time, Schilt moved his plane to the refueling station.

Sergeant Junior Wilson, who had flown up with Wodarczyk, was waiting by the pump. He studied the dried mud on the side of the tires. "How was the landing, Sir?"

"No problem. The Marines wrestled me to a full stop with plenty of space before the road dropped off. Where's the TA-1 tri-motor?"

"Won't be up 'til later this afternoon, Sir. They will haul all the wounded out at the same time. You're taking up more supplies on this run. But on the next run, you'll be flying in the new commander, Captain Peard."

"I've flown him up and back to Ocotal a couple of times," Schilt responded while inspecting the undercarriage of the plane.

"Oh? Somehow I missed that," Wilson said looking at the gas pump. "Looks like you are all topped off, Sir. See you on the return."

"Wilson, tell the top," referring to Technical Sergeant Ike Billingsworth, "that the undercarriage looks okay. Why isn't he up here?"

"He's booked on the TA-1 and will be here this afternoon; I'll pass the undercarriage information to the Top. You want him to bring anything along with him?"

"Can't think of anything, Junior. See you in a couple of hours."

One hour and forty minutes later, at 11:40 AM, Schilt landed back in Ocotal. This time he had the wounded Captain Livingston. In ten minutes, Captain R. W. Peard, the Nueva Segovia Department Commander who had flown to Managua the previous day for a brigade briefing, strapped himself into the rear cockpit. Peard would lead the attack on Chipote if Colonel Gulick believed the men were capable of doing so.

Schilt was in the air within 26 minutes from the time he hit the ground. Again, he closely inspected the plane. On the third flight, he lifted out a Guardia Nacional soldier, Gutierrez, who had been wounded with Livingston on the 30th. Once at Ocotal the plane was met by a now-growing group of spectators who witnessed the wounded men be carried to the waiting TA-1 for transportation to Managua. Privates Turner and Collins were evacuated on the fourth and fifth flights. Five flights to recover the critically

Wounded Guardia Soldier Evacuated-*USMC History Division*

wounded were flown January 6th. By all standards, the evacuations had achieved history. Echevarria's men attempted to fire on Schilt on each approach into Quilali and each takeoff, all to no avail. As they crouched in the trenches to avoid the attacking planes constant, accurate gun and were unable to fire, Echevarria found himself muttering, "Los diablos, los diablos." After the evacuation of Gutierrez, Sandino, his eyes squinting in anger, and his aide began their return trip to El Chipote.

"Sir," Technical Sergeant Billingsworth, greeted the heroic aviator, his boss and good friend.

Schilt, surprised, swung his head around while stepping in the lower wing of the aircraft interrupted, "Top! Glad you could make it."

"Sir, the major wants a full report on you and the plane. Lieutenant Frank Lamson-Schneider, who landed fifteen minutes ago, told me that his bird was flying flawlessly, he was tired and hungry and was headed for the barracks. The plane is new so I'd expect it would be flying well." Billingsworth paused and asked, "How's your plane flying?"

"Other than the darn mud I've picked up, it's flying well. But you better take a good look at the whole plane for bullet holes. I have not felt any hit, but they had been cracking nearby." Schilt paused, reflecting on a new subject. "Also, tell him that the men in Quilali really know how to stop the plane now. I was somewhat skeptical on the first landing, but they have done an outstanding job."

"Will do, Sir. Wilson and I will be here at the aerodrome a good bit of the evening looking over both planes."

"When you talk to Major Rowell, tell him, 'Thanks.' Those strafing runs are making a huge difference in me flying in and out of Quilali."

"Count on it, Sir. Hey, by the way, the parents of that Guardia kid you pulled out on the third flight referred to you and the other pilots as 'los ángeles'. They're at the Managua aerodrome with a crowd of locals waiting for the kid. I saw several of the electric company ball players there as well. The whole crowd is murmuring 'los ángeles', 'los ángeles'."

"'Los ángeles?' That's funny. I guess it depends if you're helping them out or shooting at them.

"Let me know if you find anything wrong with the plane. By the way, on the second or third run tomorrow, I'll be pulling out two at a time. That's right at or just above the payload limits. So better keep an eye on the structural components."

"Wait a minute, Sir. How many men are you taking out on a single lift?'

'Two, Top."

"You can't do that. How are they going to fit?"

"Just take the seat out and they can stand."

"Well, I have the manual with me and I am going to check out the payload limits. The old birds couldn't lift that. I don't know," Billingsworth said shaking his head. "Just don't know."

"Okay, look at it, but I'll be flying two out at a time. That's final. I am going over to the barracks. Is that driver waiting for me?"

"He is, Sir. Have a good night."

Quilali, January 7, 1928. The mountain town was characteristically damp with a cloud lingering in the valley shrouding the village. The paths leading up the hills were occupied by frustrated men unable to get a clean shot off at a slow-flying, shiny bi-plane. The Marine night security reported "All Quiet" to Lieutenant Gould and Captain Peard as they came in from their listening post, then went off to eat a bit of hardtack before taking a two-hour morning nap and arising at 8:30 AM to suppress enemy fire from the ridge. By then the tropical sun would have disbursed most of the heavy cloud cover.

Contrarily, there was a hub of activity at the aerodrome in Ocotal. Rowell, who had been concerned about fuel reserves in Ocotal initially and had been saving it for the two O2U-1s, was now confident that the operation was going well enough to allow three of the support planes to remain overnight in Ocotal and refuel there. Those three DH-4s were now lined up in the morning sun with two mechanics tending to their readiness. Billingsworth and Wilson were putting the final touches on the two new O2U-1 Corsairs. Liftoff was scheduled for 8:15 AM. To prove that he did his research, Billingsworth warned his lieutenant that the payload capacity was 300 pounds "if equally distributed."

Fifteen minutes after the DH-4s flew off at 8:00 AM, Schilt was airborne. Frank Lamson- Schneider was one minute behind him. They joined the circling DH-4s. The roar of their engines that had filled the Ocotal valley and captured the attention of many local farmers soon faded as the five planes disappeared behind the eastern mountains.

Private Ed Pamorski was Schilt's first passenger. Only a few enemy rounds were fired near the airplane. Schilt and his passenger were back in Ocotal by 10:00 AM. Gould told Schilt that, for the next five flights, lightly-wounded passengers would be flown out in pairs. The plan was the two wounded men would stand back to back in the rear cockpit and hang on to one of struts that supported the lower wing.

Back in Ocotal, after Pamorski was safely removed from the plane, Billingsworth and Wilson quickly removed the seat from the rear cockpit and installed a second strap woven through the seat's locking device. It was long enough to be wrapped around the waists of the next set of passengers. Billingsworth continued to shake his doubting head and mumble to himself. Junior Wilson managed to get an approving wink in to Schilt without the Top seeing him.

Private Hooks, wounded in his tricep on Sapotillal Ridge, and Private Coyne were the first to be flown out. Scared at the idea of flying, Hooks had been pleading with Gunny Brown to allow someone else to go. "I want to hike out, Sergeant." Brown grew impatient and told Hooks he needed him to visit Lieutenant Richal in the hospital and stop thinking about himself. Coyne was then up for the adventure. In minutes the weight-burdened plane was airborne and flying well for having transporting a third passenger's 130 pounds. Schilt looked back a couple of times during the flight and saw the two pointing at different sites as they flew west to Ocotal. He shook his head and smiled.

The impact of the landing was more pronounced than the feathery ones the pilot normally made, but soon the plane was greeted by the same two pharmacist mates who met the last few flights. Apparently no one told them to expect two wounded passengers. They laughed at the scene then quickly helped Hooks and Coyne to the ground.

"How's it look, Top?" Schilt asked while stepping to the ground. "It landed harder than normal— guess I misjudged the weight."

"Can't see anything," Billingsworth said, while rubbing his left hand lightly over the skin of the plane and studying the struts. "You be careful now."

Junior Wilson, standing with a hose in hand, soon barked, "Topped off, Sir."

And with that, Schilt crawled back into the forward cockpit for his 8th flight to Ocotal. He soloed back to Ocotal on this trip. As he approached the mountain village, one lucky round passed under the end of his top wing that did not seem to affect the flight. Schilt thought about just how lucky he had been all the while.

Suddenly, upon landing, his plane's tail snapped left and right as his tail skag caught the edge of mud rut before it stabilized in the rut. The first set of men grabbed the lower wing as they had before. They held for five seconds to slow the speed then released the wing allowing the second set of men to grab hold. One of the Marines in the first set, now sitting on the ground pointed to the plane and yelled, "You see that?" The second set of Marines stopped the plane. As instructed, they lifted the horizontal stabilizer six inches to remove the tail skag from the muddy rut and helped turn the plane around placing it in the takeoff position.

The left side of the top wing's tip was almost touching the bottom wing. Schilt, could hear the Marine say, "Something's wrong, Sir." Schilt cut the engine and climbed out of the foreword cockpit. As he stepped onto his seat he nearly bumped his head on the top wing. He saw the bent center strut. Everything else looked in tack.

Lieutenant Gould and Gunny Brown approached, accessing the situation. "What do you think, Frank?" Gould asked.

"It must have weakened in the landing. I felt something snap as it settled down," Schilt said studying the rest of the plane for any other damage.

"Did you get hit, Sir?" Brown asked while studying the bent strut.

"There was a close round near the strut as I approached the village. Why?"

"Well, right here where it's bent there's a small chunk of metal missing."

'Yeah, you're right." He paused rubbing his fingers along the bent metal then added, "They did finally get off a lucky round."

Schilt didn't say a word for a moment, while Gould and Brown were thinking what to do with their guest for the day. Schilt broke the silence. "Hey Gunny, do you have a couple of ax handles that we can use to splint this strut?"

"Sure do, Sir," Brown said, turned and briskly walked away on a mission.

"Mo, get a couple of your men to help me straighten this out."

Thirty minutes later, with the top wing raised back to its original position, the splint wrapped tightly to the strut and Privates Leonard Smith and Bernard Coyne on board, the plane roared through the village and lifted off as if nothing happened. The two passengers were far more sober then the first two as they both stared at the strut with the jury-rigged splint just waiting for it to split apart.

Billingsworth looked at the plane as it touched down then quickly to Wilson and back to the plane spitting out a "What the?" and then muttered some profanity. The pharmacist mates, Billingsworth, and Wilson rushed to the plane. The two passengers scrambled out of the plane and on to the ground waiting for the pharmacist mates.

Wilson and Billingsworth looked at the splint with amazement. Billingsworth announced, "That's it, Sir. I am grounding the plane."

"It flies okay, Top, and it's my call. Fill it up Wilson. I'll see you two in an hour and a half."

"I'll have to report it, Lieutenant. And that's my call."

"Very well, Technical Sergeant." Schilt said formally, knowing his maintenance was following procedures. Although he grinned secretly as he climbed into the cockpit.

Billingsworth followed him and looked down on him while standing on the bottom wing. At that moment, Schilt looked up and gave out an elongated, "Yessss?"

Billingsworth handed Schilt a bag and said with a smile, "I figured you'd need some sandwiches, Frank. "

"Thanks, Ike."

"Be careful, Sir."

The ninth flight into Ocotal was uneventful. At first. The touchdown of the front two wheels was normal. Then, just before reaching the first set of Marines, he allowed his tail skag to settle in the rut. The skag snapped. Without the skag finding and settling into a rut, the aft end of the plane settled onto the ground then fishtailed a foot left and a foot to the right. Schilt brought the fishtailing under control. However, the first two Marine "brakemen" were slow in grabbing the wings and couldn't slow the plane as before. This placed an additional test on the capabilities of the next two brakeman. They finally stopped the plane. As before, the panting Marines went back to the rear of the plane lifted the horizontal stabilizer and turned the plane around. Schilt cut the engine and climbed to the ground to assess the situation. Captain Peard and Lieutenant Gould rushed to him.

"What do you think Frank?" Peard asked.

Smiling as they neared him, Schilt replied, "It's flyable but needs to be replaced.

"Mo, if you don't mind, wire Top Billingsworth and tell him I'll be back in about an hour. The tail skag snapped and I need a new skag or I'll need LS's bird."

"Will do, Frank."

"I'll lift out the next two, but that'll be it for today."

"Since I don't have a skag, I'll need you to have two men lift my horizontal stabilizer and have two men hold the ends of my wings to restrain the forward movement while I get the prop speed up high enough to bi-pass the need for the skag."

"Yep," the rodeo fan comprehended aloud.

Peard, with obviously more east-coast blood in him, responded with a serious face and "Uh?"

"Mo, get the two men on board, I'll get in, rev her up, then when I waive my hand, all four Marines let go at the same time."

"Got it, Frank."

Schilt, climbing back into the plane, passed Coryell and Private Donnell and examined their safety harness. "Gunny, you two all ready?"

"Yes Sir."

"We'll be in Ocotal in 45 minutes."

"That's good, Sir"

"It might be a tricky landing once the tail section hits the deck. Hang on tight then."

With Donnell shaking his head understanding the information, Coryell said, "Will do Sir."

The flight's takeoff and landing went as planned. Schilt gave a "I told you so" thumbs up to Billingsworth with a determined wink.

Billingsworth, with the sternest look on his face, flattened his right hand into the shape of ax and whipped his fingertips over his throat signifying, "That's it for today, young fella!"

That increased the grin on Schilt's face and almost had Wilson laughing out loud at his two older mates feuding.

First Lieutenant Christian F. Schilt

Two final medical evacuation flights were planned for the 8th. Rowell had directed Schilt to make both in Lamson-Scribner's Corsair. By nightfall on the 8th of January, Schilt had delivered a new ground commander, one enlisted Marine, and 1400 pounds of medical supplies and provisions. He evacuated 18 wounded—three of whom would have died had they not been evacuated.

Managua Aerodrome, January 9, 1928. By that third day, the aerodrome became the most popular site in Managua for watching history in the making. Hundreds of onlookers from the Brigade headquarters, the ministry, Nicaraguan military, and civilians who circled the field. As George Ward, the US Charge d'affairés, said to Colonel Gulick that morning while looking at the crowd, "There are no secrets in Managua."

Rowell gathered the squadron in the aerodrome 40 minutes after Schilt landed. The atmosphere was charged with jubilation. The exhausted lieutenant, whose boyish grin never left his face, was surrounded by every man in the squadron and, for fifteen minutes, received handshakes, pats on the back, and hearty congratulations. Rowell told the young aviator that he was going to recommend him in for a Distinguished Flying Cross.

Over a megaphone, at Major Rowell's direction, Technical Sergeant Roy Jolson barked, "Squadron, Attention!"

With that, the brigade commander, Colonel Louis M. Gulick, stepped up on a wooden podium simultaneously saying, "At ease men." He paused bearing a proud look on his face. "Lieutenant Christian Schilt, would you join me?"

The men cheered exuberantly as Schilt worked his way to the front.

Once standing together, Gulick announced, "Lieutenant Schilt, today you completed an achievement of historical importance. Most significantly, at the greatest personal risk on 20 occasions, you braved enemy fire flying in and out of Quilali to save the lives of three Marines who, I understand, surely would have died had it not been for your bravery, flying skills, and unparalleled endurance. Sixteen other wounded men were evacuated. This selfless bravery will allow the seventy men remaining to march on out to safety. Secondarily, you— and your entire squadron—exhibited to all in this brigade and, as a matter of fact in this country, the unquestionable value and necessity the air squadron brings to the success of Marines fighting here in this vicious little war. Last, your achievement will be recorded in the books of Marine Corps history and will significantly eradicate any doubts in anyone's minds about whether or not the Marine Corps should or should not have its own air support."

With that, Gulick looked Schilt in the eye and shook his hand. The men cheered wildly. Gulick raised his hand to silence the men, "I had heard earlier that your boss, Major Rowell, was going to recommend you for the Distinguished Flying Cross. However, the Commander of the U. S. Special Services Squadron has directed me to inform everyone that this was not to be done." The faces on the jubilant crowd went blank and the noise ceased. "What he wants is something else," he said pausing. "So, in the morning I will be drafting a citation for this brave man to receive the Medal of Honor." The cheering erupted— this time louder than before. And for the second time Gulick raised his hand to quiet the Marines. "Gentlemen, Mr. George Ward, the ministry's Charge d'affairés, asked me earlier this afternoon if I'd mind if he would bring over a few cases of the ministry's finest wine so that we could celebrate Frank's achievement. The astonished look in my face told him all he needed to know. Mr. Ward is in the back by the hanger door. Grab a glass, and we'll raise a toast and have some well-deserved fun, Marines!"

And by the end of the 9th of January Colonel Gulik completed his draft for Medal of Honor that would be bestowed on a heroic American hero, First Lieutenant Christian F. Schilt.

EPILOGUE

El Chipote January 10, 1928. Captain Peard, the new ground force commander at Quilali, decided that the men were unable to immediately attack the nearby fortress of El Chipote. On the morning of January 10, 1928, the patrol headed north to the San Albino gold mine, 12 miles north. Once there, they were to wait for reinforcements. By midday their movement was discovered as they saw field glasses looking down on them from a mountain ridge above. Discounting the discovery, they continued on to San Albino.

Two to three miles ahead of the ground force were bi-planes. By now the grunts had grown dependent on the security provided by the aviators. Air-to-ground communications, though primitive, reached a satisfactory level of effectiveness.

Halfway to San Albino near the small village of Las Cruces, the bandits waited for Peard's force. Lieutenant Carl Byrd and Chief Warrant Officer Wodarczyk made two low passes over the front of the ground column and followed the road ahead, searching for the unusual. On their third pass, the pilots spotted the ambush. Byrd stayed on station diving on the bandits. Wodarczyk scribbled a note warning Peard of the ambush, dropped it off with lead patrol element and returned to fire on the enemy. Peard set up his Stokes mortar. No longer a surprise and under heavy fire, the bandit force faded into the jungle.

El Chipote-Sandino's Headquarters-*USMC History Division*
5427-3

Peard's patrol arrived safely in San Albino that night to learn that an infantry battalion from the 5th Marines would join them in about one week.

On the 19th of January, Major Young of 5th Marines with four Marine rifle companies and a Guardia company departed San Albino to attack El Chipote. Once on top the Marines found that the bandits had disappeared and only a half dozen cooks remained.

First Lieutenant Christian Schilt receiving Medal of Honor from President Coolidge *–USMC History Division; NARA Ref#:80-G-460270*

Managua Air Field June 15, 1928. "You got to be bullshitting me," Smitty said to his friend. "In September? I don't believe your ass!"

"Well, I ain't BS'ing you. I'll be discharged next month," Junior Wilson explained. "Burns," he noted, referring to Cook First Class Duffy Burns, "is retiring in August and we'll both be back here in September. Duffy's going to be the cook. He's happy doing that and being with his chick…er, what's her name?"

"Maria," Smitty offered.

"Right. If all goes as planned, Tun Tavern South will open in October. I have the money saved up and will be buying what we need next month, shipping it down as we get it. Duffy's doing the same thing in the San Diego area.

"Smitty, I need you down here to be the assistant manager for Tun Tavern South. I have other projects planned and I want you to be prepared for them or take over as manager for the tavern."

Being more than a bit overwhelmed by his buddy's entrepreneurial declarations, Smitty squinted his right eye, turned his head a bit to the left, and nervously stuttered, "What projects?"

Wilson's voice reduced nearly to a whisper, "Have you ever played golf?"

Smitty eyes opened wide, his stare turned upward, and his nose wrinkled, "Golf," he asked.

"Yeah golf. This place will be loaded with diplomats and senior military, and that's what they are doing these days at the bases up in the States."

"Ahhh, Wilson, you did say projects, did you not?" "Well, yeah. I guess I didn't mention the brewery."

"What, did you say 'the brewery?'" Smitty begged for clarity.

"Yeah, you remember Captain Shilling from 2/5? Well, Shilly and..."

"Did you say, 'Shilly'? Now you're buddies with the officers?" Smitty interrupted in total disbelief.

"Yeah, well his family had a growing brewery in Reading, Pennsylvania. Since Prohibition, their fermenters and other equipment are sitting idle. He said he'd help us open a brewery down here by shipping that stuff. The beer was called Sunshine Beer, and those folks up in Reading simply ask for a 'Sunny'. I like the idea, so Duffy and I are kicking this around. If we bring it down here, I'm thinking that we'll call it 'Bandit Beer'.

"Well, Smitty, can we count on you?"

"I'm not sure, Junior. Who's going to get you through the wickets here in Managua? Hell, you don't even speak enough Spanish to get through the night--let alone the day!"

"Oh yeah, Smitty, I didn't tell you about our VP for local activities, did I?"

"Noooo," he drew out, wiggling the word around long enough to underline the volume of information just given to him. "No, who?"

"Your buddy, Manuel Gonzales!" Wilson announced, adding more for the surprised Smitty. "You know Manny," further defining, "from the Shocks?"

Accessing the wide-eyed look on his friend's face, Wilson looked hard at his good friend, harder than he ever had before, and asked a second time, "So now, what do you have to say, my friend, are you in?"

Smitty replied, "Like I said earlier, Junior Wilson, you've got to be bullshitting me." Adding with a smile, "Hell, yes I'm in! I'm out in December and looks like I'll be back in January."